REVISED EDI

Soul Re-Creation

DEVELOPING YOUR COSMIC POTENTIAL

by

Robert E. Detzler

Edited by

Kathryn Hamilton

Revised Edition Edited by

Elizabeth Grobes

SRC Publishing

Lacey, Washington

The case studies in this book have been taken from actual counseling sessions and seminars. The names of the clients and students involved have been changed to protect their privacy.

Soul Re-Creation reflects the views and personal experience of the author. No medical claim is made as to the effect or outcome of the exercises described in this volume. Each person is encouraged to be responsible in the use and choice of professional healing assistance as needed.

Library of Congress Cataloging-in-Publication Data

Detzler, Robert E.

Soul re-creation, developing your cosmic potential / by Robert E. Detzler. 2nd ed.

Includes bibliographical references, glossary of terms.

1. Spiritual healing, case studies.
2. Self-actualization (Psychology)—Miscellanea.
3. Extrasensory perception. I. Title.

ISBN 978-0-9640041-4-6: $19.95

1997 Library of Congress Catalog Number 97-092398

Cover design and illustrations by Philip Brautigam Design

First Edition edited by Kathryn Hamilton

Second Edition edited by Elizabeth Grobes

Additional editing by Mary Ann Detzler and Diane Detzler

Published in the United States of America by SRC Publishing

Printed in the United States of America by CreateSpace, a DBA of On-Demand Publishing LLC, part of the Amazon group of companies.

Original Edition first printing February, 1994

Revised Edition first printing March, 1999; second printing October, 2003; third printing December, 2008; fourth printing July, 2010; fifth printing February, 2012; sixth printing October, 2013; seventh printing December, 2014

Revised Edition (*) first printing July, 2016; second printing November, 2018

Dedication

I dedicate this book to all the souls who have the courage, determination, and unwavering enthusiasm to investigate, learn, and practice the principles contained herein. I also dedicate the book to those who will use their newly-received knowledge to help others. Last, but not least, I dedicate this book to the LIGHT above all Light—Elohim, God, the GODHEAD.

Acknowledgments

My thanks to the following persons for their invaluable contributions to this book:

Dr. Clark Cameron and his wife Sharon, who brought to my attention and taught me the first eight words and the basic questioning process of Response Therapy.

My wife, Mary Ann, for her encouragement, patience, and valuable suggestions.

Mary Marie Satterlee, who taught me how to work with my High Self, and who worked closely with her own High Self to verify the accuracy of much of the material I received from my High Self.

Robert Gandrup, for channeling some of the charts, designing many of them, and with insights as to how it all fits together.

Kathryn Hamilton-Cook, for her expertise in editing the first edition, thereby helping me bring order out of chaos.

All of my clients, for increasing my awareness of the concepts involved with SRT, and for letting me use their case histories as examples. They have been some of my greatest teachers, leading me into an expanded understanding of human nature and the psychology of the soul.

My deep gratitude and very special thanks to the following beings, without whom I could not have written this book: my guides, my Guardian Angels, my High Self, the Holy Spirit, the special being who is God of this planet, the Infinite Council, I AM, ONE, and the GODHEAD.

The host of beings in the seen and unseen realms who have provided inspiration, sustenance, and direction for this work.

Contents

Chapter 1. Infinite Potential 1

We *Are* More Than We Know 1
Why Are Programs So Powerful? 2
What Is Spiritual Response Therapy? 2
What Does Clearing Do? 3
Know That You Have Help 5
Know Your Potential 6
About This Book 6

Chapter 2. The Soul's Design 9

What Is God? 9
What Is Christ? 9
What Is the Holy Spirit? 10
What Is the Trinity? 10
What Is Our Relationship to God and the Spiritual Realm? 10
What Is the Physical Realm? 11
Our Spiritual and Physical Aspects 12
18 Bodies and 90 Minds 12
The Incarnational Cycle 16

Chapter 3. The Soul Family 19

Twin Flames and Flame Mates 19
Oversouls and Soul Mates 21
Multiple Twin Flames and Flame Mates 22
The Addictive Energy of Flames 23
Soul Essence 25
Siamese Flames 26
The Purpose of Oversouls 26

Chapter 4. Infinite Service 27

Levels of Soul Consciousness and Service 28
Knowing Your Level of Soul Consciousness 34

Chapter 5. The Basic Steps of SRT **37**

Preparing to Work 37
Five Basic Steps for Clearing Programs 40
When You Are Lost or Stuck in Research 44
Review the Basic Procedure 44
Keeping Yourself Clear 45
Case Studies 45
Developing Options 49

Chapter 6. Removing Blocks to Working with SRT **53**

Removing Blocks Listed on Chart 1 54
Removing Blocks Listed on Chart 4 55
Removing Blocks Listed on Chart 5 55
Removing Unknown Blocking Energies 61

Chapter 7. Charts 1 and 4 .... **63**

Chart 1–Chart to Use; Contact or Help 63
Chart 4–Programs, When, and Cast of Characters 66
  Understand the Basic 13 Programs 66
  Understanding When Programs Become Established 71

Chapter 8. Master Programs (Chart 6A) **77**

What Are Master Programs? 78
The Elements of Master Programs 78
Clearing Master Programs 79
Case Studies 80
Master Programs Not Listed on Chart 6A 89

Chapter 9. Octaves of Learning and Soul Qualities **91**

Octaves of Learning 91
Case Study 92
Soul Qualities (Chart 2) 92

Chapter 10. Blocks to Positive Expression (Chart 6B) **99**

Case Studies 99

Chapter 11. Archetypes (Chart 8) **103**

Case Studies 104

Chapter 12. Themes and Challenges (Chart 2) **111**
Case Studies 111
Chapter 13. Negative Motivations (Chart 5) **117**
Case Studies 117
Chapter 14. Miscellaneous Blocks (Chart 10) **121**
Chapter 15. Programming Before Formation **131**
Chart 11–Soul Energy Programming 131
Chart 12–Spirit Energy Programming 133
Chart 13–Programs Before Creation 136
Chart 14–Pre-Fall of Consciousness, Creating the Illusion 139
Chart 15–I AM Level Consciousness Programs 141
Chart 16–Fall of Consciousness 142
Chart 17–Fine Tuning 144
Chart 18–Higher Level Blocks 146
Chart 19–How to Change Your Life 147
Chart 20–Refining Consciousness 147
Chapter 16. Charts 21 through 31 .... **149**
Chart 21–Final Items this ONE Universe 149
Chart 22–New ONE Universe 150
Chart 23–Spiritual Realms Programs 152
Chart 24–Rebirth Conscious Mind 153
Chart 25–Final Assurance 154
Chart 26–Freedom Is Free 154
Chart 27–Learning Is Fun 154
Chart 28–Final Forgiveness 155
Chart 29–Final Blessing 156
Chart 30–Final Light 157
Chart 31–Memory Clearing 158
Duplicate Programs 162
Programs Coming Up 162
Guarantees 162
Miscellaneous Information 166
The Maze 163
Final Draft 164

Chapter 17. Creating Health **165**

Case Studies 166
Using Colors—Chart 7 171
Using the Health Charts 172
Chart 9A—Vitamins 173
Chart 9A—Minerals 174
Chart 9B—Health and Well-Being 174
Chart 9B—Food or Diet 175
Direct Healing Processes—Chart 7 176

Chapter 18. Dreams: A Sure Guide **179**

Using SRT to Interpret Dreams 179
Case Studies 180

Chapter 19. Examples of Complete Cases **189**

Case Study 1: Alberta 189
Case Study 2: Chester 195
Case Study 3: Anthony 196
Case Study 4: Clearing an Animal 199

Chapter 20. Changing Your Life (Chart 19) **201**

Clear Blocks to Growth 201
Manifest Good 204
Re-Create the Soul 208

Appendix A. Glossary **209**

Appendix B. Charts **221**

Bibliography **257**

Suggested Reading **257**

Figures

3-1. Twin Flames **20**

3-2. Multiple Twin Flames and Flame Mates **22**

3-3. Oversouls and Looping **23**

5-1. Establishing a Yes and No Response **37**

B-1. Where to Find Information About the Charts **221**

CHAPTER 1

Infinite Potential

When I look at thy heavens, the work of thy fingers, the moon and the stars which thou hast established; what is man that thou art mindful of him, and the son of man that thou dost care for him? Yet thou hast made him little less than God, and dost crown him with glory and honor. Thou hast given him dominion over the works of thy hands; thou hast put all things under his feet,
(Psalms 8:3-6 RSV)

Within each of us there is an insistent urge to learn, to grow, to rise up, and become greater and greater. We work hard at our jobs, struggle with our relationships, often pushing ourselves to go farther faster and do more with less. But do we know where we are going?

The truth is in our longing. We chart our course by what is missing from our lives, be it love, peace of mind, prosperity, or health. We look in the mirror and ask, "Why me?" or "Why not me?" We ask, "Is there a purpose to life?" If there is, what is it and how do we fulfill that purpose? If there is no purpose, is human life merely an accident of nature? Is what we do during our brief span of life completely irrelevant? Surely there is more to knowing ourselves and understanding life than what we can see on the surface of physical reality. Somehow, we are not *there* yet, wherever *there* is.

We struggle with our own feelings and thoughts. We often have fear. Or perhaps anger, depression, confusion, or fatigue. We want help. We want to be free. And we want to *know*.

We *Are* More Than We Know

We make hundreds of decisions every day, about what to do, say, and think. Yet, not all of these decisions seem to be made consciously. We may ask "Why did I say that?" or "Why did I react that way?"

The answers lie, literally, within us. We are much more than physical brains in physical bodies. We are indeed much more than consciousness itself. To put it in simple terms, what we think of as the *mind* has three facets: the *conscious*, *subconscious*, and *superconscious*. As we will learn later, we are even more than this, but this can help us to explain some of our seemingly inexplicable behaviors and experiences.

The conscious mind is our ego self. It is the earthly identity and memory in which our soul clothes itself to survive in a physical reality. It is the judge, negotiator, and conspicuous controller of our daily experiences. The conscious mind is the part of our self with which we most often identify.

The subconscious mind, even though we are not aware of it, constantly monitors and *records* our daily thoughts, words, and experiences. It slavishly remembers things the conscious mind may have long forgotten.

While the conscious mind is often affected by the subconscious, it has the ability to *program* the subconscious. What we say to ourselves and others, and what we think to ourselves–especially if we have strong emotions about those thoughts and words–is registered in the subconscious memory banks. Unfortunately, the subconscious has no judgment. It records and replays negative thoughts, experiences, and emotions as well as positive ones.

How many times in our lives have we said to ourselves "This job gives me a pain," or "I am sick and tired of driving in this traffic every day." Then we really *do* have pain and really do become sick. Programming can also contribute to allergies, depression, illness, and can interfere with our relationships and our ability to succeed in the world.

Programming can happen in more dramatic, even traumatic ways, such as from accidents or abuse. Whatever the cause, unless we keep the subconscious clear, we will continue to replay and re-experience the programming of our negative beliefs.

Yet, even as this ability to program is our undoing, it is also our path to healing. Just as we can fill our subconscious with negative beliefs, we also have the power to *reprogram* what is negative and destructive in our lives.

And what is to guide us in positive programming? The superconscious mind. The superconscious mind is our direct link to the divine. Many call this the High Self. Jesus called it "the Father." It keeps track of our spiritual purpose and guides us through our life's lessons. If we live constantly in ego consciousness, we often do not recognize this part of ourselves. Yet it is always with us, whether we are aware of it or not.

Why Are Programs So Powerful?

To truly understand the power subconscious programming has over us, we must understand the scope of our 'life' as extending beyond this single lifetime. I believe and *know* from the vast amount of information I have obtained in doing this work that we have lived many lifetimes on this and other planets. If a single fall out of a small boat makes a person nervous around water, imagine what fifty lifetimes of death by drowning does to the subconscious.

It is also important to note that it is not *what* happens to you in any life that creates a negative program; it is the discordant or reactive energy you attach to the event. As far as your soul record is concerned, events are merely experiences–it is the emotional energy attached to those experiences that causes subsequent difficulties. For instance, it was not being a priest or nun living in poverty in a past life that blocks your current prosperity; it is the strong emotionally-charged vows of poverty you took during that life coupled with the belief that you have to be poor to please God because anyone with riches cannot "enter the kingdom of heaven" (Matthew 19:23 RSV). A strong subconscious fear of being barred from heaven when you die can energize a program that blocks your prosperity lifetime after lifetime.

Together, the subconscious and superconscious retain our past life history and spiritual future. If we could just access those records, we could consciously reprogram ourselves for positive, productive experiences. The good news is that we can. While many techniques have been developed to discover and eliminate many of the mental, emotional, and physical problems associated with being human–including psychology, hypnotherapy, medicine, drugs, meditation, biofeedback, and holistic medicine–none fully address our functioning as spiritual beings living in physical bodies. However, *Spiritual Response Therapy* enables you to access your subconscious records *and* communicate with your higher spiritual self.

What Is Spiritual Response Therapy?

Spiritual Response Therapy, or *SRT*, is a meticulous process of researching the subconscious mind and soul records to discover and release hidden blocks to health, happiness, and spiritual growth.

As explained in detail in Chapter 5—The Basic Steps of SRT, you research programs by using a pendulum to communicate, first, with your subconscious mind, and later, with your superconscious mind, or High Self. Using the charts included at the end of this book, you research past life experiences and precisely identify negative programs. You clear these programs by asking that the discordant energies be cleared. Then, you reprogram the subconscious mind with positive messages. Because you are conscious during this research and clearing, you learn more about yourself and how to effect change in your life.

Most people believe that healing comes about through medicine, and to some degree this is true. However, the greater healing, and the only permanent healing, is through attunement to Spirit and knowing ourselves as spiritual beings.

What Does Clearing Do?

When High Self clears a program or block, they literally erase the negative energy pattern from your subconscious and soul records. Instead of being driven by subconscious beliefs and desires that you do not understand, you become free to live to your greatest potential—to express your greater spiritual self. Following are some examples of how clearing programs have improved clients' lives.

Recently, a woman called me from California and asked me to research why she had allergies to food. She told me her allergies were so bad that she never ate out at a restaurant. She never visited friends because they would invite her to eat with them and she felt badly when she had to refuse. Using SRT and working with my High Self, I researched her past life programs and asked High Self to clear them. About two weeks later, she called me to report on her allergies. She stated that they were completely gone! She had seldom eaten at home since the clearing and was enjoying her freedom to visit friends and share food with them.

When I first started this work, a woman who was visiting our home mentioned that she needed to take her asthma medication as she was starting to have difficulty breathing. She had been taking medication five times a day for twelve years. When we researched her past lives, we discovered that she had died in fires in 2,689 lives and by drowning in another twenty-nine—all deaths were caused by asphyxiation. Since her programs were cleared, she has taken no medication for asthma and has remained entirely free of negative effects.

While I was teaching a class in Southern California, a student told the hostess, "I wish you didn't have cats. I am allergic to them and can't breathe." In my inner vision, I saw a panther crouched on the limb of a large tree where the student was walking along a jungle path. Questioning revealed that in that situation, a past life, he had been killed by the panther. A few moments after clearing the program, he said, "Thanks! I can breathe again." Since the clearing, he has been free of allergies to cats.

A young mother of an infant mentioned that whenever they boarded an elevator, the child would panic and start screaming when the door closed. Research revealed that she had claustrophobia caused by past life trauma. In one past life, she was trapped in the small cabin of a sinking ship. She did not drown, but died of oxygen deprivation. In another life, she was a miner. The face of the mine caved in and again she died of oxygen deprivation. We found a total of 183 lives in which she had died in a similar manner. Once these programs were cleared, the child no longer cried when elevator doors closed.

One client mentioned that he had never had a close relationship with his father. He said that he could never remember a time when his father showed him love or affection, even when he was a child. His father had never picked him up or hugged him at any time. The week after this client was cleared of his discordant energy regarding their relationship; his father visited him in his apartment, hugged him, and told him he loved him. Needless to say, the client was ecstatic about the change in their relationship.

A gentleman asked me if I could clear his fear of heights and falling. In the first inner vision, I saw him chased up what appeared to be the Eiffel Tower by two young men. They chased him to the top, cornered him, and threw him off. We found that, in another life, he was on a dirigible that blew up over the English Channel. He fell a long way before striking the water and dying. Once High Self cleared all the past lives, the client was free from the fear program.

Allergies, asthma, fears, and blocked relationships are examples of conditions that have been helped with SRT. SRT has general benefits as well. Many people find SRT to be a catalyst that gives them the extra energy and inspiration they need.

> Certainly, one of my more fortunate moments came the afternoon I discovered *The Freedom Path.** At the time I called the phone number on the back cover, I was immersed in a lengthy period of demoralization that had left me with just enough energy and motivation for basic maintenance level activities. Yes, I went to work. Yes, I did my job. ... Nevertheless, I was simply going through the motions, emptied of vitality, filled with pain. I called you on Monday. You agreed to do two hours of SRT work for me and send a report.
>
> Driving home the next day, I noticed something unusual and very subtle going on. It was almost as if a couple of people were gently tapping their fingers across my chest. I paid attention for a few moments, then shifted back to the all-news radio station and thought no more about the gentle tapping.
>
> Wednesday morning I awoke and started preparing for work. Gradually I began to honor the gnawing suspicion that something was different. Indeed, something was very different. But I couldn't put my finger on it. ...I continued the workaday preparations. Shave. Shower. Dress. Head for the car. It happened when I grabbed the handle of my brief case. Instantly I realized what was so very different. I wasn't miserable. The wet, sticky blanket was no longer wrapped tightly around me. This was an amazing and rapid transformation. I was no longer drained and fragile.
>
> The remainder of that day and that week brought me a host of unpleasant and several intensely disruptive situations. Before, to any one of those situations, I would have responded with defeat and collapse. This time the incidents were no less unpleasant and disruptive, but I responded with effort rather than collapse.
>
> Needless to say, I was impressed with SRT. I had tried several approaches to ending the reign of demoralization. Nothing else worked. SRT did. I was inspired to study with you in order to learn SRT. —J. E. of Michigan.
>
> **The Freedom Path* is my first book on SRT. The first edition of it was titled *Your Mind Net: Reprogramming the Subconscious.*

SRT is not limited to clearing past lives. It is also invaluable for clearing the negative energy you accumulate in your day-to-day activities and interactions. It is especially important to clear yourself of self-judgment and judgment of others. Once we set up energy of judgment, it is very difficult to erase it from the soul. We can spend years forgiving someone and still have negative energy on that original judgment of them. Many people pile up judgments one on top of the other without realizing that the negative energy follows them around lifetime after lifetime; these judgments are written upon the soul and stay there until erased.

Regardless of the severity of the grievance we think we may have suffered, we must immediately release the negative energy if we are to be free from destructive consequences. For example, Jesus did not condemn anyone not even those who nailed Him to the cross. Instead He prayed for them.

> *And Jesus said, "Father, forgive them; for they know not what they do." (Luke 23:34 RSV)*

His word to the disciples was:

> *"You have heard that it was said, 'You shall love your neighbor and hate your enemy.' But I say to you, Love your enemies and pray for those who persecute you, so that you may be sons of your Father who is in heaven; ... (Matthew 5:43-45 RSV)*

When you hold a grievance against anyone, there is a negative energy attached that can cause mental, emotional, or physical pain. If you would be free—really free—you must dissolve the accumulated negative energies from the past and not allow any more to accumulate.

SRT enables us to live our lives more freely. Friend and client Gary Houston put it this way:

> There is ample evidence that each of us has made far too many unconscious choices that have come back to haunt us. They show up as attitudes, behavioral patterns, and mental programs that close off the "good" of our hearts' desire.
>
> For years I have been looking for a method to root out and replace all the mental programs that bring unwanted results. I want this for myself and as a service to others. I believe I have found what I have been looking for [in SRT].

Know That You Have Help

As you learn to use SRT to clear your subconscious mind, you will become aware that you are no longer working with just your subconscious. As the negative patterns are cleared, an important channel of communication begins to open up: your connection to your High Self. While we are always receiving guidance and help from the spiritual realm, we are not always aware of it. SRT is one method of bringing yourself into close conscious contact with your own spiritual helpers. Chart 1—Contact or Help provided in Appendix B of this book lists many of the spiritual guides you may have helping you.

Everyone has a High Self. Your High Self is both a part of you and a part of the All. It is not an extension of your physical self: indeed, it is you who are an extension of the spiritual realm! Your High Self may consist of from one to an infinite number of beings. These beings may be from many different spiritual levels, from the level of Light Status (see Chart 3—Levels of Soul Consciousness) all of the way to the GODHEAD. The higher in consciousness they are, the greater their ability and the more help they can provide to you.

The members of your High Self committee have had their own incarnations in which they have experienced, learned, and grown and may have accumulated discordant energies and programs. You will find that you can ask that they also be cleared and it is important to do so.

As you grow in level of soul consciousness or wisdom and stature, the members of your High Self and your other spiritual councils may change. My High Self has changed many times as I have progressed along my path.

Using a pendulum is just one way to communicate with your High Self. My High Self also communicates with me through inner pictures, sounds, feelings, knowings, and occasionally smells. Many times while I am doing past life research, they show me images from the past lives and provide other direct information.

Like most things, communicating with your High Self takes practice. For some people, it can be like learning a foreign language. For others, it is as natural as thought. As you become clearer using SRT, pay attention to your thoughts and intuition for that is the way High Self communicates with us. They also communicate through dreams while we are asleep and through visions while we are in meditation or an altered state of consciousness.

Know Your Potential

One of the greatest fears held by mortal human beings is that their personal identity will be lost when they recognize that they are part of and one with everything. Rest assured that will never happen. You do not become less, but more. Because you are made in God's image and likeness, you have *infinite potential.*

Through the ages, we have lived on many levels of expression. We were Light in the beginning with God and we will return to Light in the final wrap-up of our individual journey from Light into darkness and from darkness back into Light. Remember that you are an eternal spiritual being, a living soul, created in the image and likeness of God. Therefore, your complete expression is not confined to or limited by the physical body. You can actually be living on many levels of consciousness and as many expressions of being at the same time. While working with various clients, I found that many of them have experienced past lives in which they were a spiritual guide, High Self, Guardian Angel, or other nonphysical entity.

Since your spirit or soul is the total accumulation of all that you have experienced and learned in all lives, it is greater than the conscious knowledge of this single life. Your soul is absolutely unlimited and greater than any of its individualized expressions. You can be living in a physical body, expressing as a human being, and at the same time your soul can be in total attunement and one with God.

Jesus prayed for his disciples:

> *that they may all be one; even as thou, Father, art in me, and I in thee, that they also may be one in us,...The glory which thou hast given me I have given to them, that they may be one even as we are one, I in them and thou in me, that they may become perfectly one,....*
> *(John 17:21-23 RSV)*

It is clear to me that the divine purpose for each one of us is to remember that we are Light, to know ourselves as God does. Everyone can accomplish this goal. Some of us may achieve it in a few lifetimes. Others may have to experience hundreds of thousands of lives before they are convinced that the world is their school and they are here to learn about God and their spiritual connection, and that they are not here just to live, earn money, raise a family, and die.

About This Book

This book serves two purposes. The early chapters present the framework you need to understand the full purpose of SRT. Most of this information was provided to me directly from my High Self or the High Selves of others.

The later chapters (Chapters 5 through 20), are designed to teach you to use SRT. If you wish to learn how to use a pendulum immediately, you may want to first read Chapter 5—The Basic Steps of SRT. You may find this useful if you want to do your own questioning as you read the first chapters of this book.

The information in this book is accurate to the degree of my current understanding, which has changed even during the process of researching and writing this material. Every time I think I have a complete system and a good understanding of it, High Self throws some new factor into the arena and I have to fit another piece into the puzzle. But that is exactly the process of SRT: learning and growing in order to move on to higher levels of understanding. It is not the knowledge, but the process of learning that is important.

There are many instances through the course of this book in which I quote the *Bible*. High Self informs me that the *Bible* is 10% history and 90%

symbolic. I use the *Metaphysical Bible Dictionary* (MBD) by Charles Fillmore to determine the meaning of the proper names involved in the *Bible* stories. Each original Hebrew or Greek name has a specific meaning or meanings. David (Hebrew) means *"beloved; loved; well-beloved"* (MBD). Jesus (Greek from the Hebrew Jeshua or Joshua) means *"whose help Jehovah is; deliverance; safety; salvation; Savior; deliverance through Jehovah"* (MBD). I use these meanings to get information about the *Bible* stories. First, I ask High Self how accurate the meanings are. Then I use the charts and the SRT questioning process to expand those meanings and the symbols involved. Many times the High Self gives me inner pictures and understanding. Once I have the inner picture or the understanding, I simply present a thought scenario in my mind to High Self about the information given. Then I ask how accurate it is. When High Self says my thoughts are 100% accurate, I ask if the information is complete or if they want to add something. Working with the High Self in this manner helps to eliminate confusion as to what the Scriptures are truly saying.

Scripture quotations are taken from *The Oxford Annotated Bible with the Apocrypha, Revised Standard Version* (RSV), unless otherwise noted in text as being from the *King James Version* (KJV). For an idea of how Jesus used parables as symbols to present a deeper metaphysical truth to the disciples, look at the Parable of the Sower and its interpretation in Matthew 13:3-9, 18-23.

Although the Scriptures use gender-specific language, the generalizations I make are not meant to be attributed only to one sex or another. Once a soul has been elevated to the level of GOD listed on Chart 3–Levels of Soul Consciousness, it no longer has gender. Elsewhere, whenever possible, I have tried to use inclusive, nonsexist language.

CHAPTER 2

The Soul's Design

What Is God?

During my training as a minister, I was taught that God is Creator. When I began to work directly with High Self, I asked if God is Creator and received a "no" response. I said, "Well! If God is not Creator, what is God?" I heard the words "Prime Mover." God is the creative force behind everything. God is Creative Intelligence, Spiritual Life, Spiritual Substance, and Prime Mover of all that is. All things that God creates are imbued with God's life, substance, and intelligence.

We could say, symbolically, that God is creative energy or the fire of creation. As the fire of creation, God is Light, a light far beyond our mortal understanding of the sun, the moon, the stars, and conventional light waves. The visible light that you perceive is stepped-down from the one great Light that is over all and through all and is an expression of that which comes out of God.

As Prime Mover, God creates *only* on the spiritual level by forming in consciousness the *divine blueprint* for all that will eventually become the formed or created heavens and the earth. That is why the Scriptures state that everything was "without form and void" (Genesis 1:2 RSV) before creation.

Normally, when the *Bible* uses the term God, it is speaking about the GODHEAD. There are two specific references in the *Bible* to the GODHEAD: Romans 1:20 and Colossians 2:9 of The *King James Version*. (Refer to Chart 3–Levels of Soul Consciousness and Chapter 4–Infinite Service, for levels of God in relation to the GODHEAD.)

There is another level of spiritual beings who take the divine blueprint which is created in the consciousness of God and construct the worlds. You might say that these beings, whom High Self calls *Vectors,* are subcontractors who work under the direction of God to bring forth the physical realms.

God (as an extension of SPIRIT) is that from which everything emanates. *God as SPIRIT is ALL: LIGHT, LOVE, and LIFE.*

What Is Christ?

If God is All, what is Christ? According to the Scriptures, Christ is the only begotten Son of God and is the Creator of all, the inheritor of all that God is (life, substance, and intelligence). Christ is a potential in everyone. The Son is *Jehovah,* which according to Fillmore in his *Metaphysical Bible Dictionary,* gives the meaning of *Jehovah,* from Hebrew as *"He-who-is–who-was–who-will-be manifest; the self-existent One; He who is eternal"* (MBD). This is, also, confirmed by *The Hebrew-Greek Key Study Bible.* Jehovah is used interchangeably with LORD in the Scriptures. Jehovah, or Christ, is the Logos or Creative Word:

> *In THE BEGINNING WAS THE WORD, and the Word was with God, and the Word was God. He was in the beginning with God; all things were*

made through him, and without him was not anything made that was made. In him was life, and the life was the light of men. The light shines in the darkness, and the darkness has not overcome it. (John 1:1-5 RSV)

Jesus of Nazareth was a man who fully demonstrated His divine nature, the Son of God potential. When Jesus is referred to as "Jesus the Christ," it means that He is one who has, through his efforts, become one with God Consciousness. Thus, Jesus is the creative word made flesh.

This creative intelligence is the Word which created all that appears in the formed world. This potential lies in every soul. For example, you use the power of your own voice to articulate the things you desire to accomplish in life. You give orders to others, which may be written or verbal. Your word is that which you individually speak and that word causes things to happen. So it is with God: He speaks forth the Word and the Word (The Son–that which comes forth from the Father) forms the manifest world in which we, the sons and daughters of God, live.

"You are the light of the world.... Let your light so shine before men, that they may see your good works and give glory to your Father who is in heaven. (Matthew 5:14, 16 RSV)

Christ is the Light that lights every man that comes into the world. Christ is the presence of God as Spirit in man and its full expression can be attained by every individual. Mankind attains Christ Consciousness by releasing discordant programming and coming into spiritual attunement. This unites man's consciousness with the inner Christ Light.

What Is the Holy Spirit?

While Christ is the Creative Word which moves all things into expression, the Holy Spirit is the instructor and counselor. The Holy Spirit is always auxiliary to the Son (Christ), for its function is to bring the soul to Christ Consciousness. The Holy Spirit does not ascend through constantly unfolding levels of awareness as the Son does.

...I tell you the truth: it is to your advantage that I go away, for if I do not go away, the Counselor will not come to you; but if I go, I will send him to you.... When the Spirit of truth comes, he will guide you into all the truth; for he will not speak on his own authority, but whatever he hears he will speak, and he will declare to you the things that are to come. (John 16:7, 13 RSV)

However, Christ never assumes the role of the Holy Spirit.

There is never a conflict between the Christ and the Holy Spirit. Each has a special function in the spiritual realm and each fulfills that function perfectly. As long as a person's conscious mind or negative programs do not interfere, the Christ and the Holy Spirit work together to bring that person into God Consciousness.

What Is the Trinity?

What, then, is the relationship between God (GODHEAD), Christ, and the Holy Spirit?
God is Light or Source which contains all life, substance, and intelligence. Light creates the perfect idea, Christ the Son of God, which manifests Itself through the creative process or spoken Word. This creative process is brought about through the Holy Spirit, which is the breath or movement of God Consciousness. (The word "spirit" comes from the Greek term *spiritus* which means breath).

Another way of stating this three-way relationship is this: Infinite Intelligence (GODHEAD) gives birth to the perfect idea of Itself (the Christ or Jehovah) by Its breath (SPIRIT).

What Is Our Relationship to God and the Spiritual Realm?

The entire universe and all things in the universe were initially blueprints in the infinite mind of God. The universe was "without form and void" (Genesis 1:2 RSV) because it was created only in Spirit (God Consciousness) and was not yet a physical reality.

The universe consisted of spiritual substance or Light. A long time after this and many steps later, man was formed, first as a 'spiritual body.'

> *Then God said, "Let us make man in our image, after our likeness; and let them have dominion over the fish of the sea, and over the birds of the air, and over the cattle, and over all the earth, and over every creeping thing that creeps upon the earth." So God created man in his own image, in the image of God he created him; male and female he created them. And God blessed them... (Genesis 1:26-28 RSV)*

The next step was to create man of the dust of the ground (dust in this case represents spiritual substance or Light). When God's breath (SPIRIT) entered man, man became a 'living soul,' which is the working consciousness of the spiritual body.

> *then the LORD God formed man of dust from the ground, and breathed into his nostrils the breath of life; and man became a living being. (Genesis 2:7 RSV)*

> *And the LORD God planted a garden in Eden, in the east; and there he put the man whom he had formed. (Genesis 2:8 RSV)*

Eden, in the east, symbolizes a place of Light or God Consciousness. We are told that man was both male and female, and that there were many such beings in God Consciousness, for God refers to this man creature as 'them.'

The story of Job also reminds us that mankind was with God in spiritual form at the time of creation. High Self says Job was not an individual real person, but represents all people.

> *Then the LORD answered Job out of the whirlwind: "Who is this that darkens counsel by words without knowledge? Gird up your loins like a man, I will question you, and you shall declare to me. "Where were you when I laid the foundation of the earth? Tell me, if you have understanding. Who determined its measurements–surely you know! Or who stretched the line upon it? On what were its bases sunk, or who laid its cornerstone, when the morning stars sang together, and all the sons of God shouted for joy? (Job 38:1-7 RSV)*

The 'morning stars' are the flames of light that are given off from the great Light that is God. These flames of light dwell in the consciousness of SPIRIT. In other words, the "morning stars" are the angels, or Light beings (spiritual beings and living souls), who have not yet come into mortal consciousness to begin the incarnational learning process.

The 'sons of God' are all of the souls, both male and female, who were within the realms of Light in the beginning. They were morning stars who chose to assume mortal bodies and undertake the testing and learning process that goes with mortal consciousness and soul growth. They had completed the incarnational process by overcoming all discordant expressions and attuning themselves to the consciousness of SPIRIT. They have returned to the realms of Light as sons of God who work with the morning stars newly preparing to incarnate for their lessons. All the souls were shouting and singing because the earth, or school, was prepared.

Since man is made in God's image we know that mankind is first spiritual, not physical. However, the physical aspect plays an important part in our development as spiritual beings, for it is through incarnating that we learn to use free will and work with energy to form our individual life. Once we learn to work with energy at the earth level, we are then able to work in the spiritual realms to assist in the creation of planets, galaxies, universes, and so on when we have returned to the spiritual realms.

What Is the Physical Realm?

Mankind was not given a physical aspect, an incarnation, or "garments of skins" (Genesis 3:21 RSV) until he partook of the fruit of "the tree of the knowledge of good and evil" (Genesis 2:17 RSV), and was sent out of the garden of Eden into the manifest world. In other words, when man obtained the knowledge of good and evil, he left God Consciousness and entered into a physical body and human beliefs. Until then, he was in the consciousness of SPIRIT and communicated directly with God. As a separation from God, the 'fall' is thus equated with a type of spiritual death:

> *but of the tree of the knowledge of good and evil you shalt not eat, for in the day that you eat of it you shall die." (Genesis 2:17 RSV)*

Separated from God, incarnated man perceived the physical world as a place of duality, where good and evil struggle for ascendancy. Thus man entered another dimension: the world of illusion. As a human being, you have been living in this world of illusion since that time, and have established in your conscious mind the belief that this world is 100% real.

In truth, there are no such things as good and evil; there are only experiences encountered and lessons learned. You choose these experiences and name them good or bad according to your beliefs, perceptions, and judgments.

We can never be separated from God, for we are in God as the wave is in the ocean and the leaf is in the tree. Without the ocean the wave would not be, and without the tree the leaf would cease to exist. You may not be aware of the truth, but "for 'In him [God] we live and move and have our being'" (Acts 17:28 RSV). Never can you be separated from God, except by your own limited beliefs and lack of understanding. This belief in separation is the true meaning of *sin*: an error in consciousness.

Mankind's purpose, and your purpose, is to renew the inner connection with the Light by seeking first the kingdom of God (refer to Matthew 6:33 KJV), and then to make proper use of all knowledge. This knowledge comes only when an individual works in harmony with the High Self. This is being born again into the pure consciousness of SPIRIT, knowing you are one in God Consciousness, and living that knowing. This is the purpose of Spiritual Response Therapy; to place you in conscious contact with your divine self and to harmonize every aspect of your being.

Our Spiritual and Physical Aspects

As explained above, we have two aspects: the spiritual or Light aspect and the physical aspect. Those aspects are expressed as bodies and minds.

18 Bodies and 90 Minds

According to High Self, we have 18 bodies: an etheric body, first astral body, mental body, emotional body, spiritual body, living soul, I AM body, Christ body, Holy Spirit body, Spirit body, physical body, second astral body, third astral body, and an additional five other bodies. SPIRIT creates the first six bodies which are considered the spiritual bodies and we form the last seven bodies. These 18 bodies have 90 conscious and subconscious minds. A conscious mind is the working consciousness of a body. A subconscious mind is the recording device for the experiences of that body. Yet, it is the mind which forms the body.

The body with which we are the most familiar, our physical body, is merely the lower vibratory expression of our greater self. The subconscious mind of our physical body records all the beliefs, perceptions, judgments, and experiences of our conscious minds. When the physical body dies, the conscious and subconscious minds also die, so to speak, and the records in the subconscious mind are moved to the soul record.

Because of our limited human understanding, the following brief discussion of these 18 bodies and 90 minds is somewhat of an approximation of this process of becoming. One confusing issue is that a body in some cases is also a mind, and in others it has a conscious or subconscious mind or both, and in others it acts as conscious and subconscious minds. It is probably best to not get too hung up on the specifics, but rather to reflect on the tremendous amount of energy and attention to detail which creates and nurtures the unique you through all these steps of becoming. You are indeed greatly loved.

The first mind, of which we are all a part, is SPIRIT, All Consciousness. SPIRIT lies behind all things and is that from which all life springs.

The first body of the spiritual man or woman is the 'etheric body' and is formed by SPIRIT at the GODHEAD level (see Chart 3–Levels of Soul Consciousness). The etheric is the basic fabric of ALL that is. It is the smallest unit of energy and the very matrix upon which the 'divine plan' is drawn. It is the whole cloth or spiritual essence that is the foundation for the spiritual realms. The etheric body has a subconscious mind that contains every idea, concept, and belief involved in the embryo, the divine plan, and the first draft (specifications for the entire ONE universe).

Astral means of the stars or Light of SPIRIT. The 'first astral body,' also created by SPIRIT at the GODHEAD level, has a conscious mind where the information in the embryo, divine plan, and first draft are recorded. As a soul completes its learning path and returns to the GODHEAD, it coordinates and harmonizes what it has learned through its many, varied experiential processes, with the original plan and intent of SPIRIT. The beliefs the soul has established during the experiential process (within both the spiritual and physical realms) are stored in the conscious mind of the first astral body. If these beliefs are not in harmony with the records in the conscious mind of the first astral body, the soul must establish harmony before it can reunite with the GODHEAD and SPIRIT.

The spiritual realms were created at the I AM level (see Chart 3). The Holy Scriptures refer to the created spiritual realms as the garden of Eden. It is at this level that the next two bodies are formed. The first formed is the 'emotional body' and has a conscious mind. This body contains the creative energy of the I AM. I AM means the self-existent ONE extending Itself through Its creation–SPIRIT becoming.

The next body to be formed at the I AM level is the 'mental body.' This body also has a conscious mind and signifies SPIRIT aware of Itself in a descending spiral through many avenues and levels of being–descending below all things unmanifest and manifest that it might rise above all things. Thus, SPIRIT extends and expands Its consciousness in ever growing circles.

Next, a unit of consciousness is formed by Elohim which are God beings at the 17th level within the GOD level (see Chart 3). This consciousness is the first form of the idea of self-expression of I AM THAT I AM. This unit of consciousness is that creation referred to in Genesis 1:26-27 RSV: "Then God said, "Let us make man in our image, after our likeness." This unit of consciousness is an instrument of God Consciousness through which ideas are expressed. It is like the shell of a seed which contains within it the idea of self-expression, just as the acorn shell contains within it the idea of the oak tree and the husk of the kernel of corn contains within it the idea of the cornstalk, and ears of corn, and the like.

A second unit of consciousness is formed at King of Kings (see Chart 3). The term King symbolizes a ruler and each of us is a ruler of our own consciousness and expression. No two of us are exactly alike, so you could say that each person is a unique King (ruling idea) of Kings (all ruling ideas). This is the ruling idea of all that will come forth as the other minds are formed and the soul travels the path of experiencing, learning and growing in wisdom and stature through many levels of expression both in and out of the physical body. There are 45,000 elements that may go into the makeup of this unit of consciousness–from one element to all 45,000 in any order or mix.

Then, these two units of consciousness are placed within the Queen of Life (see Chart 3) to form the 'spiritual body' which is both male and female according to Genesis 1:26-27. At Queen of Life there are 150 more elements (or factors) that can go into the makeup of the spiritual body—any one or all of them and in any order or mix. This is the body of ideas that will be expressed as a spiritual being and all that the spiritual being will encounter and become as it progresses along the path of experiencing at many levels of consciousness. The spiritual body contains a subconscious mind, and High Self says it has 500,000,000 compartments and each compartment may contain more information than the largest current computer that man has devised.

Genesis 2:4-7 refers to this point in our creation stating that there was not a man to till the ground, so God formed man of the dust of the ground and man became a living soul. Thus, the next body is called the 'living soul.' It is formed at the level of Lord of Lords (see Chart 3). This body contains the working conscious mind of the spiritual body and there are another 5,000 possible elements (or keys) that can go into its makeup, again in any order, number or mix. This living soul was not made of the elements of any planet, but rather of the energy or dust of SPIRIT (Consciousness). It is very difficult for many people to realize that we are not physical beings. Rather, we are spiritual beings and living souls (henceforth referred to simply as 'soul') inhabiting physical bodies and having human experiences.

The soul has its first, rudimentary existence at the level called Lord (see Chart 3). Here, the soul begins its self-expression as the conscious mind of the spiritual body. It could be stated that the spiritual body and living soul has been given birth (at Lord of Lords) and is now a spiritual being starting on its own path to development. The process so far could be compared to the birth of a physical body and the entering of a living soul into that body to experience through the process we call incarnation or human life, except that the soul's experiences are in the spiritual realms or 'garden of Eden.'

A Light body is then formed at the level of Supreme Consciousness (see Chart 3) as the next stage in the development of the soul. This is called the 'I AM body' and is the idea of self-expression of all that the soul has become during its development in the garden of Eden. This body has a conscious mind, which is called the I AM mind, but no subconscious mind. This is the first level of consciousness at which the soul begins to exercise free will. Just as our physical body has a mind that is used to learn and make decisions, so our soul has a mind that learns, makes determinations, and accumulates knowledge of the spiritual realms where it has its first existence.

In the Holy Scriptures, the spiritual realm is referred to as the garden of Eden. This is where the two sons in the story of the Prodigal Son (Luke 15:11-32) received their basic training and established a rudimentary knowledge of the spiritual realms. The inheritance spoken of in the Scriptures was spiritual life, spiritual substance, and the intelligence to work with them within the spiritual realms. Thus the two sons, who symbolize all souls, developed a basic, working consciousness while in Eden.

Next, the 'Christ body' is formed at the level of Ultimate Consciousness (see Chart 3). This body has a subconscious mind in which is recorded all that the I AM body experiences. The term 'Christ' symbolizes the idea of perfect expression of all that has gone before, all of the knowledge, wisdom, and ability that has been developed while in the spiritual realms. The Christ body also has a conscious mind that begins to express itself in other realms of experience. However, it is not counted as one of the 90 minds.

The 'Holy Spirit body' is formed next, below the level of Ultimate Consciousness and at the top level of the Universal God Consciousness level (as shown by the region of arrows on Chart 3). This body acts as both conscious and subconscious minds. This body symbolizes the movement and expression of all the knowledge and wisdom gained through the previous experiences of the soul in the spiritual realms.

The I AM body, Christ body, and Holy Spirit body are encapsulated in the 'Spirit body.' The Spirit body does not have a mind. Rather, it is the recording device (much like a computer) for all that is learned by the trinity of the three higher bodies (I AM, Christ and Holy Spirit bodies), just as the cells of our physical body record every-thing that occurs while we are in the physical—all that is experienced through the five physical senses of sight, sound, taste, touch, and smell. The Spirit body can be compared to the physical body in that it is the vehicle of expression for the three higher bodies, so it acts as a mind.

The next body is the 'physical body,' which is formed at the level of Creator Consciousness (see Chart 3) under the direction of the first through seventh levels of Gods (beings at the GOD level) which includes all of the Gods of the solar system. There are 56,000,000 elements that may go into the makeup of the physical body and its minds. The physical body has both a conscious mind, which is a sub-function of the soul, and a subconscious mind, which is made up of every cell in the body. However, these two minds are not counted in the 90 minds.

The subconscious mind of the physical body receives impressions from the High Self. Dreams come from the High Self through the subconscious into the conscious mind. The High Self can also bypass the subconscious mind and send impressions directly to the right brain or intuitive mind. These impressions are a result of the inner five spiritual senses of sight, sound, taste, touch, and smell. All people who have gone through the process of SRT, either by having their programs cleared or by taking the workshops, are capable of working with the five inner (spiritual) senses and need but become aware of and develop them.

The 'second astral body' is also formed at the level of Creator Consciousness and has a form of subconscious mind. The 'third astral body' is formed at the level of Spirit Status (see Chart 3) and contains everything that has been experienced on the incarnational path during incarnations and between lives while in the spiritual realms. The third astral body has both conscious and subconscious minds. The major mind is the conscious mind through which we experience and learn, and the secondary or subconscious mind is where we record and store all that is experienced and learned. Everything that is experienced through the five senses is recorded, every thought and its accompanying emotion is also there.

The knowledge accumulated through the actions of the previous minds and the continuing experiencing and learning process of the soul allows the whole being to expand through the levels from incarnational (earth level) to Universal God Consciousness. This is the whole person becoming aware of its spiritual nature; the soul aware that SPIRIT is the only reality and that all else is illusion; the soul aware that it is the Christ, the Son of God. There is an ever-expanding awareness of both the experiential incarnational path and the inner path of SPIRIT. There is a certain degree of spiritual enlightenment that is the seed for greater expansion of the soul's potential. You might say that it is the three loaves that Jesus mentioned in the parable found in Matthew 13:33 that received the leaven that caused them to expand and grow. The three loaves represent the mental, emotional, and physical aspects of each incarnated individual. By observing and getting in touch with our thoughts, emotions, and physical expression, we can become more aware of the process and purpose of life and aware that there is something greater that lies behind these three expressions which is the Christ or Son of God.

The fifteenth mind, the 'Universal God Consciousness mind,' is formed at the level of Universal God Consciousness (see Chart 3 where the hourglass diagram opens and the arrows begin) and is both conscious and subconscious. This mind contains all that has been experienced on the soul's spiritual path to this point. More, it contains the seed for still greater growth and expansion. At this point in our growth there are many new choices and paths open to the soul, and it is necessary for the soul to choose on which path it will proceed. This is in accord with Jesus' statement in John 14:2 KJV "In my Father's house are many mansions."

The sixteenth mind is the 'spiritual illumined mind' and is attained at the 1,999th level within the ONE level. This is the mind that has completed the experiential path and returned to a very high state of soul consciousness.

The next step is Ascension or Oneness with the GODHEAD. When Jesus appeared to Mary in the garden after His resurrection, He told her to not touch Him as He had not yet ascended to the Father (GODHEAD). His soul had attained the 1,999th level within the ONE level of the GODHEAD level, but had not yet been accepted by the GODHEAD. When we have attained the highest level of the GODHEAD (ONE), we are no longer a soul experiencing, but SPIRIT completed and the ascended consciousness (mind). We are one with ALL life, substance, and intelligence at every level. We are not the GODHEAD. However, we are one with the GODHEAD and all that is ideated by the GODHEAD. This is the point at which the plans (divine blueprint) for the heavens and the earths are drawn and we, under the direction of the GODHEAD, may take part in that work. The GODHEAD mind is the mind through which the GODHEAD CONSCIOUSNESS works and we are part of that mind. Everything in its entirety is the GODHEAD mind.

The seventeenth mind is the mind that contains within it all of the ideas that make up the spiritual and physical worlds and all that happens within those realms. It is the complete extension of the divine blueprint.

The final or eighteenth mind is the instrument of consciousness that contains within it eternal and infinite cycles of divine plans, creation of the spiritual realms, formation of the physical, and extension of all that is or ever will be into infinity.

The Incarnational Cycle

At death, you leave a physical world and enter one of the invisible astral planes (invisible, at least, to mortal eyes). You leave the physical body behind and exist in a realm where you can learn, rest, and prepare for the next incarnation.

While you are on 'the other side,' you maintain the emotional body, but without any pain. You also maintain the mental, etheric, and first astral bodies necessary for future incarnations. When you are ready to undertake new lessons and you choose to incarnate, you can return to the physical plane with these bodies to experience additional learning and soul growth in a new physical body.

Some who leave the corporeal body remain in the earth vibrations. They remain due to fear, addictive energy, lack of knowledge, or the desire to stay and comfort a loved one. These beings are known as discarnates. They may attach themselves to someone, who then becomes the host, and cause the host problems. Once there is an awareness of their presence they can be sent to their right place (see "Removing Blocks Listed on Chart 5" in Chapter 6–Removing Blocks to Working with SRT).

Since all discordant energies are established because of a desire to enter the physical realm or are set up while experiencing in some physical realm, it is in the physical where those energies will continue to be experienced and released. Any negative energy that you experience during a lifetime is actually retained in your subtle bodies. This is why releasing discordant energy using a method such as SRT is so important. If you do not, you can take negative programs with you from lifetime to lifetime.

You cannot get rid of your discordant programs while you are out of the physical body, so many lifetimes may be necessary to completely encounter, work through, and erase all discordant energy, and to establish complete oneness with God. Time has little meaning though, for in SPIRIT there is no time or space. You are an eternal spiritual being, living, experiencing, and growing until at last you are reunited with the Light of God. However, you can, through the use of SRT, research and clear all discordant programs in a single lifetime without having to incarnate lifetime after lifetime to overcome all of your individual challenges.

Eventually, when you raise yourself in spiritual awareness, you transcend the physical body and return to the Light in complete oneness with SPIRIT. Working with SRT, you can discover and release all limited beliefs and discordant energies that prevent you from this oneness. You become aware of and work directly with the High Self. Working with the High Self, you transcend the belief in good and evil and the belief that you are separate from God. There is a new birth, or a new consciousness (heaven), and a new expression of good (earth) which will then be a natural part of your daily experience.

> *"I baptize you with water for repentance, but he who is coming after me is mightier than I, whose sandals I am not worthy to carry; he will baptize you with the Holy Spirit and with fire. (Matthew 3:11 RSV)*

When John the Baptist spoke those words, he was referring to the act of receiving a purified spiritual consciousness and awareness (baptized with fire) by becoming one with Christ Consciousness. This awareness reaffirms your spiritual beingness. Remember you are first created of the substance of SPIRIT which is the very ground of your being. This SPIRIT substance contains the life, substance, and intelligence of God. However, you lost awareness of SPIRIT when you partook of "the knowledge of the tree of good and evil" (Genesis 3:6-14).

When you are reborn (born again) into spiritual consciousness, you receive once again a knowledge of the spiritual beingness. This is the awareness of spiritual consciousness that is in unity with the ONE.

> *...Verily, verily, I say unto thee, Except a man be born again, he cannot see the kingdom of God. (John 3:3, KJV)*
>
> *I tell you this, brethren: flesh and blood cannot inherit the kingdom of God, nor does the perishable inherit the imperishable. (1 Corinthians 15:50 RSV)*

When you clear up all of your discordant programs, you once more gain the awareness of SPIRIT and become one with the Light, as you were in the beginning. Then you will no longer need or desire a physical body, for your lessons are finished and further incarnations become unnecessary. You do maintain mental and emotional bodies, but they are in a spiritual realm of expanded awareness, and you do not have to deal with the accumulated discordant energies of earth until you incarnate again. However, it is possible to purify your mental and emotional bodies and gain knowledge of that spiritual plane without discarding your physical body. At such a point you could be considered "in the world, but not of the world" like in John 17:11.

> *And now I am no more in the world, but they are in the world, and I am coming to thee [God].... I have given them [the disciples] thy word; and the world has hated them because they are not of the world, even as I am not of the world. I do not pray that thou shouldst take them out of the world, but that thou shouldst keep them from the evil one. (John 17:11, 14-15 RSV)*

The 'evil one' is negative thoughts and emotions. Once you have reunited with the Light, you can form any of the bodies you wish in order to relate to others on their own level of expression. This does not mean that you will leave the Light and take upon yourself a lower vibration body. It simply means that you will, from your point of consciousness in the Light, form a body endowed with your consciousness. You will then live on both levels at once. This may seem strange to you at first and difficult to believe. However, remember that you are in the image and likeness of God and God is everywhere. As a matter of Truth, God is all there is and you are one with that Allness. You are everywhere present. Well, perhaps not yet, but that is your ultimate potential and your spiritual goal.

If you work with a pendulum, you can ask these questions yourself. (For information about learning to use a pendulum, see Chapter 5—The Basic Steps of SRT.)

Q. Do you lose your individuality when you return to the Light? (-) ("-" represents a "no" response)

Q. You still maintain your individual consciousness and your integrity when you are one with the ONE? (+) ("+" represents a "yes" response)

Q. So what really happens is that you lift your consciousness up into union with God? (+)

Q. Is there more involved than simply becoming one with the Light? (+)

Q. Do you sit around for the rest of time and eternity and just play harps and sing praises to God? (-)

Q. Is there much more involved than man is aware of? (+)

After you have ascended, you will work in and from the spiritual realms to assist other souls as they go through their learning process. The gift of life is yours to use, and how you use it is all important:

> *Every good endowment and every perfect gift is from above, coming down from the Father of lights with whom there is no variation [can be no variation] or shadow due to change. (James 1:17 RSV)*

God is the same yesterday, today, and forever—infinite Love, Light, and Life. You have the opportunity to change your soul patterns from darkness and confusion into light and harmony, thus bringing forth the Light that has been hidden in darkness.

CHAPTER 3

The Soul Family

Until I started working with my High Self, I believed, based on what others had said, that each person has one soul mate or twin flame. I believed, as many others do, that true happiness could be experienced only when you met and joined with your twin flame or soul mate. According to the information received from my High Self and from the High Selves of others, this belief is far from the truth.

Twin flames, flame mates, and soul mates are simply symbolic labels given by SPIRIT to help us understand soul relationships. The *Bible* uses many parables, allegories, idioms, visions, dreams, and symbols to describe our soul's relationship to God and others. 'Fire' and 'cloud,' as used in Genesis, are symbols denoting the presence of God.

> *And the LORD went before them by day in a pillar of cloud to lead them along the way, and by night in a pillar of fire, to give them light... (Exodus 13:21 RSV)*

High Self says that God can be symbolized as the fire of creation, although God is not fire. God is creative energy; and that energy is Light above any human concept of light. You are created in and of that one Light as an individualized package of Light and you came out of God into incarnation to learn and grow. Your goal is to again become one with God in consciousness. Jesus said:

> *"You are the light of the world.... Let your light so shine before men, that they may see your good works and give glory to your Father who is in heaven. (Matthew 5:14, 16 RSV)*

This means that as you live in the consciousness of God and become one with the Light, others will be encouraged to live in a better way so that they, too, can become one with the Light.

Twin Flames and Flame Mates

Continuing the symbolism of God as the fire of creation, a soul can be seen as a flame that is formed of and comes from God's energy. This flame is shaped something like a flower with one to nine parts or *petals*. Each petal may have one to nine divisions (souls). Thus, the maximum number of souls per flame is eighty-one (nine petals times nine divisions equals eighty-one). This is referred to as a *flame family*. Each soul within the flame family is a *flame mate* of each of the other souls. However, the flame mates within a petal are referred to as *twin flames* as a way of acknowledging the closer soul relationship of being in the same petal.

Each petal has both male and female elements (twin flames). Thus, someone who belongs to a nine petal flame with two souls per petal has eight other petals with male and female combinations. These male and female combinations are each a set of twin flames (see figure 3-1).

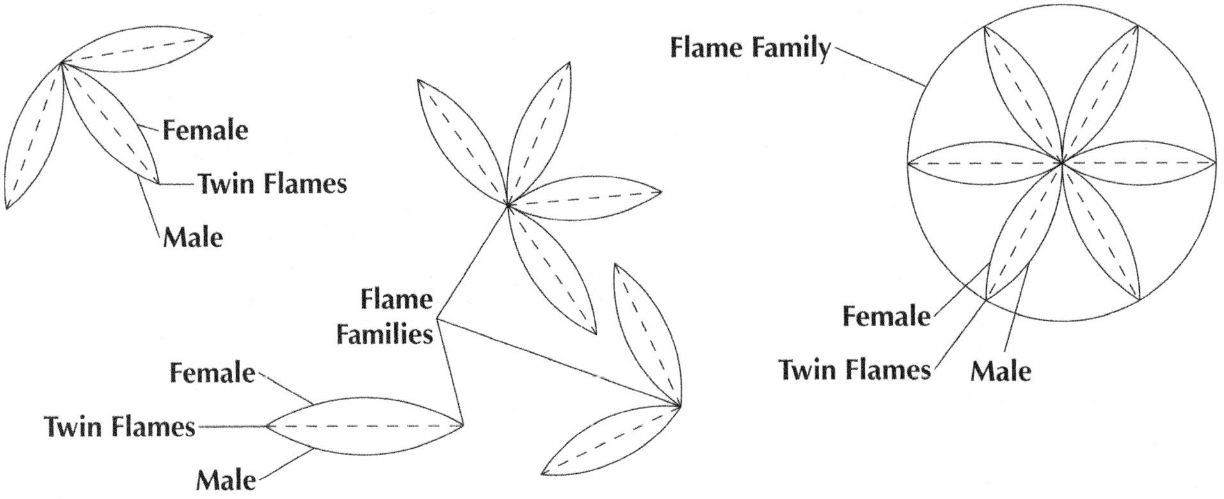

Figure 3-1. Twin Flames

When twin flames incarnate separately, each part is a complete soul. Therefore, I shall refer to each male part and each female part, regardless of being in or out of the physical body, as a 'soul.' Thus, there can be eighteen individual souls in a nine petal flame when there are two souls, one male and one female, per petal.

Every male and every female in a multi-petalled flame is a flame mate to every other male and female regardless of how many petals there are in the flame. If you are in a nine petal flame, and each petal consists of two souls, you have seventeen flame mates. However, only the flame mate in your particular petal is your male or female counterpart—your twin flame.

For example, there are six petals in my flame, each consisting of a set of twin flames. This means that there are twelve flame mates or souls in all, of which I am one. Therefore, I have eleven flame mates—one in my petal, whom I refer to as my twin flame, and two each in the other five petals.

All of my flame mates are, or were, incarnated in this life. When I was born, five of us were in one family. My father, who was killed in a cave-in when I was two, was my twin flame. He was the male half of my petal, while I am the female soul. My mother, my oldest sister, and my maternal grandmother were also in my flame. Fay, my oldest sister, died just short of her fourteenth birthday. She had two short incarnations after that and is now incarnated as my granddaughter. My grandmother left the physical body many years ago. She has since incarnated in another female form and lives in California. Three of my flame mates have made their transition and will not incarnate again.

Each soul in a petal can incarnate in either a female or male body of flesh and bone, whether or not the soul is a male soul or a female soul. I am the female half of my flame and a lovely woman (my father reincarnated) is the male half. Of course, it is obvious from working with past lives that my twin flame and I have both been incarnated many times as males and many times as females. Never have I found that a person has lived every incarnation solely as a male or solely as a female.

In addition to male and female souls, I have found androgynous souls. Androgynous souls are both male and female because they did not split when they were created. In some instances, they are part of a petal or flame and in other instances they are not, they are a petal all by themselves. Occasionally, they are complete loners and do not even belong to an oversoul (see the next section, "Oversouls and Soul Mates").

I was curious about why the maximum number of petals in a flame is nine, so I asked my High Self some questions. The number nine is the number of spiritual completion; for it is the Trinity squared (a number that is squared is considered to be completed). Man's number is 12 and when man is squared (12 x 12 = 144), he is completed spiritually, for 144 totals up to nine (1+4+4=9). Man has twelve spiritual faculties that are represented by the twelve special students that Jesus called apostles. On Chart 12—Spirit Energy Programming, these faculties are referred to as 'twelve aspects of Spirit as genetic coding.'

Many people believe that they have to meet and marry their twin flame in order to be fulfilled, complete, and happy. Here are some questions I asked my High Self regarding this belief.

Q. *Is it guaranteed that, if you meet your twin flame, the energy between you will be loving, positive, and harmonious as so many people believe? (-)*

Q. *Can there be conflict, pain, and unhappiness? (+)*

Q. *So, coming together with a twin flame does not guarantee love and order in a person's life? (-)*

Q. *Does a twin flame ever come into our lives to test us? (-)*

Q. *Does a twin flame ever come into our lives to assist us in meeting and overcoming a challenge in the process of soul growth? (+)*

Q. *Then a twin flame may be the means through which we are set up to face a challenge in the process of soul growth? (+)*

Q. *And, this can be both painful and difficult? (+)*

Oversouls and Soul Mates

Groups of flames join together to form an *oversoul.* This is the extended soul family, and their joining as an oversoul has a common purpose—to fulfill some soul function in the process of growing and unfolding spiritually. *Soul mates* are all of the souls that belong to an oversoul and work together just as all of the cells in a fingernail belong to the fingernail and work together to form the nail and fulfill its function. In other words, everyone in an oversoul is a soul mate to every other soul in that oversoul. There can be a large number of soul mates in an oversoul (my oversoul contains three hundred souls), or only a few. The smallest number I have found in an oversoul is three, and the largest number is infinite. Infinite simply means there are too many soul mates involved to realistically assign a number.

Although it seldom occurs, the number of souls in an oversoul can change during the last incarnation, but only under the direction and intervention of SPIRIT. SPIRIT can, at its discretion, and under certain circumstances, remove a person from one oversoul and place them in another. This does not happen very often and the circumstances requiring the move must be very critical to the welfare of the soul being moved. I have only run into one such case, where the soul was part of a dark oversoul. Because she was growing spiritually, the soul was taken out and placed in another oversoul where she could continue her growth without the negative influence of other souls in the dark oversoul.

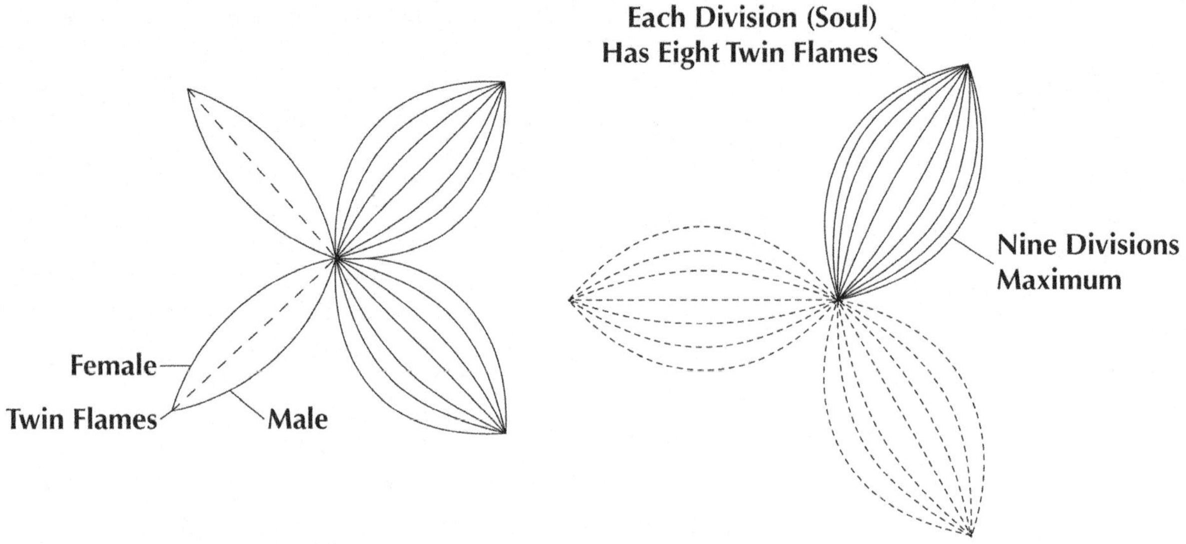

Figure 3-2. Multiple Twin Flames and Flame Mates

Multiple Twin Flames and Flame Mates

To further complicate your search for the right and perfect spiritual mate, you may find that you have up to eight twin flames and seventy-two flame mates in your soul family. Remember, a flame can be made up of as many as nine divisions or petals. Each petal can have up to nine divisions of male and female souls (see figure 3-2). If there are nine souls in a petal, there could be four female souls and five male souls or five female souls and four male souls. You would, in this case, have eight twin flames. Which one will you find happiness with? Or, which one should you search for and marry? Perhaps you would be better off with a flame mate from one of the other petals or a person who is not even in your soul family.

There can also be 'looping' between adjacent flames or between oversouls, adding another twin flame. Looping gives the two souls, one in each flame or one in each oversoul, one additional twin flame (see figure 3-3). For example, my grandmother and brother are twin flames, and my grandmother is my flame mate. For a long time I questioned the accuracy of this information given by my High Self. I would ask if my brother was in my flame or my oversoul and would get a "no" response. Yet my High Self insisted, again and again, that my brother and my grandmother were twin flames. I finally understood what my High Self was trying to get across: there may be looping between flames within an oversoul or between flames in adjacent oversouls. If you are looped with another flame you would have one more twin flame. My brother is part of a flame in an adjacent oversoul and he is looped with my grandmother (the woman in California) in my flame.

Looping also answered another twin flame question that came up during a workshop. I had questioned High Self about a possible soul relationship between Jesus and Mary, His mother, and was told that they are twin flames. I presented this information to people in the workshop and was immediately challenged by one of the students. She insisted that I was wrong because, she said, "Raphael is Mary's twin flame." I did some more questioning about Mary and Jesus and continued to get the same answer: "Yes, they are twin flames."

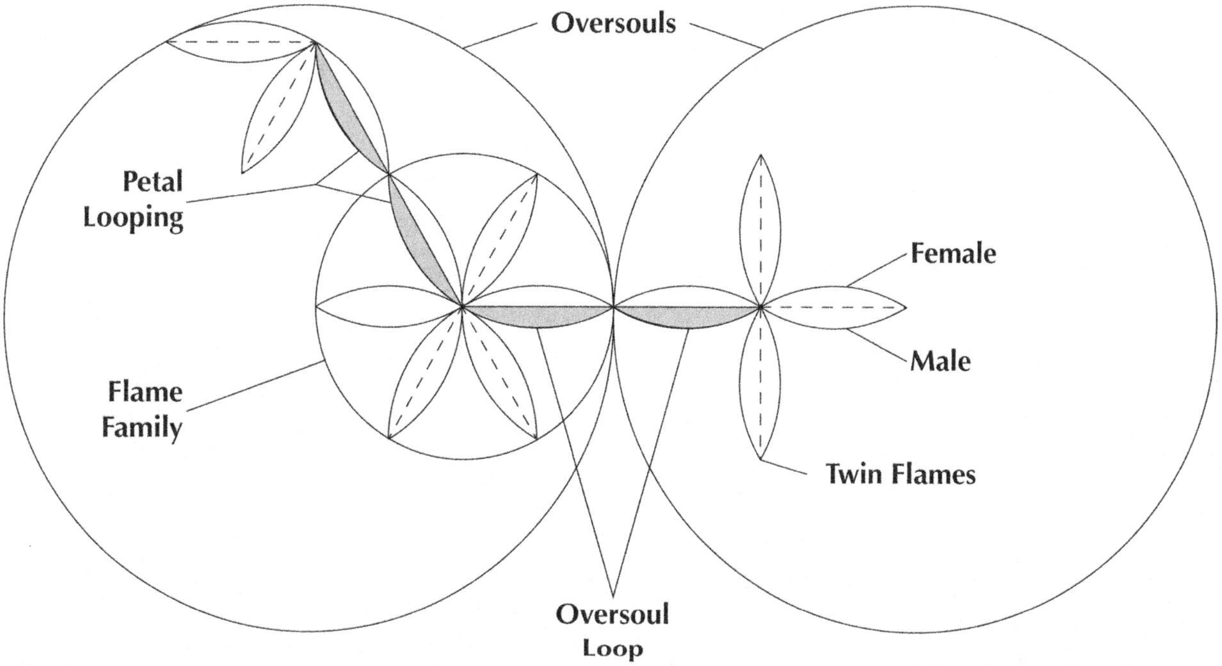

Figure 3-3. Oversouls and Looping

When I finally became aware of looping, I found that Jesus and Mary are not in the same flame or even the same oversoul. They are twin flame loops between two adjacent oversouls. Jesus is in a nine petal flame with nine divisions per petal. He has eight twin flames in His petal (one of whom is Mary Magdalene), and has one additional twin flame by being looped with His mother, Mary, who is in an adjacent oversoul. Thus, Jesus has nine twin flames.

Twin flames may also be adopted. Every person I work with I adopt into my flame family as a twin flame. This establishes a mind connection so that I can research and clear their programs. By the time this book goes to press, I will have placed over 10,000 people on my twin flame list. Only one is part of my original flame family.

While working with a client, we found that she had one twin flame. About a year later she questioned the accuracy of what we had been told. "Didn't you tell me that ... was my only twin flame?" I assured her that the answer we had previously received was correct. She said, "Then why do I now have two twin flames?" Questioning High Self revealed that she did indeed have two twin flames and I told her I did not know why this was so. The next week, she helped me facilitate a workshop. After the workshop, she had two more twin flames. They were two people with whom she had worked one-on-one, and had adopted them as twin flames. That was when I realized I probably had adopted as a twin flame everyone I had worked with, and a check revealed that this was correct. Later, I learned that it is not necessary to adopt anyone; you can ask your High Self to make sure that this is not done.

It is important, when researching your original flame family, to tell your High Self you want to research the flame family as it existed before any adoptions. Once you establish the number of petals in your flame and the number of souls per petal in your original flame family, you can then ask about any souls you may have adopted into your soul family as twin flames.

The Addictive Energy of Flames

According to Jesus, this is the first and greatest commandment:

and you shall love the Lord your God with all your heart, and with all your soul, and with all your mind, and with all your strength.' The second is this, 'You shall love your neighbor as yourself.' There is no other commandment greater than these." (Mark 12:30-31 RSV)

These commandments may pose a very real problem where twin flames or flame mates are concerned. An individual may be married to one person but have a very strong attraction to another person. Working with SRT, you usually find that the third person is a twin flame, flame mate, or soul mate and that there is addictive energy between them—the energy of attraction is so strong that it is an addiction. When a person is addicted to something, the draw is so strong that everything else is sacrificed to fill that addiction. When souls are addicted to each other, they will give up everything else including God. Thus, addictive love for a twin flame has even supplanted love of God, relegating God to second place.

Here is one case that demonstrates the addictive energy of twin flames (all names have been changed). Sam was married to Terri, but found that he loved Rita very deeply. It wasn't that he did not love and respect Terri, because he did. However, the addictive energy between Sam and Rita was very strong and was creating pain and conflict in all three lives. Here are the questions I asked Sam's subconscious mind.

Q. *How many past lives have you and Rita had together? (Infinite)*

Q. *Are you in the same oversoul? (+)*

Q. *Are you in the same flame family? (+)*

Q. *Are you in the same petal? (+)*

Q. *Then you are twin flames? (+)*

Q. *How many petals did your flame divide into? (7)*

Q. *How many per petal? (2)*

Q. *You have thirteen flame mates? (+)*

Q. *One of the thirteen is your twin flame? (+)*

Q. *How many past lives did you and Terri have together? (86)*

Q. *Are you twin flames or flame mates? (-)*

Q. *Are you in the same oversoul? (-)*

Sam had a very strong desire to be with Rita, due to the addictive energy built up in their past lives together. The fact that he and Rita were also twin flames only increased the attraction, for there is usually a strong natural attraction to any soul in your soul family. This attraction can be even stronger for a twin flame.

Sam was not Terri's twin flame nor had the two of them had many lives together. Therefore, their attraction and love for each other was not based on addictive energy, but simply a need to be together and work on other programs.

To a degree, twin flames, flame mates, and soul mates are always together in Spirit. They can be very sensitive to each other's energies. For instance, my twin flame lives some 900 miles away, yet each of us can still be aware of the other's energies. When either of us is aware of the other person running some energy, we can work with our High Self to research and clear the program.

Once you have had some experience in using SRT, there is an easy way to find out if there is a soul connection—simply ask if there is one. When I get a "yes" response, I ask what the connection is. To do this, I designate the upper-left corner of the chart as twin flame, the middle as flame mate and the upper-right corner as soul mate. When I asked if there was a soul connection between Sam and Rita, I received a positive response. When I asked what the connection was, the pendulum pointed to the left corner, indicating twin flame.

I found Sam's addictive energy on Rita to be 100%, and her's on him to be 87%. High Self indicated that they needed to break the addiction and that is one of the reasons they incarnated together. High Self indicated that if Sam and Rita did not break the addiction in this life, they would have to face and resolve it in another life. Should the addiction not be resolved in this life, it would be more difficult to resolve in a subsequent life. Thus, each lifetime of addiction tends to add to the energy and make it more difficult to resolve.

Addictive energy between twin flames can show up in other ways. Alice came in for counseling to discover why she was not physically attracted to her husband Gary. Eighty-eight of their past lives together included addictive energy. Both of them had an addictive energy of 100%, and both had the desire to clear up the addictive energy in this life. To learn when this energy was set up, we researched their past lives (researching past lives is explained in detail in Chapter 5–The Basic Steps of SRT).

We found out that in one past life, Alice was a male and Gary was a female, and that God was involved. We discovered that God was trying to help them break the 100% addiction they had established in previous lives. However, this incarnation only increased their desire for each other. In the second past life we researched, they were both Light beings and the other cast member was God. This was before their first incarnation and they believed that God caused them to incarnate. They were both angry at God and believed he was unjust and unloving.

This is another case where the beliefs of the person or persons involved do not make much sense to the rational mind. Alice is the male half of the soul and Gary the female half. In the current life, Alice was not physically attracted to Gary, because she is female, and to be attracted to him would indicate a homosexual relationship.

After clearing the negative energy, Alice and Gary were more attracted to each other, but without the addictive energy. God has first place in their relationship and human love comes second.

Soul Essence

There is another complication that comes up from time to time regarding soul families and relationships. After asking if two people have a soul connection and receiving a positive response, when I ask what the connection is, High Self may indicate that it is not on the chart. Often High Self is trying to tell me that the two people share the same *essence*.

Having the essence of someone simply means that you have some of the basic elements that make up the other person's nature. For instance, each person has the essence of God, which is love. As the wave is in the ocean and has the essence of the ocean, so we are in God and have the essence of God. The leaf on the tree is not the tree; however, it has the essence of the tree.

I have met many people who have the essence of Mary Magdalene. When I ask if the person is the incarnation of Mary Magdalene, I get a "yes" response. When I ask the same question again, I get a "no" response. This form of mixed response indicates that the person is not the actual reincarnation of Mary Magdalene, but has some of her nature (essence) and hence some of the same programs.

When a soul has risen high enough in consciousness, they do not need to incarnate again. However, they may continue to experience physical life by investing their soul energies in a person who is incarnated. You might say they are living and experiencing vicariously through the other soul's experiences. The incarnated soul may run some of the same programs that the other soul ran when they were in physical body. Every person who has Mary Magdalene's essence, for instance, has a program of anger. I have seen several inner pictures of various people (as Mary Magdalene) standing at the foot of the cross. Mary Magdalene was very upset and angry at Jesus for not using His power to save Himself from the crucifixion. She had witnessed many of His miracles and knew He had the power to save Himself. Her anger was also directed at the apostles who were not there to defend Jesus, the people who reviled Him, and the soldiers who crucified Him.

Siamese Flames

Another variation on the soul family is back-to-back or *Siamese* flame families. Imagine a flower with two sides. The side facing you is one flower and the other side looking away from you is the other flower. The souls in the back flame are in your oversoul, and there is a soul connection, which High Self says are soul mates. However, they are not flame mates or twin flames; they are more like Siamese twins. So, you see, soul families can seem a little complicated until you understand all of the ramifications and variations. And this understanding only comes about through practice.

The Purpose of Oversouls

Chart 2–Themes and Challenges, which is included in Appendix B of this book, lists themes and challenges. You can use these to determine the basic purpose of your oversoul. The basic purpose of my oversoul is to learn and reflect love and affection in every aspect of life. Love and affection are also the basic themes for everyone else in my oversoul.

You can also use Chart 2 to determine the personal programs that you came into life to work on.

Q. *Does the number of themes chosen to be worked on by other souls in my oversoul vary? (+)*

Q. *When someone in the oversoul grows in spiritual awareness, does it affect all of the other soul mates in a positive way? (-)*

Q. *Does it affect the entire universe in a positive way? (+)*

Q. *Is that what Jesus meant when He said, "if I be lifted up from the earth, [I] will draw all men unto me" (John 12:32 KJV)? (+)*

Any person (soul) who has cleared sufficient subconscious programs and has grown into a conscious awareness of SPIRIT is one with everyone and has an infinite number of soul mates. At the GODHEAD level there is only one consciousness and one oversoul, as each soul has completed its work and has returned to ONE. This oversoul is called the master oversoul. When you return to the GODHEAD, you become part of this master oversoul.

Q. *Does Jesus belong to a master oversoul? (+)*

Q. *So everyone is His soul mate? (+)*

Q. *When Jesus began His ministry in Israel, was He in a master oversoul? (-)*

Q. *Was He in a master oversoul before His ministry was completed? (-)*

Q. *Did He enter the master oversoul when He was crucified? (-)*

Q. *Did He enter it upon His ascension? (+)*

Q. *Is that when He became one with the Light that is God? (+)*

Q. *Then, His ministry was only complete when He ascended? (+)*

Q. *Is Jesus now one with the Light of God? (+)*

Q. *Is there a link between each individual oversoul and every other oversoul? (+)*

The Scriptures instruct us to love God, and love our neighbors as ourselves. I like to put it in these words: Love God, the Source and Substance of all life, animate and inanimate. Love all living souls, male and female, for they are the essence of God. Then, regardless of a soul being a flame mate, twin flame, soul mate or just another person having no soul family connection, choose the one you would like to share your life with. If you love everyone, it makes it easier to find someone you can be happy with.

Remember, you are complete in God, not in another person. As your soul rises in consciousness, you become one with every soul in the universe. You are twin flame, flame mate, soul mate, essence of, and brother and sister to all.

CHAPTER 4

Infinite Service

Each one of us establishes a basic divine plan before we come into life. Every soul has certain goals that it wishes to accomplish in each incarnation, so it sets up a plan of action. Each soul picks the galaxy, planet, country, nationality, body, sex, parents, and so on, in order to fulfill his or her basic goals for the particular incarnation. If you successfully accomplish those goals, you grow upward in infinite potential.

One way to fulfill our potential is to serve as a guide or High Self for others, even while we are simultaneously incarnated in physical form. During my workshops, after the students have gained some expertise in using a pendulum, I suggest that they ask their High Selves if they are also serving any other soul in any capacity. Almost always the answer is a strong "yes." They are usually serving as High Self to an infinite number of souls. This means that, while they are sitting in class practicing, their soul, which is infinite, is serving at other levels of awareness!

If you have learned to use a pendulum, you can ask the following questions for yourself. (For details on learning to use a pendulum, see Chapter 5—The Basic Steps of SRT.)

Q. *Am I serving other incarnated souls as their High Self? (+)*

Q. *With an infinite number of souls? (+)*

We can also serve as some form of angel, such as Guardian Angel or Seraph. A Seraph may serve as guide, Guardian Angel, High Self, or Angel of Light. These positions of service are listed on Chart 1—Contact or Help, which appears in Appendix B of this book.

We find the term *seraphim* is used only once in the Scriptures.

> *In the year that King Uzzi'ah died I saw the Lord sitting upon a throne, high and lifted up; and his train filled the temple. Above him stood the seraphim; each had six wings: with two he covered his face, and with two he covered his feet, and with two he flew. And one called to another and said: "Holy, holy, holy is the LORD of hosts; the whole earth is full of his glory." And the foundations of the thresholds shook at the voice of him who called, and the house was filled with smoke. And I said: "Woe is me! For I am lost; for I am a man of unclean lips, ... Then flew one of the seraphim to me, having in his hand a burning coal which he had taken with tongs from the altar. And he touched my mouth, and said: "Behold, this has touched your lips; your guilt is taken away, and your sin forgiven."*
> *(Isaiah 6:1-7 RSV)*

Seraphim in Hebrew means, *"the burning; fiery ones; consuming with fire"* (MBD). They represent purity, the cleansing power of exalted ideas, and the healing power of SPIRIT. Wings symbolize our ability to fly, or rise, above all limitation of the material world. Those who have cleared their discordant programs are spiritually quickened and have gone a long way in the development of spiritual intuition. Once the intuitive faculty has been developed, the soul grows through higher levels of purification into the total consciousness of God Light until there remains no impurity whatsoever.

The wings covering the face of the seraphim symbolize that the spiritual work is going on at a level that cannot be seen and is too deep for human understanding. This work is done on levels of consciousness that, we as humans, have little awareness of. When you work with SRT, you learn very quickly that there is much that goes on as a result of this process that is unseen. As you clear most of your discordant energy, checking with High Self may reveal that only a small fraction of one percent of your total soul energy is used to maintain earth-level consciousness. The rest is manifesting at other levels of being. These could be parallel lives, lives in another universe, future lives, or simply working on levels of spirit far beyond your mortal understanding.

Levels of Soul Consciousness and Service

Chart 3–Levels of Soul Consciousness, which appears in Appendix B of this book, shows the levels of consciousness a soul can attain as it works on its creative potential lifetime after lifetime, in and out of the physical body. As your soul attains higher and higher levels of consciousness, it is able to fulfill greater and greater levels of service to other souls. A soul often provides this service by being assigned an office such as High Self or Guardian Angel, where they help other souls on their spiritual journey.

Although it took me twelve years to accumulate this information, it is still mostly a bare framework with many missing pieces. As this information is needed to clear negative programs, I here present what I know.

The ***Incarnational Status*** (at the bottom of Chart 3) is the level at which you begin your physical incarnations. At this level, your soul is caught up in the challenges and difficulties of experiencing life on some planet. Because most of your soul's energy at this level of consciousness is invested at a planetary level, you do not serve others as High Self, guide, or Guardian Angel. Beyond this level of soul consciousness, your soul can express as you and simultaneously serve others. When your soul consciousness is at the level of ***Spirit Status*** and you are between incarnations, you can serve as a guide or Guardian Angel. The soul you serve may be incarnated or out of the body between incarnations.

At the level of ***Holy Spirit Status*** you can serve someone who is incarnated as their personal Holy Spirit. At the level of ***Christ Status*** you can serve someone who is incarnated as their personal Christ.

Souls that are not incarnated do not have a soul serving as their personal Holy Spirit or personal Christ. They sometimes do have guides and almost always a High Self. From time to time I encounter an incarnated soul that does not have High Self or Guardian Angels. When I discover this, I ask that they be assigned.

The Holy Spirit Status and Christ Status levels of soul consciousness are not to be confused with the Holy Spirit or the Christ. The Holy Spirit and the Christ are aspects of the GODHEAD and are above and interpenetrate the entire hierarchy of soul consciousness. Metaphysically, the Trinity may be presented as God as Infinite Consciousness which creates ideas while Christ is the perfect idea of self-expression in God Consciousness and Holy Spirit is the movement of that idea into expression.

A soul at the level of ***Light Status*** can, when out of the body between incarnations, serve in the office of guide, Guardian Angel, or High Self for another soul. The soul they serve may be incarnated or out of the body between incarnations.

Sometimes they serve a soul as both guide and High Self, or they may elect not to serve anyone, but simply mark time and rest until their next incarnation. High Self says there are five other positions (they are not offices) a soul may occupy when at Light Status. However, it says that it will not and cannot reveal what those positions are because I would have no understanding of them.

Once a soul has reached Light Status (the upper portion of the hourglass diagram on Chart 3), there are two paths that lead to the higher realms. They are the Savior Path and the Ascended Master Path. The ***Savior Path*** I call the 'greased pole,' since it is the hardest path that a soul can choose. There can be no deviation from this path and the requirements are rigid and unalterable. Jesus is one who chose the Savior path, and as you can tell from His life, it was not an easy one.

There are two levels of savior. The first-level of savior is any spiritual teacher who comes to reveal a higher principle to receptive souls incarnated on a planet. There are about 92,000 of these on planet Earth and the number is increasing. There is only one second-level savior per planet, and the savior for this planet is Jesus of Nazareth. He is not Savior for any other planet. Jesus directs all of the first-level saviors on Earth, and guides and counsels them. Those on the savior path go through the same levels of consciousness as those on the Ascended Master Path but the functions they perform that are associated with those levels are different.

The second path through the levels of Light (the upper portion of the hourglass diagram shown on Chart 3) starts with the level of ***Ascended Master***. The basic responsibilities that a soul at this level undertakes are greater than those at Light Status. There are eighteen offices in each level of Ascended Master, and there are 144,000 levels.

Souls in the first office of the Ascended Master level can serve as Guardian Angels for souls that are incarnated, but not for souls out of the body. Souls in the second office can serve as guides for souls out of the body, but not for souls in the body. Souls in the third office are Angels of Light and may be called upon to lend their light energy to incarnated souls or to work in a variety of ways. For instance, I used to ask them to take out discarnates that were in possession or in the aura of a client. Now I simply ask my High Self to take care of all discarnates. High Self informs me that they do not do the actual work, but call on the appropriate beings for whatever is needed. (For more information about clearing blocks and interference, see Chapter 6–Removing Blocks to Working with SRT.)

The fourth office of the Ascended Master level is High Self. SPIRIT says that souls in this office can serve two, four, seven, or nine incarnated souls. They do not serve souls who are not incarnated. Souls in the fifth office are council members and serve a physical planet, actually working with planetary energy. There are seven souls on the council, called the Council of Seven. The sixth office is also a Council of Seven, and souls in this office serve the people on some individual planet by working with energy.

The seventh office is an Angel office of Holy Spirit. These souls serve under the Holy Spirit and work with incarnated souls as assigned. The eighth office is sometimes an Angel office and sometimes not. I have no information as to the function or duties for this office. Souls in the ninth office serve as a guide for someone in the physical body. Souls in the tenth office are Angels of Light that work with plant life on the planet.

Angels of Light from the eleventh office work with the lesser organisms on a planet. Office twelve works with the animal kingdom of a planet, including the fish and fowl. They work with all lower life forms.

Souls in office thirteen work on committees under Ones (beings listed on Chart 3). Ones are in charge of planetary systems under the direction of the Gods of that system. Office fourteen consists of Guardian Angels for souls out of the body.

Souls in office fifteen serve as High Self for souls either in or out of the body. The souls serving as High Self may be incarnated or out of the body. Souls in office sixteen serve souls who have left the physical plane and need time to rest and renew before considering their next incarnation. Souls in office seventeen serve as High Self for souls who are not incarnated, and can serve two, four, seven, or nine souls at a time.

Office eighteen totals numerically to a nine and this is where the Council of Nine has its origin. These souls work with souls who are planning to incarnate and continue to work with them as needed while they are in the flesh.

As you have probably realized, you can serve as guide, Guardian Angel, or High Self from many levels of consciousness. You can serve as a guide at Spirit Status, Light Status, or Ascended Master levels. As you attain each subsequent level, you are higher in consciousness and should be able to do a better job for the soul you serve—providing, of course, you do not have your own programs.

Just because a soul is serving as a guide does not mean that they are the best guide there is. At the Ascended Master level, for instance, there are 144,000 levels of soul consciousness within this level—so there are 144,000 levels of a guide. This also holds true for each of the eighteen offices that are within each of the 144,000 levels of the Ascended Master level. I find many of my clients, especially after they have taken the workshop or had their programs cleared, are serving as High Self for other souls who are incarnated or out of the physical body, or some of each. When I ask how many souls a person is serving as High Self, the answer may be in hundreds, thousands, or even infinite.

In the level called ***One***, there are 70,000 levels and each level has seventy offices within it. A soul's primary function at this level is to be a council member for a planetary system. However, there are many other functions, some of which are guide, Guardian Angel, Angel of Light, and High Self.

A soul's primary function at the level of ***Vector*** is to serve as a council member for an entire solar system, which includes the sun or suns, planets, and moons of that planetary system. There are 144 offices and 144,000 levels at the Vector level.

In physics, a vector is a quantity that has magnitude and direction. When the term came up while working with a client, we found a parallel. We were researching a past life and had asked Iris what she was in that past life. Her pendulum was moved across the bottom of the chart indicating that the answer was not on the chart. I speculated as to what it could be and Iris, who is very intuitive, said, "I am getting the word 'vector.'" I said, "What in the world is a vector?" Immediately I had an inner vision of Zeus standing on the mountain with thunderbolts in his hand. I asked if vectors were Creative Forces and Iris' pendulum moved to indicate a "yes" response. Vectors are the sons of God spoken of in Genesis 6:1-2 and Job 38:7.

The level of ***Free*** has infinite levels and contains 756 offices within each level. The primary function of souls on this level is to manage a planetary system, excluding the sun. They work under the direction of the God of the planet. I have not identified any of the offices other than guide, Guardian Angel, High Self, Angels of Light, Holy Spirit, and Christ. There are simply too many unknowns and too many possibilities.

The level of ***Holy Spirit Consciousness*** is a presence (these would be considered, by humans, divine or supernatural spirits) and there are infinite levels containing an infinite number of beings. The only information given on this was that they become one with active and creative forces.

The level of ***Christ Consciousness*** has infinite levels. These beings are a presence and are like divine or supernatural spirits that work under the office of the Holy Spirit. They are in charge of planetary systems including the sun or suns, and are council members for a universe.

Beings at the level of ***Mentor Consciousness*** are in charge of a universe, under the direction of the I AM THAT I AM of that universe. (For more information about the I AM THAT I AM, see the Glossary in Appendix A of this book.)

Beings at the level of ***Creator Consciousness*** take part in the creation of planetary systems and solar systems. Spirit Substance permeates all space, and Creator Consciousness moves upon the face of this Spiritual Substance and forms it into physical matter. This is also where the physical, human body is formed.

Beings at the level of ***Universal God Consciousness*** take part in the creation of a universe. Universal God Consciousness, along with Mentor Consciousness, and Creator Consciousness beings are all of God and work as a team. Universal God Consciousness is shown opening up into many paths and levels. This is in keeping with Jesus' statement, "In my Father's house are many mansions" (John 14:2 KJV). There are infinite levels at the Universal God Consciousness level, and that is the only information High Self has given.

High Self gave ***Ultimate Consciousness*** as the next level which contains infinite offices, levels, and beings. Next, there is the ***Supreme Consciousness*** level with infinite offices, levels, and beings. The same three factors are found in the next level called ***Majestic Consciousness***.

Beings at the level of ***Lord*** work with the laws of creation. This is often called the law of mind action. What we think and feel creates that which we think about. This is true on all levels of consciousness, whether it be on the level of the rock, amoeba, plant, fish, bird, animal, human, or beyond. Of course, a rock does not have the same consciousness that higher forms have, but it does have life, substance, and intelligence, and it does think (but not as man thinks) at its own level of consciousness.

The next level given has three levels within it: King of Kings, Queen of Life, and Lord of Lords. Let's start with the ***King of Kings*** level. King means 'the ruling power or idea.' The highest ruling power is the idea of God in self-expression. However, every idea has its own power of expression, so we have the highest idea, King (God in expression) of all the ideas or Kings (which contains all ideas).

The highest ideal of God was to form mankind in the image and likeness of Self (Genesis 1:26-27). But, before anything can be brought forth at any level of the creative process there has to be some idea involved in that creation. High Self says there are 45,000 different elements that can go into the makeup of mankind. These elements may be present in the individual in any quantity, from one element to all 45,000, and in any order. Thus, High Self indicates that the number of possibilities for the makeup of the different ideas called man is ten to the infinite squared. This is the King, or ruling idea of each individual.

The level of ***Queen of Life*** is the womb of creativity where the ruling idea called man is placed during its gestation or formative period. High Self says this is a black hole and is called anti-time. Just as the egg and the sperm come together in the womb of the female to form the body, so the divine idea of mankind goes into the womb of creativity (Queen of Life) for its gestation and formation into the 'spiritual body,' which was created in the image and likeness of God (Genesis 1:26-27). High Self says that at Queen of Life there are another 150 elements that may go into the makeup of the spiritual body in any order or combination.

Lord of Lords is the level where the working consciousness of the spiritual body is formed, called the "living soul" (Genesis 2:7 KJV). 'Lord' means the individual idea expressing as one soul from among all of the Lords or souls. Here there are 5,000 additional elements that go into the makeup of the living soul, in any quantity and combination. All of this occurs before the formation of man as a physical being. It was not until spiritual man partook of 'the tree of the knowledge of good and evil' that he was given the physical body, or the "garments of skins" (Genesis 3:21 RSV). High Self says that 'the tree of the knowledge of good and evil' is a catalog containing 900,000,000 possible life scenarios that a soul can chose from when they desire to start on their incarnational path. The soul can choose up to a combination of any twenty scenarios. Also, the soul may chose up to three other life scenarios which it can switch to at any time. In addition, there are 56,000,000 elements that can go into the makeup of the physical body at the time of incarnating, in any quantity or combination. That is why every person has individual fingerprints.

The next level given on Chart 3 is ***GOD***, which has infinite beings at infinite levels. High Self gave information on eighteen groups (or levels) that are within this level. God at this level is known as I AM THAT I AM. Level 1 is a single God being (I AM THAT I AM) over a single planet. And, since there are an infinite number of planets in a universe, and they are at different points or levels of expression, there are an infinite number of Gods at infinite levels of consciousness.

Level 2 is a God over each two planets in a solar system. Level 3 is a God over every four planets in a solar system. Level 4 is a God over eight planets in a solar system. Level 5 is a God over sixteen planets in a solar system. Level 6 is a God over the sun or suns in a solar system. Level 7 is a God over an entire solar system.

From here on there is always a council of Gods and it is called an ***Infinite Council of Gods*** or ***Elohim.***

Level 8 is an Infinite Council of Gods over a set of solar systems consisting of three or more systems, up to an undetermined number (depending on the level of consciousness of the God beings who make up the Council). This is also called a *quadrant* of a galaxy.

Level 9 is an Infinite Council of Gods over a galaxy. Level 10 is an Infinite Council of Gods over a set of galaxies, numbering from three to nine. Level 11 is an Infinite Council of Gods over sets of galaxies consisting of three to nine galaxies each. The way this was communicated by High Self was, "Level 11 resides over sets of nine galaxies, consisting of from four sets of nine galaxies to eighty-one sets of nine galaxies."

Level 12 is an Infinite Council of Gods over groups of eighty-one sets of nine galaxies. The minimum number is one set of eighty-one, and the maximum number is twenty-seven sets of eighty-one. Level 13 is an Infinite Council of Gods over twenty-seven sets of eighty-one times nine galaxies. Level 14 is an Infinite Council of Gods over three sets of twenty-seven.

Level 15 is an Infinite Council of Gods over thirty-six sets of three times twenty-seven sets. Level 16 is an Infinite Council of Gods over seventy sets of thirty-six sets. Level 17 is an Infinite Council of Gods over 144 sets of seventy.

Level 18 is one I AM THAT I AM (one being) over a universe. This one being is called Elohim and is made up of countless beings acting as one. You could describe this being as a melded consciousness working as **One**.

High Self says that at the next level, the ***I AM*** level there are another 2,000 levels. Each of which is presided over by an Elohim (many Gods). All of the 1,999 beginning levels within the I AM level are called an Infinite Council. Each level is over a larger and larger group of universes up to super universe, much as the GOD levels are over the planets, solar systems, and galaxies up to the level of universe. The 2,000th level is the I AM or Yahweh level and is over a super super universe. A super universe is made up of many universes. There is no minimum number, although the maximum number is 700,000. A super super universe is made up of a maximum of 9,000 super universes.

I was told by High Self that the I AM over a super super universe forms the working model, or prototype, of the manifest realms, which is created of life, substance, and ideas. The prototype is in SPIRIT only and the energy is squared, or vibrating at an extremely high rate. Thus it would be invisible to the human perception. This is the beginning of Beingness, or Yahweh. According to Fillmore's *Metaphysical Bible Dictionary*, Jehovah (the Hebrew name for God or Yahweh) means *"the self-existent One."* Another way to say this is 'He who reveals Itself to Its creation, through Its creation, as Its creation.' From *The Hebrew-Greek Key Study Bible*, teaching comments on Exodus "3:14 The phrase "I AM" in Hebrew is closely related to God's personal name (Exodus 6:4; Jehovah or Yahweh... seems to suggest the timelessness of God, the very foundation of all existence." Another way of saying this is Yahweh is the one who was, who is, and who shall be.

Next, at the ***GODHEAD*** level there are ten levels of which the lower nine levels are called Supreme Council, and the top or tenth level is called ONE. Each of the nine levels of Supreme Council below ONE is made up of unnumbered beings who act as a Supreme Council to ONE. They are over groups of super super universes. Here is the breakdown of what the nine groups are council over:

- Supreme Council 1 is over 2 super super universes
- Supreme Council 2 is over 8 sets of 2 super super universes
- Supreme Council 3 is over 30 sets of 8 super super universes
- Supreme Council 4 is over 12 sets of 30 super super universes
- Supreme Council 5 is over 9 sets of 12 super super universes
- Supreme Council 6 is over 84 sets of 9 super super universes
- Supreme Council 7 is over 2 sets of 84 super super universes
- Supreme Council 8 is over 9 sets of 2 super super universes
- Supreme Council 9 is over 9 sets of 9 super super universes

Everything that has been listed so far constitutes what is called the ultimate universe. The maximum number of super super universes in an ultimate universe is 900,000,000. There are many ultimate universes, 8 quadrillion, and the GODHEAD is over all.

ONE is Source of all that is, Creator of all that is, Prime Mover of all that is and contains all life, substance, and intelligence. Everything has its beginning at ONE, which is the 'God' mentioned in Genesis 1:1 RSV:

> *In THE BEGINNING God CREATED the heavens and the earth.*

We are told that when the heavens and the earth were created, they were "without form and void" (Genesis 1:2 RSV). The reason for this is that when they were created at the ONE level, the energy was cubed and everything that would eventually become the manifest realms was first formed as the divine blueprint in the consciousness of ONE. There are 2,000 levels within the ONE level and each is infinite.

The GODHEAD is made up of the infinite beings who have gone through the incarnational process to gain knowledge, wisdom, and understanding and who have returned to the GODHEAD.

There is nothing higher than the GODHEAD. However, there are five consciousness energies behind the GODHEAD. They are ***SPIRIT***, ***LUMINOUS***, ***WELLSPRING***, ***GRAND-I***, and ***WHOLE***. SPIRIT is the SOURCE of all that is, both spiritual and physical. LUMINOUS is the LIGHT beyond all Light. WELLSPRING is the fountain of living water from which all life, substance, and intelligence springs. GRAND-I is the GREAT-I. WHOLE is the culmination of all that is; the grand finish of the whole creative process.

As you can see, this is a bare framework of the hierarchy, and it would take volumes to explain it all. When I ask what percent of the hierarchical structure has been revealed to me, I get 13.7 %. There are other bits and pieces that have been given, but High Self does not want me to confuse the issue more by presenting them now. Even as I write this, more has been given which, according to High Self, will be presented in a future book.

Knowing Your Level of Soul Consciousness

You might ask, "What is the importance of knowing all this?" The only importance is to know that we are spiritual beings with an infinite potential; that what we do in this life to balance our energies as we learn and grow is important, because we are part of a greater whole and to a degree, we do affect the whole. Knowing also gives one a greater purpose than just existing from day to day. We are goal-oriented and what greater goal is there than to open our consciousness to spiritual light, understanding, and wisdom, and to grow in awareness of our unity with the ONE and with all life?

During workshops, while explaining soul levels on Chart 3 and demonstrating how to determine a student's soul growth from incarnation to present, I am sometimes accused of getting into ego. However, when my High Self indicates that I am to give a client information regarding their soul status, it certainly is not ego. Here is how High Self points out that I am to give a client information on their soul process and current status.

Q. *Is there something else we need to do? (+)*

Q. *What chart is it on? (Chart 3–Levels of Soul Consciousness)*

Q. *You want me to show them what progress they have made on a soul level? (+)*

Turning Chart 3 sideways and holding the pendulum a few inches off the chart, I ask what the soul level was when they incarnated. Here is an example.

Q. *Please indicate on Chart 3 what their level was when they incarnated into this life. (Incarnational Status)*

Q. *What level were they before we started clearing their programs? (Light Status)*

Q. *So they have accomplished soul growth this life? (+)*

Q. *What is their level of soul now? (Free)*

Q. *Clearing some of their programs made a difference in their soul's status? (+)*

One of the toughest questions to answer from the human perspective is, "Have I made any progress in my spiritual growth?" With SRT you can answer that question. For example:

Q. *What was Bob's level of soul consciousness when he incarnated into this life? (One)*

Q. *What was his level before clearing? (Incarnational)*

Q. *Bob picked up a lot of earth energies which caused him to go down in soul level? (+)*

Q. *What is Bob's soul level at this point in the clearing? (The area of arrows on Chart 3)*

In the following example, the pendulum was moved to indicate the area of the level of GOD.

Q. *Is this person's soul level in one of the first eighteen GOD levels? (+)*

Q. *What number are they? (4, God over 8 planets)*

I always emphatically stress to the client, or student in the class, that regardless of their soul level, their experiential level in the physical body is human and they have to deal with day-to-day physical, mental, and emotional encounters. Everyone is a spiritual being, living in a physical body, dealing with the stuff of life, regardless of their soul status.

We came out of LIGHT and eventually we return to that LIGHT. How long it takes is up to each individual soul and the path chosen. When we incarnate, we come into darkness and no longer know the truth, for we have forgotten our SOURCE. Thus a way-shower, or Savior, is needed–one who has overcome darkness and revealed the LIGHT of Divine Presence, and who can then show us by example how we, too, can overcome and find the LIGHT within. Jesus is that person for this planet, although we do not always understand His message of truth and freedom.

> *...Jesus spoke to them, saying, "I am the light of the world; he who follows me will not walk in darkness, but will have the light of life." ... I have come as light into the world, that whoever believes in me may not remain in darkness. (John 8:12, 12:46 RSV)*

> *Ye are the light of the world.... Let your light so shine before men, that they may see your good works, and glorify your Father which is in heaven. (Matthew 5:14, 16 KJV)*

SRT reveals that everyone has infinite potential, and that includes you. However, you must have singleness of purpose and actively work to change your life if you want to express that potential. Chart 1–Contact or Help shows a number of offices in which you can serve as you accomplish higher and higher levels of soul consciousness. We have specifically mentioned guides, Guardian Angels, and High Self. As you move higher in spiritual consciousness, you can serve in the offices that are listed on Chart 1 (starting with guides and the farther you go from left to right to GRAND-I/WHOLE, the greater the responsibility of the office). Whether you are in or out of the body, you are constantly learning, experiencing, and gaining greater knowledge and understanding.

CHAPTER 5

The Basic Steps of SRT

We are cognizant of the world through our five senses. We perceive events around us, then build a belief system based on those perceptions, establishing the judgments–right or wrong, good or bad, positive and productive or negative, destructive, and limiting–that become the framework of our lives.

The heart of SRT work is *research* and *clearing.* Working with High Self, we *research* the cause of negative programs and belief systems. Then we ask High Self to *clear* the negative energy.

Preparing to Work

As a spiritual being, you already possess the qualities you need to use SRT–connection to High Self, and your own intuition. All you need is a little patience and a lot of practice!

Using the Pendulum

The subconscious mind is in charge of all of your body functions. Once you learn how to crawl, run, chew, or any other of thousands of tasks, your subconscious allows you to perform those acts automatically, or with very little prompting. The subconscious also performs many automatic functions without any conscious direction. For example, it beats your heart and expands your lungs so you can breathe. Your subconscious is, also, a silent monitor of your conscious and superconscious state, and a recorder of all your experiences.

You can access the information retained by your subconscious by using a pendulum. Swinging a pendulum is one way to set up recognizable muscle responses to yes or no questions so your subconscious can visually answer any questions you ask. This is called an *ideomotor response.*

Here is how to start. Draw a circle on a piece of paper and bisect it with two straight lines at right angles to each other. It should look similar to the drawing in figure 5-1.

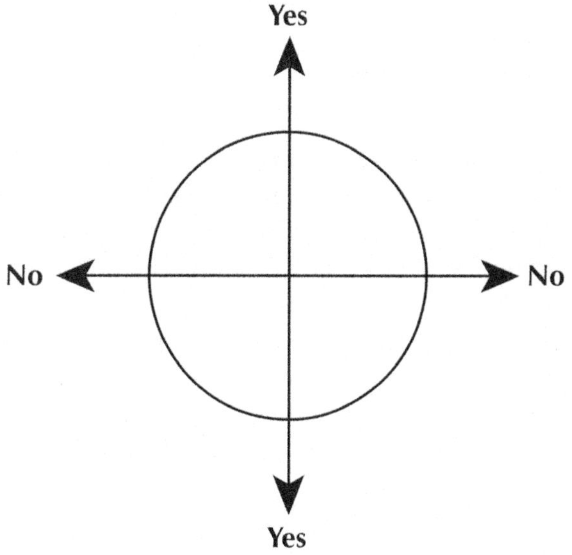

Figure 5-1 Establishing a Yes or No Response

Place the drawing on a flat surface. Then place your elbow on the surface, and, with a relaxed hand, dangle the pendulum over the point of intersection of the two lines. Make sure your pendulum is a fairly light object that will swing easily. Swing the pendulum forward and back while saying, "This is like nodding my head 'yes.' It is everybody's 'yes' and it will be my 'yes' also." Mark the chart you have drawn to indicate the direction of movement for a yes. Then move the pendulum from side to side while saying, "This is like shaking my head 'no.' It is everybody's 'no' and it will be my 'no' also." Then mark the chart to indicate the "no" direction. After saying this several times, hold the pendulum still and ask for a "yes," and then a "no" response. The pendulum should move in the appropriate direction for each question.

If you cannot get the pendulum to work for you, you may have blocks to using the pendulum. This may be caused by something as simple as your conscious mind believing you cannot use the pendulum. You might also have been killed or sustained some injury in a past life for using your spiritual knowledge. A subconscious fear of this happening again can block your ability to use the pendulum in this lifetime. Speaking one or more of the following clearing statements out loud should help you get the pendulum to respond to your questions.

> "I release all fear of using the pendulum. I release all belief, perception, and judgment that I cannot or should not use a pendulum. I release all need and desire to believe that I cannot or should not use a pendulum. I now completely accept and believe and instruct my subconscious to accept and believe on every level of my being conscious and subconscious that I can use a pendulum and that I will receive strong signals and accurate information."

Sometimes the subconscious simply does not want to answer a question which may embarrass you or cause you emotional pain. Instead, it will try to protect you by refusing to give a direct answer. This situation may be indicated by the movement of the pendulum at a forty-five degree angle or by no movement at all. This situation can be easily handled with the following releasing statements:

> "I release all fear of answering the question. I release all resistance to the answer. I give my subconscious mind permission to answer the question."

These clearing statements reprogram the subconscious mind to replace fear or resistance. In the beginning, you may find it necessary to use the releasing statements several times to obtain a yes or no response from the subconscious mind.

If for some reason you are physically unable to use a pendulum, you can train your subconscious to use another ideomotor response such as an eye blink or head nod. For example, my subconscious will also answer "yes" with a single eye blink, and "no" with a double eye-blink.

Using Your Intuition

Soon after I began using SRT as a spiritual counseling method, people started asking me why I seldom asked a question that elicited a "no" response. I stated that I simply know what questions to ask in order to get correct answers. Later, I found that my High Self was impressing upon my conscious mind the questions they wanted me to ask the client. After that time, I began to pay more attention to the inner pictures and thoughts that were being impressed upon my consciousness. As a result, my intuitive ability has expanded in a wonderful manner. I now see pictures of situations, especially past lives, and have a complete knowing about the picture. I then use the pendulum to check my interpretation. That way, if I am interpreting falsely, High Self gives me a "no" response. Sometimes, High Self actually gives me a spoken message which comes as a quiet, inner voice or impression. At other times, there is simply a knowing.

You, too, can develop your intuitive ability by clearing your subconscious blocks and learning to tune into your High Self. Many students of SRT get to the point where they receive all of their responses from High Self without using a pendulum. Then they use the pendulum to check their interpretation of what they intuitively receive.

How to Use the Charts

The charts included in Appendix B of this book comprise the remainder of the tools you need to practice SRT. These charts make it easy for you to identify a wide range of programs that are blocking you or a client. To use a chart, place the chart on a flat surface. Then place your elbow on the surface and dangle the pendulum over the circle located in the center of the 'fan.' When you ask your research questions (which are detailed later in this chapter), your subconscious, and later your High Self, provide an answer by swinging the pendulum in the direction of one piece of information or another. The chapters in this book provide information and examples for the programs listed on the charts.

Attuning Yourself to SPIRIT

All things have a starting point. Because SRT is a system based on working with your High Self, the starting point is prayer. Your prayer does not have to be complicated or long. Rather, it can be quite simple, like the one Jesus used: "I and the Father are one" (John 10:30 RSV). Do not pray with the hope of changing God, because prayer is not for changing God, but for attuning yourself spiritually to SPIRIT.

I often paraphrase Zechariah 4:6 for my prayer: "Not by my might, nor by my power, but by your Spirit, Father, let this work be done."

Even something as simple as, "I am one with the presence, power, and consciousness of the universe." will attune you to High Self.

Never put yourself down while praying. High Self has taught me some very wonderful lessons about positive versus negative prayer. One day I was blocked from getting correct answers. In fact, I was not even able to find out why I was blocked. Finally, I asked my daughter to see if she could find the problem. Using Chart 6B–Blocks to Positive Expression, she found I was blocked in two positive areas–self-esteem and worthiness. For five years I had been using the prayer, "Of myself, I do nothing. The Father within does the work." My High Self blocked me so that I would pay attention to how I was praying. They were trying to tell me that I am valuable and worthy and should maintain my self-esteem–and that I should not limit or put myself down by affirming that I did nothing.

I immediately changed my prayer to, "The Father and I are one. We work together as a team." Jesus said,

> *..."My Father is working still, and I am working." ... Do you not believe that I am in the Father and the Father in me? The words that I say to you I do not speak on my own authority; but the Father who dwells in me does his works. (John 5:17, 14:10 RSV)*

Affirm your oneness with SPIRIT and you will be guided to perform marvelous work for many of your brothers and sisters on this planet.

Making Certain You Are Clear

You cannot work accurately or effectively with SRT unless you are clear and working with your High Self. Some people unknowingly work with discarnates (souls who have left the physical body, but not the earth plane) or satanics, demonics, or dark forces (discarnates that have even stronger negative energy). Their work is inaccurate and misleading and it takes them a long time to research and clear programs. In fact, you can never clear all programs when working with discarnates because you do not receive correct answers. So make certain you are a clear instrument and that you are working with your High Self. Here are the questions I ask before starting the actual research for myself or for a client.

Q. *Do I have any blocks or interference? (If you receive a "yes" response, use Chart 5–Blocks and Interference, and the information presented in this chapter and Chapter 6–Removing Blocks to Working with SRT to research the cause. Then ask High Self to clear the block or interference. Continue to ask this question and clear blocks until you receive a "no" response.)*

Q. *Will I get correct answers? (If you receive a "no" response, you must work with High Self and the charts to clear yourself. Continue to ask this question and clear blocks until you receive a "yes" response.)*

Q. *Will I receive wrong answers? (If you receive a "yes" response, you must work with High Self and the charts to clear yourself. Continue to ask this question and clear blocks until you receive a "no" response.)*

Q. *Am I working with my High Self? (If you receive a "no" response, ask that you be cleared and that you be placed in direct contact with your High Self. Continue to ask this question until you receive a "yes" response.)*

Q. *Can I start work now? (If you receive a "no" response, you must again work with your High Self and Spirit and the charts to clear yourself.)*

Sometimes you may be so blocked that you cannot even use the pendulum. In that case, speak clearing statements out loud as described earlier in this chapter, or work with another person who knows SRT to clear your blocks. As you clear more and more of your own blocks and programs, you should find it easier to get clear answers.

Obtaining Permission to Work

If you intend to work on someone other than yourself, and they are not with you, ask permission from High Self to do the clearing work. Should you not receive permission, ask if there is a self-punishment program. Usually there is. The self-punishment can usually be broken by asking that the soul be given a spiritual kick. Once the spiritual kick has been administered, the person's programs can be researched and cleared.

Recording Your Research

Because the charts can reveal a lot of detail, you will probably want to record your research on a sheet of paper as you work. This is not only a valuable record that you can give to your client at the end of a counseling session, it is also a very effective way to track your progress as you work, so that you do not miss any steps.

Five Basic Steps for Clearing Programs

Before researching programs for yourself or for a client, it is important to ask your High Self to clear everyone on your and your client's committees and councils; educate, elevate, harmonize, balance, and uplift them; reduce them to minimum size for maximum effort; and to establish proper supervision.

Once you have attuned yourself to High Self through prayer, cleared your own blocks and your committees and councils, and obtained permission to work, you are ready to research and clear programs for yourself and others. To research programs, you will need your pendulum, the charts located in Appendix B of this book, and paper to record your findings. The basic steps for researching and clearing programs are:

1. Identify the first program that needs to be cleared using Chart 1–Chart to Use. One of the numbers on the outside of Chart 1 will be indicated.
2. Determine the program on the chart indicated.
3. Determine when the program was established, and who was involved using Chart 4–When; Cast of Characters.

4. Identify the situation: who was harmed and who did the harming; or if there was no harm, find the negative energies using Chart 6A–Discordant Energy.
5. When enough information is found, ask High Self to clear the program and the associated negative energy.

You then begin again with step 1 for the next program that needs to be researched and cleared. These steps may vary slightly depending on which program you are researching. See the rest of the chapters in the book for details on researching and clearing different types of programs.

1. Identify the First Program that Needs to Be Cleared

The first step is to ask if there is a problem area or program that needs to be cleared. Use Chart 1–Chart to Use to locate the first program to be cleared. (To make the questions less wordy, I use the symbol "+" to represent a "yes" response, and the symbol "-" to represent a "no" response throughout this book.)

Q. *Is there a program that needs to be cleared for [the client's name]? (+)*

Q. *On which side of the center line will I find the program? (High Self indicates the right or left side by pointing diagonally in either direction on Chart 1.)*

Q. *What chart is the program on? (The pendulum should swing to indicate which chart.)*

You then turn to the chart that is indicated. For example, if the pendulum swings to indicate Chart 5–Negative Motivations; Blocks and Interference you know that the client has discarnates, some other form of blocking energy, or negative motivations. There are many programs–so many, in fact, that the greatest portion of this book is devoted to explaining them. For most programs, you can continue researching and clearing as outlined in this section. For more details on particular programs, however, you will probably want to consult other chapters in this book.

Remember to note your findings on the note pad as you work.

2. Determine the Program on the Chart Indicated

Most of the charts have more than one program listed. Hold your pendulum below the chart if there is more than one type of program and ask which one it is. For example on Chart 2–Soul Qualities and Themes and Challenges are listed. Should the pendulum be moved to indicate Soul Qualities, hold the pendulum over the darkened circle and ask which soul quality. See Chapter 9 on Soul Qualities for further information.

3. Determine When the Program Was Established and Who Was Involved

Once you have learned the reason for the program, use Chart 4–When to ask when the program was established:

Q. *When was the program established?*

More often than not, High Self indicates that the program was established during past lives. (For details about the other time periods listed on this chart, see "Understanding When Programs Become Established" in Chapter 7–Charts 1 and 4.) The first thing you do when you have a past life to research is determine what you were, if it is your program, or what your client was in that past life, if it is his or her program you are clearing. The same holds true for a life in other dimensions, a future life, a parallel life, or a parallel universe. Always, and I cannot stress this enough, find yourself (or your client) first and then find the rest of the cast members. Use Chart 4–Cast of Characters to help you determine the gender, familial or spiritual relationship, or other role you played in the life you are researching.

Q. *Who was I in this past life [or who was the client]? (The pendulum swings to indicate the role played by you or the client.)*

Q. *Is someone else involved that we need to find? (If "yes," ask "Who?")*

Continue to ask this last question until you have identified all major players. Sometimes the subconscious wants to give you a list of people (often the family) as the cast. When this happens, I ask the subconscious if we can lump the family as a group, if we do not need to know who particular individuals are. Here is how High Self indicates a group to me.

Q. *Is there someone else involved? (+)*

Q. *What were they? (The pendulum moves in a circle.)*

Q. *Is it a group? (+)*

When I get a circular motion of the pendulum, I ask if it is a group. When I get a "yes" response, I ask what the basic unit size of the group is. If the pendulum is moved to indicate the left corner of the chart, I know the number is in tens, if to the middle, the number is in hundreds, and, if to the right corner, the figure is in thousands or greater.

Q. *What is the basic unit? (The pendulum is moved toward the upper-left corner, indicating the figure is in tens.)*

Q. *What is the first digit? (7 is indicated by pointing to 70; for 1 digit, drop the 0.)*

Q. *What is the second digit? (3)*

Q. *So the total is 73? (+)*

Q. *What are they? (Sisters) (Sisters, in this instance we determined they were a group of nuns.)*

The movement of the pendulum might have indicated brother which means they would have been a group of priests or monks (identification of a person as a sister, brother, mother, and father can also indicate a religious figure; just ask your High Self if this is so). If the pendulum had moved in a circular motion when I asked what the seventy-three were, it would mean they were a mixed group of people.

4. Identify the Negative Energies

The final piece of information you often need when researching a past life is the negative energy that you carried away with you (or that the client carried away, if you are working with another person). This is important, as the retention of this negative energy can be a chief cause of disease and disharmony in this life and future lives. First, you must find out if you (or the client) sustained harm in the past life.

Q. *Was there harm? (If "yes," ask the next questions.)*

Q. *Who was harmed? (The pendulum swings to indicate which person in the past life was harmed.)*

Q. *Who caused the harm? (The pendulum swings to indicate which person caused the harm.)*

Q. *Was the harm mental? Emotional? Physical? (If the answer is "physical," ask the next question.)*

Q. *Was it simple harm? Serious harm? Was it death?*

Sometimes you may get the signal that the person harmed him or herself, which could mean suicide. If there was no harm, ask whose energy needs to be cleared.

Q. *Whose energy do we need to find?*

Use Chart 6A–Discordant Energy to identify negative energies. First, ask where the energy will be found–inside or outside and on the right or left half of the chart. (These indicators are printed at the top of the chart on either side of the center line.) Once you have identified the area of the chart, ask High Self to indicate the word. Always check to see if you are getting the correct word by asking if that is the word.

Q. *Where will I find the first energy? Left or right? (The pendulum swings to indicate where the first energy will be found–on the left or right side of the chart.)*

Q. *Inside or outside? (The pendulum swings to indicate where the first energy will be found–in the inside circle or the outside circle.)*

Q. *What is the energy? (The pendulum swings to indicate the first energy.)*

Q. *Is it [fear, alcoholism, hate, or whatever was indicated]?*

Q. *Any other negative energy? (If you receive a "yes" response, repeat the process until all energy is found.)*

Continue to ask this last question until you have identified all negative energies held by you (or the client) on this past life. Again, do not forget to record details on your note pad.

It is at this stage that your intuition may come into play. Now that you know the players, the level of harm, and the energies, you can often get a general picture of the situation or event. It is no coincidence when this situation often bears some resemblance to a difficulty or problem in the current life!

5. Clear the Program and Associated Negative Energy

There are two ways to clear programs and the associated negative energy. One is to repeat aloud, or have the client repeat aloud, statements of affirmation. These statements alter the subconscious record so that the negative effects stop manifesting. For example, if you discover through research that you have a fear of abandonment program based on past lives in which you believed you were abandoned by God or other important people. You could use the following clearing statements to remove the program from the subconscious.

> "I release all belief, perception, judgment, need, and desire to believe that I have ever been abandoned by God and those I love and that I ever will be abandoned."

> "I now completely accept and believe, and instruct my subconscious to accept and believe on every level of my being that God, and those I love, love and support me, and that, furthermore, I love and support myself on every step of my life's journey."

The first statement removes the negative programming. The second statement introduces positive programming, so that it is more difficult for the negative belief to reappear. For thorough clearing, use both statements.

The second and easiest way to clear a program is to ask your High Self to do the work. Just ask these questions.

Q. *Do we have enough information to clear this program? (+)*

Q. *Can you clear this program? (+)*

Q. *Will you clear this program now? (+)*

Please clear and replace with good. Thank you.

The pendulum will be moved in a circle to indicate High Self is working. Once the new program is in, the pendulum is moved in a forward and back "yes" position to indicate the work is completed. Always check to make certain the work is completed.

Q. *Are the discordant beliefs removed? (+)*

Q. *Has a new, positive program been installed? (+)*

Thank you.

Q. *Is there anything else we need to do on this issue? (-)*

If you receive a "yes" response, return to Chart 1—Chart to Use and ask on which chart the program will be found.

When you have finished clearing the first program, find the next program to be researched and cleared using Chart 1, and begin the five-step process again.

When You Are Lost or Stuck in Research

I receive many calls for help from students and practitioners of SRT. They tell me they are trying to research and clear some program and are having difficulty with blocks, or are lost and do not know what to do. The first thing I do is to make certain I am clear to work with my High Self and receive correct answers. When I am clear, I ask if I can ask questions on behalf of the caller. Once I am ready to begin, I ask the following.

Q. *Are they having a problem getting correct responses? (+)*

Q. *Is there a clue on one of the charts as to why? (+)*

Q. *Which chart? (Use Chart 1–Chart to Use, to determine on which chart the block can be found.)*

Often the block is listed on Chart 5–Blocks and Interferences. Moving to Chart 5, I determine what the blocks are–discarnates, satanics, dark forces, or other interferences. Once I have identified all of the blocks on Chart 5, I ask High Self to clear them. Again, I check to see if there are any other blocks. If there are, I determine what chart they are on, research them, and ask that they be cleared. When I cannot find any more blocks, I ask the following:

Q. *Are they lost in procedure? (+)*

Questioning the caller may reveal that they are not using the correct procedure to find out what chart the program is on, or they are not using correct procedure in researching the program once it is identified.

Review the Basic Procedure

People often get lost when researching past lives. Even in workshops, after repeating the instructions many times, students sometimes forget the basic steps in research. Review the steps again and again until they become automatic.

Steps in Research (97% of all research is past life research)

1. Is there a program to clear?
2. What chart is the program on? (Use Chart 1–Chart to Use)
3. What is the program? (Use chart indicated)
4. When was it established? (Use Chart 4–When)
5. Find the cast of characters (only major participants). Use Chart 4–Cast of Characters. List across the page.

   For past life research, find out who the client was and who the remaining cast members were.

   For present life research, just find out who the other cast members are. Determining the age at the time of the program is often helpful.

   Example:

Client	Other	Other	Other	
Female	Husband	Son	Daughter	etc.

6. Was there hurt or harm?
7. Who was harmed? By whom?
8. Was it mental, emotional, or physical harm?
9. Was it simple, serious, or death? (Mental or emotional harm can be early death or suicide.)
10. If no harm, whose energy do we find?
11. Is this enough information to clear? (Sometimes age of cast helps.)

    (When researching parallel lives, ask:
    Is this enough information to clear the program? ...the life? ...all parallel lives? You may need to research more lives to clear the program and/or the set of parallel lives.)

12. Please clear all lives. (When researching parallel lives, be sure to clear and block all parallel lives between each other and between the parallel lives and this life so that they can't bleed through.) Once you have become skilled at the process, and the

necessary research had been accomplished, High Self may clear and block parallel lives automatically.

When Spirit has cleared the program, begin the process over again by returning to Chart 1 and asking if there is another program.

Memorizing this simple procedure can keep you from getting lost while doing SRT. You would not start out to drive across the country, if you had never been, without consulting road maps, making a plan, and following your plan. To do so might get you lost. If you get lost or stuck while using SRT, stop and retrace your steps, you may have missed an important part of the process. Remember, also, that recording your work on a sheet of paper will help you keep track of your place.

Keeping Yourself Clear

When you work with other people to help them clear their discordant programs, you not only bless them, you bless yourself. Be assured that you are eliminating a lot of your own negative programs at the same time.

Even if you work regularly with others, you should make a conscious effort to clear your own programs daily. Because you are on this planet to learn and grow, you will often encounter new programs and negative energies. Some programs may not activate until you reach a certain age, or until some event or circumstance in your life triggers them.

Case Studies

Case Study 1: Clearing the Counselor

During March of 1988, something of great significance happened to me while working with a client, whom I will call Mary. We had researched a program that was causing Mary trouble and had listed a whole page of material that needed to be released.

When High Self indicated that no other programs needed to be researched, I said, "All right, let's clear it." Putting her hand up to her chest in a clutching motion, Mary pulled her hand forward as though she were jerking something out of her chest and said, "Yes! Let's rip it out of here." There was an instant flash of pain in my chest that was so intense it brought tears to my eyes.

"Don't say that," I exclaimed. "That really hurts!"

"I'm sorry," was her response. "I didn't mean to hurt you."

"That's all right. I just have some energy running that I need to check out," I assured her.

We proceeded to clear her programs and finished our counseling session. Later, when I had time, I researched to see if there was some reason for the pain. I found that there were three future lives involved.

During the first future life, I was male and there was a twin brother involved. Further questioning revealed that I was a spiritual teacher. For some reason (I did not research to find what it was), my twin brother betrayed me and I was killed by the people. The manner of death was having my heart ripped out. That is why the pain triggered when Mary said, "Yes! Let's rip it out of here."

Q. *Can I change what happens in this future life by releasing that they rip my heart out? (-)*

Q. *Must I go through this experience? (+)*

Q. *Is there something I need to change? (+)*

Q. *Is it my attitude and reaction to what happens? (+)*

Q. *Am I bitter and angry? (+)*

Q. *Can I set it up by responding as Jesus did at His trial and crucifixion? (+)*

Q. *Will this clear up any karmic energy? (+)*

Q. *Is that the right way to handle it? (+)*

These are the basic statements I used to clear the energy on the future life:

"I release my belief, perception, and judgment that in this future life I am angry, bitter, or upset. I release all need and desire to believe that I am angry, bitter, or upset. I release all need and desire to believe anything except that I am calm and at peace. I realize they can kill my body and drive my eternal soul out of the body, but they cannot kill *me* for I am an eternal spiritual being and I live and move and have my existence in Light. I pray for all these who seek to cause me harm: 'Father, forgive them, for they know not what they do.' I love you, bless you, and set you free from any sense of offense or spiritual debt."

After releasing, I checked to see if I had done it correctly.

Q. Is there any negative energy remaining on this future life? (-)

In the second future life, I was female. My father, mother, and a group of people were involved. Research revealed that I was involved in the black arts. Because of that involvement, the people killed me and my parents. My own death was accomplished by being tied to a stake, having my heart ripped out, and my body burned. Again, I could not change the process of my death. However, I could change the negative reaction by going through a series of releasing statements similar to the ones used to clear the first future life. This was done and a check revealed that the desired results were accomplished.

In the third life, I was male. The other cast members were my brother, daughter, and a group. Additional questioning revealed that I was psychic (most of the time, neither the subconscious nor the High Self perceive any difference between psychic and spiritual gifts, unless the psychic energy is involved with black magic). The brother and daughter were also psychic. All of us were killed by the group of people. Again, the only thing that could be changed was the attitude—the reactive energy—that I held. This future life was cleared and I checked to make certain that no discordant energy remained.

There is a very important lesson demonstrated in these three lives. It is not what happens to you in any life that requires you to incarnate again to balance the record; it is the negative, reactive energy you attach to the event. Jesus, our elder brother and the perfect example of how to live a spiritual life, stood silently before his accusers.

But when he was accused by the chief priests and elders, he made no answer. Then Pilate said to him, "Do you not hear how many things they testify against you?" But he gave him no answer, not even to a single charge; so that the governor wondered greatly. (Matthew 27:12-14 RSV)

When Jesus was nailed to the cross, He held no enmity toward His persecutors. He even went so far as to pray to the Father for them.

And Jesus said, "Father, forgive them; for they know not what they do."... (Luke 23:34 RSV)

Notice that He did not say, "I forgive them," because there was no criticism, judgment, or condemnation in Him. Had Jesus held any discordant energy against any person, He would not have been resurrected. Nor can anyone else ascend into the presence of Light with negative energy in heart or mind. The only way is through love, for only love can return to the presence of Love, which is God.

So we know and believe the love God has for us. God is love, and he who abides in love abides in God, and God abides in him. (1 John 4:16 RSV)

Jesus was the full expression of God's love.

During June of 1988, my wife and I were in Florida attending the national conference of the church to which we belong. While there, I was talking to a fellow minister about my book, *The Freedom Path*. He was very interested and asked if we could get together after the conference ended. We did so and I began to explain SRT to him and the use of the charts. When we got to the area of future lives, he became very excited and asked if it were really true that you could be living future lives while you are still in this present life. I assured him that it is true and that while working with people and clearing their programs, I occasionally run into future lives. I also showed him how to use the charts by asking questions about possible future lives I was living at the time.

He asked if I could find out if he was involved in future lives. I asked High Self for permission to ask questions in regard to this man and any possible future lives he might be living, and received an okay to do so. He was living thirty-two future lives.

Ted asked, "Do I make it?" He wanted to know if, through the process of living the future lives, he would clear all of his karma and not have to incarnate again.

I had a very uneasy feeling in the pit of my stomach, so replied: "I don't want to ask that question. I don't feel good about asking it at all."

"That's okay," Ted said, "I probably blew it anyway."

Instantly, I was caught up in an energy that was pure agony. My breath came in deep, shuddering sobs. I became rigid and could neither speak nor move. I could not break out of the energy, and it held me locked in its grip for what seemed an eternity. Finally, the agony subsided and my breathing became easier. When I could finally speak, I said, "Wow! What was that?" I knew that it had something to do with the future lives that Ted was living, but not what they might be. I could have researched it at that time and found out what was going on, but I probably was afraid of having the truth revealed, or that the agony might start again.

During the night, the energy continued to manifest itself, although with greatly decreased intensity. I would drop off to uneasy sleep only to awaken a short time later feeling like I was burning up. I experienced the high energy several times during the night and it kept me restless and disturbed until nearly morning. The next day we returned home.

Once a month we hold a meeting and invite all of the people who have gone through SRT workshops. The meeting was held the day after our return from Florida and I related what had happened to me. Mary Satterlee, who taught me how to work with my High Self, began to question her High Self to find out what had happened to me.

"Robert," she said, "you know what that was, don't you?"

"No, what was it?"

"Remember you told us about the future lives in which you had your heart torn out. The energy and agony you felt in Florida was the effect of the future life. That was the moment in which the people tore out your heart. Now it is completed."

When I asked my High Self if that was the case, I was assured that it was. Later, I asked some additional questions about the incident and the more than six thousand future lives I had been living. All of them were clear except for the other two in the series of three that were previously revealed. About a week later I made a further check and found that the other two lives had cleared.

Q. *Am I involved with any future lives at all? (+)*

Q. *How many? (Infinite)*

After the three future lives were cleared, further questioning revealed some very interesting facts.

Q. *What level of consciousness am I now? (Light)*

Q. *You mean that my soul has returned to Source? (+)*

I have learned since this questioning was done that there are infinite levels within the Light realms and I was only a beginner on the path of Light, and had not yet reached the level of Ultimate Light, or ONE. I have continued to clear myself of programs and negative energies, and, according to High Self, have finally reached the level of GRAND-I/WHOLE. Yet the path is infinite, and every day I find more to clear, and more to learn.

Case Study 2: Mary Jane

Mary Jane sat in my office in what appeared to be a total state of anxiety, verging on panic. She clasped and unclasped her hands and her whole body was tense. It looked like she was ready to jump up, run, and hide. The first program I discovered was self-punishment, which was established in past lives. In the past life we researched, she was a Light being. God and a Council of Nine were involved. Mary Jane was planning to incarnate for the first time. When I asked her questions to determine if all of them were in agreement about her incarnating, she received "yes" responses. This left me rather nonplused. I expected to find that either, or both, God and the Council of Nine were averse to her incarnating. Then the reason for self-punishment would have been disobedience, or rebellion against God or the Council of Nine. "High Self, I don't understand," I said. "What is going on? Why is she punishing herself?" I heard the words "dumb" and "stupid." I asked Mary Jane if she was punishing herself for incarnating because it was a dumb, stupid thing to do, and received a "yes" response. That was the only reason for the self-punishment.

Mary Jane also had a program of panic. She had been a Guardian Angel in charge of making Guardian Angel assignments and believed she had fouled up. She was in a panic, believing that God was going to get her for being so dumb and stupid.

Mary Jane, based on her perceptions and beliefs, had judged herself to be dumb and stupid because she left the realms of Light and incarnated. We used clearing statements to alter the inner perceptions and beliefs that she had recorded in her subconscious computer, and which had become the judgments causing her anxiety in the current life. Here are the statements I had her repeat.

> "I release all belief, perception, and judgment that it was a dumb, stupid thing to leave the Light and incarnate."
>
> "I release all need and desire to believe that it was a dumb, stupid thing to incarnate."

These two statements cleared the program from the subconscious mind. We then replaced the dumb, stupid judgment with a new, positive program.

> "I now completely accept and believe, and instruct my subconscious to accept and believe on every level of my being that it was a wise and wonderful thing I did when I chose to incarnate for I have gained knowledge, wisdom, and stature in the sight of God."

We used the same type of clearing and replacement statements to remove the belief that she had fouled up as a Guardian Angel, and to establish a new sense of having done exactly right as a Guardian Angel. It worked! When Mary Jane left my office, she was completely at peace.

Sometimes clients or students question that they can clear something by affirming that it did not happen, because to do so would be a lie. I assure them that, according to Eastern teachings, everything is *maya*, or illusion. Therefore, we are simply removing a discordant, limiting, or potentially destructive illusion and replacing it with a positive, constructive illusion. As the Scriptures state: "Death and life are in the power of the tongue, and those who love it will eat its fruits" (Proverbs 18:21 RSV). "For by your words you will be justified, and by your words you will be condemned" (Matthew 12:37 RSV).

The Gospel of John states that, "In THE BEGINNING WAS THE WORD and... all things were made through him" (John 1:1, 3 RSV). We are told that this WORD became the life of men and dwelt among (within) us. Whatever you speak, whatever you think (the silent word), when it is charged with constructive or destructive energy, will produce after its kind and become your expression of life. With SRT you can use the power of your word to delete any conscious or subconscious programs that are causing problems from your 'bio-computer' and put in new, positive, constructive programs. And it works!

Jesus was able to perform many miracles, because He knew that the physical world and everything in it is an illusion. He could change the illusion of illness into the illusion of health, the illusion of death into the illusion of life, the illusion of two fish and seven loaves of bread into the illusion of food enough to feed 5,000 men, women, and children. He could walk on water, because He recognized that the illusion of the physical body could walk on the illusion of the physical Sea of Galilee. Above all, Jesus knew that He was Spirit, created in the image and likeness of the one great SPIRIT called God, and that like God, he was unlimited. He stated time and again that what you believe and what judgments you make determine the course of your life.

There is, according to High Self, only one thing that is not illusion–God. And no one really knows what God is. We only have beliefs about God, which are mostly erroneous and often counterproductive to a balanced, harmonious, and productive expression of life.

Developing Options

Each person will find that their High Self has a particular way of working with SRT. My High Self gives me a lot of past life research in which the client is part of a religious order. Others get more of what is called the 'cosmic soap opera': love triangles, work situations, and harm between what I would call ordinary people.

I use the corners of the chart I am working on to determine many things not printed on the chart. Example: On Chart 4, if "Father" is indicated when I ask who was involved, I ask "Father as in what?" A direct move to the right corner would indicate father as head priest of a religious organization. When the middle is indicated, it is a father with one or more children. If the pendulum is moved to indicate the left corner of the chart, it means head monk or high priest. When I ask if that is head monk or high priest, the pendulum may stay at the left corner which is head monk or be moved to the right corner which is high priest. If the options were typed in on my chart, this is how it would look (see following page).

Location of Option:

left	center	right

——— across top of chart ———

Options

head monk	father of family	head priest
high priestess	mother of family	mother superior
monk	brother in family	priest
priestess	sister in family	nun
student monk	son only child	student priest
student priestess	daughter only child	student nun

When I ask for the form of harm in a past life, I use these options:

mental	emotional	physical

If I want to know how serious the harm was, I use these options:

simple	serious	death

Why were they harmed?

teaching	healing	channeling

——— other ———

What were they channeling?

information	both	healing

The three positions are used to indicate common forms of death.

burned	stoned	crucified

——— other * ———

* Other forms of death such as hanging, beheading, torture, arrows, etcetera are indicated by a horizontal movement across the bottom of the chart.

The same process works for numbers. Ask for a starting point.

tens	hundreds	thousands

Or, ask for the number of digits in the total. Then ask for each digit in turn.

There are many occasions when I do not need to ask the above questions as I get inner pictures of the past life scenario and know exactly what happened and why. Be aware of your own inner pictures or knowing.

You can set up multiple positions on any chart or simply in your mind. Eventually you learn the charts to the degree that much of the information is committed to memory. Then you can work the system without having the charts in front of you. This works best for me when I am driving the car. I cannot stop to use a pendulum, so I simply ask High Self questions and they respond with an inner knowing. The charts can become a crutch and I have a tendency to depend on them instead of intuition. However, you can use the pendulum and charts to check the pictures, words, and knowing that you do receive intuitively. You can ask if you are receiving direct from High Self or if you are head tripping.

from High Self   head tripping

Once you have determined the information is from High Self, you can formulate the meanings in your head and ask the percentage of accuracy of what you are thinking. When I am very clear and receiving a strong impression from High Self, they will give me a straight line across the bottom of the chart telling me that my perception is infinitely accurate–I do not have my own head in the way. Sometimes, I simply say, "Are you trying to tell me ...?" If my interpretation is correct, they give me a good solid yes signal. If the interpretation is flawed or incomplete, they give me a yes but move it to the left of center to indicate I have mixed my own beliefs in or have somewhat misinterpreted the internal picture that was given.

CHAPTER 6

Removing Blocks to Working with SRT

Many people have programs that block them and keep them from working with SRT. If you are already working with SRT, you may have a blocking program, and may not be getting consistent, correct answers. When this happens, you could need the help of someone trained in the work to help you discover and clear the blocks. The trained counselor is able to work with his or her High Self in order to research the client's blocking program and clear it.

If you are just starting to learn SRT and find that you are getting crazy answers, ask your High Self if you can research and clear any blocks to working with the system by yourself before you call for help from another person. Every time I sit down to work for myself, or for any client, I always check to make certain I am not running a program or have blocks to getting correct answers. First, I spend a few minutes centering myself through prayer. Then I ask if I am clear to work for myself or with the other person. As often as not, I have blocking energy that must be cleared before I can work. When I am unable to clear the blocks, I call on my wife or daughter for assistance, both of whom are trained in SRT.

When I ask if I am clear and I get a negative response, I use Chart 1–Chart to Use; Contact or Help to determine what chart lists the blocking energy. (Again, if you are blocked and cannot get accurate responses, you may need to get some help from another trained person). You may experience blocks from the following sources:

- Guides, Guardian Angels, High Self, or other spiritual helpers and counsel (Chart 1–Contract or Help, on the inside of the fan).
- Energy from past lives, past lives in other dimensions, or self-punishment programs (Chart 4–Programs). You may have been killed for using a pendulum or for developing your psychic abilities.
- Discarnates, separates, imprints, or other negative energies (Chart 5–Blocks and Interference).
- Master programs or discordant energy (Chart 6A–Master Programs; Discordant Energy).
- Any program listed on Charts 10 through 31.

In addition, High Self may indicate that the blocks are not listed on any chart (my High Self indicates this by giving a "no" response across the bottom of Chart 1). In that case, just ask if they can clear the block without research.

This chapter discusses blocks listed on Charts 1, 4, and 5. For detailed information on master programs and negative energies listed on Chart 6A, see Chapter 8–Master Programs.

Removing Blocks Listed on Chart 1

Chart 1–Contact or Help lists those beings who are a part of your spiritual council (see Chapter 4–Infinite Service). When High Self indicates that the blocking energy is listed on Chart 1, it usually means that one or more of these beings is causing the problem. Ask which are blocking and then ask what High Self recommends be done with them. High Self provides me with three options:

- Clear them.
- Clear and remove them.
- Clear, remove, and replace them.

For example, here are the questions you would ask:

Q. *What is the blocking energy on Chart 1? (High Self)*

Q. *Do you want to clear them? (-)*

Q. *Do you want to clear and remove them? (+)*

Q. *Do you want to clear, remove, and replace them? (+)*

If High Self does not want to remove the being that is blocking you or the client, ask High Self to clear the being.

To make questioning easier, I made the following agreement with my High Self. When I ask the question, "What do you want to do with the High Self?" the pendulum is moved to the upper-left corner of the chart to indicate clearing the energy. To indicate clearing the High Self's energy and removing them, the pendulum is moved to the middle of the chart. To indicate clearing, removing them, and replacing them with other beings, the pendulum moves to the upper-right corner of the chart. After receiving an answer, simply ask that what has been indicated be done. Set it up with your High Self to use the same procedure I use with my High Self, and it will simplify the questioning process.

When the required action is to remove the beings who are blocking, request that they be replaced with higher level beings who will be in harmony, order, and cooperation. Sometimes, High Self simply wants to clear and remove beings that are blocking rather than replace them. There are usually enough beings remaining who are in harmony with you to do a good job.

Always ask that beings of infinite level consciousness be assigned when High Self wants to replace the souls serving you, whether those souls are Guardian Angels or High Self. This assures that you, or the person you are clearing, has the highest possible guidance for their present level of soul consciousness and spiritual growth. Of course, it is always up to the individual to learn to work with their High Self, and to follow the spiritual path. Learning to cooperate with your High Self and the other souls assigned to work with you, and knowing when you are working with them, is not always easy. However, it is a vital ingredient to successful spiritual growth, and is a natural outcome of your consistent practice and desire to clear your own programs.

Every soul that serves you–guide, Guardian Angel, High Self, or others from Chart 1–may be of any level of consciousness (as indicated on Chart 3–Levels of Soul Consciousness). Guides and Guardian Angels must have attained at least Spirit Status to serve you. Beings in your High Self must have attained Light Status. Beings that serve you may even have reached the infinite consciousness of the GODHEAD. The possibilities and levels appear to be endless. High Self assures me that all of the beings who serve us in any capacity, regardless of their level of soul consciousness, are learning as they serve. This certainly becomes obvious as you research past lives and find that guides, Guardian Angels, or High Self are emotionally involved with the souls they are serving. For example, it is not uncommon to find a twin flame serving as another twin flame's High Self, Guardian Angel, or guide.

Once a soul has reached the Infinite Council levels at the I AM level on Chart 3, guides can no longer serve you so they are removed. The primary spiritual committee you need to work with SRT is High Self.

Regardless of the level of soul growth a being has attained, or the capacity they are serving in, they can cause problems. I have found Angels of Light, Masters, Council of Seven, High Council, Forces of Light, Holy Spirit beings, and beings of God Consciousness causing problems. I do not know how high a soul has to be in consciousness before it is so clear and pure that it does not have any reactive energy to what is happening in the life of the person they are serving. Remember that each soul—whether or not that soul is in a physical body—has its own lessons to learn, and may still be carrying discordant programs from their own incarnations in the soul record.

Removing Blocks Listed on Chart 4

Several things listed on Chart 4—Programs may be a source of blocking energy. They are past lives, past lives in other dimensions, self-punishment programs, and discarnates (which are also identified on Chart 5—Blocks and Interference).

Shortly after a lecture that I gave at a dowsing convention, a lady approached me and said she could not use a pendulum with any degree of success. Research revealed that she had used a pendulum in a past life and had caused much harm by giving false information. Research into another life revealed that she had been accused of witchcraft because of using a pendulum to work with her High Self and was burned at the stake. In the current incarnation, she was blocking herself so she could do no harm to others or be harmed herself because of using a pendulum. Once we cleared the programs, she received strong movements of the pendulum.

Most of the people with whom I have worked, either one-on-one or in a workshop, have had some blocking energy based on past lives or past lives in other dimensions. Many of these people can overcome the blocks without research, while others cannot use the pendulum until their programs are cleared. One person had so many blocking programs while taking a workshop, that it took five of us (me and four graduate assistants) working with her over a period of fifteen hours to clear her so she could work with her pendulum. We had to ask High Self to remove her High Self committee and replace it with beings of higher spiritual understanding. Jesus came in as her High Self, and immediately she began to get good pendulum responses.

Self-punishment programs are also common causes of blocks to using a pendulum. They are usually based in past lives or past lives in other dimensions. Some people also punish themselves for coming into this life and may block themselves in every aspect of living, not just in using a pendulum. To clear self-punishment programs, follow the steps outlined in "Five Basic Steps for Clearing Programs" in Chapter 5—The Basic Steps of SRT.

Removing Blocks Listed on Chart 5

Chart 5—Blocks and Interference, lists a number of common blocking energies. High Self can remove all of them.

Discarnates

Discarnates are souls who have left the physical body, but not the physical vibrations of the earth plane. After physical death the soul has ninety hours to leave the planet. If they do not leave within that time, they are stuck and cannot escape the earth vibrations without help from an incarnated being. When a soul leaves the carnal body, they carry into the invisible realm with them whatever they have learned or experienced in the flesh. They are not suddenly enlightened beings that know all things, but are stuck at whatever mental, emotional, and spiritual level they attained in life. They carry with them any likes, dislikes, emotions, and beliefs that they had when they were in the human body.

Discarnates in the Aura; Discarnates in Possession

Discarnates that are shown as being in the aura or in possession are not usually deliberately destructive or harmful to the host. They may be stuck in earth vibrations because of an addiction to someone or something in the physical realm. They may be reluctant to go into the higher realms after death because of a fear of punishment or retaliation from God. Or they fail to move on because they don't believe they are dead or they don't believe in an afterlife. These discarnates can, however, cause difficulties for the host if the host is susceptible to their energy. I have asked High Self to clear discarnates from people who had symptoms of physical disease and the symptoms have disappeared.

During September of 1989, I gave two lectures at the American Society of Dowsers annual convention in Danville, Vermont. As part of the demonstration of SRT, I checked to see if anyone at either lecture had discarnates. There were thirty-six people with discarnates at the first lecture, so I asked High Self to clear them.

About an hour after the lecture, a gentleman came up to me and with considerable emotion said, "Thank you for clearing the discarnates. I had a healing. I walked to the lecture with my cane and walked back free." Research revealed that he had picked up a discarnate who had massive injuries on one side of the body when he was in physical form. The discarnate was still running the pain and trauma of the injuries while attached to the host and the host was manifesting the trauma.

I have found that nearly one hundred percent of all the people I work with have had discarnates at some time in the past or still have them. Although some people are not blocked from using SRT by the discarnates they have, discarnates can and do cause other problems. If the host person is sensitive to the vibrations of the discarnates, they can experience the same energies that the discarnates had when they were in their physical body. High Self says, that as long as the discarnate is stuck in the physical realms, they can carry the same energies that they had while in their physical body. Only when they have left the vibrations of the earth and moved on into the spiritual realms can they be free of the earth energies they accumulated.

I never leave discarnates attached to anyone. I question High Self regarding every person I work with to make certain they are clear of all blocking energies—especially discarnates. I ask High Self to clear the person, and then check to make certain all of them have been removed. Clearing discarnates is quick, easy, and painless when you work with High Self.

It is my observation that you can never drive discarnates out using anger, hate, rage, or any discordant energy. They simply feed off the discordant energy and become more strongly entrenched. Patience, gentleness, prayer, talking them out, or asking High Self to remove them is the simplest and best ways. Many discarnates will exit if you can convince them that there is no criticism, judgment, condemnation, or punishment on the other side. You can also inform them that they will have the opportunity to learn and grow and even form their own new incarnational body, one to their own personal specifications. Relatives that have stayed because they feel needed or who are addicted to a loved one need to be told that they are blocking their own spiritual progress as well as the progress of their loved one and, therefore, need to move on to the higher realms.

Never use your own energy to clear discarnates. One day an individual called me and said a friend told them they had discarnates and to call me. I made a quick check with my High Self and discovered that the caller did indeed have discarnates. Later that day another person called with the same complaint, I told both people that

I would ask High Self to clear the discarnates before I retired that evening.

I had already retired and was half asleep before I remembered my promise. Quickly, I said, "I now release these discarnates into their right and perfect place." A check revealed that the two people were clear and I drifted off to sleep. The next morning when I awoke and started to get out of bed, I found I was exhausted. I have never felt so completely drained, even after an illness. I instantly realized what the cause was: I had used my own energy to clear the discarnates when I made the statement "I now release ..." and had seriously depleted it. That taught me a very valuable lesson. Always work with High Self. Let them do the work. Never use your own energy to clear.

Discarnates in Past Lives

There are times when a client is using the pendulum and everything seems to be working smoothly as we research past lives. Suddenly their pendulum stops moving or goes into a circle indicating some blocking energy. Checking with my High Self, I often find that they have discarnates from the past life they were researching. The client may have killed or caused the death of these souls in the past life. The instant we open up a past life, discarnates may show up in the current moment and have to be removed so you or the client can work with the pendulum.

It is difficult for people to understand or even believe that opening up a past life can cause the discarnate souls involved to come into the current time. I explain to them that in SPIRIT and in truth there is no such thing as time and space, and when you open up the past life, to all intents and purpose, you are living it now. Just as when you regress someone under hypnosis, they actually relive the events as though they are occurring now.

Imprints

An imprint is a statement that is registered in the subconscious mind during an emotionally charged time. Imprints of brain damage may cause blocks. Usually, an imprint of brain damage is made at birth. Either because the birth process was slow and pressure was put on the head, or because a doctor or someone else in attendance made a negative comment. This is especially true when the doctor uses instruments to assist the birth and he or she makes a statement or expresses a thought regarding a fear of damaging the child's brain. Brain damage imprints can also result from a fall in which the head is bruised and fear of brain damage is expressed. A blow to the head, even if not serious, may result in a brain damage message if some statement is made to that effect, and emotions are running high. This usually occurs within the first year or two of life. Seldom do I find an imprint of brain damage later than the first couple of years after birth.

The program, Imprint–Other, listed on Chart 5, always has its origin in past lives and often involves a message of brain damage. There is even a master program labeled 'brain damage' found on Chart 6A–Master Programs. Some imprints of brain damage from past lives can be cleared without research; others have to be researched before clearing can be accomplished. Just ask your High Self. I find four things from past lives that can register as brain damage. They are Alzheimer's, Down syndrome, syphilis, and a conviction that you were insane.

Another blocking program that may interfere with the use of the pendulum is a statement you have made in some previous life to the effect that you did not want to communicate with your subconscious mind or your High Self. The following case is an example.

Arthur had worked for about eight months with SRT. He loved the system and was thrilled by the difference it had made in his life. From time to time he had difficulty getting correct answers, but patience and persistent questioning usually paid off. Sometimes, the answers were so conflicting that he became upset and accused both his subconscious and High Self of lying to him. He began to suspect there was a serious problem when he received the following responses.

Q. *Can I speak to my High Self? (-)*

Q. *Can I speak to my subconscious mind? (-)*

Arthur called me and set up an appointment. When he came in, most of the work had to be accomplished by my asking the questions through my High Self. We found two past lives involved. In the first, Arthur was at Holy Spirit Status and others involved were a being at Christ Status, a male, his High Self, God, a Council of Nine, and a Guardian Angel. The Christ Status being is Arthur's daughter in this life, and the male figure is his wife. Both the High Self and the Guardian Angel were assigned to the male. Arthur, as a being of Holy Spirit Status, and his daughter, as a being of Christ Status, were trying to cause the male (current wife) pain. This conflict between the three of them had its roots in the time when they decided to leave the Light realms and incarnate. Arthur believed that he and his daughter were in rebellion to God and the Council. He refused to talk to the Council or listen to them on a meaningful level.

Q. *So you did not want to communicate with the Light beings (God and the Council)? (-)*

Q. *Are your subconscious mind and your High Self trying to fulfill your program of blocking communication with your High Self? (+)*

Q. *Was your subconscious upset when you accused it of giving false answers when it was only trying to fulfill your program of non-communication? (+)*

During the second past life, Arthur was a spirit body, or discarnate. There was a female involved who was his present wife. Also, infinite dark energy came up three times in a row. This is the first case in which I received a second, let alone a third, response of infinite dark energy. The dark energy belonged to the female (current wife) and Arthur believed she was inflicting that energy on him. He believed it was a form of retaliation for hurts experienced in previous past lives. Arthur believed she was attacking him with the discordant energies in the present life and the fear engendered was blocking their current communication.

Arthur wanted revenge and the desire for vengeance never works, it simply causes more problems. One of the hardest lessons we have to learn as living souls is that forgiveness and non-judgment are essential to our soul's spiritual growth and freedom. These things we have to learn and express on the human level and on every level of soul. When we do, we will have peace within and peace on earth.

Discordant Thought Forms

Every thought you think takes a form in the invisible realm. If you have the same thought again and again, it gains strength and may manifest in the visible world. For example, when you think strongly enough about going to the grocery store to restock your cupboard shelves, you will eventually go to the store and purchase groceries.

Our consciousness, or mind, produces results either good or bad in our lives. For example, a man may fear that his wife will run around on him. That fear is nurtured day after day and week after week, perhaps for years. Eventually his wife finds another man and leaves him. His thoughts have created an untenable situation for the wife; she looks elsewhere for fulfillment, and is blamed for her infidelity. We must understand that our fear creates.

The basic message in the book of Job in the *Bible* is that fear produces that which is feared.

> *For the thing that I fear comes upon me, and what I dread befalls me. I am not at ease, nor*

am I quiet; I have no rest; but trouble comes. (Job 3:25-26 RSV)

When you are troubled in your mind and fearful in your heart of what may happen to you in life, there is no rest or quiet in your consciousness; and it is busy creating that which troubles you. Therefore, it is vital that you think positive thoughts, for positive thoughts build good results.

Years ago, a man came to me on several occasions to have his programs researched and cleared. During one session, he stated that a friend had told him he had a very strong negative thought form attached to him. She informed him that the thought form believed that, if it could accumulate just a little more energy from him, it could separate from him and have an independent existence of its own. Since I had some doubt, I queried my High Self concerning the validity of the woman's statement. High Self revealed that what she had told him was correct. We asked that the negative thought form be cleared and it was done. Once the thought form was gone, the client actually felt the difference.

High Self assures me that a negative thought form could never gain enough energy to become a separate expression for any extended length of time. Thought forms can and sometimes do work independently of their source, but soon start to diminish in strength when they are not continually sustained with more discordant thought energy. Just as a leaf or a flower that is cut off from its source of energy soon dies, so a negative thought form dies when it is no longer nourished by additional negative energy.

One day a client asked me if I could tell him what was turning on lights in their home. High Self indicated the answer was on Chart 5. Using that chart, I was shown "discordant thought forms." The creator of the negative thought forms was the client's wife. Several years before, she had been diagnosed as having an incurable disease. Because of the doctor's negative diagnosis, she was creating a great amount of fear-filled thoughts, which then created more emotional pain, fear, and anxiety. It became a vicious cycle. Her thoughts were constantly filled with hate of her own physical body and belief in its inability to heal itself, hate of life for giving her such a rotten deal, unforgiveness, rejection of self, and bitterness.

Eventually the thought forms accumulated so much energy that they were actually beginning to think. Here is the amazing part: They were trying to tell her, by turning on the lights, to see the situation in an enlightened way. She was to understand, despite the doctor's opinion to the contrary, that there is no such thing as an incurable disease. As a minister and follower of the teaching of Jesus, my message to my congregants is "There is no such thing as an incurable disease. There is nothing to heal. There is only something to know. You are a spiritual being created in God's image and likeness. Since God is SPIRIT, you are SPIRIT. SPIRIT cannot be sick or less than perfect." You can, however, believe that you are diseased, or that your life is out of order, or any other negative thought, and that thought will be made manifest and maintain itself as the appearance of disease in your physical or as disorder in your life.

Negative thoughts have a strong effect on some people. During workshops, in which we teach SRT, I demonstrate the power of both negative and positive thought. A volunteer is asked to stand in front of the class. Using a pendulum and working with High Self, I locate the edge of the subject's auric field. The class members are then asked to send negative thoughts to the person. When I measure the aura again, it has usually collapsed, sometimes to within inches of the physical body. I then ask the students to send positive thoughts to the subject. A subsequent check of the volunteer's auric field shows that it has expanded outward past the point at which it was originally measured.

Many years ago I attended a workshop, titled "Alpha Truth Awareness," in which the teacher told us that sending out a negative thought was like writing a letter with a carbon copy. You send out the carbon copy and keep the original. Unfortunately for the sender, they register the original discordant energy in their own consciousness. And fortunately, the intended receiver of the carbon copy thought-letter does not have to take delivery.

The benefits that may be derived from controlling your negative thoughts, saying no to them, and holding only positive thoughts, are beyond measure. And, it is up to each individual to control his or her own thoughts and emotions. No one else can do it for you.

When negative thought forms are blocking, have them dissolved. Even if they are not blocking, you can have the accumulated energy dissolved. One good practice when you retire for the night is to have the High Self clear any discordant energy you may have accumulated during the day. It is a wonderful way to maintain a greater balance of good and create more harmony in your life. Having High Self clear your discordant energy is a powerful process of giving up or 'forgiving' anyone or anything that may have offended you or caused you to think or react in a discordant way. It is a grand feeling to feel free of discord and offense toward anyone and anything.

Conscious Control

Occasionally, in one of the workshops or when working one-on-one with a client, a conscious control program will block the movements of the pendulum. One client, John, had a conscious fear of losing control. He would allow me to question his subconscious for about an hour before he would shut down. Questioning my High Self revealed that we had reached the limit of his ability to allow someone else to question or control him. When we asked questions of his subconscious mind, we found that John had a fear of losing control that went back to when he was fourteen.

There were times in his youth when John was fearful that he was going crazy and struggled to maintain control. He set up a program that, even as an adult, was causing him to shut down when anyone questioned him or pushed him too far. Clearing the program gave John great relief and assurance that he could communicate with others without losing control.

Alfred had problems getting responses from his subconscious mind during the workshop. His fear that he would give someone wrong answers was blocking any response whatsoever. There were several past lives involved in which Alfred had used a pendulum to question his High Self concerning other people. He deliberately gave false information, causing harm to the people with whom he was working. Now he was fearful of again harming someone. The assumption was that, if he could not get any answers at all, he could not give information that was in error or harmful to anyone, including himself.

Satanics, Demonics

People often ask me what the difference is between discarnates and satanics or demonics. The simplest answer is, "Their attitudes and programs." Just as souls in physical bodies (people) have different degrees of positive or discordant temperament, energy, and action, so out of the body souls (discarnates), whether they are satanics, demonics, and so forth, also has varying degrees of positive or discordant temperament, energy, and action. As they are listed on Chart 5 from the left to right, the discordant energies and negative attitudes of the souls get progressively worse.

Dark Energies

Dark energies are discarnates who carry a lot of dark, discordant energy. Their typical energies are anger, hate, sexual abuse, and spiritual suicide. The anger, hate, and sexual abuse have caused them to cut themselves off from the Light within–spiritual suicide. These energies, when carried by discarnates of dark energy level, can set up a lot of conflicting currents in the host's mind, physical body, and emotions.

Dark Forces

Dark forces are discarnates with dark energy who band together and sometimes deliberately try to cause problems. Their additional dark energy is jealousy of any soul that is not like them. Some psychics actually channel dark forces and do not realize what their source is. They think they are receiving information from guides, and they are not. Part of the information given will be accurate, but much of it is false. That does not mean that you should never consult a psychic or that all psychics are inaccurate and present false or misleading information. Just make sure you check out the psychic's accuracy with your High Self.

There are occasions when I pick up dark forces and find that they have attached themselves to me because they either want to have their programs cleared or they want to be released from the earth realms. They are tired of playing the dark game and want to go on to whatever awaits them in the spiritual realms. They are like lost children who want to go home. For a long time they have caused problems, but are now willing to face the music, pay the price, and balance the scales.

Satanic Forces; Demonic Forces

Satanic forces are simply souls that have satanic energy who have joined together as a group. Demonic forces are the same.

Removing Unknown Blocking Energies

Occasionally, you or a client may be blocked with an unknown energy (when you ask what chart the energy is on, High Self will swing the pendulum in a "no" position across the bottom of the chart). Simply ask the following questions.

Q. *Can you remove the blocking energy without me knowing what it is? (+)*

Q. *Will you please remove it now? (+)*

Q. *Is the energy gone? (+)*

The pendulum will now move freely under the direction of the subconscious mind or High Self, and reflect the correct answers. If it does not move, continue to work with the High Self searching for and removing blocks. Anything can be found and cleared. However, sometimes it takes a lot of persistence and patience.

CHAPTER 7

Charts 1 and 4

Chart 1—Chart to Use; Contact or Help

We have previously mentioned Chart 1 and the fact that it is used to determine where to find the programs that need to be cleared. Those to call on for help are also listed on the chart from Guardian Angels all of the way to GODHEAD and into Infinity. This chapter contains an explanation of the rest of the items on the inside of Chart 1, starting on the inside left at the bottom of the chart.

Siamese Souls

When the soul is created, it may have other souls attached to it like a string of paper dolls. There can be a maximum of nine Siamese souls attached. They must be cleared and removed before the soul is free since all of the Siamese souls carry the same records as the person's soul. Just ask High Self to clear them and cut them loose.

Extra Souls

Second round, advanced souls may have extra souls in their physical body. These attach to the person's soul for one of three reasons. Either the person who is the host harmed the extra souls in past lives, or the extra souls harmed the host, or they are part of the host's soul family. The past life discordant connections need to be resolved, so the host allows the extra souls to enter at birth. When the clearing process for the host soul is begun, the extra souls are discovered. Once the extra souls are cleared and removed, they do not have to incarnate again as they are clean and have returned to the GODHEAD. Always double-check how many souls are left in the physical body after clearing anyone. When the host has harmed the extra souls they are harder to remove as they desire to stay attached and give the host a bad time. Extra souls are one of the reasons why a person may demonstrate multiple personality syndrome or schizophrenia.

Another reason a person may acquire extra souls occurs when the person doing the SRT research is also serving as High Self for another soul. When the soul being served leaves the physical body (through death), their High Self may send that soul to the SRT researcher for clearing and healing. This is not necessary. As soon as the researcher is aware of what is happening, they can give direct orders and permission to the other expressions of their own soul who are serving as High Self to clear the souls under their care the moment they leave the physical and enter the spiritual realms.

People, who have been cleared through using SRT but who do not use the system, can also pick up extra souls this way. Asking High Self to clear and remove any and all extra souls as part of the SRT clearing process for yourself and others will ensure that you and your clients stay free of extra souls.

To understand this, it may be helpful to reiterate some information presented in earlier chapters. When a soul is at the level of King of Kings (see Chart 3–Levels or Soul Consciousness) or higher, it may serve countless other souls as their High Self even while still experiencing a physical life. I find many people who have been cleared, and/or who may be working with SRT, are serving an infinite number of souls as their High Self. We know that when a soul leaves the physical body through what we call death and enters the spiritual realms, that soul can be cleared of all discordant programs. This frees them from the need to incarnate again.

However, this clearing of the soul's records must be done from the level of the experience–physical incarnation. This is why a High Self would send a soul to another human for clearing. These extra souls can cause problems for the host, usually in an effort to get their attention so that the host will ask for them to be cleared, healed, and removed. Thus, it is important to do so to keep yourself and your clients free of interference from extra souls.

Soul Family

Every person has a soul family just like we have human families and relatives. There are times when we can clear members of our soul family which can be of tremendous benefit to them. When High Self indicates soul family, it is an indication that some of the soul family is ready to be cleared. It is not necessary to know how many need clearing or what the programs are, just ask that it be done.

Spiritual Kick [and Rap in Head]

High Self first indicated the use of a spiritual kick when a student's husband was giving her a very bad time about attending the SRT workshop. Asking High Self to apply a kick dramatically changed the husband's attitude and he was completely open to her attending the workshop although he admitted he did not understand what SRT was about. Later, High Self indicated that some people need a spiritual rap in the head. That works also. Occasionally, the person needs more than one kick or rap to help them open to greater spiritual awareness. You can ask for these on a daily basis for yourself or your clients. Many students of SRT have stated that there had been a dramatic change in attitude and receptivity for someone they had asked to be given a spiritual kick or rap in the head.

There are times when a person may be benefited by ongoing spiritual kicks or rap in the head. When this is indicated, I ask High Self to set up a kicking wheel with boots on it so that additional spiritual kicks are administered as it revolves.

Soul Programs

These are set up when a soul has left the physical body at the time of death but is still emotionally attached to it. These programs do not go to the conscious or subconscious mind of the physical body where they can be modified or deleted. They go directly into the soul fully charged. High Self cannot clear soul programs, but they can work with the soul to get them to release the energies. Soul programs are very strong and can cause a lot of pain, suffering, and turmoil lifetime after lifetime until the soul releases them.

Conscious Mind; Subconscious Mind

When conscious mind or subconscious mind is indicated, I always turn to Chart 3–Levels of Soul Consciousness, for the answer as to which conscious or subconscious mind has the problem. Then I go to Chart 6A–Discordant Energy, to determine what the discordant energy is. High Self says any or all of the 18 bodies and their associated minds can have a problem. In Chapter 2–The Soul's Design, information was given as to the bodies and minds and their points or origin.

Here is one example of a subconscious mind program held in the etheric body of a female client. The energy on Chart 6A was fear. It was carried over from the embryo and the divine plan. High Self calls the etheric the blueprint paper or whole-cloth from which everything is created and which contains the complete design for the entire ONE universe.

The second example was presented as a conscious mind program for a male. The living soul was indicated and the energies were hate and extreme hate of God. Remember, there are always two sides to the coin. The other side is love and love of God. Because each soul has free will to exercise choices to love or to hate, once it partakes of 'the tree of the knowledge of good [love] and evil [hate]' and incarnates, the challenges of love or hate are set in motion and must be faced. Hate is to be overcome and love must be brought into ascendancy.

Contact or Help – Guides or Other Beings

The contact (person or group) worked with to research and clear programs in the SRT process is High Self. When you sit down to work, always check to make certain you are clear; and using Chart 1, ask who you are working with. If anything other than High Self is indicated, ask that everything be cleared so you are working with High Self.

You can ask for help for yourself or other people. For instance, I just asked if someone in the hospital needed some help and received a positive response. Using Chart 1, I asked what we could send and was shown High Self, Masters, Council of Seven, High Council, and Holy Spirit. Since so many Councils were involved, I asked if this was a mental and emotional condition that needed healing and was assured it was. When I asked for help to be sent to someone who needed physical healing, Angels of Light and Forces of Light were indicated. I do not have a clue as to who was receiving the help. I really don't need to know. You also can ask for help for people. For me it is a way of tithing my time and talents to my fellow souls and to the universe.

Behind the GODHEAD

There is something behind the GODHEAD. The first thing I found was SPIRIT. SPIRIT is the source and expression of all that is; all knowing, energy and consciousness. Next, the word LUMINOUS was given to me. This is a reflection of SPIRIT as all knowledge and intelligence. Next was WELLSPRING, which is a reflection of SPIRIT as all creative energy. It is the pool of energy from which SPIRIT draws to extend Itself as all knowledge and intelligence through both spiritual and physical expression.

Behind SPIRIT is GRAND-I and WHOLE. GRAND-I is the complete and final expression of SPIRIT as a ONE universe. WHOLE is the complete balance, harmony, and perfection of the completed ONE universe and everything that is experienced in that universe.

Additional Items Chart 1

When the individual soul ascends to SPIRIT—returns to SOURCE—it becomes one with SPIRIT and everything that SPIRIT extends. There is no time or space in SPIRIT, thus as SPIRIT extends a new ONE universe, the soul is everything that will be experienced both above and below Chart 3—Levels of Soul Consciousness. So it is vital and important to clear everything 'above Chart 3' and 'below Chart 3' and back to SPIRIT. This is called 'looping' on Chart 1. Then the soul continues to experience and learn at all levels which is called 'beyond looping.' Then there are items 'not on charts.'

Since there is never a time when SPIRIT stops extending Itself or a time when the soul stops being a part of that extension, the soul can pick up additional energy that can cause conflict with the physical incarnation you are presently experiencing. I ask that programs be set up at all levels to keep the soul clear as it continues to expand and grow along with SPIRIT. I also ask for infinite guarantees raised to the infinite level that the soul will stay clear.

Chart 4—Programs, When, and Cast of Characters

Understanding the Basic 13 Programs

In my first book, *The Freedom Path,* I explored thirteen programs that might cause problems in the present life. These programs are listed on Chart 4 as: *inheritance, identification, imprint, experience or trauma, benefit, conflict, self-punishment, organ language, past lives, past lives in other dimensions, future lives, discarnates,* and *fear.*

These thirteen programs are basic causes of problems, although the effects they can have on a person's life may be complex, and have major, far-reaching consequences. I shall present these thirteen programs only briefly in this book, since all of them are covered extensively in *The Freedom Path.*

During my basic workshop, I use these thirteen programs and my first book, *The Freedom Path,* to teach students how to research and clear problem areas. After students have mastered the fundamentals, I introduce them to the advanced programs. If you have not read *The Freedom Path,* you should begin your SRT work by learning to clear programs caused by the thirteen programs listed in this section.

Inheritance

Inheritance is usually a belief that you picked up from another life and carried over into the present life. Another common source of inherited beliefs is your parents' genes. You can also inherit a belief from someone else by associating with them and accepting and believing what they say. However, this form of inherited belief is not as common as the genetic belief.

Every cell in the human body is a mini-computer that stores a complete record of everything you have experienced through your five senses from the moment your soul attached to your incarnational body. (For an expanded understanding of this concept, you may wish to read some information on holography. I recommend the book *Stalking the Wild Pendulum* by Itzhak Bentov.)

The soul can attach to the physical body at the instant of conception (the joining of the sperm and egg), anytime in the womb, or anytime up to 2½ days after birth. Before the soul enters the physical body, the only programs that are registered in the cellular memory are those of the parents. This is because parents' programs are carried in the cellular memory of the mother's egg and the father's sperm when these join to form the physical body of the fetus. This is often referred to in scientific terms as the inherited DNA in the genes.

Once the soul attaches to the fetus, it starts to pick up and register new programs based on its beliefs, perceptions, and judgments, even while it is in the womb. Remember, the soul is eternal and while attached to the fetus, it is aware of all that is being thought, felt, and acted out by those around it.

Once the baby comes out of the womb, it begins the human process of eating, sleeping, working, and so on. During sleep periods, which usually add up to many hours out of each twenty-four hour day, the child may dream as much as eight hours. High Self tells me that, during the dream state, the soul is programming his or her akashic or soul record into the cell structure of the physical body. This may take one to two weeks to complete, depending on the age of the soul and the accumulated programs in the soul record.

After programming is complete, the child's cells hold the memories, programs, and beliefs of the mother, the father, and the soul that now inhabits the physical body. The child may also have the grandparents' programs, which can also be passed to the child by the parents. (I have found some people who have inherited genetic beliefs from eight generations back.) From the time that programming is complete; the child can experience any of them, especially if his or her own past life programming and chosen soul path reinforces the genetic programs. However, a child is most likely to run his or her own personal programs.

High Self says that you never under any circumstance inherit disease. You may inherit the belief in disease because of genetic programming. Then, if you have a disease program of your own, or a desire to punish, limit, or afflict yourself in some way, you may run the program, thus producing the disease. There is a limit on genetic inheritance, however. High Self says the belief cannot sustain itself after the third or fourth generation unless it is constantly reinforced by a belief in the disease in subsequent generations. In fact, if each generation cleared the inherited beliefs of disease and discord, these programs would not be passed on at all, as the chain would be broken.

> *'The Lord is slow to anger, and abounding in steadfast love, forgiving iniquity and transgression, but he will by no means clear the guilty, visiting the iniquity of fathers upon children, upon the third and upon the fourth generation.' (Numbers 14:18 RSV)*

Iniquity, or sin, is an erroneous belief or wrong thinking which causes a separation from God and good. This belief was set up prior to our first incarnation when we partook of 'the tree of the knowledge of good and evil.' We often continue these beliefs. When we stop filling our minds with discordant beliefs, we will stop experiencing all of the painful things in this life and in any subsequent incarnations. Certainly, we need to clean up our thinking. We also need to research and clear any programs or beliefs that we have picked up through our parents' genes.

A program of inheritance may also originate in the bardo (a term referring to the time between lives from *The Tibetan Book of the Dead*), past lives, past lives in other dimensions, parallel lives, parallel universe, and may even originate at the beginning of the creative process before the universe and worlds were formed.

Once you have determined that there is a program of inheritance causing a problem, you ask when it was established (Chart 4–When), identify the cast of characters (Chart 4–Cast of Characters), find out what happened (use Chart 6A–Discordant Energy, to find the energies), and clear it.

Identification

What are you? Or, rather, what do you perceive yourself to be? Often we see ourselves as models of one or both of our parents. We identify with them and take on their traits. This is okay, as long as the traits are positive and constructive. However, it is not okay if the traits are discordant, destructive, or addictive. Sometimes you may simply be identifying with yourself and your own negative traits or experiences from a past life or early childhood. Identification can have its beginning in the current life, bardo, past life, past life in other dimensions, parallel lives, or in a parallel universe. Regardless of when the identification program was established, or the reason for the discordant energy, you can research and clear it using SRT.

Imprint

An imprint is a message or belief that is received by the subconscious mind during a time of emotional stress. The imprint becomes fixed in the subconscious mind and can later manifest itself when external circumstances are conducive. Although most imprints are totally erroneous or greatly exaggerated, they still cause the person to react in specific, disruptive patterns until the imprints are revealed, released, and replaced with beneficial messages. It is as though a post-hypnotic suggestion was made and is being carried out without the conscious volition of the subject. The person simply has no awareness of the imprinted message or control over it. Only by researching the program, clearing the old imprint, and reprogramming the subconscious mind can a person take control of their life.

Experience, Trauma

You are experiencing many things at this very moment, although you may take these experiences for granted and be unaware of them. You are breathing, and your heart is beating and circulating blood which carries oxygen to every part of your physical. You are seeing, hearing, sensing, and thinking—all of which you accept as an ordinary part of your life. However, if one or more of these experiences were drastically restricted or eliminated, you would have a traumatic experience.

Traumatic experiences may create deep-seated phobias and have long lasting effects. Sexual molestation as a child can affect you the rest of your life and into future incarnations unless the energy is released.

Another example of a program that can be caused by trauma is asthma. When researching an asthma program, I often find past lives in which the person died in a fire, was drowned, hung, or strangled—any trauma that cut off the air passages to the lungs. This creates a strong negative energy program in the subconscious mind. If the program runs in the present life, asthma may occur. Strangling in a past life is also one of the reasons a person may stutter in this life.

Benefit

A benefit is a form of payoff. The payoff can be positive and beneficial or negative and destructive. Self-esteem, love, joy, abundance, and health are all positive benefits. Unfortunately, I have found people who derive a benefit from punishing themselves. One client had a strong benefit of getting attention by creating symptoms of illness. As a child, she felt starved for affection. The only time her craving for attention was fulfilled to her satisfaction was when she was sick with a childhood disease. Attention was then lavished on her, and she loved it. As an adult and wife with a very considerate and attentive husband, she could never get enough attention. So she constantly ran symptoms of disease in order to get more attention. She was stuck in her own negative benefit. When I suggested to her that we clear up her programs causing illness, she said "No." She was afraid that if she were not ill, her husband would not give her the attention she needed and might even leave her.

Conflict

A program of conflict is often a want colliding with a taboo: "I want to love you but I can't because you do not love me. You do not meet my needs. You do not fulfill my shortcomings and make me okay. I want to be at peace, but you make me feel inferior and inadequate." Conflict with another person is often a result of being in conflict with yourself. If you have the inner programs of low self-esteem, anger, hate, fear, frustration, and so on, you will find that life will reinforce your programs and you will be in conflict with the world.

Conflict may be a source of guilt which can cause you to set up programs of self-punishment, self-limitation, or self-destruction. If you have such programs, you may inflict mental, emotional, or physical pain on yourself. You may even seek to kill yourself to escape the conflict. Many people are completely unaware of the source of conflict in their lives because they blame everyone else. Any possible awareness that they could be at fault is denied and they make no attempt to find the cause or source within themselves. With SRT, you can find the causes, clear them, and have a new expression of life, a new birth.

Self-Punishment

Seldom have I worked to clear someone's subconscious programs and not encountered self-punishment. There are a myriad of reasons why a soul sets up such programs. Many people set them up based on religious lives and a belief that, in some way, they failed to live the teachings of the Church. These are often based on a false understanding of God, a belief in the devil, and so forth. Another reason for self-punishment is that the first thing we may be taught as a small child is that we are bad and therefore guilty. Toddlers are curious and may get into things that are forbidden. If they are told to leave things alone, fail to do so, and end up breaking some priceless possession of a parent, they may be made to feel guilty and receive punishment. Too frequently the punishment may be done 'because I love you.' In later years, the individual may look for punishment as a form of love. Or, they may punish themselves for doing something that was foolish; something they should not have done. I have even found people who have punished themselves lifetime after lifetime for incarnating the first time.

Organ Language

Organ language comes in two categories: body comparison and body statement. For example, if you have been compared to another family member, and do not measure up to their good looks, stature, physical capabilities, or mental brilliance, you can run an organ language program. When this happens, you may have a sense of being imperfect or unworthy. Another body comparison is having a physical resemblance to someone. This is fine as long as the person you are compared to has your respect and love. You would probably have a strong reaction if you were told you looked like Hitler, or some other infamous person.

The body statement form of organ language refers to how the body is used, treated, or affected. You may use the body in a forceful, cruel, mean, or angry way. You may mistreat your body by not exercising, eating badly, using drugs or alcohol, or by overworking. One client had a body statement form of organ language programming on her son, who got in a fight and had a tooth knocked out. This was misuse of his body.

Many organ language programs are a result of past lives in which the physical body was tortured, crucified, burned at the stake, stoned, beheaded, thrown off a cliff, drowned, and so on. Through the ages, man has devised many ways to cause suffering to his fellow man, much of it deliberate and often in the name of God. I have seen many different forms of physical abuse when past life pictures are given to me by my High Self.

Your own spoken word can cause a program of organ language. I often hear people make statements that could set up a negative result in the body: "You give me a pain in the neck" or, "That turns my stomach." Since the subconscious does not have the ability to make judgments, but simply takes things at face value and plays them back, constant repetition of a discordant statement can and often does cause a negative reaction in the body. Watch your words and try to use only positive statements. After all, it is your life you are affecting in a positive or negative way.

Past Lives

Past lives can be a program or the time when a program was established. Many people do not believe in past lives. However, once you begin to use a pendulum and the charts, and start asking what the programs are and when they were established, past lives come up again and again. About 97% of all the research I do for clients involves past lives. No one can really prove the reality or non-reality of past lives. However, I have obtained dramatic results by researching and clearing past lives, and that is proof enough and reason to continue the work.

There are many good books on past lives and reincarnation. You may wish to expand your knowledge by reading some of them.

Case Study:

During a lunch break at one of our workshops, ten of us went to a nearby restaurant and sat at the same table. One young lady said she would love to have waffles and cream but dared not since she was allergic to milk and wheat products and would have an immediate and painful reaction if she ate them. I had two inner pictures. One was of a huge vat of steaming milk in a dairy and the other was of a farm with a blasted wheat crop. I handed her a pendulum and asked her if she had fallen into a vat of milk and drowned in a past life. She got a "yes" response. I asked her if, in another life, there was starvation because of a blighted wheat crop and if she had said she would never again have anything to do with wheat. Again, the response was "yes." We cleared the programs and asked if she could have waffles and cream without having an allergic reaction. We again received a positive response. She ordered waffles and cream, ate them, and was delighted to be free from any negative effect.

Past Lives in Other Dimensions

Past lives in other dimensions are lives on other planets, in other solar systems or galaxies, or even in other universes. They may also be lives lived at other vibratory levels or in other forms such as Guardian Angels, guides, High Self, Angels of Light, Masters, and so forth. You research them just like any other past life.

Future Lives

As eternal spirit beings, we are not bound by time and space. Albert Einstein pointed out that in the absolute or spiritual reality; space and time do not exist. This is also the premise underlying the concept of simultaneous lives described in the *Seth Speaks* writings, authored by Jane Roberts. Even though all energies from past, present, or future lives may have impact on the current life and moment, you can research and clear them. The process for researching future lives is the same as it is for any past life—determine the cast of characters and what happened, and then ask High Self to clear the program.

A person may find, through questioning the subconscious or High Self, that they are not living any future lives at the present time. However, as they research and release discordant programs they may find that they are beginning to live future lives. High Self says this is because a person may have all or most of his or her soul energy invested in the current life in order to handle discordant programs. Once they start to clear subconscious programs, they free up soul energy that can then be used by the soul to live future lives or parallel lives, thus speeding up the process of learning and growing.

There is another intriguing factor involved with future lives. You may discover, through questioning, that this is your last incarnation. Yet, you may find that you are living future lives. You may be puzzled and ask how this can be. Ask the following questions when High Self indicates future lives.

Q. *Is this truly my last incarnation? (+)*

Q. *Yet, I am living future lives right now? (+)*

Q. *Then will these future lives be finished before I leave this physical incarnation? (+)*

Q. *Will they then become past lives and be added to the total number of past lives I have lived? (+)*

Although we may not understand how we can live a future life while we are still in this physical body, clearing future lives can and usually does change the present life.

Discarnates, Entities

A discarnate, defined for SRT, is any living soul who has left a physical body through the process called death, but has not yet left the physical vibrations of the planet. Discarnates are 'stuck' on the earth plane. Questioning reveals that ninety hours is the maximum time a soul can stay in the physical vibrations of earth after the physical body dies and the soul exits the body. If they stay beyond that time, they are stuck and someone has to assist them in leaving. I never clear discarnates by using my own energy. I ask High Self to do it.

Fear

I often encounter fear programs when researching a client's blocks to a balanced, productive life. Fear programs can have their inception in this life or anywhere back to the beginning when only the GODHEAD existed. You research a fear program like any other program.

Understanding When Programs Become Established

You also use Chart 4—When, to determine when a program was established. The time may be any time from the moment we were first created as spirit beings to the future of this current life.

Present Life Already Happened

Let's suppose that, when you ask High Self when a program was established, the pendulum is moved to indicate 'present life already happened.' Using a chart with numbers (such as Chart 4), you ask for an age and find that the pendulum is moved somewhere between 0 and 10. Because this is too broad a time to pinpoint a problem, you ask that the zeros be ignored and that the age be given in single digits. Then, when the pendulum is moved somewhere between the numbers 30 and 40 on the chart, you know the age is between 3 and 4. Verify the time by asking a question like this:

Q. *Was the program set up between three and four years of age? (+)*

When the movement of the pendulum indicates a time between two numbers that are higher than 9 (such as 10 and 20), ask for the second digit. Let's say the pendulum indicates a figure between 20 and 30.

Q. *Did this happen when I [or the client] was between twenty and thirty years of age? (+)*

Q. *Please indicate the second figure. (4)*

Q. *Was I [or the client] twenty-four years of age? (+)*

The system is so comprehensive and exact that, if you wanted to, you could find the exact moment when you were born and took your first breath. I was born late on the evening of July 4th, but I did not know the exact time. Questioning High Self revealed that it was 11:36.5. The only value for such an accurate answer would be if you were having an astrological reading. Approximate ages usually suffice for determining when programs are established.

Present Life Yet to Come

Most of the events in our lives, at least the major ones, seem preplanned. That does not mean, however, that you cannot alter your life. One student wanted to know if there was some reason why that very day, she had, out of the clear blue, told her sister she would take care of her children. High Self indicated that the student and her sister had also been sisters in a past life, when the sister had two children. Further questions revealed that the sister had been depressed and had killed herself. The surviving sister (the SRT student) had taken the responsibility of caring for her two children. This had happened in 672 past lives and was a well-entrenched suicide program for her sister. In each case, she had left the surviving sister with the care of the children.

Further questioning revealed that the sister was planning suicide in the current life and the spiritual agreement was that the remaining sister would take care of her children again. We made the appropriate clearing statements regarding the past lives and the planned suicide for this life. Then we verified that the program was cleared.

Q. *Is your sister planning suicide in this life? (-)*

Q. *Will she live out her life and die of natural causes in old age? (+)*

Q. *So you will not have to take care of her children? (-)*

This is only one case of many in which a client, while out of the physical body, had planned something traumatic for the present life yet to come as a way to fulfill a karmic belief. I have researched programs for auto accidents, illness, family upsets, suicide, murder, and many other situations. Of course, none of this can be proven. However, based on the wonderful and often miraculous changes that have occurred as a result of clearing clients' discordant programs, I have to believe it is true. These programs had been planned to take place at some future time and place in the present life and will not happen because the situation has been defused.

Bardo

According to the Whitton and Fisher book, *Life Between Life*, "bardo" is a Tibetan term that means "space or time between lives" and High Self says the definition is correct. Prior to incarnating in the present physical body, you were in the bardo. You met with a Light Council (your High Self), which consists of two or more beings of higher consciousness. You reviewed your past life (akashic) record and considered what you needed to work on in this present life. You chose your birth parents and, if you were to be adopted, your adoptive parents. You knew they would provide you with a lot of basic programming and launch you into the situations and challenges you needed to encounter, learn from, and overcome. Sometimes a soul is very reluctant to incarnate because the challenges they choose to face may be difficult and painful. You may come in kicking and screaming, but come in you do.

Some of the factors from the bardo are extended into the womb, the birth, and finally are experienced through the life process. When these three times are indicated, research past lives because past lives are the root cause of the programming. You can research bardo, womb, or birth but it usually does not clear the past life roots. Whereas, if you clear the past lives, that clears the bardo, womb, and birth as well.

Miscarriages, still births, and crib deaths are usually a result of a soul changing its mind about incarnating. A soul may decide that he is not ready to face life in the physical realm. He may decide that the task chosen would be too difficult, or he may realize that things have changed and he will not be able to accomplish what had been planned for this life, so he simply withdraws. Also, the need to incarnate to continue soul growth may no longer be there.

A client came to me for counseling. She was about eight weeks pregnant and she wanted me to check on the soul who was coming in to see if it had any programs that could be cleared. We found that the soul had attached to the fetus at the moment of conception. There were programs to be cleared and permission was granted by High Self to do the work. We were given the necessary help to research and clear the soul's programs.

About two weeks later, the client returned and said she had a miscarriage. I asked High Self why this had happened. We found that after clearing the soul's programs, the soul no longer needed to incarnate and work so they chose to withdraw. The client was comfortable and able to accept what had happened. High Self assured us that we had done what was best for all concerned when we asked that the soul's programs be cleared.

This experience taught me a very important lesson: Never research and clear programs for a soul attached to a fetus. Now, when asked to check on an unborn child, I always ask if it is right and proper to clear the fetus but not the soul. I also ask if the soul will still incarnate with the fetus' programs cleared. Clearing the fetus can sometimes make the pregnancy easier and the fetus healthier. Then I wait until a few weeks after the child is born, and again checking with High Self, I ask if the research and clearing for the soul can be done safely and the soul will stay in the physical body.

When a program is set up in the bardo, we can find out who else is involved, what is planned, and clear the energy of self-punishment, fear, anger, hate, and so on. However, knowing that the plans for this life that we make in the bardo are based on past lives, I prefer researching and clearing past lives.

Death

There are two possible scenarios that can come up when death is given as the time when a program is established. First, there can be the physical death experience in a past life and the resulting energy. In this case, the discordant energy is experienced after the death has occurred and may automatically become a soul program. When the energy is recorded in the soul after a death has occurred, and the soul is already out of the physical body, the High Self cannot automatically clear it. They must work with the soul to release the energy. (See "Soul Programs" explained earlier in this chapter.)

The second scenario involves the present life yet to come, when the soul may be planning a traumatic death. You can research and clear this program so that the experience of exiting the physical body, called death, can be simple and free from trauma. Often the soul decides to stay in the body longer.

Transition

Transition can be one of four possible time frames in our soul journey: death and dying in a past life, leaving the bardo to incarnate, a dramatic change of consciousness (transition or transformation) in the present life, or one soul leaving the incarnational body and another entering.

When the subconscious or High Self indicates transition as the time a program is set up, ask:

Q. When was the transition experienced?

If the transition was experienced at death, ask:

Q. When was the death experienced?

The second type of transition, Bardo, is that time in your soul journey when you are between lives, and you are reviewing your past lives to determine what you need to work on in the next life. It is not always easy for you to choose what you are going to work on. Once the choice is made, you experience a major transition from a state of peace and harmony on the etheric plane to the physical incarnational process and turmoil. Sometimes you pick horrendous programs to face, work on, and clear up in an attempt to bring about major shifts in your soul status. You may even decide to face all of your remaining 'stuff' and finish up so you will not have to incarnate again. Since programs are chosen but not established in the bardo, you must research the past life in which the program was actually established.

The third type of transition, a dramatic change in consciousness, can be triggered by a traumatic experience in the present life. The experience could be divorce, illness, injury, death of a loved one, or a catastrophe such as a flood, tornado, or earthquake. Narrow the times down by asking when in the present life the program of transition was experienced (use a chart with numbers, and ask what your age was at the time of the transition).

In one case involving transition, a client revealed that the family had moved from the Midwest to the West Coast, leaving friends and relatives behind. This caused a decided change in life styles and relationships. The move instilled a sense of total transition from one form of life expression to another.

Perhaps you have heard someone use the phrase, "He (or she) is a walk-in." A walk-in is a spirit being who takes the place of another soul when the original soul determines that they have had it with life and want to leave the physical body. According to my High Self, the soul coming in prefers being called an exchange student, because there is always an agreement between the previous occupant of the physical house, who moves out, and the new occupant. In the workshops I teach, I have become aware of many exchange students and the number keeps growing.

Another form of transition involves soul qualities, which are addressed in Chapter 9—Octaves of Learning and Soul Qualities. This type of transition is the transition from discord to harmony, from not knowing to knowing, from not being to being. For instance, you may have accumulated a lot of energy in past lives, future lives, the present life, parallel lives, or even a parallel universe that is blocking your understanding and love. This blocking energy may keep you from knowing and being your true potential—that of a spiritual being, a child of God Consciousness. When you research and clear the soul qualities, you experience a transition from darkness into greater Light. As this transition or transformation occurs, you become enlightened and aware that you truly are a spiritual being having a human experience. Jesus did not tell us to *become* the Light of the world, He said, "Ye are the light of the world.... Let your light so shine before men, that they may see your good works, and glorify your Father which is in heaven" (Matthew 5:14, 16 KJV).

Parallel Lives

Parallel lives can be compared to a clump of birch trees; there is one major root cluster, but several trunks. Another analogy for parallel lives is a tree with one trunk but many branches. In some paranormal studies, parallel life is called "bi-location." Regardless of any attempt to describe parallel lives, it is difficult for most people to believe that they can be in more than one place at a time. The thing to remember is that you are created in the image and likeness of God (Genesis 1:26), and God is everywhere. You are a spiritual being, living soul, expressing through a physical body. Therefore, it stands to reason, if you will simply open your mind to the idea that the soul can express through more than one incarnational body at a time.

The first time I ran into parallel lives was with a young man in San Jose, California. We had cleared all of his programs that we could find when the dimension of parallel lives was revealed.

Q. *Is there something else we need to do? (+)*

Q. *What chart is it on? (Chart 6A—Master Programs)*

Q. *You mean he has more master programs? (+)*

Q. *Are they a result of this life? (-)*

Q. *When were they established? (Not on the chart)*

The signal for "not on the chart" is the movement of the pendulum in a "no" response across the bottom of the chart. I then asked when the master programs were established and heard the words "parallel lives."

Q. *Do you mean the client is living other lives at the same time? (+)*

Q. *Are they on this planet? (+)*

Q. *How many parallel lives are there? (5)*

At this point, the client became very excited. He asked me if he had just recently met one of his parallel expressions. He said he had met a young man that reminded him of himself and he had a very strong feeling that he had known the man before and that they had a connection. Questioning revealed that the person was one of his parallel lives.

Another client had met two of her parallel life expressions and they were both male. However, most of my clients' parallel lives are being lived in other galaxies.

Q. *What percent of all people living on this planet who have parallel lives have them on this planet? (1.5%)*

Q. *What percent of those who have parallel lives have them on other planets in this galaxy? (70%)*

Q. *What percent of those who have parallel lives have them in other galaxies? (9.5%)*

Q. *What percent of all people on this planet have parallel lives? (16%; this percentage fluctuates over time)*

Some people are living more than one set of parallel lives. The most I have run into is ten sets. However, there is no maximum number of sets of parallel lives a soul can be living.

A soul may not be living any parallel lives when I first work with them, then days or weeks later they may be living hundreds or even thousands. The only answer to this puzzle seems to be the infinite nature of the soul and the fact that in SPIRIT there is no such thing as time or space. As the masters of the Far East have said, "all is maya." Everything exists only because we believe it does. Another way of saying it is, we are part of a dream that God is dreaming, and we are actors in the dream.

Sometimes it is necessary to research several of the parallel lives in a set in order to clear the client's programs. For the first parallel life, research and clear all programs in the parallel life until there are none remaining. Then ask High Self to clear the parallel life and block the energies from affecting another life. Let's say that we have found soul qualities, master programs, and negative motivations and they have been researched and cleared.

Q. *Can you (High Self) now clear and block this parallel life? (+)*

Q. *Please clear, replace with good and block. (The pendulum should move in a circular motion.)*

Q. *Is there another parallel life to research? (+)*

Then research the second parallel life, starting with the following question.

Q. *What is the first program we need to research? (Use Chart 1–Chart to Use)*

Research and clear programs as described earlier in the chapter. Repeat this procedure for each parallel life until there are no more parallel lives to be researched and cleared. Then ask the following questions.

Q. *Can you now clear and block all parallel lives? (+)*

Please clear, replace with good and block.

The smallest number of parallel lives I have found is five and the largest is 4,262. However, High Self says the quantity can be as little as one, with no maximum number. To date, the most parallel lives I have had to research to clear all of the lives in a set is twenty-six, and that was for a client with 2,600 parallel lives.

Living parallel lives is another reason for schizophrenia. Schizophrenia happens when access between parallel lives is open, and the person flips back and forth between one or more of the lives, becoming disoriented. This is the reason, once all of the necessary parallel lives are researched, that I ask High Self to clear and block all parallel lives. High Self actually puts a block or shield between each parallel life and the current life, so none of the lives can bleed over and cause confusion in another life.

Parallel Universe

In contrast to parallel lives, I have never found a person who has lived in more than one parallel universe. As with parallel lives, use the necessary charts to do the research, and then clear everything. Then ask if there is another program, research and clear until no programs remain. After all of the clearing is completed, ask High Self to block the parallel universe so energy cannot bleed over into this life. Bleed over from another universe is another reason for schizophrenia.

CHAPTER 8

Master Programs

Your soul's growth and learning in the spiritual dimension can be understood using an analogy of human life here on planet Earth. You are born of physical parents and enter a world where day after day and year after year you study, learn, and grow. Your education consists of home life, worldly experience, and guided learning through the school systems. You may leave school and go out into the working world before or after you graduate from high school, or you may go on to college before joining the working world where you provide a service and earn a living. The education received and your personal desire and ambition will carry you to some level of accomplishment in the world. That level can be perceived as low or high depending on the social and working structure of a country, a locale, or the business world.

During your incarnation on Earth, you may decide to quit your job and return to school for additional education, believing you are as high as you can go in the business world without your master's degree. Your employer might be upset and try to keep you as an employee by offering you praise for a job well done, by offering advancement, or by telling you how foolish it would be of you to leave a secure position and start the difficult task of returning to school for a higher education. However, your decision is to gain more knowledge and improve your skills, so you may go higher up the corporate ladder. Therefore, you quit your job and return to school to attain your master's degree.

The same pattern holds true for the soul. Lifetime after lifetime you incarnate to experience, learn, and grow. When this is accomplished to your satisfaction and you feel your education is complete, you are through with your first cycle of incarnations and begin to work in the spiritual realms.

The maximum level of soul consciousness that anyone can attain as a result of the first round of incarnations is the top level of the Ascended Master level, which is level 144,000th. When a soul has reached the highest level of the Ascended Master level, High Self indicates that level by giving the number 900, which is the numerical total of adding up 144 (1+4+4=9). High Self says the number nine equals the Trinity squared and symbolizes the number of spiritual completion. Thus, when you reach the top level of the Ascended Master level, shown on Chart 3–Levels of Soul Consciousness, you have completed all the requirements of the first round. However, as you can see on Chart 3, the level of Ascended Master is only a modest achievement in soul growth. To reach the higher levels, a soul must continue on with a second round of incarnations. The majority of the people who come to me for SRT have attained the 900th level (of the Ascended Master level), and have chosen to continue their learning.

What Are Master Programs?

Master programs are the concentrated courses of study that we choose to undertake in our second round of incarnations. When we reach the top level of the Ascended Master level (see Chart 3), we have completed our first round of incarnations, much like finishing college. When we choose to incarnate for our second round, we are choosing to pursue our master's degree in spiritual growth.

A master program is a course of study we construct by planning lives that have specific spiritual challenges. If we feel we have not learned enough about forgiveness or love, we may deliberately set up a life in which we must face and overcome unforgiveness and hate. High Self has revealed basic master programs that souls choose, which I have listed on Chart 6A–Master Programs.

The Elements of Master Programs

The difficulty with master programs, despite their prestigious name, is that your soul can get lost in them once they enter the physical body, or forget the original purpose of taking on the programs in the first place. Because of the level of commitment you often have to a master program on a soul level, there are specific steps you must follow to clear the program successfully.

Hidden Agenda

While teaching a workshop, we found one person with an infinite number of master self-punishment programs. We would clear them, checking to make certain there were none left, only to find, sometime later, that they had been rebuilt. Finally, I asked my High Self if there was something causing them to rebuild, and received a "yes" response. When I asked what it was, I got the words *hidden agenda*. I was amazed at this revelation; just like a computer, the subconscious backs up master programs with a file that is protected and cannot be released unless you become aware of its existence and specifically ask the High Self to clear it.

Backup Programs

Another factor that can cause master programs to rebuild is *backup programs*. Just like a computer operator who makes a copy of programs and files them in a safe place, so that the original work can be replaced if destroyed, so the subconscious also protects against losing the master programs studied.

Original Sin

Original sin is a belief that results from the decision to incarnate for the second round. When a soul deliberately takes upon itself the knowledge of good and evil by incarnating, it can feel cut off from God, High Self, and Source, and may feel that it has sinned. This deep-seated fear of being cut off from God is exemplified in the Book of Genesis:

> *And the Lord God commanded the man, saying, "You may freely eat of every tree of the garden; but of the tree of the knowledge of good and evil you shall not eat, for in the day that you eat of it you shall die."*
> *(Genesis 2:16-17 RSV)*

Yet, this is not so much a warning of punishment from God as a statement of the difficulties of incarnation. While we enter the physical, manifest realms in order to experience, learn, and grow, we forget that we are spiritual beings having a human experience. 'Dying' is really forgetfulness. The 'original sin' factor of master programs is really our misunderstanding and fear surrounding the act of incarnation.

Identifying with the Serpent in Eden

While doing a workshop in Lee's Summit, Missouri another piece of the puzzle fell into place. One of the women in the workshop was having a difficult time staying clear of master programs. I would ask High Self to clear her and they would. Then the master programs kept rebuilding. Once, as I started to walk away, my High Self gave me an inner message. I heard the word, "serpent." I continued to silently ask questions of my High Self and was told that she had a subconscious belief that she was the serpent in the garden of Eden who caused everyone else to sin. When a soul partakes of 'the tree of the knowledge of good and evil,' they are given the coats of skins (the physical body) and are driven out of the garden of Eden or consciousness of God. Quite simply, they incarnate. If they convince others to partake of 'the tree of the knowledge of good and evil,' and incarnate with them, they may establish the belief in their soul record that they are the serpent. This is in keeping with the symbolism of the garden of Eden story presented in the first three chapters of Genesis.

Turning to the client, I asked her to use her pendulum to get a subconscious response to the question, "Do you believe you were the serpent in the garden of Eden who caused everyone else to sin?" Her response was, "I don't even have to ask that question. I feel it in my solar plexus. That is it!" And it was.

Rebellion to the High Council

Before you can incarnate for the second round of learning to undertake your master programs, you go before a High Council and receive approval. As in the story in Genesis, if the LORD of the garden (High Council) tells you not to eat of the forbidden tree, and you eat anyway, you establish a belief that you are in rebellion. This belief can cause master programs to rebuild until the belief is cleared.

Abandonment of Levels

When you leave the level of Ascended Master, attained as a result of first round studies, and incarnate to gain more knowledge, you establish a belief called 'abandonment of office' or 'abandonment of levels' that must be cleared to prevent master programs from rebuilding.

Compartments

When your soul makes several, or even many, copies of a program and places them in a safe place, you are using *compartments*. That way, your soul has reasoned, if some of them are destroyed, or your master studies become lost, you can pull up one of the compartments and replace the programs.

Clearing Master Programs

High Self indicates that you or your client have master programs by directing you to Chart 6A–Master Programs (although an indication of a program listed on Chart 6A does not always mean you have a master program–make sure you verify). The first thing you do when clearing master programs is to determine which of the eight elements you have. Here is a typical case. (High Self indicates an infinite number by swinging the pendulum in a straight line across the bottom of any chart.)

Q. *Do I have master programs? (+, Infinite number)*

Q. *Do I have hidden agenda? (+, Infinite number)*

Q. *Backup programs? (+, Infinite number)*

Q. *Compartments? (+, 69)*

Q. *Sin? (+)*

Q. *Serpent? (+)*

Q. *Rebellion to the High Council? (+)*

Q. *Abandonment of levels? (+)*

Once these questions have been answered, you ask High Self to burn all of them, "root, branch, and seed" so that there is nothing that can rebuild the master programs. Then you ask if there are any left to be researched and cleared.

Q. *Is anything left that can rebuild master programs? (-)*

Q. *Are there any programs remaining? (+, 497)*

Q. *How many do we research to clear the rest? (7)*

Turn to Chart 6A and determine the first master program to be researched.

Q. *What is the first master program? (Helplessness)*

Master programs are always cleared by researching past lives, just as you learned in Chapter 5—The Basic Steps of SRT.

There is always a flip side to any master program. For instance, a hate of God program always has a counterpart program, love of God. We learn from both types of experiences, and sometimes the greater soul lesson and resultant soul growth is accomplished through the negative experience.

Case Studies

Master programs manifest in many different ways in our lives. Because of this, there is no single way to research and clear a master program. That is why most of the following descriptions of master programs are based on case studies. You do not need to read all of the case studies to understand how to clear master programs. However, the cases will give you many examples of how the programs are set up and how they are researched and cleared. If you are researching master programs for the first time, you may find the examples will help you understand how it all fits together.

Abandonment, Separation

In the first past life we researched for Betty's abandonment program, she had been serving in the office of Seraph—which represents wholeness or completeness—when she decided to incarnate for the second round. The other cast members consisted of God and a Council of Nine. Betty had a program that she had abandoned her office of Seraph in order to incarnate, and that symbolized abandoning her own good, both then and now.

The second past life was a continuation of the process of incarnating and found Betty as a Cherub—which means angel of life and truth. The other soul involved was a Seraph and was her twin flame. The negative subconscious message she retained from this life was that she abandoned her twin flame in the process of incarnating so deserves to be abandoned now. She anticipated being abandoned by good, wholeness, truth, and those persons who are close to her and have a special meaning.

In the third past life, Betty was a Light being. She had dropped her angel offices and retained only her status as a Light being. Others involved were dark energy (Satan), an infinite number of souls called dark energy, a Council of Nine, and many guides. Satan is the serpent in the garden of Eden who caused everyone else to sin, or partakes of the knowledge of good and evil. Betty and countless others followed the soul called Satan into a second round of incarnations. They were accompanied by an infinite number of discarnate souls who would act as their guides. Betty believed that by following Satan into incarnation, she had committed spiritual suicide, and cut herself off from the Light. She felt she had abandoned God, the Light Council, and good, and that God, the Light Council, and everyone who has special meaning in this life would abandon her now. As a result of this master program of abandonment, Betty had put some very strong stumbling blocks in the way of her own good and any meaningful relationship. Any time she started a meaningful relationship, her program caused her to be abandoned.

You can know your oneness in God even as Jesus knew His. In chapter 17 of John, Jesus prayed to the Father for the preservation of His apostles and for all those who would come to believe the message brought by the apostles.

> *...Holy Father, keep them in thy name, which thou hast given me, that they may be one, even as we are one. ... I have given them thy word; and the world has hated them because they are not of the world, even as I am not of the world. ... Sanctify them in the truth; thy word is truth. ... "I do not pray for these only,*

but also for those who believe in me through their word, that they may all be one; even as thou, Father, art in me, and I in thee, that they also may be in us, so that the world may believe that thou hast sent me.
(John 17:11, 14, 17, 20-21 RSV)

If we are one in the Father, as Jesus prayed that we might be, there can never be separation between me and you. We can only *believe* that we are separate. The belief in separation that was established through Adam and Eve partaking of 'the tree of the knowledge of good and evil' was the beginning of mankind's present and prevailing belief in separation from God and from each other. (Remember that when Adam and Eve ate the forbidden fruit, they ran and hid—separated themselves—from God.) That is the major cause of conflict in the world today. When we begin to realize that we are all one and that what we believe, say, feel, and do affects the entire universe, then and only then, will harmony and peace be established and maintained, first in our individual souls, and then on our planet.

Abuse

In her present life, Lucille was physically abusive to her son and emotionally abusive to her own inner child. She had 253 past lives involving child abuse. The first past life we researched revealed her as High Self for a fourteen-year-old male, who is her son today. The male was mentally, emotionally, and physically ill and had devised many ways of abusing himself. This son is her twin flame and not only did Lucille pick up the programs, she is continuing to run them in this life.

As a female in the next life, Lucille's energies were hate, bitterness, and abuse toward herself, which caused her inner child to feel neglected and abused. As a forty-six-year-old male in the next life, she was physically ill and had reverted back to a very childlike state of mind. Lucille believed that she was being mentally and emotionally abused by her son and daughter in the current life.

In this present life, Lucille had a program of excessive, childish complaining and was constantly expressing hate and bitterness toward her children and herself. That has changed since clearing her programs, and Lucille is now building a good relationship with her children and her own inner child.

Addictions

When the High Self indicates that a soul has an addiction, they are simply indicating that the soul is stuck in some compulsive behavior; the person is so caught up in an energy that it becomes a strong habit.

Martha had a master program of addiction to hate. The reason for the hate was easily understood when we looked at the past life in which it was set up. She was female and her father was involved. Martha believed that her father forced her into prostitution, so she hated him. High Self indicated that it was her own choice to become a prostitute. However, Martha was angry and upset at her father. She left home, found herself without means of support, and turned to prostitution. Martha's father loved her, but she felt he did not give her enough attention. Her pride drove her from home and kept her from returning because her respectability was destroyed.

Adultery

Jesus told us to keep our minds free of impure thoughts. He stated that if a man looked at a woman to lust after her in his heart, he had already committed adultery (Matthew 5:28). Adultery, in this sense, is to contaminate one's consciousness with wrong thinking and feeling.

Occasionally I find programs of adultery that involve excessive sexual experiences with married people. At other times, adultery is simply an adulteration of consciousness with a belief in good and evil. Here is one example.

Susan was a Cherub and her twin flame was a Seraph. She was incarnating and her twin flame was not. She felt she adulterated her consciousness with a belief in good and evil by incarnating and was no longer in the pure consciousness of SPIRIT.

Alcoholism

Alcohol is a major form of addiction. Many times when researching master programs of alcoholism, the only person involved is the client, and the usual energy is alcohol. Lucille's programs were more complicated. During the first past life we researched, she was a male and had a Guardian Angel. Even the Guardian Angel could not keep her from escaping life through alcohol and finally committing suicide. In the second past life, she was an eighty-six-year-old male. She was extremely depressed, stingy, and cruel toward herself. She drank herself to death and it registered in her soul record as suicide.

As an alcoholic male in the third past life, Lucille caused mental and emotional harm to her entire family. As a male during the fourth past life, she was depressed, mentally and emotionally sick, addicted to alcohol and had abandoned all meaning and purpose in life. Her energies were the same in the fifth past life, in which she was again a male who drank himself to death—he literally drowned himself in alcohol. During the sixth past life as a female, she deliberately committed suicide through the consumption of alcohol.

Anger

The cause for master anger programs can take some strange twists, as did this one for Arthur, Lisa, Dawn, and Jane. Lisa and I were working to clear her master programs and this is what was revealed in past lives. In the first life we researched, Lisa served in the office of Holy Spirit. The others involved were Dawn as a female, Arthur as a male, and God. Lisa wanted to be personal Holy Spirit for Dawn, and she was angry at God because she was not allowed to. She feared she would lose Dawn to Arthur and she set up a hate of God energy.

In this current life, both Arthur and Lisa feared that one would win the love and affection of Dawn and the other would lose out. This has caused a great deal of struggle and anger between them.

In the second life, Lisa was out of the physical body serving Arthur, a male, as guide. Dawn was a guide for Jane who was incarnated as a female. Lisa was angry at Arthur for being with Jane, and Dawn was angry with Jane for being with Arthur. Both of the guides were trying to keep Arthur and Jane apart in an effort to break the addiction. Lisa felt guilty because she felt she had abandoned her responsibility and chosen task to break the addiction and believed God was going to get her.

God is Love and never 'gets' anyone. However, we often set up heavy programs of guilt and self-punishment which cause us to 'get' ourselves.

Bitterness

There were two past lives to be researched and cleared in order to dissolve Rita's bitterness program. During the first past life she was a ninety-five-year-old woman. She was ill, but did not want to die. When her family decided to perform euthanasia, she saw it as murder. This concept of being murdered when euthanasia is performed, even when the person asks for it, comes up quite frequently when researching past lives.

In the second past life, Rita was born with a serious deformity and her family put her to sleep when she was one week old. She was angry and bitter because they did not allow her to experience life in the physical body that she had selected. The soul always designs its own physical body in order to experience the lessons needed to learn and grow. When a child is killed because they are deformed, the soul's progress is delayed and they have to make other plans to fulfill their soul desires.

Brain Damage

Programs of brain damage from past lives, even if there was not actual brain damage, can cause serious problems in the present life, as the person may conduct their present life as though they really do have brain damage.

Zeb was a male in the only past life we researched. There was a grandmother who is his twin flame and present-life father. There were also six daughters and an aunt involved. The grandmother believed the family had caused her brain damage. Zeb picked up the message of brain damage from his twin flame and was acting out the message in this life by being unbalanced, out of control, and mentally spaced out.

Zeb is living parallel lives and they were causing problems. In the first one, he was a ninety-four-year-old male with Alzheimer's disease. Alzheimer's disease often registers in the soul as brain damage, and there is a good possibility that the person will repeat the disease of Alzheimer's in the current life unless the program is cleared.

During the second parallel life, Zeb was again male. The others involved were a wife and a grandfather who is his twin flame. The wife accidentally harmed the grandfather causing brain damage, and Zeb picked up the program because of the twin flame connection.

Complaining

Excessive complaining is one of the most common energies that I find causing conflict in a person's life. Complaining reinforces the discordant programs and drives them deep into the subconscious where they lie in wait to explode into manifestation in subsequent lives. That is what was happening in Greta's present life as a result of past lives. In the first past life we researched, Greta was a male whose wife abandoned her because she was a habitual complainer, stingy, self-destructive, and unjust. Her life was so filled with discordant elements that she could see no value remaining in the physical body, so she used suicide as a means of abandoning life. Since these discordant programs were not faced and overcome in previous incarnations, Greta's life this time was a perfect example of having to face and work through unresolved issues.

Depression

Martha's master program of depression started when her Spirit body was formed (see Chapter 2—The Soul's Design, for an explanation of the spiritual bodies). The only thing that we had to find to clear the past life was that she felt depressed and suppressed. In the next past life, Martha was dark energy. Also involved were Lucifer (a flame mate) and the Mother of Darkness (her twin flame). The title, Lucifer, is used here to symbolize some soul that decided to incarnate for a second round and convinced others to incarnate with him, thus establishing a belief in his soul record that he is the serpent in the garden of Eden. The title, Mother of Darkness, is used here to symbolize any female soul that leaves the Light realms and incarnates with the belief that they gave birth to darkness when they took upon themselves the knowledge of good and evil. Martha left heaven and followed them into the darkness of incarnation. She believed that she must suppress the Light in her because she was darkness and followed darkness. This resulted in a very strong program of depression that has continued for many lifetimes.

Escapism

Greta blamed everyone else for the problems she was experiencing in life. She was also filled with her own dark energy of intolerance toward life, as well as believing that life treated her unjustly. These current life beliefs were supported by 253 past lives during which she built her master program of escapism. During the first past life we researched, she was a male who believed that the world and everyone in it was unjust and abandoned her. She retaliated by abandoning everyone around her. She withdrew from life and finally killed herself. During the second life

Greta was female. She was sick and felt everyone had abandoned her so she killed herself to escape a life that she felt was unfulfilling and unproductive.

Failure

Oliver was having trouble succeeding and prospering in the present life. This problem involved 625 past lives. In the first past life we researched, he was a priest. Making up the rest of the cast were sixty other priests, forty-five nuns, the mother superior, the head priest, and a group of angels. Oliver believed that the others had rejected him because he believed that mankind could be prosperous and still be spiritual, while they did not. They caused him mental and emotional harm. He felt like a failure and killed himself.

Oliver was a male in the next past life we researched. The other characters were his father, brother, and an uncle. He felt like a failure. His family believed he was a failure and killed him, which reinforced his belief that he was a failure. We cleared Oliver's failure program. When I last checked on Oliver, he had a good job and was prospering.

Fear

When we are in human form, we often create and experience many fears and phobias. What we do not understand is that those fears and phobias are not restricted to this earth life only. They become a part of our soul record that can come back to haunt us life after life, whether we are in the physical body or out.

Fear has a tremendous power to create what we fear.

Pearl is a sweet and gentle person, rather shy and timid, but one who would do anything for you. She had a strong master self-punishment program and a lot of fear that kept her from living life fully. It was necessary to research and clear three past lives in order to free her from the fear. In one, she was a High Self who was assigned, along with two other High Selves, to serve a soul who was planning to incarnate. Pearl had an intense fear that she would foul up her assignment as High Self. Questioning revealed that she performed her task extremely well, but her intense fear was recorded in her soul and had limited her in the current life.

In another life, Pearl was a discarnate soul filled with the dark energy of fear. There was another dark energy (hate) and an androgynous person involved. This was an interesting scenario. Pearl was trying to possess the androgynous person and felt she was being possessed by the dark energy of hate. This caused Pearl to develop a fear of possession and of opening up to life. When we tried to work with SRT, we found that Pearl was blocked by the fear that working with SRT would open her to possession by discarnates.

In the third past life, Pearl was a female. There was a male who is her twin flame, two Cherubs, a Seraph, a Guardian Angel, and a High Self. The Guardian Angel and High Self were serving Pearl. Her twin flame (the male) was very ill and the two Cherubs and the Seraph had come to receive his soul and guide it into the Light realms. Pearl was aware that he was dying, and was filled with fear that she would lose her twin flame forever when he died. Pearl set up such a strong fear that she carried it for 8,156 more lives.

Greed

Vic was male in a past life and a leader of a group. He and his brother were forcing the people to support them. They caused much hardship and lived well at the expense of others. Vic was blocking his own prosperity today as a result of 164 greedy past lives.

There were 367 past lives causing Olive to limit her financial success in this life. In the one we researched, she was female and there was a father involved whose energies were illness, injustice, bitterness, abandonment, and suicide.

Olive had energies of cruelty and a double program of stinginess, or greed. Olive took care of her father. He was unjust and bitter toward her, so she retaliated by being cruel and miserly. He abandoned life by killing himself. They were both involved in all 367 past lives. This is a terrific example of energy set in motion that continues to be experienced life after life.

Guilt

Have you ever felt guilty about what someone else has done? Every parent has probably felt guilty about something a child has done or not done, for they usually feel responsible for the perceived shortcomings or actions of their children. Guilt for the actions of another can even be established when we are their guide, Guardian Angel, or High Self. Here is a case in point. Linda had a master program of guilt centered in two past lives. The first past life she served as a High Self for a female who had committed suicide. Although Linda was not at fault, she blamed herself and thus set up a guilt program.

During another past life Linda was in the bardo making plans to incarnate into this current life. There was a Light Council of 144 working with her. The Light Council felt her decision to incarnate was unwise and unnecessary. She felt guilty for not heeding their advice. Yet, her purpose in this life was to clear up guilt and other remnants of ego consciousness. My High Self indicated that she could not have cleared up her guilt and other programs without incarnating.

Hate Programs

The only thing we found when researching the first past life in Randall's hate program was that he had a real hate of everything. High Self gave me an inner vision of Scrooge from Dickens' *A Christmas Carol*. In the second life, he was a Guardian Angel for his twin flame, who was in male form. The twin flame had the same energy as Randall in the first life—he was a real Scrooge. Randall picked up the programs. During the third past life we researched, he was male and lived with his grandfather and an aunt. The aunt sexually abused him. Many times he told his grandfather about the sexual abuse, and his grandfather refused to believe him. He had a program that his grandfather had abandoned him to his aunt's sexual abuse, and he hated all of them, including himself. The interesting thing was that he did not hate his aunt because of the sexual abuse—he simply hated her.

Greg had a hate of God program. In a past life, he was counselor to the ruler of a country. The ruler accused him of betrayal, and ordered that he be stripped of his citizenship and all that he possessed. He was then ostracized and exiled from the country. Greg decided to commit suicide and failed in the attempt. He blamed God for his failure to kill himself. He decided that God was torturing him and thus established the hate of God program. He also held 100% discordant energy of hate on the ruler and the man who carried out the ruler's orders.

Illness

Often, when I am researching why someone is experiencing physical problems in this life, I discover a master program of illness. Here are Ula's programs involving 623 past lives. In the first life, she was male with a grandmother, who is a twin flame. Her grandmother was ill and Ula picked up her program. Ula was cast as a grandmother in the next past life. She was ill with a female disorder, hated being a female, and was tired of life. She refused to face the illness and handle it. Instead she abandoned life by taking an overdose, which caused mental and emotional pain to her son. The pattern was repeated in the next life, in which she was a grandfather, and there was a daughter who suffered because of her suicide. This was repeated a total of seventy-six lives. Ula set up the master program of illness in many lives and then refused to face and handle it. Finally, she set up the illness program for the current life and has done a good job of facing and working with it. Now she is free, as the program has been faced, completed, and cleared.

Injustice

Binny established her program of injustice after she started her second round of incarnations. Her soul had incarnated many times and had accomplished a high level of consciousness. Both Binny and her twin flame had reached the level of consciousness called Creator Consciousness (see Chart 3). We found that Binny had infinite addictive energy on her twin flame, although her twin flame had none on her. The twin flame decided to incarnate and Binny did not want to. Because of her addictive energy on her twin flame, Binny was fearful of losing the twin flame when he incarnated. She felt forced to incarnate. She felt it was unjust of her twin flame to force incarnation upon her.

Jealousy

Some interesting factors came to light in Kelli's jealousy program. In one life we researched, Kelli was the niece and granddaughter. Her aunt and grandmother were jealous of her because she was beautiful. They are her twin flames and she picked up their programs of jealousy. In addition, she developed the belief that it is wrong to be beautiful because it causes separation and jealousy. She punished herself for creating jealousy and separation. Kelli believed being beautiful was the same as being spiritual. Since it was wrong to be beautiful, her subconscious made her wrong to be spiritual.

Murder

Seldom have I run into a master program of murder while researching past lives. Here is one case of euthanasia that was a master program that registered as murder. The client is Ula. Ula was a female whose mother was terminally ill. The mother asked Ula and her son to perform euthanasia on her. Although they did as their mother asked, Ula believed that she had murdered her mother. Further questioning revealed that neither the mother nor the brother registered it as murder. Sometimes one or more of the people involved will see euthanasia as murder and sometimes none of them will. Other times the person who asks to be killed is the only one who sees it as murder.

When Karen came to see me, she admitted that she was terrified of John, who had threatened to kill her. He wanted to date Karen, but she was afraid he would carry out his threat. He also threatened to kill her if she did not date him, so she was between a rock and a hard place. We found that John had a master program of murder and had killed her in 374 past lives.

In the first past life we researched, Karen and John were both male and John murdered her. In the second life, she was a Guardian Angel for John who was a male. John had a lot of discordant energy in this past life—anger, insanity, panic, self-destruction, self-limitation, self-punishment, and suicide. He blamed Karen for his discordant energy and suicide. He registered in his soul record that she had murdered him because she failed to protect him from murdering himself.

In another life, Karen and John were Seraphim and God was involved. They are twin flames and there was conflict between them even before first incarnation. They both believed that God had thrown them out of heaven because of their conflict with each other. John took the blame for the situation and felt as if he had killed them both spiritually.

Negativity

Frank had great difficulty living his life in a positive, constructive way. He had very low self-esteem and a strong conscious program of self-hate. We were able to clear his subconscious programs but had great difficulty keeping him clear of his conscious programs because he rebuilt them as fast as Spirit dissolved them. We discovered he had a master program of negativity.

In the first life we researched, he was a priest and God was involved. His energies were hate of God, negativity, separation, abandonment, hate of women, unworthiness, intolerance, addiction to alcohol and lying, frustration, self-punishment, jealousy, adultery of consciousness, hate, mental and emotional illness, violence, negativity, and apathy.

During the next life he was a Guardian Angel for a female who is his twin flame. He picked up her energies, which were negativity, injustice, hate of self, unforgiveness, intolerance, addiction to hate of life, intolerance, and negativity.

Revenge

I have not encountered many people with master programs of revenge. I have encountered the energy of revenge involved with other situations, and found that it is always destructive to the person who desires it.

I have worked with several women who have been raped in this life. Researching past life programs for them often leads to a past life rape. The rapist is usually the same soul that raped them in the present life. This is because holding the emotions from the past life rape–which can include hate, bitterness, anger, intolerance, injustice, and revenge–can actually attract the same soul and cause the rape to be experienced again.

Once in a while, when we uncover the facts and ask the client if she is ready to release negative energies on the rape a client may say, "No! I want to know how to get revenge." I ask her if her discordant energy is harming the person who mistreated her and she will readily admit that it is not. I ask if it is harming her and she may reluctantly say it is. I suggest that the best way to get even is to get free. And the only way to do that is to release belief, perception, and judgment that she was molested or raped. The moment the client makes the clearing statements and puts in a new program, she feels free and at peace. Even though High Self clears the program, it is usually necessary and always beneficial to make clearing and reprogramming statements when the issue is sexual abuse.

Self-Destruction

We had to research and clear four past lives to free Linda of her self-destruction program. Linda was identified as dark energy in the first past life we researched. The dark energy was researched and found to be Linda's fear, anger, and suicide, which were self-destructive. In the second life, she was in spirit form. She believed she was in conflict with God, and had committed spiritual suicide by separating herself from God.

Another life found Linda as a Light being, with God and the Council of Nine involved. She believed she was in conflict with God and the Council because she wanted to incarnate and had committed spiritual suicide. After we made the clearing statements, further research revealed that we cleared not only the self-destruction program but a program of alcoholism. This piqued my curiosity and led to further questions.

Q. *Was the alcoholism a way to fulfill your program of self-destruction? (+)*

Q. *Did the alcoholism program clear because there was no longer a need for Linda to self-destruct? (+)*

Self-Limitation, Self-Punishment

Many times we experience limitation in this life because we have limited ourselves in past lives. Where does self-punishment end and self-limitation begin? It was difficult to decide in the case of Pamela. She wanted to know why she seemed to attract men who have an extremely miserly consciousness. They were often wonderful in most ways, but stingy in the extreme. We found she had a program of self-limitation laced with self-punishment. Three past lives gave us an insight into the problem.

In the first life we researched, Pamela was a Light being and Seraphim were involved. Pamela believed the Seraphim were barring her from her good and were limiting her expression. Although Pamela had decided to incarnate, she changed her mind and wanted to return to the Light realms. However, once she had made the decision to incarnate, she had to follow through and carry out that decision. The Seraphim guarded the gates of heaven and Pamela believed that they would not let her return to the Light realms. This was simply not true. Her strong desire to incarnate and learn did set up the program. Then, when she tried to alter her decision, the momentum was already established and it brought her into incarnation. So, rather than accepting responsibility, Pamela passed the blame on to the Seraphim.

There are many reasons why we leave the Light realms and incarnate. One is because we feel that we are limited and always would be if we simply stayed in the consciousness of Light. Eve was not tempted by Satan because the fruit looked good. She was tempted by the desire to learn and become knowledgeable like God. Eve represents the feeling nature of every human being, and like all of humanity, Eve believed she was limited in the spiritual realms and wanted to incarnate to gain knowledge.

> *But the serpent said to the woman, "You will not die. For God knows that when you eat of it your eyes will be opened, and you will be like God, knowing good and evil." So when the woman saw that the tree was good for food, and that it was a delight to the eyes, and that the tree was to be desired to make one wise, she took of its fruit and ate; and she also gave some to her husband, and he ate. Then the eyes of both were opened, and they knew that they were naked; ... (Genesis 3:4-7 RSV)*

Their eyes being 'opened' and finding they were 'naked' means that they realized they had entered a new dimension and were exposed mentally and emotionally to all that dimension contained (Adam represents our mental nature, and Eve represents our emotional nature).

Selfishness

In one past life involved in Peggy's selfishness program, Peggy was a male that refused to take responsibility for his wife's and daughter's welfare. Rather, she wanted to escape from the reality of a family life and sought only to fulfill her own selfish desires. She was cruel to the wife and daughter. The daughter became a prostitute to support herself and her mother, after Peggy killed herself. In another life Peggy was a father with a son who was born deformed. Peggy killed the son because she did not want to care for him and because the child would have been a social stigma. Again, Peggy thought only of herself and her own selfish goals and desires.

Sexual Abuse

During a past life, Eva was molested by her father. She experienced strong conflict over the sexual abuse because she loved her father as well as hated him. Eva had a desire to destroy him as well as a desire to be with him for the rest of her life.

Marti had 530 past lives in her sexual abuse program. In the first one, she was a daughter abused by her father. In another life, she was a niece abused by her uncle. During the third life, the situation was reversed. She was the father and sexually abused her daughter. In the final life researched, Marti was a mother with a small daughter. There were also Marti's father and an uncle. The uncle sexually molested the child and Marti blamed herself. She was bitter and felt the whole situation was extremely unjust. She was self-destructive, self-limiting, mentally and emotionally ill, and killed herself.

Spiritual Suicide

Grace believed that she had committed spiritual suicide by leaving the realms of Light (heaven) and incarnating. She felt that she had rebelled against God, failed God, hated herself, and feared that she might fail again. The combination of fear, guilt, and self-hate were causing Grace to limit her life. She had a deep soul fear that if she were successful she would blow it all again.

Leaving heaven is symbolized in the Holy Scriptures as being tempted by the serpent to eat of the forbidden 'tree of the knowledge of good and evil' and having to incarnate. This caused a sense of separation from God, or spiritual death. For only a pure consciousness free from a belief in good-versus-evil can remain in or inherit the kingdom of pure Light. While physical suicide is a deliberate separation of the soul from the physical body, spiritual suicide is a belief in separation from God (Light) by taking upon ourselves a divided consciousness of good and evil. There is no such thing as evil—there are only lessons to be learned and spiritual realization to accomplish. Even the lessons that seem evil are useful for they cause us to seek change and they forge us into a fit vessel for the infilling, once again, of the Light of God. This tempering, or purification, brings us into the kingdom of heaven where we remain forever. Since we are formed in the image and likeness of God, we cannot fail—we can only succeed.

Unforgiveness

Jesus told us to forgive and we would be forgiven (Luke 6:37). Yet, most people hold programs of unforgiveness lifetime after lifetime. The unforgiveness may be toward someone else or toward oneself. Regardless of toward whom the unforgiveness is directed, it is of vital importance to clear it. Many times, all that is needed once the client's programs are cleared is for the client to speak the statements of forgiveness.

In the first past life we researched in Gwen's unforgiveness program, she was an elderly female American Indian, who was no longer a valued member of the tribe and was put out to starve by her daughter. She registered that her daughter had killed her, and she was still carrying the energy of unforgiveness in this life. In another past life, she was a guide for a female who is her flame mate. There was a male who raped the woman and the woman refused to forgive him. Gwen picked up the woman's unforgiveness program.

Unworthiness

Monica wanted to discover if she had any blocks to relationships. A master program of unworthiness was the main culprit. In the first past life we researched, she was a husband, and the rest of the cast was a wife and the wife's sister. Monica and the sister-in-law were in love with each other, and they killed the wife so they could be together. Monica loved her wife, but was caught up in an emotional situation with the sister who led Monica into the unhealthy relationship. Their marriage only lasted about two years and Monica realized the sister-in-law was unstable, and that she had made a bad mistake in killing her first wife and marrying the sister. Monica thus had a program of being unworthy of a good relationship.

In the second life, Monica was a male and the whole family was involved. She was unjust to everyone, hated women, and killed herself, which caused mental and emotional trauma to the entire family. This reinforced the belief that she is unworthy of love or any semblance of a familial or marriage relationship.

Master Programs Not Listed on Chart 6A

You may run into other master programs from time to time that are not listed on Chart 6A (when you ask what the program is, the pendulum moves in a straight line across the bottom of the chart). Just ask High Self to reveal the program to you. Then listen to your inner guidance and you will get the information necessary to do the clearing work. Sometimes you do not even need to know what the program is. Simply ask if it can be cleared without research.

CHAPTER 9

Octaves of Learning and Soul Qualities

Octaves of Learning

Years ago, when I was in ministerial school, one of the instructors taught from the works of Gurdjieff. The instructor stated that, according to Gurdjieff, you go through many octaves of learning in your soul's evolution from darkness into Light. Soon after starting my training in Response Therapy, I asked my subconscious mind if this were true and received an affirmative response. An octave of learning, as you will see, is simply an eight step process of experiencing, learning, and growing

You do not clear octaves of learning. You simply clear the accumulated garbage that tends to limit the expression of your good qualities. Initially I didn't have a single idea how to clear octaves of learning and free myself from reincarnating lifetime after lifetime. However, as I continued to study and practice SRT, I found that there was no need to worry; the octaves simply cleared one after another as I worked with others, and within fourteen months they were all cleared.

The octaves of learning you incarnate to work on involve eight basic steps. The steps are:

1. Awareness
2. Desire
3. Faith
4. Willingness
5. Setting goals
6. Doing the work
7. Completion or rest
8. Return to awareness

You never accomplish anything in life without taking these basic steps. You may take the steps with full realization of what you are doing, or you may take them as a natural result of daily living without conscious knowledge that there is even a process involved.

For example, you come to an AWARENESS that your cupboard is getting bare. You DESIRE to see it full again, and you have FAITH that you can make a trip to the store to procure what is needed. You make a WILLING DECISION to go to the store and purchase what you are short of. You have thus established a GOAL. You make out the necessary list of supplies you will purchase. You travel to the store. There you make your selections and pay for them–the WORK. You return home where you put the groceries in their proper place in the cupboard. The awareness is now COMPLETED and you REST in the realization that the buying and stocking of your cupboard is accomplished, and you have food to eat. Now, you are ready to take up the next task or octave of learning. There is a new AWARENESS–preparing the food to eat–and you find yourself involved with the continuing process of life.

Going to the store fulfills a goal of providing food and supplies that sustain life in the physical body. However, it is of far greater importance to work at clearing blocks to your greater physical and spiritual potential–the programs you came into life to experience and clear. That is the only way you can avoid returning to physical form again and again until you have finished the work that sets your soul free. Octaves of learning will clear as you work with High Self and SRT to research and clear other programs. I have never had to specifically research octaves of learning, they simply clear.

Case Study

When Sandra came to me, she had twenty-nine octaves of learning remaining of the sixty-six she chose to clear in this life. The first program we worked to clear was a block to her prosperity.

Q. *What is the major block to your prosperity? (Conflict)*

Q. *When was this conflict established? (5 to 6 years of age)*

Sandra knew what this program was.

Q. *You were molested at that age? (+)*

Q. *Was it your fault? (+)*

After clearing this program, we discovered that Sandra had eliminated twenty-two of her octaves of learning by clearing this single program. Next, we worked on her master self-punishment program. When we finished with that, there were no octaves remaining to be researched or cleared. I have found from experience that souls deliberately come into this life to clear their octaves of learning quickly and easily by working with the system of SRT. That was the case with Sandra.

Like Sandra, there may have been experiences in your own life for which you felt responsible. Sandra was a defenseless child when she was molested and was not responsible for what happened. However, her subconscious mind said she was responsible and recorded the molestation that way. Therefore, as far as her subconscious programming was concerned, she was guilty. Sandra's desire for self-punishment was blocking her own prosperity. Sandra also felt unclean and unworthy of prospering her life because her mother refused to believe her when she told her of the molestation.

The trauma of sexual molestation is extremely difficult for the human psyche to handle. And for a child who must depend on an adult for her defense, and for helping create self-esteem and self-worth, it is even more critical. Deep scarring can occur in the soul of a child when he or she is molested and the parent refuses to believe the story. For example, it is not uncommon for the mother to fear that her own relationship with her husband will be damaged or threatened and might even blame the child for being attractive to the husband. Regardless of the circumstances or the depth of the program in the molested person's subconscious mind, the energy that is causing difficulty is easily released by using the proper clearing statements. Even though High Self clears the program, it is usually necessary and always beneficial to make clearing and reprogramming statements when the issue is sexual abuse. The memory of the actual occurrence is not erased. However, there is no longer negative energy or stigma attached.

Soul Qualities

High Self gave the information on soul qualities listed on Chart 2–Soul Qualities, to a friend, Robert Gandrup, in 1987. The information has proven to be extremely valuable and vital to clearing programs for complete freedom of the soul and for spiritual growth. There are ten sets listed on this chart and all of them are positive characteristics that are keys to a constructive, balanced expression of life. Occasionally, only one of the words in a set applies to the situation being researched.

High Self has revealed that soul qualities are part of the genetic coding of a soul when it is created (see Chart 11–Soul Energy Programming). There are a total of eighty-six characteristics, twenty-two of which are listed on Chart 2. Soul qualities, as part of our basic coding, are vitally important to the development of our spiritual abilities. Therefore, any accumulated discordant energy which may block their full and complete expression must be cleared. See Chapter 15—Programming Before Formation, for a more complete explanation of the soul's genetic coding.

Most people have discordant programs that have to be cleared on at least one and usually several of these soul qualities. When High Self indicates that soul qualities need to be cleared, you always research past lives to find and clear the discordant energy (see Chapter 5—The Basic Steps of SRT). Some students fail to listen to the instructions to research only past lives when soul qualities are encountered. Instead, they use Chart 4—When, to ask when the program was experienced, and are often lead to other time such as bardo, womb, or birth. Just research past lives, it is faster and more complete.

Understanding, Love

Bert started to accumulate his discordant energy on the soul qualities of understanding and love before his first incarnation. He was not in a physical body, but was a Cherub preparing to incarnate. Bert did not understand the purpose, process, and meaning of incarnation. He believed he committed spiritual suicide when he incarnated, felt guilty, and failed to understand and love himself.

As you continue to work with SRT, you may frequently find a belief of spiritual suicide involved with leaving the presence of God and beginning the process called incarnation. This concept fits perfectly with the symbolism of the garden of Eden story in which Adam and Eve are cast out of the garden and cut off from the LORD because 'they ate of the tree of the knowledge of good and evil.' This caused them to have a consciousness filled with error and a resultant belief in separation from God. This is the 'first death' implied in Genesis 2:17.

Jesus told everyone that they would know the truth and that the truth would set them free (John 8:32). The 'truth' is you can never be cut off from the LORD of your being, although you may feel that you are. Jesus taught that there is only one Father, God, that the kingdom of heaven is within and that the Father dwells in that heaven within. We can walk in darkness of consciousness not knowing the Father is within, but in truth we can never be separated from the God presence.

In the second life we researched, Bert was High Self for a female (his twin flame) who had programs of apathy and suicide. She is his mother in his current life. Because Bert lacked a consciousness of self-love and understanding, he blamed himself for the female's apathy and suicide and picked up her programs.

Picking up another's soul programs, while serving as their High Self, Guardian Angel, or guide, is a common occurrence. This is especially true when there is a soul connection between the two people such as twin flame, flame mate, or soul mate. While serving as High Self, Bert picked up the programs because he did not understand the error and futility of doing so and because he is his mother's twin flame.

Communication with my High Self has revealed that programs are most often based on what you perceive through your five senses, which then becomes your beliefs, and, finally, the judgments you set up regarding yourself, others and the happenings of life. "For with the judgment you pronounce you will be judged" (Matthew 7:2 RSV).

We were researching the problems Velma was having with food allergies and her self-image when the soul quality of understanding and love came up. In the first life we researched, she was High Self for a male who is her twin flame. The twin flame's programs were lack of understanding and love, expressed as stinginess, child abuse, self-destruction, resentment, hate of women, rejection of self, rejection of women, and rejection of life, and suicide. Velma picked up his programs.

Control, Restraint, Harmony

Mike had blocks to this soul quality involving 362 past lives. Fortunately, we only had to research two lives. In the first life, he was a father. The remaining cast members were a wife and two daughters. The first daughter had brain damage from an injury, which caused her to be emotionally unbalanced. To compound her difficulties, she was conceived out of wedlock, and her mother harped on the subject. The second daughter caused the injury to her sister and was made to feel guilty by her mother. Because of the pressures of a dysfunctional family, the second daughter was out of control, complained all the time, was depressed, and finally killed herself. Mike was caught up in the inharmony and felt completely out of control.

In the next life, Mike was a seventy-nine-year-old male who was terminally ill and in the hospital. His family wanted him out of his pain and asked the doctor to perform euthanasia. Mike had depression, negativity, self-destructive energy, and hate of women because his family abandoned him. He did not want to die, and after euthanasia was performed, he wanted revenge on the doctor and his family. Mike felt out of control regarding his right to determine his own destiny. There was no harmony in the situation, and he possessed an unrestrained desire for revenge. Mike called the Spiritual Response Center shortly after his programs were cleared and informed us that he could really feel the difference in his energy. He said his whole attitude had changed for the better.

Passiveness, Humility

Lack of passiveness and humility can lead to impatience. This was the case with Melanie in the current life. She was running her past life soul quality of lack of passiveness and humility and was extremely impatient. In the past life we researched, she was the head priest and the other member of the cast was a male. The male was a political leader and the priest was his religious and political advisor. A strong sense of injustice, bitter complaining, and rejection were the political leader's energies. He asked the priest for counsel and then rejected it. Melanie's energy was anger, hate, a strong belief that she was treated unjustly, unforgiveness, frustration, and anger.

Faith, Joy

In the first past life we researched for Lucille's soul quality of faith and joy, Lucille was a Seraph. She had accumulated a lot of negative energy during her many incarnations. We found fear, apathy, anger at God and people, failure, guilt, bitterness, escapism, depression, stinginess toward self (she was selling herself short and refusing to give herself any credit), hate of women, and hate of self. This was her condition immediately before coming into this life.

Lucille was living parallel lives. As a Cherub in one of them, her energy was guilt, bitterness, and spiritual suicide which blocked her faith and joy. She was not serving another soul as guide, Guardian Angel, or High Self, so there simply did not seem to be any reason for her discordant energy. Since we did not have to know anything else in order to clear the program, we asked that it be cleared, and it was.

Sometimes we sacrifice our joy because of religious commitments. This was what Yolanda did in two past lives we researched. In one she was a nun and in love with a priest. She and the priest sacrificed their love and joy because of their religious vows. Neither of them believed that they could share their lives together, as husband and wife, as they would be sacrificing their salvation.

Yolanda was a nun in another past life, and received great joy from her work with the church. She was involved with another nun and a priest in a small discussion group seeking a greater understanding of God. Several nuns accused the three of them of heresy because of their liberal views and they were burned at the stake by a group of priests. Her faith in God and joy of serving Spirit was destroyed, and she was filled with negative feelings and hate of God.

Clarity, Forgiveness

Lucille and her mother in this life are twin flames, and the discordant energy between them started before their first incarnation. We researched only two lives out of 836. During the first one, Lucille killed herself with fire. After her death, she felt guilty for taking her own life and refused to forgive herself because she felt the need to punish herself.

In another past life Lucille was a Cherub. There was a Council of Nine, God, and a Light being who is her twin flame and mother in the present life. The twin flame (Light being) was addicted to her and Lucille wanted to break the addiction by incarnating. Her twin flame believed Lucille was mentally, emotionally, physically, and spiritually ill for even thinking about incarnating. When Lucille incarnated anyway, she believed that Lucille had abandoned her and was filled with bitterness and depression. She also felt incomplete and limited without her twin flame. The unfortunate thing was that Lucille picked up her twin flame's programs of bitterness and depression and has run them ever since. Fortunately, both Lucille's and her twin flame's programs are cleared and the addictive energy has been dissolved. They now have the opportunity to live in clarity and forgiveness, harmony and peace, if they so choose.

Courage, Purpose, Direction

The life we researched for Andy's soul quality of courage, purpose, and direction was before first incarnation. Andy was a Seraph. The only other cast member was a Council of Nine. Andy wanted to incarnate, and the Council suggested that he not do so, since he did not understand either the purpose of incarnation or the direction he would take.

Alfred was a Cherub and his twin flame was a Seraph. Alfred was incarnating and the twin flame felt he was being abandoned. Alfred was fearful of being separated from his twin flame and did not know if he had the courage to fulfill the new direction and purpose he had chosen without his twin flame along to encourage and support him.

No one has to concern themselves with the actions of another soul regarding the right of choice, good or bad, for the law of cause and effect will eventually balance the scales and the price will be paid. Regardless of our relationship to another soul, be it mother, father, brother, sister, husband, wife, or Guardian Angel, we need to stay objective and not become emotionally involved to the degree that we lose our own perspective. When we become too emotionally involved, we become part of the problem and not the solution.

Innocence, Patience

Before first incarnation, we are innocent of all knowledge of evil. We are spiritual beings knowing only good. Every soul that partakes (eats) of 'the tree of the knowledge of good and evil,' and that is everyone in a physical body, loses their innocence by doing so. High Self says that many souls are impatient to leave the Light realms and incarnate into physical form. Dirk was one. In the first life we researched, he was dark energy. The other cast members were the Council of Nine and God. Dirk was impatient to incarnate and believed that neither God nor the Council wanted him to. When he incarnated, he believed that he lost his innocence and patience, committed spiritual suicide, and was cast out of the garden of Eden because he was no longer in pure consciousness and unworthy to stay in the Light realms.

The garden of Eden represents the consciousness of God or Light. It is indicated in the Scriptures that only the pure in heart can enter into the "kingdom of God" (see 1 Corinthians 6:9-11). There must be a purification of all that is discordant and limiting, for we must be as white and as pure as snow. When you partake of the knowledge of good and evil, you have contaminated your pure consciousness of SPIRIT and are separated from God Consciousness. Only through purification of mind and heart can you return to the Light realms. SRT is the science of research and purification of all levels of being. Every false belief and discordant energy may be revealed and washed away so you can rebirth this life and all lives and return home to SPIRIT.

In the second past life, Dirk was a Seraph. The remaining cast consisted of seventy Light beings and a Council of Seventy. Dirk was taking the next step in the incarnational process. The Council tried to convince Dirk not to incarnate, but he did anyway, entering into male form. As a result, Dirk had a program that he was in rebellion to SPIRIT.

The same theme of rebellion was carried out at the beginning of Dirk's second round of incarnations (the round in which he began his work on master programs). In the first life of the second round, Dirk was listed as thought. The rest of the cast consisted of a Council of 144 and God. The major energy listed was hate. Dirk hated being stuck at the top level of the Ascended Masters level (the 144,000 level). He could not go higher unless he incarnated again to undertake his master programs, so he felt trapped and limited. From this level, Dirk could see that he was a simple neophyte and that there were infinite levels above his present position that could be attained through the process of incarnating, so he did. Further questioning revealed that he had the belief that he deserted his position in the realms of the Ascended Master level, was in rebellion to God and the High Council (Council of 144), and committed original sin when he once again partook of the knowledge of good and evil. He carried the soul quality of loss of innocence and patience as a soul belief for 747 incarnations. Now, for the first time, Dirk is free of that program.

Composure, Benevolence

This soul quality does not come up as frequently as some of the others. When it does, benevolence seems to be the major issue. Lucille had 449 incarnations involving this soul quality and all of them were centered around benevolence. In the first one she was a male who lacked benevolence toward herself and was self-destructive. In the second past life, she was a king who lacked benevolence and caused hardship, poverty, and starvation among her subjects.

Unity, Compassion

There were 827 incarnations involved with Felicia's soul quality of unity and compassion. In one life, she was a student priest. Because of a strong sense of disunity and separation from God, she had hate of self, unworthiness, and lack of compassion.

As a priest, in a past life, Arthur felt that the people had refused to support him when they did not provide the money for a large, impressive church. Arthur had no compassion or consideration for the poverty status of the people and was very unforgiving when they didn't provide the money to build his ego-centered dream. In the second life, Arthur was a nun and at odds with the entire congregation. He had a lot of hate for almost everything about life, which seriously limited his own self-expression and caused a complete lack of unity.

Selflessness, Obedience

In the one past life we researched for Jonah's soul quality of selflessness and obedience, he was a priest. There was another priest who was the Dalai Lama (the life was not on this planet, nor in this galaxy). Jonah was strongly involved with ego and believed he would make a better Dalai Lama than the other priest. One of the principles of the teaching was selflessness, and he blew it.

Here is another case in which a client, Roger, picked up a flame mate's programs. Roger was a

High Self for a male in a past life whose energies were hate of life, unforgiveness of others, and frustration. Although he knew the law of forgiveness, he was disobedient and refused to forgive anyone because he was self-centered and could see only his side of things. Roger picked up the flame mate's programs and was running them in this current life.

CHAPTER 10

Blocks to Positive Expression

In previous chapters we learned that a soul can accumulate negative energies as a result of past life experiences. In addition to clearing negative energies listed on Chart 6A–Master Programs; Discordant Energy, you may need to clear blocks to positive expression. Use Chart 6B–Blocks to Positive Expression, to identify words or areas in which you may be blocked in expressing positive traits or actions. One of my students, George Nummer, listed the words on this chart and gave me a copy. For a long time I did not use the chart because I felt it was superfluous; after all, you clear the negative, not the positive. Then one day High Self indicated I was to use the chart to clear a client's programs. Subsequently, we listed Chart 6B, positive words, on Chart 1–Chart to Use. Since then I have been directed to use it time and again to get rid of my clients' blocks to positive expression.

Case Studies

I will not present a lot of case histories or detail regarding blocks to positive expression, because the process of research is the same you use for other programs. When High Self indicates the problem is on Chart 6B–Blocks to Positive Expression, simply ask what the word is and it will be indicated. Use Chart 4–When; Cast of Characters, to determine when the program was established and who was involved.

Blocks to Abundance

Roxanne had a program that is common to a lot of people–she was blocked from receiving abundance. Using Chart 4, we found the program was established during past lives. In the only life we researched, Roxanne was a nun who believed God was cruel, vengeful, stingy, and angry. She set out to prove her saintliness by being poor and especially by withholding from herself. Roxanne took vows of poverty, for only in this way, she believed, could she please God and keep Him from being angry and cruel to her. She was doing her best to fulfill that program in the current life as well. Once the past life programs were cleared, we counseled her to make the decision to prosper and to give praise to God for her overflowing prosperity, because Jesus said it is "your Father's good pleasure to give you the kingdom" (Luke 12:32 RSV). Roxanne needed to know and affirm that she is a child of God and an heir to all that the Father has, gladly accepting His good into her life.

Blocks to Prosperity

Edith had a prosperity block that resulted from being a Guardian Angel for her twin flame and picking up the twin flame's negative motivation of greed. As a result, she established energy of self-punishment which she used to block her prosperity in this life. Edith also had blocks to success and enthusiasm.

In another life we researched, Edith was a nun who believed God was greedy and angry, and that He rejected and refused to communicate with her. She believed God wanted everything and gave nothing. She took vows of poverty, obedience, discipline, and silence. The nuns were not allowed to speak or have any self-expression. Edith was very bitter toward God, hated herself, and was unforgiving of herself and God. These energies were carried over into the present life and were blocking her prosperity.

Edith sold an herbal product for a living, and she could not seem to get ahead–she seemed blocked at every turn. The problem was past lives. She had 2,703 past lives as a healer, 839 of which she lived as an herbal healer. During 287 of those lives she was accused of witchcraft and killed and so developed energies of fear and unforgiveness toward those who harmed her. Her fear of being killed if she again dealt in herbs was the major blocking energy in this life.

Blocks to Health, Purpose, Self-Esteem

Willa had blocks to health, purpose, self-esteem, and self-worth. Only one of the issues, purpose, involved a past life. In that life, Willa was a Cherub. She did not want to be a Cherub; in fact she did not have any purpose at all. She felt that the other Cherubs refused to accept her and she ended up with a lot of frustration. Willa ran the program for an additional 369 lives and was running it in this life also.

Willa's blocks to health were established during early childhood. Her father was quite ill and received a lot of nurturing and attention. Willa imprinted herself with the belief that she had to be ill in order to get the attention and love she needed. Her father was also involved with her block to self-esteem and self-worth. Willa and her father are twin flames, and she believed that she had inherited his traits, including his low self-esteem and low self-worth. She also believed she inherited his propensity for illness and felt it was very unjust.

Blocks to Sincerity, Enthusiasm

Cara's block to sincerity had its roots in past lives. The first life we researched, she was the head priest of a universal church on another planet in a far-off galaxy. She was very insincere in her desire to serve God and mankind and wound up with a hate of God program. This translated into a hate of good since God represented the good in her life. In another life she was a mother superior on a different planet in the same galaxy. She was 374 years of age and hated being old, worn out, and unable to do everything she wanted to. Cara built up such a strong self-destructive energy that it caused her death. In the third past life, Cara was a priest on the same planet where she was mother superior. She was very unjust to others and felt like she had committed spiritual suicide because of her injustice.

Cara also had blocks to enthusiasm. In the first past life, Cara was a priest. She was so fearful of displeasing God; she became apathetic and did nothing. Cara believed it was better to do nothing than to do something and make a mistake. This 'do nothing' program was affecting her in the present life. In the second life, she was a guide for a male who is her flame mate. The male had apathy, hate of life, and suicide programs. Cara picked up his programs and ran them for 723 more lives. When I asked if Cara lacked enthusiasm in the present life, we received a "yes" response.

Blocks to Self-Control, Worthiness

Another block Cara had was a block to self-control. She was a nun in the first past life with hate of God, bitterness, and self-limitation energies. In the second past life she was an alcoholic nun with a strong fear of God. The fear was not that God would punish her or that she would end up in hell, but rather that God would 'get her.'

Cara had a block to her career with a benefit of self-limitation. During the only past life involved she was a mother superior with the energies of sexual promiscuity, fear, and failure. She felt completely unworthy of God's love and was limiting herself to prove her unworthiness.

Blocks to Love of Self, Intelligence, Cheerfulness

Lily had three programs on Chart 6B. They were blocks to love of self, intelligence, and cheerfulness. Her block to intelligence was established in early childhood. She was just fourteen months old when she decided she was incapable of learning. No one else seemed to be involved. However, she had set up energy of unforgiveness which she carried until this program was cleared.

Lily had only one past life that blocked her love of self. She was a Seraph who had hate of self and an intense hate of life in general. In contrast to the single life in the love of self program, Lily had 916 lives involving blocks to cheerfulness. In the first of two lives researched, she was a male, 345 years of age. She had a long-term physical illness that kept her in a constant state of depression.

Blocks to Understanding, Consideration

Betty Jane had two blocking programs to clear—lack of understanding and consideration. Both involved past lives. In one past life, Betty Jane was a priestess and one of her functions was to sacrifice people as part of a religious rite. She hated sacrificing human beings and developed a hate of God program because she was taught that God required sacrifice. She felt it was wrong to kill people in the name of religion. She hated life and the people who required her to perform the sacrificial act. She lacked a true understanding of God and the courage to break from being a priestess because she had been trained and prepared from age three to do the work. In the next life, she was a priest. Again, she lacked a true understanding of the nature of God and her purpose in life. She had hate, hate of God, hate of life, and hate of self programs.

Blocks to Self-Preservation, Self-Forgiveness, Supportiveness

Ida had all three of these blocks all of which were rooted in past lives. In one past life Ida was head priest with hate of God and apathy programs. She had been sexually abused by others and came to the conclusion that she was without value or she would not have been sexually assaulted. Since things that have no value are destroyed, she killed herself. In the current life, Ida has been struggling with the same sense of unworthiness and finds it extremely difficult to establish a sense of peace and well-being. She believes everyone is against her and she becomes angry and out of control very quickly.

Ida also had blocks to supportiveness, strength, and freedom. Ida was a priest in the only past life we researched regarding her blocks to supportiveness. There was also a group of priests involved. Ida was very paranoid and believed she had brain damage. She was angry at the other priests because they did not support her and she believed that they were intolerant of her condition. She was intolerant of the priests and had hate of life and hate of self programs. She also had a strong energy of unforgiveness towards everything and everyone and she harbored feelings of resentment and hate toward the other priests. The number of lives involved was 274½. The ½ indicated that some of the energies were running in the present life. Those energies were intolerance, hate of life, unforgiveness of everything, and hate both toward and from others.

Blocks to Faith, Success

Ned had blocks to success that involved 767 past lives. In the first life we researched, he was a priestess with hate of life, unforgiveness, and hate of God programs. In the second life, he was a priest filled with hate, unworthiness, and self-destruction. Ned found himself so blocked lifetime after lifetime that he killed himself in 714 of the total lives involved.

Ned also had blocks to faith in 871 ½ lives, of which we had to research three. In the first one, he was a mother superior with a sense of unworthiness; fear that God would abandon him because of his unworthiness, hate of God because he believed that God did abandon him, and intolerance toward himself for his lack of faith in God. In the second life he was a male and the only energy he had was hate of God. In the third life, Ned was a nun with hate of God, for which he was punishing himself. He took his frustrations out on others, became very intolerant of people, and rejected them because he felt they did not support him. Finally, he hated himself for not having more faith in God and for acting the way he did. The most significant energy that was running in this life was anger.

Blocks to Love of God, Love of Men, Love of Women

Ned had blocks to love of men. In the one life we researched, he was High Self for his twin flame who was in male form. The twin flame started out in the past life by hating her father (she is female in this life). Later she turned to a life of crime because she hated all men and was determined to get even. She was finally executed by men as a criminal and this locked the hate energy in. Ned picked up his twin flame's program while serving as her High Self.

Quentin had blocks to love of God, love of women, and love of men. In one past life, he was a mother superior with the energies hate of life and frustration. Quentin blamed God for his frustration, and so ended up with a hate of God program. In the program involving blocks to love of women he was in a male/female form and had hate of self and hate of women. He hated the female part of himself and ran this program for 175 lives. In the life involving his hate of men program, he was a priestess and the only energy was hate of men.

Blocks to Forgiveness

Olga had blocks to forgiveness and worthiness. We researched one past life in which she was a priest involved with a group of people and a nun. There was a love relationship between Olga and the nun. Their relationship was discovered and they were stoned to death by the people. Olga had never forgiven the people who had harmed her and the nun.

Blocks to Truthfulness

Percy had blocks to truthfulness involving 368 past lives. In the first of two lives, he was a female. There was a love relationship with a male who was a gangster. The male was a murderer, intolerant, and untruthful. He was involved with other women and lied about it. Percy was harmed mentally and emotionally by the man because of his relationships with other women and set up a program of jealousy, hate of life, and the belief that other people would lie to him. In the second past life he was a husband. His wife was a hateful, unjust person and ran around with other men and lied about it. Percy was mentally and emotionally harmed by her actions and turned to alcohol as a form of escape. He was addicted to both alcohol and tobacco. It was not Percy who was untruthful; it was the people he associated with. He built a strong program of believing that other people would lie to him and it was running in this present life.

Blocks to Friendliness

Ellie's block to friendliness was a huge program with 2,849 past lives. When we asked what we needed to research to clear the program, we were given the word *trauma* based on past lives. In the only life we had to research she was a nun. A large group made up the rest of the cast. Ellie was channeling healing through her High Self. She was accused of witchcraft by the very people she was healing and whom she trusted, and she was burned at the stake. She channeled healing in 72% of the 2,849 lives and was killed for healing in 83% of them. That was a pretty strong reason not to trust people.

CHAPTER 11

Archetypes

Part of our basic makeup is a set of patterns or *archetypes* that help us create and shape our identities in the physical world. When we are balanced and in harmony, these archetypes act to motivate and inspire us. However, when the archetypes are blocked or in conflict, we can experience pain and confusion.

There are twenty archetypes listed on Chart 8—Inner Archetypes. The first twelve terms were adopted from James Maynard's *Transpersonal Hypnotherapy*. Here is the basic meaning of each.

Inner Child. The urge to play, to create. The aspect involving relations with children, especially the inner child.

Adult. The desire to communicate with and to be nurtured by a loving, wise, understanding parent figure.

Critical Parent. The urge to be criticized, called to task, and corrected when error is encountered.

Paternal. The urge for external security. The aspect involving career, job situation, success, and one's standing in society.

Maternal. The urge for inner security and nurturing. The aspect involving family, domestic and emotional life, and balance.

Group instinct. The urge to affiliate with others. The aspect involving friendships and group involvement.

Inquirer. The urge to acquire knowledge. The aspect involving mental life. The state of one's communication.

Creator. The urge to create good in all levels of our expression.

Producer. The urge to acquire and to produce. The aspect involving finances, net worth, and self-worth.

Perfectionist. The urge toward purity and perfectionism. The aspect involving tidiness, hygiene, diet, practical techniques, mechanics, and domestic responsibilities.

Dreamer. The desire to dream and, through higher levels of consciousness while in the dream state, communicate with Spirit.

Guide. The urge for direction and meaning to life. The aspect involving spiritual and philosophical life.

Mentor. The urge to be open and receptive to higher guidance from Spirit.

Feminine. The urge and desire to love. The aspect involving primary relationships of life and their fulfillment.

Masculine. The urge to assert yourself by fully expressing your talents and abilities. The aspect involving self-image, sense of identity, outer appearance, and physical vitality.

Merger. The urge to merge with others. The aspect involving sex life and joint resources shared with another.

Suppressed Child, Feminine/Masculine. This is a block that is found at the soul level. Either or both the masculine or feminine aspect may be blocked.

Healer. The desire to be whole mentally, emotionally, and physically. This archetype helps with self-healing when blocking programs are removed.

Mystic. The urge for transcendence. The aspect involving spiritual activities and escapist activities.

Case Studies

The following cases present examples of how to research and clear archetypes that are blocking you or your client's full, free, and balanced expression of life.

Maternal

Ellen had separates blocking her inner maternal self. She also had a program that was based on trauma experienced during 329 past lives in other dimensions and we researched two. Ellen was a nun in the first life. There was a group of priests who accused her of heresy and she was stoned to death. Her energies were hate of life, self-limitation, negativity, unworthiness, and suicide of her own maternal instincts and inclinations. She felt she couldn't express her maternal instincts ever again because she had loved the priests and they killed her.

In the second life we researched, Ellen was a guide for a mother superior who hated God and committed suicide. Ellen's energies were unworthiness, hate of God, selfishness, and jealousy. Ellen believed she was unworthy because to her a mother superior represented the highest and best example of the maternal archetype and she had been unable to keep her from killing herself. She hated God because she wanted to enter the physical body of the mother superior and take over to fulfill her own selfish desires. She was jealous of the mother superior because she could not take her place and fulfill the perfect example of the maternal.

Paternal

Heather's block to the inner paternal was based on the theme of love and affection. It was necessary to research three of fifty-six future lives in order to clear the energy. In the first life, she was High Self for an androgynous person whose energies were spiritual suicide, intolerance, guilt, and bitterness. The androgynous person felt that he had cut himself off from God who represented the great father or paternal image to him. He also felt that he was giving up his masculine part because the feminine was too strong. He was intolerant of and bitter toward the feminine part of himself. Then, to top it off, he felt guilty about the whole thing. Heather is the androgynous soul's flame mate and she picked up his programs.

Heather was a student priest in the second future life with the energy hate of life. The reason for the hate of life is that she wanted to be a female and not a male. She saw herself as maternal in nature, not paternal. Consequently, she was blocking her male expression and was unable to fulfill her desire to have a maternal expression. This was keeping her from expressing and enjoying her paternal nature in the present life.

In the third future life we researched, she was a priest working under the direction of the head priest. The head priest's energies were spiritual suicide, sexual indulgence, guilt, frustration, bitterness, unforgiveness of self, and suicide. Heather's energies were jealousy, anger, hate, negativity, and intolerance. The head priest felt that he had cut himself off from God because of his indulgence in sex. He felt guilty, frustrated, and bitter because he could neither give up nor control his sex drive. Heather was jealous of the head priest's position which she saw as the ultimate expression of the father figure, the paternal archetype. She was angry at the head priest and intolerant of his sexual involvement. She considered him to be in flagrant disregard of his father image. Then she hated herself for being intolerant of him and ended up being intolerant of herself and filled with conflicting emotions.

Producer

Kay was blocking her prosperity—her inner producer—because of 253 past lives. In the only life researched, she was a priest who had taken a vow of poverty. She was a priest in 225 of the 253 past lives and had taken the same vow of poverty. In the remaining twenty-eight lives, she was a nun who took the same vow.

Merger

Paula had only one life to clear regarding her inner merger. She was a nun and the other character involved was God. The problem, in part, had to do with her concept of what God was like. She saw God as angry, judgmental, and rejecting. Paula had hate of self and unforgiveness because she believed she failed to live up to God's judgment of what a nun should be. She had taken vows of chastity and separation from all male figures and was very unhappy with the situation. She also perceived God as a masculine figure and her source of good. Therefore, for her, separation from males caused separation from God and the lack of togetherness or merging.

Inquirer

Gordon's inner inquirer archetype program involved 516 past lives. In the only one researched, he was an unassigned Guardian Angel and the only other character was God. He believed God was unjust and he felt separated from knowing the will or desire of God. Gordon questioned the meaning of life and his divine plan. He felt cut off from God and unable to inquire and get answers to his dilemma.

Guide

We researched one of 476 lives in Colleen's inner guide program. She was a female and there was a male involved who wanted her to enter a convent while her inner guidance—her High Self—told her not to. Her life was in turmoil and she was uncertain of the path she should choose. She failed to listen to her inner guidance, allowed the man to influence her, and became a nun. Colleen experienced a strong sense of unworthiness which caused her a lot of mental and emotional pain. To strengthen her inner guide, she is to become aware of her inner guide (her High Self), listen to it, and make better choices.

Inner Child

Faith's blocks to the inner child were established in this life. Faith's first block was set up on the first day of her birth by her father who wanted a boy. Faith felt rejected and worthless. At just over four weeks of age, her father called her a squalling brat, and again she felt rejected. The next block was established at ten weeks when she continued to cry and her father told her to shut up or he would kill her. He also told her she was a worthless brat and wished she had never been born. At five months, her mother gave her a message of rejection. The next person to give her a discordant message was her older sister who told her she was dumb and worthless when she was eight years old. At age sixty-five, her aunt said something that blocked her inner child. This was the final block to be cleared. Her current age is ninety-four and we were given the age of her inner child as 101. This indicates that her soul can remain in the physical body to age 101 if it so chooses.

Group Instinct

We had to research three past lives to clear Hal's inner group instinct. In the first life, the cast members included Hal as a nun, a mother superior, a head priest, a group of nuns, and a group of priests. The head priest's energies were hate of life and hate of God. He was in open rebellion to the Church and was teaching the people principles contrary to the accepted doctrine. The group of priests, pretending to be his friends, asked him to secretly teach them what he believed. Using this pretense, they lured him away from the Church to a secret meeting where they attacked and killed him. Hal found out what had happened and told the other nuns and the mother superior. There was nothing they could do about what had happened because the group of priests was too powerful. From this experience, Hal set up a strong inner resistance to working with or trusting any group.

In the second life, Hal was the Guardian Angel of a novice nun. The remaining cast consisted of a group of 107 nuns. The novice was accused of heresy by the group of nuns and burned at the stake. Her energies were hate of God for deserting her and allowing the nuns to kill her and anger at the group. Hal picked up the nun's programs. This increased his fear of groups and caused him to avoid group functions.

Hal was male in the final life we researched, and a group of fifty-two men who were robbers and outlaws were involved. They attacked Hal, robbed him, and beat him to death. Here, again, he had a bad experience with a group that was recorded in his soul memory. His task in this life is to release all of the energy and memories from these past experiences and learn to trust and work with groups. Then, Hal can move on to positive group experiences.

Perfectionist

Here are the two past lives we had to research to clear Sadie's inner perfectionist. She was a male in the first one and her energies were hate of the world, hate of people, negativity, bitterness, adultery, self-limitation, and abandonment of all things of value or productive of any good whatsoever. She had abandoned all concepts of the archetype of inner perfectionist.

In the next life, Sadie was a sixty-seven year-old retired mother superior. Her energies were adultery, hate of life, guilt, bitterness, self-castigation, and hate of God. She was overcome by temptation and had sex with a married man at the retirement home. She hated life for being put in the situation where she was tempted, and she blamed God for not helping her resist temptation and maintain her perfection.

God does not care if we are perfect or imperfect as human beings. God doesn't expect any more than we can do. Even our High Selves are not perfect. I often find that a person's High Self is causing problems. High Self beings are like you and me and may still be running some programs.

Mystic

There were 164 past lives blocking Glenn's inner mystic connection. During the only life researched he was a priest. The cast was a group of 370 priests. Glenn was channeling his guides and High Self and was very accurate. The group of priests accused Glenn of witchcraft and stoned him to death. Glenn was a channel during all 164 lives involved in the program and was killed each time. No wonder his spiritual expression was being blocked in this present life! Glenn felt a tremendous shift in energy as we cleared these programs. He is now free to develop his inner mystical potential and use it to channel and bless many people on this planet.

Religion, not only on this planet but throughout the universe, has taught that we are to seek, find, and know God. Yet, if you truly find the God within yourself, you may be accused of witchcraft, heresy, blasphemy or of working with the devil. Often, when I tell people that I am able to work with the Father within to research and clear problems so people may be healed, I too am accused of working with the devil. My answer is, "That is okay, if it works, it works." And it does work!

Sometimes, I believe that people have more faith and belief in the devil than in God. Fortunately, they do not, at least here in the United States, burn at the stake, stone, crucify you, or do any of the other nasty things I have seen done to others in past lives.

Dreamer

Ted had twenty-six past lives blocking his inner dreamer. He was the head priest in the first life we researched, and there was an androgynous person involved, as well as a group of 3,730. His guides were giving him information through his dreams. Ted was accused of witchcraft by the androgynous person who was jealous of him, and he was stoned to death by the group. The androgynous person is Ted's wife in the present life. In the next past life we researched, he was male. He was receiving information from his High Self while in the dream state. Ted's energies were panic that he might be killed again and unforgiveness of his High Self for not protecting him in the twenty-five past lives in which he received information from his guides or High Self and was killed. He set up a program of self-hate and felt he was neglecting his spiritual potential because he feared being killed again, even though people were no longer being killed for channeling.

Mentor

Arthur was running an imprint in a future life that was based on being killed in past lives for listening to his inner mentor. There were a total of 1,967 past lives involved and he was killed in 70% of them because he channeled and the people thought he was a witch. In the first past life, he was guide for a mother superior who was channeling him. A group of nuns accused her of witchcraft and burned her at the stake. There were 262 such lives in which Arthur was either a guide or High Self that gave information to others who were killed for channeling. Arthur gave himself a two-fold imprint which he was trying to fulfill in the future life: first, he felt he had to punish himself for causing the death of others; and second, if he channeled, he thought he would be killed again. This program is cleared and Arthur is able to receive information from his guides and High Self without fear of being killed or setting up a desire to punish himself in some future life.

Critical Parent

Colleen's inner critical parent problem was set up in the current life. She was just over six years old when she started becoming very critical of herself. I asked High Self if she would be at peace with her critical parent and stop beating up on herself and received a "no" response. There were other programs that had to be cleared before Colleen could be loving and gentle with herself. They were cleared, and further questioning revealed that she could, and would, be nicer to herself.

Healer

Gary's block to the inner healer was set up in the womb when she was about eight-and-a-half months old. Gary's mother contracted the flu. As a result, she was having difficulties with the pregnancy and the doctor told her that it might have a detrimental effect on Gary's health. Gary registered it in his subconscious as an imprint of poor health which had been running off and on ever since.

Ula's blocks to her inner healer were set up in 924 past lives in other dimensions, and it was necessary to research two. In the first one, she was head priest. She was channeling healing through her High Self, was accused of heresy, and burned at the stake. In the second life, Ula was again head priest channeling healing through her High Self. There was another priest who accused her of witchcraft and she was burned by 779 people who laughed, danced, rejoiced at her predicament, and ridiculed her. She vowed that never again would she allow the healing power to flow through her. This woman is a nurse in this life and has had a lot of difficulties with having a whole and fulfilling life. Her life, not her physical body, was sick.

Adult

There were 386 past lives blocking the harmony of Sid's inner adult. He was a priest and the only person in the first life. He was very immature and childish and was completely in a panic about life and his relationship to God. He became very depressed and ended up committing suicide.

In the second life, Sid was head priest, and there was another priest involved. He was very jealous of the other priest's popularity with the people. One day Sid, in a fit of childish temper, struck the priest in the head with a statue and killed him. He told the authorities that the priest had fallen down the stairs and hit his head on the altar. Sid's actions in this life indicated a certain immaturity and childishness which was blocking the expression of his inner adult.

Creator

Dick's inner creator was blocked at one year of age by his father, who ignored him and never worked with him to help him learn and express his creative ability. Dick told me that this was a common occurrence for him, that his father never seemed to have time for him or showed any interest in his creativity.

Suppressed Child, Feminine

Virginia began her suppression of her feminine aspect while in the womb. Her father was also involved. She was the first born, and she knew that he wanted a male child. Therefore, Virginia believed that she would have to suppress her feminine nature in order to win the approval and acceptance of her father. They are twin flames and that explains why she had such a strong need for his acceptance and approval. Also, she had a long-standing lack of self-approval that began when she was created as a female soul, as she wanted to be a male soul. This suppression of her feminine aspect had caused problems in many past lives and she was desperately seeking her father's approval in this life as the female half of the flame. She felt that if she could get his approval she would be okay and could then accept her own feminine nature.

We researched two lives to clear Jason's blocks to his suppressed child, feminine self. In the first one, he was a female who was 262 years old. His energies were hate of life, spiritual suicide, self-punishment, and a strong hate of women and anything feminine. Jason saw women, and himself, as weak, ineffectual, and unproductive.

In the next life, Jason was a mother superior, 202 years old, with a group of parishioners involved. The parishioners made him take an early retirement and he felt that they had abandoned him because he was female. He had a sense of unworthiness, hate of self, hate of women, and anything feminine. Again, he saw women as being weak, ineffectual, and unproductive. It was suggested to Jason that he balance and integrate the inner feminine and that he learn to respect, honor, love, and develop the softer qualities of his feminine side. He was to bring about a marriage of the masculine traits of self-image and wisdom and identity with the feminine, intuitive, and caring aspects.

Suppressed Child, Masculine

Leann's suppressed masculine child problem started when she was created as a living soul. Her soul energy was created masculine and she harbored a lot of negativity because she wanted to be a female soul. During subsequent incarnations, she suppressed her own male instincts and looked down on all males as inferior.

In a previous incarnation, Fawn was a head priest. She believed her life was very difficult and rigorous while the nuns had it easy. She had a burning desire to be a female because she believed her life would be easier, so she suppressed her masculine nature. This set up a program of being weak, soft, feminine, and ineffectual at the expense of her masculine side of strength and wisdom. Her lives, since this basic program was established, have continued to be weak, ineffective, and nonproductive. It is astounding how one lifetime can have such a strong discordant effect on many subsequent incarnations. The fortunate part is that there is now a system that can be used to track down and eliminate discordant energy and replace it with good, productive energy, allowing a new and better expression of life.

Becky had a block to her suppressed child, masculine self. When we asked what chart to use in order to clear the blocks, we were directed to Chart 5–Blocks and Interference. She had 357 separates which had attached themselves to her when she was five years old. (For more information about separates, see Chapter 6–Removing Blocks to Working with SRT.)

Becky was a nun in a past life and there was a group of 357 people. Her energies were intolerance, injustice, hate of life, hate of men, hate of women, and negativity. She accused the 357 men and women of heresy and they were crucified. They then bound together in a common state of consciousness as separates, and when Becky reached five years of age, they attached themselves to her to try and block her and limit her self-expression as she had limited theirs. Her inner masculine was blocked and she did not have the power to throw them off.

CHAPTER 12

Themes and Challenges

A theme or challenge is a set of lessons we choose to address in a particular lifetime. We choose our themes and challenges for the coming lifetime while in the bardo. Some people come into life with a strong desire to 'clear it all up this time around' and may have chosen to work with many or all of the themes and challenges listed on Chart 2–Themes and Challenges. They have taken on a tremendous task in an attempt to finish the work and ascend into the Light realms. They meet challenge after challenge and must not weary in well-doing; they have made the free-will choice to tackle their remaining work and finish it. Fortunately, there is plenty of help given to such people and the chance of succeeding is high. Once they start on the spiritual path, they are assigned many guides and Light beings to assist them. As they continue on the path, they are given more help as needed. When High Self indicates that you or a client need to clear programs related to themes and challenges, you always research past lives.

You can also use Chart 2 to identify your personal spiritual goals. Here are some of the questions I have asked about my own goals.

Q. *What is my personal goal for this life? (Affection, love)*

Q. *Do I have this goal because I failed to give love and affection in past lives when I had the opportunity to do so? (+)*

Once we have finished the experiential path and cleaned up the discordant programs, we will not have to incarnate again. We will be as it states in the book of The Revelation:

> *He who conquers, I will make him a pillar in the temple of my God; never shall he go out of it, and I will write on him the name of my God... (Revelation 3:12 RSV)*

'Name' means 'nature of.' As used here, it means that you have overcome, risen above the physical life, and have become one with the consciousness of God. You have taken on God's nature–Light. This is the atonement, or reconciliation (at one with Light) spoken of in Romans 5:11.

Case Studies

Control, Power

Amy had a control and power problem and was in conflict with her husband, Jim, who had the same program. The conflict was creating bad feelings and distance in their marriage, and Amy wanted it cleared. We started the research by checking the discordant energy on Jim. The energy originated in past lives in which he had exercised power and control over her. In the first life, Amy was a female and Jim was her spirit guide. He was trying to force his will on her and she resented it.

In the next life, both Amy and Jim were androgynous and there was a soul who was their

Guardian Angel. Amy had subjugated Jim and the soul serving as Guardian Angel to her will in previous incarnations by exercising unrighteous control and power. According to Amy's subconscious record, the Guardian Angel decided to pay her back by trying to control her. Her husband, Jim (an androgynous being in this past life), was supporting the Guardian Angel's desire for revenge. When I questioned her subconscious mind further, I discovered that Amy thought she deserved what they handed out (she felt guilty and had set up self-punishment). Clearing this program completed the clearing work for Jim. However, a check revealed more energy on Amy's control and power program.

During another life, Amy was male and dark energy was involved. There was a power struggle going on between her and the dark energy, but there was no winner. The dark energy was her current husband, Jim, incarnated with her in male form. They were trying to control each other in that life and both of them lost out. Nothing of soul value is ever gained in this kind of situation because discord never has any positive benefit.

High Self informs me that a soul can practice black magic while in discarnate form (out of the physical body). This makes the soul a *satanic discarnate* (satanics are identified on Chart 5—Blocks and Interference). While a satanic discarnate that uses black magic can exercise some control and power over incarnated souls, the incarnated souls can work to keep themselves clear and in the Light realms.

What happens when a soul receives divine illumination and does nothing with it? Linda received illumination as a male in a past life and did nothing with it. She felt powerless and out of control in the current life because she did not use the spiritual gifts God had given her in the past life. Like the parable of the talents, you either use it or lose it. When you lose it, you become powerless. You are bound up and limited.

> *For to every one who has will more be given, and he will have abundance; but from him who has not, even what he has will be taken away. And cast the worthless servant into the outer darkness; there men will weep and gnash their teeth. (Matthew 25:29-30 RSV)*

'Outer darkness' is separation from God. When we receive a spiritual gift and do not use it, we are separated in consciousness and spiritual knowing from our Creator and have to incarnate again and again until we once more receive spiritual illumination and use it for the benefit of our fellow man. Sitting in a cave and praying for others may be okay, but passing your knowledge on through the use of spiritual power, as Jesus did, is the better way. Thus you control your life and use your power to bless others.

Personal Integrity

When we asked what was blocking Dave's prosperity, High Self indicated personal integrity on Chart 2. The first two blocks originated in past lives. In the first life we researched, Dave was a father and God was involved. Dave, because he had incarnated, believed he was in rebellion to God, gave birth to darkness, and showed a lack of personal integrity. In the second life, he was one of eleven High Selves serving a female. There was a division of purpose in guiding the female, and Dave believed the rest of the High Selves harmed the female because they blocked him in the use of his personal integrity and zapped him out across the universe. Real or not, when this belief was cleared, Dave felt the change.

The next block was set up when Dave was nine years old and he cut his hand with an axe. He saw this as a lack of personal integrity (if he had been aware, he would not have cut himself), and was punishing himself by blocking his prosperity.

Dave's final block was organ language, established at birth. First, he believed he was valueless in the eyes of his father. Then, his mother had a difficult pregnancy, and Dave believed that he had been a threat to her life. He wished that he had never been born and believed he must block his own good or destroy himself since he lacked personal integrity and caused his mother pain.

Sexual Relationships, Sex

There were 153 incarnations in Nellie's theme of sex and sexual relationships, but it was necessary to research only one. She was a married female who left her husband because she could not satisfy her sexual desires with him.

We researched two past lives to clear blocks to Laura's sexual expression. In the first life, she was an eighty-four-year-old female. The rest of the cast consisted of a group of thirty-six people involved in black magic. The group took Laura and sexually tortured her. The experience was extremely painful and disturbing for her, and this soul memory has restricted her sexual expression in the current life.

In the second life, Laura was a Guardian Angel for a nun. The nun broke her vow of chastity by having intercourse with a priest. As a result, the nun set up a heavy program of guilt. Laura picked up the program from the nun who is one of her flame mates. She also sees sex and sexual relationships as detrimental to a happy physical expression, limiting to spiritual growth, and a creator of guilt.

Health, Fitness

Many times High Self indicates a health and fitness theme when a person is simply not taking care of himself or herself while in the physical body. One such case involved a female client who was a male in the only past life we researched. She simply failed to take care of herself and was sickly all her life.

A theme of health and fitness can be more complicated. Bruce was a male slave in one of the southern states. Although his owner did not abuse him, Bruce was filled with rage. The rage opened him to possession by satanic discarnates. The combination of rage and possession by satanics compromised his health and fitness and drove him insane.

Out of a total of 687 past lives, we cleared only two for Ula. In the first one, she was a ninety-three-year-old female with serious challenges to her health and fitness. She developed a strong hate of herself and of her physical weakness and abandoned life through suicide. In the second life, she was a sixty-five-year-old male who committed suicide because of a terminal illness. High Self says that when a person fails to meet a challenge like terminal illness, as in Ula's case, they will have to reincarnate and face that energy again until it is overcome.

Career, Work

Children sometimes have big dreams about what they want to be when they grow up. Perhaps they have a dream to be a doctor, lawyer, musician, or a computer operator. But, what are the dreams of each living soul? How do souls choose what they want to be and when do they make the decision? Perhaps, they have a hard time making up their minds. Here is such a case. Janet was a Light being before first incarnation. She was eagerly looking forward to her first life in the physical plane. There was only one problem—she had too many choices. She simply could not make up her mind as to what line of work or career she wanted to undertake when she did incarnate. High Self says she has been confused ever since.

Karen was a 106-year-old male in the past life we researched to clear her career and work theme. The average life span on the planet where she lived was 400 years, so she had lived about one quarter of her expected life. She was out of work, had no specific career or hope for a good life, became despondent, developed a hate of life, and killed herself.

Family, Life, Children

The case of Emma was fascinating. She had a theme of family life and children with a strong addictive energy attached to it. We researched and cleared only one life. Emma was High Self for a male (her twin flame and mother in the current life) and God was involved. She wanted to incarnate with the male because she was infinitely addicted to him. Emma was very angry at God because she believed God refused to allow her to incarnate because of the addictive energy she held on her twin flame. Therefore, she hated God and cursed God.

We found that Emma was punishing herself for cursing God by having broken relationships in this life. She was fearful that God had blocked her from having any meaningful family life or relationship. She felt guilty for hating God and believed she had closed herself off from heaven as well as good here on earth. This energy cleared easily, and Emma was no longer addicted to her twin flame. Neither did she hold the discordant energies of hate and anger on God.

We researched two past lives for Perry. In the first one, he was a Cherub and Guardian Angel. There was a group of Cherubs serving as Guardian Angels, a group of females, and a group of males involved. Perry was assigning Guardian Angels to souls that were incarnating as male and female children. He had an intolerance of children and did not like the responsibility of assigning their Guardian Angels. Perry abandoned his principles of common sense and his work.

This program was actually established before first incarnation, when Perry was an imp (baby angel) and there was a group of baby angels involved. Perry was mischievous and getting into trouble. He wanted to do his own thing, try his own wings. He went too far and ended up incarnating as a new soul. That was why he did not want to assign Guardian Angels to new souls who were incarnating for the first time. He felt that they were unprepared to incarnate and were making choices based on ignorance. After all, look what his own ignorance had brought about—he was stuck in the incarnational process.

Affection, Love

A psychic told me many years ago that there were four past lives in which I had gained a very high level of spiritual knowledge. Rather than using that knowledge fully as a blessing to others, however, I blew all four lives. Each time, I lacked love and affection. In the first life I researched, I was male and there were fifty-six females and seventy-five males, all of them teachers. There was also another male who was my brother. We were both students of "The Way," as it was called. My brother harmed me physically, although it was not serious. I was angry at him, refused to forgive him, and killed him. Anger and murder are dark energies and they canceled out the Light of Truth that I had received. This life was in Egypt at the Karnak temple. I have met this past-life brother in this life and have cleared the energy we held on each other.

In the second life, I was male and my older sister was involved. There was another male who was my spiritual teacher, and He was Jesus of Nazareth. I turned back from following Him because my older sister was ill, and she was my twin flame on whom I held addictive energy. The purpose of love would have been better fulfilled had I let someone else take care of my sister, so that I could follow the Master and become a teacher to many. I blew that life and soul purpose because of my addictive love for my sister.

During the next life, I was a male. God, another male, and dark forces were involved. The other male and I were spiritual students and received illumination. The dark forces were my anger, health abuse, terror of God, hate of self, hate of men, unforgiveness, helplessness, jealousy, and revenge.

In the fourth life, I was again male. The Holy Spirit, my High Self, and a male teacher were involved. I had gained spiritual knowledge through the Holy Spirit, my High Self, and the spiritual teacher. I failed in that life because I did not respond to the needs of others and pass on the knowledge I had gained. I did not fail out of neglect; I had flatly refused to pass the teachings on. I lacked a love of God and of my fellow man. Since I did not use the spiritual gifts to "feed my [Father's] sheep" (John 21:16-17 KJV), I lost out.

SRT is the method that allowed me to complete all of my own themes. I have researched and cleared a few of my own programs using SRT. However, most of my own negative programs were cleared while I worked to clear the programs of others.

Recognition, Prestige

Ingrid's recognition and prestige program seemed rather simple according to the information required to clear it. Two past lives were involved. In the first one, she was a Light being and believed that God failed to give her recognition or prestige. Ingrid wanted to do something for which she was not qualified. Spirit could not use her in the way she desired because she lacked the training and soul qualities for the task. Ingrid felt she was qualified–she was caught up in ego.

In the second life she was a priest. A female and a soul at Christ Status were also involved. Ingrid was in a position of leadership. She felt her talents and abilities were ignored and that Christ had failed to bring her the recognition and prestige she desired and rightfully deserved. Ego was involved in this life also. Ingrid felt rejected by both the female and the soul at Christ Status and committed suicide. The program cleared easily when we made the necessary clearing statements.

Money, Income

Ingrid had 363 past lives blocking money and income and we researched four. In the first life, she was a religious leader with several groups of priests and sisters involved. The other cast members were a single male (Ingrid's father today) and God. The religious organization was building a lot of monuments to God. Because Ingrid herself lived extravagantly, causing the priests and sisters to live in poverty, she is blocking her own prosperity now as a form of self-punishment.

In the second life, she was a female owner of a male slave (her father in this life). High Self identified the other character as dark energy. The dark energy was not a soul. Rather, it was her energy of guilt. Ingrid had beaten the slave, kept him in poverty, and starved him to death.

In the third life, Ingrid was androgynous (both male and female). There was a stepson, a stepdaughter, and a group of males. The father of the children had deserted them and she was forced into prostitution in order to maintain herself and the children. She stole from her customers and felt guilty. Her guilt was blocking a full expression of good in the present life.

Life Meaning, Purpose

How many of us feel lost in a world without meaning or purpose? Kari had established a program of self-limitation when she decided to incarnate. In the first life we researched, Kari was dark energy. God and a Council of Nine made up the rest of the cast. She believed God wanted her to incarnate and the Council did not. Since there was a difference of opinion between God and the Council, she was confused and uncertain about her purpose in incarnating and about the direction she should take to please both God and the Council. Although this program cleared easily, High Self informed me that it had affected 80% of Kari's past lives.

In the past life we researched in Goldi's life meaning and purpose program, she was an eighty-four-year-old female who was physically ill. She caused her daughter mental and emotional pain by abandoning her. Goldi could see no meaning or purpose in living further so she took an overdose of pain pills. Then she established energy of guilt because of the suicide.

Security, Resources

We researched three lives to clear May's blocks to security and resources. In the first life, she was a female with energies of self-limitation, alcoholism, depression, guilt, self-punishment, and suicide. In the second life, she was a female with a husband. She had an affair with another man and her husband kicked her out. She blew her security and resources and ended up killing herself. In the final life, she was a fourteen-year-old male. Her parents had died and she was living with an uncle. She hated her uncle and life and destroyed her security and resources by killing herself.

When we researched Sean's first past life, we found that I was involved. He was a female leader on one of the islands of Tahiti. I was one of many people who were his subjects. A sailing vessel was wrecked by a storm off the coast because the sailors were infected with the plague and could not handle the ship. The natives took care of the sailors and contracted the disease from them. Many of the natives died because they had no natural immunity or physical resources to combat the disease. Their security from disease was in their isolation, which they sacrificed when they took care of the sick sailors.

In the second life, Sean was again a female. There were a lot of people involved who wanted him to be their leader. Sean tried and failed because he could not manage people or resources. He was having the same problem in this present incarnation. His financial resources were strained, and he was having difficulty with his co-workers.

Recreation, Play

Pat was a male in the past life we researched to clear her recreation and play program. She gave up her own expression to impress a female and then was rejected. She felt she had been caught up in playing a game that was a waste of time and effort.

Gay was in spirit body in the past life we researched to clear her program. She was not involved with any specific task but was simply playing around. She has been punishing herself for playing around for the past 2,483 incarnations.

CHAPTER 13

Negative Motivations

A negative motivation is an improper desire to control or manipulate another person or to limit one's own self-expression. There are nineteen major negative motivations listed on Chart 5–Negative Motivations. Seldom do you find a person with all nineteen of these negative motivations. However, some people run two, three, or even four of them at one time.

Negative motivations are easy to dispose of; you simply research and clear past lives as described in Chapter 5–The Basic Steps of SRT.

Case Studies

Desire, Ambition

Only one past life was involved with Bets' program of desire and ambition. High Self says that one life affected 145,504 subsequent lives. The energy was not removed until this present life, when it was researched and released. The negative motivation was established before her first incarnation into first round. Bets was a Light being and there was another Light being who was her twin flame. Another Light being who is Bets' flame mate was also involved. Bets and her twin flame (her maternal grandmother in this life) were infinitely addicted to each other. Bets wanted her twin flame to incarnate and break the addiction. The twin flame felt that Bets–and God–were applying undue pressure. The twin flame developed a hate of God program because she felt that God was trying to force her into incarnating in order to break the addictive energy. The flame mate (not presently incarnated) felt that Bets was being unfair and intolerant of her flame family and he set up his own program of intolerance, which he is still carrying to this day. Then, to top it off, Bets picked up both her twin flame's and her flame mate's negative energy on the situation. Bets had, before clearing, the belief that her twin flame's desire and ambition was negative and she was angry at her. She was intolerant of both her twin flame and her flame mate. Bets also had energy of injustice on herself, as well as on the other two because of her own negative reaction to the situation and her desire to force her twin flame to incarnate.

Questioning revealed that both Bets and her twin flame are free of the addictive energy they held on each other. Their negative motivation of desire and ambition has also been cleared. However, the flame mate still has an adulteration of consciousness program, with the energy of intolerance, and will have to face it and clear it in some future incarnation. High Self indicates that the flame mate has many incarnations yet to experience in order to complete his education.

Appeasement

Appeasement is a desire to pacify another because of some perceived shortcoming, fault, or hurt to the other person, even if this appeasement causes harm to oneself. Anne was a guide in the one past life we investigated. There was also a large group of other guides involved. The group of guides believed they were in rebellion to God. Anne was trying to make peace between the guides and God and failed. Anne was willing to give up her own self-expression on behalf of the other guides, even to the extent of damaging herself emotionally.

We only researched one life to clear Darlene's appeasement program. She was a young mother and the other character was her brother. The brother sexually molested her while he was drunk and out of control. He later asked her forgiveness and she refused to be appeased. The brother felt so badly about what he had done that he killed himself. Darlene was blocked from full expression in the current life until this past life was researched and cleared.

We had to research two past lives in order to clear J.J.'s appeasement program, which involved a total of 3,424 incarnations. In the first one, she was a father. There was also a daughter and her son, who was born out of wedlock. The remaining cast included a grandmother and a grandfather. The grandmother harmed the granddaughter physically by beating her with a stick. She also harmed her mentally and emotionally by rejecting her and her son. The father and daughter had been living with the grandparents, and the grandmother kicked the young mother and her son out. J.J. tried to achieve peace by appeasing her mother, but she failed. We asked if the program was blocking her from being gentle and loving now and received a "yes" response.

In the second past life, J.J. was a mother whose daughter (who is also her daughter in this life) hated life and was filled with anger and general hate. J.J. tried to appease the daughter but was rejected. This hurt J.J. mentally and emotionally. She became depressed and committed suicide. They are at last free from those old programs and can, by putting forth the effort required, have a wonderful relationship as mother and daughter in this life.

Power, Manipulation

One of the most important lessons each soul needs to learn is that no soul has the right to manipulate or exercise unrighteous power over any other soul regardless of a soul's level of consciousness or degree of soul growth. Every soul is a free-will being with sovereign control and power over his (or her) own life and destiny. However, it is obvious that some people want to manipulate others because they have lost control of their own self-expression.

Bert's energy of power and manipulation was established before his first incarnation. He was a Cherub and decided he would incarnate and force others to live the way he believed they should. He could see the evil in the world and wanted to change it so everyone would have to be good.

Most people are not aware, or do not believe, that there is life on other planets in our solar system. I am assured by High Self that there is life on all planets, although the life may not be at the same vibration as life here on earth. The past life we researched for Anne's power and manipulation program was on Venus. Anne believed that Venus was the planet of love. Yet she could see that love was not always expressed, so she decided she would incarnate and make the people express love.

Coercion

Coercion means to curb or constrain another, or to compel another to do things against his or her own sense of right or personal will. Coercion stymies the soul's authority over his or her own chosen path and weakens the will. Sometimes we weaken our own self-will or ability to express our life freely because of fear. Coercion takes many forms.

There were 396 incarnations in George's coercion program. In the first life, he was a Seraph serving as a guide for a female. The only other character was God. The female was killing her own good by being sexually indulgent. She was afraid that she had offended God and that God would condemn her to hell. George was depressed and filled with guilt. He felt responsible for the female's conduct. Since he could not influence the female to live a better life, he resorted to coercion. Although he decided that coercion was not the right way to do things, he continued the practice and set up a boomerang energy that was haunting him in the current life.

There is a saying that what you hate, you manifest, and that whatever you hold energy on, you will get to experience. George was Thought in the second life that we researched in his coercion program (Thought is one pre-incarnational form of existence for a soul). The other character was a Light being from the level called Free (see Chart 3–Levels of Soul Consciousness), who was serving as George's High Self. George felt that his High Self was trying to coerce him into incarnating when he did not want to. He became angry at what he believed was undo pressure and began to complain bitterly to the other beings in the Light realms. He did incarnate, but his High Self did not coerce him to do so. It was George's own energy–that which he set up and resisted propelled him into incarnation.

Coveting

Coveting seems to be a part of the human makeup and may be defined as wanting something ardently and with envy.

Rex had a negative motivation of coveting. We researched two of the 722 lives involved. During the first life, he was a priest who coveted wealth and acclaim. During the second incarnation he was a female who coveted wealth, the power the wealth would bring, and the acclaim of others.

Beulah's zealous, burning desire to know God caused her a lot of unhappiness and grief in the only incarnation researched. She was a nun who strongly coveted God. She wanted to be known as a holy person, "the nun who knew God." Beulah was very bitter and frustrated when her greedy desire to know God on a personal basis was not fulfilled. She only succeeded in causing herself a great amount of mental and emotional pain.

Conscious Control

Colleen's negative motivation of conscious control involved ten past lives. We researched only one, in which Colleen was a male. Two other males were involved, one of whom is her husband in the present life. The three of them were partners in a business. Colleen hated life and took it out on her partners by consciously controlling them, lying to them, and defrauding them. They had her tried for fraud and sent to prison where she died.

Negative Motivations Not Listed on Chart 5

Occasionally, you encounter a negative motivation that is not listed on Chart 5. High Self indicates that a program is not listed by swinging the pendulum in a straight line across the bottom of the chart. When this happens, use Chart 1–Chart to Use, and ask if there is a clue on one of the other charts. If there is no clue, just ask High Self to clear it without research.

CHAPTER 14

Miscellaneous Blocks

When I have completed researching a person's basic and major programs and they have been cleared, High Self usually directs me to Chart 10—Miscellaneous Blocks. Chart 10 identifies miscellaneous items that, like other programs, can cause problems in your life. I identify all of the Chart 10 items that the client has and then ask High Self to clear the blocks as required (each is slightly different). I will present here, to the extent of my current understanding, how to identify and clear each of the blocks listed on Chart 10.

You can also ask if everything the client has on Chart 10 can be cleared without identifying individual items. If you receive a positive response (as I often do), ask High Self to clear the programs, and then verify that the blocks have been cleared.

World Energies (Positive and Negative)

These are negative energies that we accumulate from our daily experiences. They can be any type of energy listed on Chart 6A—Discordant Energy. You clear world energies from the subconscious by asking High Self to dissolve the energy. You can ask your High Self for a daily removal of any discordant energy you may accumulate.

Subconscious Clutter

Sometimes, when I have asked if there is something else to clear, my High Self would point to "subconscious mind" on Chart 1—Contact or Help. Further questioning would reveal that it was not a program or discordant energy. Not understanding what they were trying to tell me, I would simply ask them if they could clear it and have been given a "yes" response. Finally, I asked High Self to give me a picture of what was involved. I saw a Christmas tree with all of the presents unwrapped and stacked under it. The wrapping paper, boxes, ribbons, and bows completely covered the floor. I inquired of my High Self if they wanted to dispose of all subconscious clutter, and they gave a positive response. It appears that each discordant program has its own wrapping that needs to be disposed of when the programs are cleared.

Conscious and Subconscious Memory

When we are created as a spiritual body, we are vested with a subconscious mind where all of the knowledge gained through our many experiences is stored. This stored knowledge is called the *akashic record*. The next step in our creation is to become a living soul (which is described in the second chapter of Genesis). The living soul, I am informed by my High Self, is the working consciousness (conscious mind) of the spiritual body. Eventually the soul partakes of 'the tree of the knowledge of good and evil,' and God gives the soul a physical body (coats of the skins of animals)—the soul incarnates. God provides the physical body with a conscious and subconscious mind in which daily experiences and their attached energies are stored. High Self indicates that the stored material gained while in the physical body does not go into the akashic record until the person leaves the physical body by the process known as death. If before death, you clear all discordant energy from the happenings experienced while in the physical body, all that is written into the akashic or soul record is the knowledge and wisdom gained during the life.

While you are out of the physical body, your experiences and their attached energies go directly into the subconscious mind (spiritual body) and the conscious mind (living soul), where they remain until they are researched and cleared using SRT or some other method. High Self assures me that only someone in the physical realm who works with his or her High Self using SRT or other methods can research programs and have them cleared. Clearing the conscious and subconscious memory banks of both the physical body and the soul helps to release all discordant energies that may have been causing problems or might later cause difficulties. Then it is up to each individual soul, whether in or out of the physical body, to keep themselves free of all discordant energies.

Heart Vows

People normally make heart vows during religious lives, although they may make them under other conditions as well. They are called heart vows because they register in the emotional or heart center. There are twelve basic vows identified by High Self that can often be destructive to our physical life and limiting to our soul development. Many of these concepts are a part of the accepted requirements of religions today. They may have a positive effect on a person's life and religious path when taken with complete understanding of their true meaning and purpose. However, High Self indicates that 90% of the people who have taken religious vows experience a negative, often destructive, result as a direct or indirect consequence of those vows.

These vows are listed in no particular order of seriousness; I have simply listed them in the order in which I became aware of them. The vows and the reasons they are taken are:

Separation, from others that we might be true to God.

Loneliness, so we can hunger and thirst after God.

Silence, so we can hear God.

Poverty, because all physical nature is evil and our reward is in heaven, which we attain only after death. Yet Jesus implied 'the kingdom of heaven is within.' Many religious people generally accept the idea that wealth is evil and must be shunned in order to prove spiritual worth.

Chastity, which equals purity and singleness of purpose to worship God.

Celibacy, which equals righteousness.

Suffering, which purifies and cleanses.

Obedience, which proves our spiritual value.

Sacrifice, which is giving up everything, that we might be like God–having nothing but being all.

Illness, which proves that we are worthy of God's love through suffering–our reward will be great in heaven (in truth, heaven is now).

Anxiety, which causes us to pant after God–Him only will we search for and cling to.

Fear of God, which keeps us in line so that we will not go astray after false gods.

These vows are so strong and have been repeated in so many incarnations that they often have a powerful, discordant effect on subsequent lives, even when they are totally out of context with their original purpose. For instance, many people are blocked in their financial well-being and experience abject poverty because of vows of poverty taken in past lives. Others suffer illness because they set up past life programs of illness, believing it proved they were worthy of God's love. God, according to Jesus' teachings, is Love (1 John 4:8). Why would Love require us to suffer? It does not make sense.

Inhibitors

An inhibitor is anything that tends to limit or inhibit our full spiritual potential. Inhibitors that are set up before our first incarnation discourage us from incarnating. If set up after a soul incarnates, inhibitors become defense mechanisms that prevent the incarnational body from having a negative reaction, such as self-destruction, self-limitation, suicide, murder, guilt, negativity, or hate of mankind. Another purpose of inhibitors is to keep us from blocking our own paths so that we can successfully complete our soul's purpose of learning and growth. Unfortunately, inhibitors sometimes block our true response to stimuli.

Inhibitors are set up by an individual in a fashion similar to heart vows. We carry them with us until they are removed. However, unlike heart vows, they are not considered sacred and have not been inspired in response to universal laws. Rather, inhibitors exist because of the defense mechanisms of the incarnational body. Therefore inhibitors, if labeled as such, are negative defense systems carried over from lifetime to lifetime which inhibit the soul's growth.

Inhibitors are insidious, yet they often appear to be positive in nature because they seem to protect. However, inhibitors, more than programming, often work in a discordant fashion. Unfortunately, they are so deep within the psyche (at a cellular level) and the soul consciousness that their presence is seldom detected. Fortunately, High Self can identify and clear them from all levels of your being.

Curses

There are two common forms of curses. The most common form is when a person has cursed someone else. Even though a thought is sent forth to another, as in a curse, the sender retains the belief and the energy of that thought which act as a judgment against the self. Thus, it has a definite negative impact on their soul. The thought or curse sent forth is merely a photocopy. The intended recipient can accept or reject it. Another form of curse is when someone curses you and you accept it. I also meet clients who believe they have been cursed by life or by God. Regardless of the form, High Self can clear the program.

Contracts

There are two forms of contracts. The second form will be covered when we get to decaying universes later in this chapter. The first form has to do with second round souls and the serpent message that is often a part of master programs (see Chapter 8—Master Programs). When we incarnate second round and persuade others to incarnate with us, we sometimes believe that we are the serpent in the garden of Eden who caused others to partake of 'the tree of the knowledge of good and evil.' Souls with the serpent message have a contract with the souls they persuaded to incarnate—they agree to pick up the souls' load of programs if they cannot handle them. These 'rescuing' souls may have a savior complex which can cause them to believe they have to save everyone by taking on their programs. However, the other people still have their own discordant programs and will have to work with them in this lifetime or some future lifetime in order to clear them. When you encounter contracts, ask High Self if the contracts can be broken and the serpent and savior beliefs released.

Genetic Beliefs

The *Bible* states that the LORD will be "visiting the iniquity of the fathers upon the children and the children's children, to the third and the fourth generation" (Exodus 34:7 RSV). (See Chapter 7—Charts 1 and 4, under the section titled "Understand the Basic 13 Programs," then refer to "Inheritance" for a more extensive discussion.) The question is why should the LORD cause a child to suffer for the iniquities of their parents, let alone their grandparents? The answer is the LORD doesn't. Beliefs are inherited from previous generations through the mother's egg and the father's sperm. Inheritance is a spiritual version of holography, where every part contains the whole. Each cell is a minicomputer that contains the whole record and programs of the individual. Therefore, when the mother's egg and the father's sperm come together to form the physical body, all of the programs that they have as part of their belief system, and which are registered in each cell, make up and become part of the cellular memory of the infant body. I have found genetic memories that have been passed on for as many as eight generations. Thus, if you inherited a belief in some disease from one of your parents, and you have your own reinforcing programs, you may run the beliefs you inherited. Fortunately, High Self can clear all genetic programming from the cellular memory so that only your own personal programs remain. Then, as long as you do not consciously rebuild them by listening to other people's beliefs, you will be free of all inherited messages.

Karmic Beliefs

Karma is a belief system. Here again, we set up some very strong negative beliefs. These can and often do play out the *Old Testament* scenario of, "eye for eye, tooth for tooth" (Exodus 21:24 RSV). Our belief that we must be punished for our shortcomings is often strong and deep. Forgiveness and love are the keys to breaking the bonds of past actions, beliefs, and energies. When we learn to love our fellow travelers upon the earth plane, forgive them of any perceived trespasses, and bless them with our prayers, we are free. Remember, everything is based upon our own personal beliefs, perceptions, and judgments.

Blocked Chakras

There are seven major chakras associated with the physical bodies. There are also eighteen chakras that extend above the physical body into the spiritual realm. Some of the chakras, both in and above the body, may be blocked. They can be cleared, balanced, and opened by High Self.

A complete discussion of chakras is beyond the scope of this book. There are a number of good books on the market, one of which is *Wheels of Light* by Rosalyn L. Bruyere. For information on this book and other books, see the bibliography.

Balance Positive and Negative Energy

Everything has a positive and negative pole—a person, a plant, a leaf on the plant, a house, and so on. The poles can be out of balance. Just ask High Self to clear and balance them.

Toxic Streams

Toxic streams are called geopathic lines of force by the American Society of Dowsers. They are energy streams that run below the surface of the ground and carry negative or destructive energy. Where two of these lines cross, a vortex of discordant and often harmful energy may develop. If you spend time in these vortices, you can be negatively affected mentally, emotionally, and physically. If toxic streams run under your home, your place of business, or any place where you spend a lot of time, it is best to have them removed. You can call on a dowser to locate and divert them. However, the simplest way to handle toxic streams is to have High Self fill them with Light energy. The streams then become positive and constructive.

Decaying Universe

For some time I had been working with a client who was picking up energy from another realm. I knew it was there, but could not put my finger on it. Then, one day, while working with him and finding the same energy, I said, "You are still picking up energy from some other realm, and I do not know what that realm is. I hope Spirit will soon reveal what it is." Instantly, I heard the inner voice say, "Half universe." At almost the same instant my wife, who was listening to my end of the conversation said, "I am getting that it is a half universe." My daughter, who was in the room, said, "Dad, I am getting half universe also." Later questioning revealed that, indeed, the client was picking the energy up from a half universe.

Some quantum physicists have stated that the universe was created with a big bang, and that it emerged from a white hole. High Self says that their belief is correct. Astronomers have also determined that matter disappears into a black hole. This is also true according to High Self. Here is what High Self has revealed through the questioning process and inner pictures. Imagine a huge donut in space. Through the center there is a hole shaped like an hourglass. A universe that has completed its cycle gradually decays and eventually collapses, going into a black hole that is one side of the hourglass. It goes through the narrow opening as solid matter and explodes out of the other side of the hourglass (white hole) as pure energy. That energy, under the direction of very high beings, begins to coalesce into the many galaxies and other components that make up an unfolding universe. Eventually, the planets within a galaxy evolve to the point where they sustain life forms. The universe proceeds on its way and over eons of time, like other universes before it, travels full circle around the donut, goes into decay, collapses, and starts the process all over again.

I often encounter people who have contracts with the souls who inhabit decaying universes (which can be down to one-half, one-quarter, or one-eighth of their full energy). These souls are not far enough along in their evolution to have gained the amount of knowledge and energy they need to be self-sustaining. Unless rescued, they will dissolve along with the decaying universe they inhabit and cease to exist as individual souls—there will only be pure energy.

Some souls make contracts to take upon themselves the discordant energy of these young souls in the decaying universe. The contracts cannot be broken, as in the case of the serpent or savior contracts (see "Contracts" earlier in this chapter). However, since there is no time or space in SPIRIT, you can ask High Self to complete them. SPIRIT then removes the souls from the decaying universe and places them in an expanding universe where they will continue to experience, learn, and grow as they progress on their soul paths.

Race Beliefs

Even if a person feels he is not prejudiced against other races in this life, he can carry prejudices over from past lives. If there is one thing that SRT has taught me, it is that I have been every race, nationality, creed, and color on this planet and on other planets. Race beliefs cause separation, hate, pain, and destruction—let us all get rid of them.

Multiple Souls

High Self tells me that multiple souls are souls that attach to another soul at the time of birth, always with the host soul's agreement. Although they do not normally cause any problems, multiple souls can interfere with the host's vibrations. Multiple souls can cause some people to show signs of either schizophrenia or a split personality. The reason these souls attach to a person at birth is that they want their programs cleared without having to incarnate. When you discover them, have High Self clear their programs and take them to their right and perfect place. There are three reasons why a soul may have multiple souls. The host soul may have harmed them in past lives, the multiple souls may have harmed the host soul, or the multiple souls are part of the host soul's soul family.

Transfer Student

Ruth Montgomery, in her book *Strangers Among Us*, talks about walk-ins. These are souls who have come into a physical body vacated by a soul who is disillusioned with earth life and wants out. There normally is complete agreement between the two souls that the exchange will take place. High Self says that the new soul occupying the physical body as a result of the exchange prefers being referred to as an exchange or transfer student, not as a walk-in. These exchanges can be made any time after birth. However, the new soul is not referred to as a transfer student unless the body they inhabit is at least three years of age.

I have encountered quite a few transfer students in my workshops. Some of them knew they had made the transfer and others did not. When there is no memory of the transfer, I usually find the exchange was made at an early age. Sometimes, when the transfer is made between three and eight years of age, the person has little or no memory of the years prior to the transfer. I can sometimes spot an exchange student in my workshops by realizing that they are clearing two sets of programs, theirs and the previous occupant's.

Exchange students usually come from a more advanced galaxy. They bring with them a desire to help souls on the planet to learn and grow. Or, they bring some new technology or teaching that if properly used can bless and lift the consciousness of the people and dramatically shift the energy on a planet. These exchange students are often multiple souls who express as one consciousness, one being. You can ask High Self to clear all of the programs of the previous occupant so that the exchange soul or souls do not have to deal with previously-recorded messages in the cellular memory or the subconscious mind. Sometimes an individual soul makes the exchange and later, when everything is in order; additional souls will come in to form a multiple consciousness.

Clear the Cellular Memory

Every cell is a minicomputer that contains all the records of the conscious and subconscious minds. It is, therefore, of vital importance that you ask High Self to clear the physical body's cellular memory of all discordant and hurtful issues once you have researched and cleared the other programs.

Major Beliefs

Major beliefs can also be called separation beliefs, as they are set up when we, as spiritual beings, began the process of leaving the Light realms and incarnating. They include negative fundamental beliefs about separation from God and our compromised state as incarnated beings. As with other miscellaneous programs, just ask High Self to clear them. Following is the listing of all twelve beliefs.

Eternal Damnation—Eternal damnation is the belief that mankind, as a result of incarnating, is forever damned to wander in the earth, alone, lost, and separated from Source. As the wave is in the ocean, we are one in God, and we can never be separated from Source. To be separated means that we would have no energy to sustain life and would cease to be. The truth is that we have our being in God as life, substance, and intelligence—we are One with God.

Emotional Imbalance—According to the symbolism of the *Bible*, Eve, who was influenced by the serpent (sense-consciousness) in her desire to gain wisdom, led mankind into the incarnational process that was a natural result of partaking of the knowledge of good and evil. Eve represents the feminine or feeling nature of all mankind. Since it was the emotional nature, represented by Eve, that led us into a difficult physical life, many people have a fear of their emotions. Since emotions are the creative energy that we use every day, many people are blocked because they have a fear of emotional imbalance. Unfortunately, the fear can create what is feared.

At a lecture, quantum physicist Fred Alan Wolf, Ph.D., indicated that thoughts are particles and emotions are wave forms which move the thought (particle) into being. Without the wave form, the thought has little possibility of moving into manifestation. It does not make a difference whether the thought and emotion is positive or discordant; emotion moves it into being. Unfortunately, having fear of the emotions can create more reason to fear the emotions until a person is completely out of balance. One whole book of the *Bible*, Job, is devoted to what happens when the mind is filled with a consciousness of fear.

For the thing that I fear comes upon me, and what I dread befalls me. (Job 3:25 RSV)

Let go of fear. Know that SPIRIT is more powerful than anything in the world. Know that God is both the source of all good and the expression of all good, and God is unlimited. Know that you live, move, and have your being in SPIRIT. You are SPIRIT. Control fear, eliminate it from your life, and use your positive emotions to create good.

Eternal Vows—These are the same as heart vows which are listed on Chart 10. The only difference is that eternal vows are set up when we first come out of the Light realms into physical incarnation. I will list them here, but not repeat their meanings. They are: separation, loneliness, silence, poverty, chastity, celibacy, suffering, obedience, sacrifice, illness, anxiety, and fear.

Creator Fragmentation—This is the belief that God fragmented in order to create us which caused a sense of separation to be established in the soul.

Belief in the Devil—This is the belief that there are two powers, one good and the other bad, God and the devil. High Self says it is a limiting, destructive, false belief. It is an attempt to escape personal responsibility for what happens on our soul path of learning while experiencing in the incarnational realms.

Both SPIRIT and my High Self assure me that there is no such being as the devil. The serpent in Genesis symbolizes sense-consciousness or any soul that becomes involved with the incarnational process. In the Book of Job, Satan is simply Job's own consciousness of fear that created what he feared.

The devil is referred to by other names in the Scriptures, including Abaddon and Apollyon (Revelation 9:11), Beelzebub (Matthew 12:24), Belial (2 Corinthians 6:15), and Satan (Luke 10:18, Job 1:6). Satan, in Hebrew means *"lier in wait; an adversary; an enemy; hater; accuser; opposer"* (MBD). Metaphysically, it means the deceiving phase of the sense mind that holds fixed ideas in opposition to the truth of our unity with God. Satan is the destructive state of mind that is adverse to or believes in lack, limitation, separation from God (good), and death. The devil signifies the mass of discordant thoughts and beliefs that have been built up in human consciousness through many generations of earthly experiences and have crystallized into what is called human personality, or carnal mind.

Spiritual Imbalance—This is the belief that we are weak and ineffectual because we are only fragments of God and separated from Source. It is the belief that God has abandoned us to an unjust, cruel, difficult existence in a cold, harsh world. In some cases, it is a belief that we were cast out of heaven as a means of punishment. One person I counseled had a belief that he was so distasteful that God spit him out of His mouth.

Spiritual Suicide—This is the belief that we created separation from God by partaking of the forbidden tree and are eternally damned. This belief is completely adverse to the teachings of Jesus that God is love. Love would never cast out or eternally cut off its own created beings. Only humans would do that. Unfortunately, many humans have created God in their personal image and likeness with all of the imperfections and weaknesses of the human personality.

Cursed by God—Many believe that we are cursed by God. Genesis 3:17-19, states that the ground was cursed because Adam and Eve, representing all mankind, ate of the tree of good and evil:

...in toil you shall eat of it all the days of your life; thorns and thistles it shall bring forth to you; and you shall eat the plants of the field. In the sweat of your face you shall eat bread till you return to the ground, for out of it you were taken; you are dust, and to dust you shall return." (Genesis 3:17-19 RSV)

This does not mean, as many believe, that God really cursed man. Earth life can be a trial to the incarnated being. We daily face challenges (thorns and thistles) and overcome them only by conscious effort (sweat of your face). The field represents earthly consciousness, which partakes of all kinds of ideas, good and bad, and brings forth both good and bad (see the parable of the wheat and tares in Matthew 13:24-43). We believe that earth life is the only reality and partake of it (take it into our consciousness), then have to deal with it until we have overcome all challenges, learned our lessons, and completed the soul's education. Then we leave the physical realm and once again return to dust (the spiritual realms) where we were created of the substance (dust) of SPIRIT. For a review of the incarnational cycle, see Chapter 2–The Soul's Design.

Suffering Is Ordained of God–This is a belief that there is a divine law of compensation, and we must pay for our sins through suffering. The truth is that our experience is the result of what we set in motion with our thoughts and emotions, that which we plant in consciousness and allow to take root and flourish. If our minds hold only thoughts of good, good is produced. When the consciousness is filled with belief in thorns and thistles, thorns and thistles are produced. Jesus told us that our enemies were of our own household. These enemies are our own discordant thoughts and emotions that give birth to more discordant happenings. The secret of freedom is to know the truth. The truth is we are spiritual beings having human experiences. This planet and other planets are the classrooms, life is the teacher, and earthly experiences provide the lessons by which we learn. When we complete our lessons and overcome all discord, we will return to the spiritual realms with the wisdom we gained over many lifetimes.

Pain Is Ordained of God–This is a companion belief to the belief that suffering is ordained of God.

> *To the woman he said, "I will greatly multiply your pain in childbearing; in pain you shall bring forth children, yet your desire shall be for your husband, and he shall rule over you." (Genesis 3:16 RSV)*

'He' is the law of mind action (what you think or fear you create). Eve represents the feeling nature and Adam the intellect. We would like to have our thoughts rule our world and too many times that is exactly what seems to happen. The truth of the matter is the intellect (the masculine aspect of mankind) forms the thought, but the feeling nature or emotions (the feminine aspect of mankind) moves that thought into being. Working with SRT, we quickly realize that it is the emotions (female energy) that we attach to the events of our lives that sets up and returns to us a subsequent result, good or bad. This has held true from the moment of our conception in the consciousness of SPIRIT.

Anxiety Is a Way of Life–Mankind seems to have a natural propensity for worrying. This is understandable given our deep-seated belief that we are separated or have separated ourselves from our Source (the consciousness of God) by incarnating. We also fear that we will be forever separated from God. When we understand the truth, we will know that "'in him we live and move and have our being'" (Acts 17:28 RSV). Just take time to be still, enter into the awareness that your High Self is constantly with you and seeking to bring to your awareness that presence. When you do this, you will begin to hear the still, small voice of High Self. Inner pictures will begin to form and you will know what they mean, for a complete understanding will flash upon your consciousness. Then, if you have developed the ability to use the pendulum as a tool, you can ask questions of the Father within to ascertain the accuracy of what you are seeing, hearing, and knowing.

A Death Wish So We Can Return to God–Many religions teach that the only way you can be one with God is after you die and go to heaven. This seems to result in some people having a strong wish to die so that they might return to God. Yet, Jesus told us that He and the Father were one and prayed for all those that believed on Him, that they might be one in God even as He was. So, can we know God before we die? Certainly! The Scriptures also state, "Then you will call upon me and come and pray to me, and I will hear you. You will seek me and find me; when you seek me with all your heart" (Jeremiah 29:12-13 RSV). The heart represents the feeling nature (the feminine), and it is with the heart (feelings) that we find God, and not with the intellect (the masculine).

Anti-Time Conflict

There were several stages in your development as a spiritual being that ultimately led to the incarnational life you are presently experiencing. Before you entered the physical body, you were a spiritual body with a living soul or consciousness. Before that, you were an idea in the mind of God. Prior to that, you were thought in the consciousness of First Cause, SPIRIT. According to High Self, even before that, you experienced infinite levels of existence. (Refer to Chart 13–Programs Before Creation, and the explanation of that chart, in Chapter 15–Programming Before Formation, for more information).

The womb of creativity–where we are formed as idea, then as a spiritual body, then as a living soul–is before time as we know it from the incarnational experience. This is *anti-time*. When we come out of the womb of creativity into time, we are often in conflict as to our purpose in doing so. We may also feel that we were cast out of the garden of Eden where we had been placed as a soul during the gestation period. High Self indicates that we can clear the conflict by becoming consciously aware that we were not cast out of the consciousness of God. We chose to incarnate as part of the continuing process of learning and growing. Simply ask High Self to clear the anti-time conflict.

Soul Programs

Soul programs are set up when you are out of the physical body. One client, as a female in a past life, was raped and killed by a gang of teenage youths. After she was out of the body, she set up about fifteen negative energies such as hate, revenge, bitterness, and anger. Those were recorded directly in the soul, and not in the conscious and subconscious mind. Therefore, High Self could not clear them, but had to work with the soul so that she could release the energies and forgive the ones who had harmed her.

Polarity Beliefs

A polarity belief is any belief that tends to separate or polarize. These can be a belief in good and evil, a belief in two powers (God and the devil), or a belief that one race of people or color of skin is better than or worse than another. These are all prejudices that separate and cause conflict. All things are equal in the sight of God. We who are in the image and likeness of God should be the first to recognize and attempt to live from that knowledge. We have collected polarity beliefs in our computer banks over many lifetimes. It is time to clean out the computer, forgive the old beliefs, and replace them with ideas of the unity and oneness of all life.

Astrological Beliefs

Have you ever known anyone who would not leave the house until they had read their daily horoscope in the newspaper? I have. And if the horoscope indicates trouble in the offing, they believe it, establish energy of fear, and thus set in motion the very thing they fear. High Self tells me that there is not one person on the planet who has not picked up some negative astrological beliefs and stored them in their computer banks. Then, when circumstances in the present life are supportive, they run the destructive belief. Ask High Self to clear all destructive, discordant astrological beliefs.

Loss of Subconscious Integrity

When we are born into the physical body, the subconscious mind is completely sound and pure. The moment we take into our subconscious mind a discordant thought, belief, or emotion, we compromise the integrity of the subconscious mind. Never have I found a person who has not to some degree compromised the integrity of their subconscious. When you encounter loss of subconscious integrity, just ask High Self to restore it.

Dissipation of Vital Energies

There are over 450 ways that a soul can dissipate vital energy. One of them is to take on the belief in good and evil during the process of incarnating. Then, when the soul incarnates, it picks up the world energies that cause dissipation. You do not need to know all of the ways, just ask High Self to clear them.

Desire to Escape

There is a host of programs that come under this heading. Here are the ones most often encountered: a desire to escape responsibility for our actions; a desire to experience all of the good things of life and never encounter pain, challenge, or difficulty; or a desire to escape life and the process of learning through experience. High Self informs me that there are over 800 programs included under this heading.

Belief of Beliefs

These are often called "old wives' tales." This includes such things as believing that walking under a ladder is bad luck. A black cat crossing your path is even worse. A rabbit's foot and a four-leaf clover will bring good luck. There is no truth in these tales. A thought held in consciousness, charged with creative energy, and coupled with action creates the result. These beliefs divert our attention from the real cause of good or bad—our own beliefs and the positive or negative energy we attach to them.

Scarring

Scarring is a result of the soul being wounded and healed. The only thing I have discovered regarding scarring is that it may occur even before first incarnation. One client had so many programs that I was beginning to despair of them ever being completely cleared. I asked High Self if they could clear the soul completely, from top to bottom. They said they could, and I asked them to do the work. Immediately they gave a symbolic representation of the soul, and I saw with my inner eye a huge stainless steel cylinder. The cylinder appeared to be about four feet in diameter and twenty feet deep. When they started to clear the programs, it was as though a huge roto-rooter was going down into the cylinder to clean it. The steel sides began to appear and they were bright and shiny. However, there was a crack quite far down in the cylinder, and later a welded bead. Another image I have received is a mottled, dirty gray patina on the steel that seemed to be in the steel itself.

I verified these insights regarding the symbolism of the stainless steel cylinder by questioning my High Self. The mottled gray patina represents discordant and harmful soul programs established while the soul was out of the physical body. A crack indicates that the soul has been wounded, but not yet healed. When I asked them if they could and would heal the wound, it was as though a large thumb touched the crack, moved along it and it was healed—the area was smooth and free of cracks. The welded bead symbolizes a soul wound that has been healed, although scarring remains. These scars can be completely removed by asking High Self to heal them.

CHAPTER 15

Programming Before Formation

During late June of 1991, when we finished creating Chart 10–Miscellaneous Blocks, I asked High Self if there were going to be any more charts. They said "yes," and that there would be nine items on the next one. During the first part of July, 1991, while conducting a workshop in southern California, Charts 11 and 12 were given to me by SPIRIT. They are entitled Chart 11–Soul Energy Programming and Chart 12–Spirit Energy Programming. Since then, SPIRIT has given the additional charts numbered 13 through 31.

The programs listed on Charts 11 through 31 represent the steps we take on our soul's spiritual journey from our inception as an idea in the consciousness of the GODHEAD to the spiritual realms in which we were first formed as spiritual beings, to the physical worlds and the process of incarnation, and, finally, to our return to the GODHEAD. Although there are many pathways from the GODHEAD to physical expression and back again, the goal is the same: to learn to use creative energy so that when we return to the GODHEAD, we may assist in the creation and government of the next universe.

To clear programs listed on these charts, just ask High Self to clear them. I seldom go to any chart from 10 through 31 and research individual items. When any of these charts are indicated, I simply ask High Self if they can be cleared without research and have them cleared.

Chart 11—Soul Energy Programming

In Genesis, chapter 2, we are told that after the heavens and the earth were finished,

> *...there was not a man to till the ground. ... And the LORD God formed man of dust of the ground, and breathed into his nostrils the breath of life; and man became a living soul. (Genesis 2:5, 7 KJV)*

In Chapter 2–The Soul's Design, we discussed how the LORD God gave Adam and Eve (mankind) physical bodies or "garments of skins" (Genesis 3:21 RSV), and how they began the incarnational process. Genesis also tells us that before mankind became flesh, he was formed of God Consciousness ("dust of the ground" Genesis 2:7 RSV). The LORD God invested this being of consciousness with Its breath (life force) and man became a living, thinking extension of God Consciousness. As you will see, we existed in some form even before this time. But, for now, let us cover the programs that were set up when we were created as living souls. I call this programming "soul programming." This programming is part of our very soul makeup. Most souls that I research have all eleven items on Chart 11. These can be and usually are in layers. When you clear these programs, always ask if the programs are in layers, and, if they are, ask that they be cleared completely at all levels.

Programs the Soul Is Unaware of

The first item is 'programs the soul is unaware of.' No information has been given as to how these programs are set up. That they do exist and can cause problems becomes self-evident, for when the programs are cleared, many clients feel the shift in energy, and changes usually take place in their lives. Just make certain that if they come up to be cleared, you ask High Self to see that the work is done in depth.

Preprogramming

There are 5,000 basic elements that can go into soul programming. A particular soul may have from one to 5,000 of the aspects in any combination or order. Not being a mathematician, I can only guess that the total possible numerical combinations would be somewhere in the neighborhood of ten to the fifth power. These elements can be positive or negative.

Dysfunction of the Mind

Each soul is created in and of the consciousness of First Cause, SPIRIT, and held within the infinite mind of SPIRIT. The Hebrew word Jehovah means *"He-who-is–who-was–who-will-be manifest; the self-existent One"* (MBD). We exist because we are part of the manifestation of the ONE presence, power, and consciousness of the universe. Jehovah can be said to mean "he who extends himself; he who becomes himself as a living soul." Since Jehovah or SPIRIT is all there is, we are quite literally an extension of that ONE Consciousness working through individuated expressions of SPIRIT.

However, if SPIRIT, or Jehovah, extended and duplicated Itself, there would still be only SPIRIT, and since SPIRIT is perfect, there would only be a perfect duplicate of Perfection. Therefore, programming was introduced into all living souls that would bring forth an imperfect or flawed creature through dysfunction of the mind. You might say SPIRIT created a diamond in the rough so that it could be polished over time. Over eons of time, the diamond, by contact with many levels of consciousness and expression through the incarnational and other processes, would be self-polishing and self-learning and would grow into the brilliance of SPIRIT's purity and beauty.

Codependency of Different Aspects of the Soul

The basic path of the living soul was established by SPIRIT long before the soul entered the physical body. Each individual's path was based on the elements that went into the soul as preprogramming. The complete structure of the soul programming and the many aspects cannot be compromised as every aspect is dependent on every other aspect functioning in perfect order and harmony. High Self says that if inharmony occurs at the soul level and is not resolved, dissolution could take place and the soul would then go back to basic spiritual energy within the consciousness of SPIRIT.

Dysfunction of Thought

The thoughts of SPIRIT are orderly, harmonious, and pure. Therefore, a dysfunction of thought must be introduced or there are only perfect thoughts and there is no opportunity for the living soul to perfect itself as it follows the incarnational path. Thus, nothing would be learned or experienced except perfection, and the soul would not develop the ability to correctly use power and creative energy, a skill that is learned as a result of experiencing dysfunction incarnation after incarnation.

Genetic Soul Coding

There are certain SPIRITUAL qualities that are programmed into the soul as genetic coding. There are eighty-six total elements, twenty-two of which are listed on Chart 2–Soul Qualities. The task of each soul is to acknowledge, appreciate, and learn to use these characteristics in an orderly and harmonious way so that good is produced. When we fail to use them correctly in peace, love, wisdom, and order, discordant energy is accumulated and must be researched and cleared as described in Chapter 5–The Basic Steps of SRT.

Preprogramming of the Experiential Path

SPIRIT decided to extend Itself into being and experience something other than being absolute good. This could only be done by creating beings like Itself within Itself and have them experience. Each individuated expression of the ONE Consciousness–including you and me–has been keyed for a different experience–a preprogramming of the experiential path. Thus, no two of us are alike, yet we all began and are still contained in the consciousness of SPIRIT. High Self informs me that this is correct to the extent of my present understanding, and that is all that will be given at this time.

Dysfunction of Soul Consciousness

Because the soul is formed of SPIRIT substance (the "dust from the ground" spoken of in Genesis 2:7 RSV) and filled with SPIRIT Consciousness and Life (the breath of SPIRIT), it was created perfect. This, again, precluded any expression except a perfect clone of SPIRIT until dysfunctional factors were built in as part of each soul's makeup. Thus each soul was programmed to express in a unique and individual way.

Dysfunction of Expression

When a soul chooses to incarnate, an automatic dysfunction of expression engages so that every human being is different.

Miasma of the Soul

"Miasma" is a foreboding or deathlike atmosphere; a stain or pollution. We can understand incarnation as a miasma because the soul seems to enter into a deathlike state. Remember that Adam and Eve were told they would die the day they ate of the forbidden fruit. Thus, when they ate, they entered a deathlike atmosphere called incarnation. They did not actually encounter a physical death (as we think of death). Rather, they polluted or stained the pure essence of their soul consciousness and entered a state where they were, for all intents and purposes, dead to the reality that they were spiritual beings. They found themselves naked, exposed to a new realm of things which involved an impure consciousness (a belief in good and evil) and the physical or incarnational world. Certainly, the incarnational world is considered a dangerous, foreboding atmosphere.

Cleanse the Soul of Evil [and Karmic Penalty]

The other program that appears on Chart 11 has two aspects. The first program aspect that is vital to a complete clearing is the 'cleanse the soul of evil' program. When the soul partakes of 'the tree of the knowledge of good and evil,' it believes that the soul is filled with evil. This sets up another belief that there is an unavoidable 'karmic penalty' that will cause the soul to experience continuing pain, trouble, and sorrow for as long as it exists throughout space and time. Every incarnated soul has these programs, so make certain you ask that they be cleared.

Chart 12—Spirit Energy Programming

The programs listed on Chart 12 are the basic programs that go into the makeup of the spiritual body when it is formed at the Queen of Life level (see Chart 3–Levels of Soul Consciousness). Like the programs listed on Chart 11, the soul programs on Chart 12 can be in layers. It is important that you do not miss clearing any of the layers, or the programs will crop up later.

Preprogramming of Spirit by GOD

Before we were formed as living souls, we were created as spiritual bodies 'in the image and likeness of God' (Genesis 1:26-27). There are 150 elements that can go into the programming of the spiritual body by GOD or SPIRIT. Any number of the elements can be employed in any order or combination. This increases the number of possibilities for individualization. The spiritual body has a subconscious mind but no conscious mind. The conscious mind is the 'living soul' whose formation is discussed in Genesis 2:7 KJV. These two bodies (spiritual body and living soul) can be compared to the physical body in the mother's womb. It has a subconscious memory in every cell but does not have a conscious mind until the soul attaches to the fetus.

Potential Dysfunction of Spiritual Consciousness by GOD

There must be a dysfunction established as part of the makeup of the spiritual body, or there would only be a perfect expression of GOD or SPIRIT. The built-in dysfunction allows the spiritual body to express in its own unique way.

Codependency of Spirit on GOD

We are completely dependent on SPIRIT for our very existence, for in SPIRIT we live, and move, and have our being. We are what we are, because we are part of SPIRIT, an extension of SPIRIT's energy and likeness–we are forever in and of SPIRIT. All that we have is of SPIRIT, because SPIRIT is both source of all good and the gift–all is spiritual substance in myriad form.

> *Beloved, we are God's children now; it does not yet appear what we shall be, but we know that when he appears we shall be like him, for we shall see him as he is. (1 John 3:2 RSV)*

Jesus called himself the Son, the enlightened one of God. We too are sons of God and when we are enlightened, we will know the ultimate and complete truth of our being–we are SPIRIT. Many people have a belief that they are separate from GOD or SPIRIT and have their own creative powers and life. This is not true, as they are part of SPIRIT and can never be separated from SPIRIT except in their own beliefs. Separation would be like the leaf in the tree saying it is separate from the tree and has a life of its own. We are codependent on SPIRIT and when we attempt to separate, or believe we are separate from SPIRIT, we set up negative beliefs that must be eliminated. We are because SPIRIT (GOD) IS, and SPIRIT IS because we are that which SPIRIT expresses and expands consciousness through.

Dysfunction of Spirit by Thought

As pure spiritual bodies, our thoughts could only be functional and good for we lived in an absolutely pure state of being within the consciousness of SPIRIT. There had to be a means whereby each being would have the potential of learning lessons in order to use and expand consciousness. Until this means was introduced, we are only in Spirit consciousness and serve as a Cherub in the Light realms. The potential for imperfect or dysfunctional thoughts was set up so the process of manifestation could occur for those beings who choose the incarnational path of learning.

Twelve Aspects of Spirit as Genetic Coding

Jesus chose twelve special students whom He called apostles. Each of the apostles represents one of the twelve spiritual characteristics that every being is endowed with from the moment they are created. Thus there are twelve genetic codes that are part of each person's spiritual nature and potential. Peter symbolizes the spiritual characteristic of faith; Matthew, will; Thomas, understanding; Bartholomew, imagination; Simon, zeal or enthusiasm; Philip, power; John, love; James the son of Zebedee, wisdom; James the son of Alphaeus, order; Andrew, strength; Thaddaeus, elimination or denial; and Judas, life.

Very few people know that they have all of these characteristics as a genetic code that is programmed in when they were created as spiritual bodies. Like Jesus, each person must call forth and work with these characteristics in order to magnify his or her full spiritual potential. Ask to be cleared of any blocks to the full expression of these characteristics.

Dysfunction of Creative Energy by Emotions

Emotions move our thoughts into manifestation. Therefore, what we think and the emotional energy we attach to the thought determines to a great extent the framework of our experience. As spirit beings in the consciousness of SPIRIT, our emotions could only be of love and harmony. Partaking of the forbidden tree brought forth new experiences that were no longer pure. The first thing Adam said to God after eating the forbidden fruit was, " I heard the sound of thee in the garden, and I was afraid, because I was naked" (Genesis 3:10 RSV). Fear was the first dysfunctional emotion projected by the spirit being called Adam (representing all mankind), and we have been dealing with it ever since. Many people know that their fear creates more reason to fear, and, yet, they have a difficult time letting go of that fear. They have so much faith and belief in bad things happening, and so much fear supporting that belief, that they continue to create discordant experiences.

Dysfunction of Spirit by Error Consciousness

Created as spiritual bodies, we would always remain pure unadulterated Spirit unless the possibility of error consciousness is introduced. Once we have completed the incarnational, experiential path, these error beliefs must be cleared in order for the soul to return to the GODHEAD.

Dysfunction of GOD Consciousness at Spirit Level

We were created as spirit beings as an integral part of SPIRIT Consciousness, which is absolute Good. Dysfunctional factors were programmed into each spiritual body so that there could and would be a differentiation of the individual spirit beings. Otherwise there would only be SPIRIT Consciousness as one whole. Once the soul has completed the learning process through many incarnations, it returns to the GODHEAD and is ONE with ALL.

Loss of Seeing GOD

Each spiritual body is an independent expression of the ONE. A loss of seeing GOD or SPIRIT was set up so each soul would seek to follow its own path of learning and experiencing. Had we never lost sight of GOD, we would know completely the truth of our being, would expect GOD to do it all for us, and would never try our own wings. Just look at any person today who expects everything to be done by his mother, father, government, or a savior. He becomes dependent and nonproductive. If we constantly look to GOD to do it all, and GOD does it for us, we become slaves or automatons, taking no part in our own particular destiny. Our CREATOR gave us life, substance, and intelligence, and a world in which to access and work with our spiritual potential. It is obvious that when we refuse to exercise our own power and dominion to be and to become, and we expect someone else to do it for us, we are limited and dysfunctional. Still, many people expect and desire others to do everything for them.

Loss of Hearing GOD

Jesus said:

> *For this people's heart has grown dull, and their ears are heavy of hearing, and their eyes they have closed, lest they should perceive with their eyes, and hear with their ears, and understand with their heart, and turn for me to heal them.' (Matthew 13:15 RSV)*

We are fully aware that there are five physical senses. What we are not aware of is that there are also five inner spiritual senses. Unfortunately, we have lost contact with the five inner senses. Of these, seeing and hearing are the two most important. Yet many times we are blocked from our inner hearing and seeing because of programs that were established long before first incarnation. We can, over a period of time, reestablish these two important spiritual senses through the practice of prayer and meditation, by becoming still, and looking and listening for the still small voice within.

Several times in the past I have been told that I had psychic, intuitive abilities. However, it was not until I started work with SRT that I began to be aware of the inner pictures and sounds I was receiving directly from my High Self. My High Self tells me that they are giving me information 100% of the time when I am working with them. Sometimes I am very aware of that information and at other times I am not. It depends on whether I am looking outward with my consciousness, concentrating on the charts and pendulum, and depending on them for the information, or if I am working with my inner eyes and ears and looking inward for the answers. Your High Self is giving you information right now. Learn to look and listen within and you will be amazed.

Miasma of Spirit

Each person, before incarnating, was created as a spirit being: complete, perfect, eternal, wise, intelligent, and indestructible. The potential for imperfection (miasma) was necessary, or there could never be an extension of the spirit being into materiality. It would forever remain as a perfect potential within the body of SPIRIT and nothing more.

Chart 13—Programs Before Creation

It is fascinating to see, from my present perspective, how SRT has unfolded. In the beginning of my training, there were no charts, only eight words. Gradually, over a period of twelve years, the system has expanded and the knowledge increased until there are now thirty-three charts. By means of the charts, and the information contained therein, High Self has taken us backward in time until now we are clearing programs that go back to the very beginning of all things when "God CREATED the heavens and the earth" (Genesis 1:1 RSV). Charts 11 and 12 present the programs that were set up prior to first incarnation when we were created souls, and before that when we were created as spirits. Chart 13 takes us back even farther.

When High Self indicates that you or a client have a program on Chart 13, you find out at what stage it was established. Chart 13 lists the stages of development in which we lived before creation. All of the programs on this chart may be in levels, so make certain you ask High Self to clear all levels.

Idea

Before anything comes into fruition, there is first an idea. Consciousness holds the idea in mind and works on it, molding and shaping it into a blueprint that will finally be produced as the final product or happening. SPIRIT had the perfect idea of self-expression. That idea was placed in the womb of creativity where it was worked on, molded, shaped, and given its basic characteristics.

Chart 3–Levels of Soul Consciousness presents a level that has three levels within it and they are: King of Kings, Queen of Life, and Lord of Lords. King of Kings is the perfect idea of self-expression, or the ruling thought that is in the process of becoming. Queen of Life is the womb of creativity where the idea of self-expression is placed for nurturing and maturation of the spiritual body. Here the spiritual body is given its basic characteristics of what it will be when it begins to manifest, much as the human body is formed and shaped in the mother's womb. The womb of creativity, according to an inner picture I received, is a black hole, and when I asked my High Self if this were true, they said it was. There are 45,000 possible elements or factors that can go into the makeup of the idea. There can be anywhere from one to any number of these 45,000 possibilities in any mix or combination, making the total possibility ten to the infinite power squared. Lord of Lords is the law of the idea's expression, how it will project itself upon the screen of life–the living soul.

Thought

Before idea, there was thought. There has to be a consciousness, working through a mind, before anything can take shape and form. On the highest level, that consciousness is the GODHEAD and the Prime Mover above and behind all that is SPIRIT. This Consciousness works through an infinite mind to think into being ideas that form the divine blueprint of all that is and will be.

There are programs that were set up even at the level of thought and before that have to be cleared if the person would be totally free.

Infinite Levels Before Thought

I find through questioning my High Self that thought can go back infinite levels before Idea. This simply means that the GODHEAD is Alpha and Omega, without beginning or end, and the ideas, thoughts, and energies produced by the GODHEAD are also without beginning and end. Make certain you get all of the levels of thought when you are clearing. When thought comes up, I simply ask how many levels are involved and usually find that the number is infinite.

Levels 1 through 6

The paths called Levels 1 through 6 are found before thought and were established at the GODHEAD level (see Chart 3). I do not have much information on these paths, and fortunately, nothing other than the awareness that they exist is all that is needed to clear them.

High Self does indicate that there are 2,600 pathways by which we may come into being as a spiritual being and living soul. Contrary to Darwin's theory, High Self tells me that there is no direct link between the apes and a gradual transformation into the human form. There are links to the animals and other creatures, but not as Darwin and others have envisioned.

Level 1 has to do with the path of the sea and dolphins. Some of the sea creatures go through many incarnations as various sea creatures until at last they have graduated (grown in consciousness) to the level of dolphin. Then beings at the Supreme Consciousness level (see Chart 3) invest a quantum amount of energy into the dolphin soul and they become human beings in their next incarnation. Thus, slightly over 8% of the humans on this planet came through this path.

Level 1 also has to do with the birds and land animals which provide paths for humans. The bird with the highest consciousness is the eagle, and the consciousness of all other birds has to progress up to and through the eagle. That is the final goal and conclusion of the bird consciousness. Therefore, killing an eagle is a crime against the path of soul evolvement and should under no circumstance ever be done.

The land animal with the highest consciousness is the cow, and the only four-footed creature that has the ability to think to the same degree as man. That is why the East Indians consider the cow to be sacred. However, the cow is not the only path from animal to human. High Self says there are 540 animal paths that finally lead to human expression. Once the animal soul has completed its rounds of incarnation in order to experience, learn, and grow, very high beings at the level of Supreme Consciousness invest a quantum amount of energy into the animal soul and it is transformed directly into a pre-Neanderthal, Neanderthal, or human soul. The soul can then incarnate into the form of body which depicts the level of consciousness they have attained on a planet where their particular form of life is evolving.

My dog, Josh, a Chinese pug, had been with me during 261 of his previous lives, five of which were in this, my current, life. I have known him in past lives as elephant, tiger, lion, horse, dog, cat, chicken, rabbit, and many other animal forms. This was Josh's last incarnation as an animal. His next step is as a pre-Neanderthal man. I do not know the criteria that determine a being's next physical form, but I am certain each soul travels its right and perfect path.

Level 2 has to do with fire planets—ones that are in the fire or molten state in their formation. These planets are under the direction of the God of the particular solar system where the planet is being formed. Over this God is a High Council of beings who work with Vectors, beings who actually mold and shape the planet. Vectors also create mineral and microbe consciousness and invest the planet with the possibility of good and evil in preparation for the higher life forms of man, whether that life form is pre-Neanderthal,

Neanderthal, or human. Mineral consciousness can eventually be transformed into microbe consciousness, but never into pre-human or human consciousness. Microbe consciousness, after an extended period of time, can be invested with a quantum amount of energy by beings at the Universal God Consciousness level (see Chart 3) in preparation to becoming pre-Neanderthal. From pre-Neanderthal consciousness, they would graduate to Neanderthal or go directly to human form in their incarnational round, depending on the situations encountered, the lessons learned, and the attitudes and energy of consciousness they have established.

Level 3 has to do with plankton and land plants, either of which can be transformed directly into pre-Neanderthal. Plankton can also take the path of transformation into the higher level of sea creatures and eventually into dolphin before moving on into the human framework of expression.

Level 4 has to do with fish. Fish can come through the path of plankton or directly from the generation of atomic coding (see Level 6).

Level 5 is the direct transplant of humans from other planets by space ships who have been visiting our planet for many thousands of years. That is how both Lemuria and Atlantis, in the beginning, were peopled by higher level humans.

Level 6 has to do with the atomic coding of matter. This coding takes place before physical manifestation, but after the Big Bang, while the universe is still pure energy. Beings at the levels of Holy Spirit Consciousness, Christ Consciousness, Mentor Consciousness, Creator Consciousness, and Universal God Consciousness (see Chart 3) are the ones who do the genetic coding. As the universe begins to manifest by the vibration of the energy that makes up the as yet unformed galaxies and planets, the automatic genetic coding within the forming energy unfolds into the various atomic structures of the earth elements. There is a different genetic coding for all that will become manifest: earth, plants, microbes, fish, birds, animals, and so on.

There is also an atomic emotional coding that eventually becomes the physical human being inhabited by a living soul. This atomic structure is the first physical body form that the soul inhabits. It is the first form that has the life of the GODHEAD (Prime Mover) coupled with it, and it is filled with life, substance, and intelligence. This soul, when incarnated, must work to overcome the negative aspects of that emotional coding. The prime purpose of the incarnated soul is to learn to work with creative energy, the emotions, in the highest and best way.

There must be the investiture of emotion in the physical body, or the soul that inhabits it would not be challenged or tested, and thus would not learn and grow. The illusion is that the soul takes upon itself the limitations of the physical expression, and this illusion must be overcome for full expression of the soul's inherent potential. Emotions = energy + motion, or E-motion. Without emotion, there is no movement of thought or idea except on the spiritual level.

There are different levels or expressions of emotion, from inert matter, to physical being, to living soul, to spiritual body, and on up the ladder to the GODHEAD or Prime Mover. In the beginning there was an expansion from the GODHEAD of the E-motion or energy of creation which interpenetrates all. That "emotion" is a potential for expression by which we experience, learn, grow, and create. The mind is an instrument of consciousness, and the physical brain is an instrument of the mind and of consciousness. Emotions are the working energy of infinite SPIRIT, GODHEAD, Prime Mover moving into expression as it manifests Itself as all that is. That is why love is the most powerful creating and healing energy, for it is like GOD or SPIRIT and is SPIRIT.

Any dysfunctional energy that is set up through Levels 1 through 6 has to be cleared so the soul is free from all limitation and can return to the

GODHEAD with a full understanding of its creative potential and the ability to use that potential wisely and for the benefit of all.

Levels 7 and 8

High Self has revealed nothing about Levels 7 and 8, that were established at the GODHEAD level (see Chart 3), other than that these levels exist and can cause problems. When Level 7 or 8 is indicated as a problem area, just ask High Self to clear the energy.

Subconscious Stuff

When I ask High Self what subconscious stuff is, they simply show me a picture of leaves falling off a tree and being blown around by the wind.

Subconscious Odds and Ends

I have no information on this either. High Self simply shows me a garbage bag full of odds and ends (white elephants) that need to be dumped.

Fire Planet Energy

A person may be in the physical body and still be working on other levels of consciousness and in other places. One person who had fire planet energy had red blotches appear on his arms, and the palms of his hands would get flaming red. The red blotches would have little blisters. From the appearance, you would say he had been scalded. When he showed me these spots, I had an inner picture of fire on an extremely large scale. It turned out that he was a council member for a fire planet—a planet in the molten stage of formation. He was picking up the energy of the vectors who were doing the actual work of formation as well as the energy of the God of the solar system where the planet was being formed. When we cleared that energy and a belief that he was responsible for the vectors and had to pick up their energy, the red marks and blisters faded. Since that time, I have encountered several people who were working with fire planets, and as a result had been experiencing discomfort. Remember, you are in God's image and likeness. Since SPIRIT is everywhere present, you can be also. You can live parallel lives, future lives, lives in a parallel universe, serve others as their High Self, guide, or Guardian Angel or in some other office, all at the same time you are here on the planet in physical form.

Animal Energy

One of the major issues that has come up from Levels 1 through 6 is a carry-over of animal energy from animal incarnations. One child would not stay in her crib. She was okay in her brother's or her parent's beds, but would scream and carry on every time she was placed in her own crib. When the parents mentioned her problem, I saw an inner picture of her as a tiger. She had been captured and placed in a cage where she was tortured to death by being jabbed with spears. It was a slow and painful death for her and the crib reminded her of the cage.

Imprint of Brain Damage

This program is established before infinite levels of thought. Imprint of brain damage is not a correct term regarding this energy; however, High Self says there is no adequate term in the human language to describe what they are presenting. Just ask High Self to clear it when it comes up.

Creator Programming

These are programs that are set up by the Creator in order to bring forth the ultimate expression of the manifest realms and the testing of the souls as they incarnate to learn and grow. These programs may be made up of any of the items listed on the charts found in this book. Just research as necessary and have High Self clear them. There will be times when all you have to know is that there is a program, and High Self will clear it.

Chart 14—Pre-Fall of Consciousness, Creating the Illusion

Chart 13—Programs Before Creation lists steps and paths in the creative process. This is the process of entering lower and lower vibrations until at last the soul enters a physical body as part of the learning process. This is seen as a fall in consciousness. Programs listed on Chart 14 were established prior to this lowering of vibrations, and are thus designated 'pre-fall of consciousness' programs. The physical worlds are the realms of illusion that we enter when we incarnate and where we believe we are separated from SPIRIT. This illusion is created by the GODHEAD that there might be a process of experiencing and learning.

Although High Self says items on Chart 14 need to be cleared and the energies balanced, there is in reality not much for us to do, other than to ask High Self to clear any discordant beliefs or energies involved and to balance all of the energies so they are positive and in harmony. We can know that on a spiritual level all is well for we have never left the consciousness of SPIRIT—we are ONE now and always. Affirm this truth; know it with every fiber of your being, "I AM ONE with Yahweh, the SPIRIT. In Yahweh I live and move and have my being. I am whole, complete, and at peace." Yahweh is the expression of all life, substance, and intelligence beginning at the GODHEAD. High Self says that Yahweh was lonely, wanted companionship, and to experience Itself, so extended Itself. Jehovah (the Hebrew name for God or Yahweh) means *"the self-existent One"* (MBD). Another way to say this is "He who reveals Itself to Its creation, through Its creation, as Its creation." (For more information, see the explanation about the GOD level in Chapter 4—Infinite Service.)

Conscious Mind Programs Type I

Type I programs are pre-programmed and are eventually established in the conscious mind of the physical body. These are set up by beings at the lowest level of the Universal God Consciousness level when the soul begins its incarnational process. There is no limit to the number of items that can be stored in the conscious mind of the physical body.

Conscious Mind Programs Type II

Type II programs are set up in the conscious mind of SPIRIT, or I AM. Another name for I AM is Yahweh, and it is at the I AM level that the prototype (spiritual manifestation) for all that is to be formed physically is created, and the basic programs for the individual souls are installed. The maximum number of these programs is 999. However, there can be unlimited layers of the 999 programs.

Light Energy Discord

This has to do with the discord set up at the Light, or GODHEAD, level in order to bring forth the Light beings who eventually incarnate in human form. Each Light being is intended to reflect the image and likeness of its CREATOR. However, there had to be discord at the Light energy level in order that the individual expressions of SPIRIT are different and unique. For if there were no discord there would only be perfect SPIRIT. There would be no formed universe containing individual worlds. In Job 38:7 RSV these beings are called "morning stars," and they existed before the worlds were formed.

Misuse of Life Meaning

The ultimate meaning of life is to be spiritual, or perfect beings of Light, not physical beings struggling in a world of illusion. We were never intended to incarnate just to wander in a dream-like state. We were to remain in spiritual consciousness and be companions to SPIRIT in whose image and likeness we were created. Each Light being was given the spiritual gifts of life, substance, and intelligence. Some of them chose to take their spiritual gifts and incarnate, "took his journey into a far country" (Luke 15:13 RSV of the Prodigal Son parable Luke 15:11-32 RSV). When we misuse life meaning, we are not awake to our true spiritual existence.

Misuse of Energy in Creating

When we were simply Light beings, we deliberately chose to partake of 'the tree of the knowledge of good and evil' and incarnate, which was a misuse of spiritual energy in creating. We fell from the consciousness of Yahweh and entered the state of consciousness called illusion, or the physical world. Yahweh is The Pure Consciousness of All Wisdom, Light, and Love–SPIRIT. We wanted to experience physicality, the consciousness of good and evil, that we might learn, gain wisdom, and become like our CREATOR. In doing so we entered into the consciousness of good and evil and have a difficult time believing that there is no evil, only lessons to be learned. Thus, we misuse creative energy when we set up discordant beliefs and energies that we continue to experience thousands of lifetimes until we learn that the only reality is love.

Animal Consciousness Programs

These are the programs each incarnated individual inherits by partaking of the "tree of the knowledge of good and evil" (Genesis 2:17 RSV). We were cast out of the garden of Eden, or consciousness of SPIRIT, given the physical body called "coats of skins" (Genesis 3:21 KJV), and began the learning process. One of the major things that happened was our belief in separation from SOURCE. This was implied as the "first death" (Genesis 2:17). Upon incarnating, we adopted the belief that we are animals in nature and those beliefs have caused us difficulty, pain, and all of the inherent ills and problems of the human condition.

Energy Forms Attached at Higher Levels

These are actually beliefs having to do with the symbolism of the 'tree of the knowledge of good and evil,' which brought about our descent into the darkness of the physical realms. A belief is simply mind energy and has no true reality. Therefore all beliefs of human consciousness are illusions. All false, or illusory, beliefs will eventually give way to the ultimate knowing that there is only SPIRIT.

Other Souls Bonded to the Soul

A soul is a living thought form created by Yahweh, and all souls are bonded together as one in the consciousness of SPIRIT. What we do as individual human beings affects all souls. Not until all souls are in harmony with all other souls is there a complete reunion with SOURCE. Clearing the energy between souls that are bonded together brings harmony and peace and a return to Oneness.

Subtle Ethers

The subtle ethers are the creative fibers of the universe that tie each individual to the GODHEAD. They have to be cleared that we might know that we are one with the GODHEAD and that the SPIRIT of Truth and Oneness moves within us at every moment when we allow it to do so. We can tune into that SPIRIT and find peace, harmony, order, love, joy, and all things good as we become still and know the Yahweh presence.

Etheric Body Out of Balance

The etheric body is the pattern for the physical body. It is important that it be kept balanced and in tune with SPIRIT. This can be accomplished by simply knowing that we are one with Yahweh, and that in Yahweh there is only truth and balance. Yahweh is the perfect idea of self-expression of the SPIRIT. It is the Son of God, the Christ.

Chart 15—I AM Level Consciousness Programs

In Chapter 4–Infinite Service, I explained Chart 3–Levels of Soul Consciousness. Near the top of that chart, I listed *two thousand levels* and indicate that the top level (or the 2,000th level) is called I AM or Yahweh. That is where programs on Chart 15 were established.

High Self compares the first seven items on Chart 15 to the seven days of creation as outlined in the first chapter of Genesis. The eighth item is the living and experiencing of the soul through the process of incarnation in a physical world.

The programs on Chart 15 are set up at the I AM level of consciousness (see Chart 3) and only I AM or higher level beings can clear them. Some of the programs are in layers, so make certain to ask that all programs be cleared in depth.

In order for Yahweh to extend Itself, a duality had to be set up or there would only be the ONE, I AM–Yahweh. Therefore, the first factor on Chart 15 is ***Duality of the I AM Level Consciousness***. Yahweh established a belief of something else besides pure single consciousness. This is a dream state or illusory state of the I AM Consciousness. At this stage, Yahweh formed the mental image of all that would become–the divine blueprint of self-extension. This divine blueprint did not have form or substance. "In THE BEGINNING God [the GODHEAD (Yahweh; Elohim; I AM)] CREATED the heavens and the earth. The earth was without form and void" (Genesis 1:1-2 RSV).

The next step taken by Yahweh was the expansion of the ideas of dualism, which caused a war or discord in the pure consciousness of heaven. Thus the second factor was given as ***War in Heaven (the I AM Level Consciousness)***. Dualism always sets up energy of conflict, and the proliferation of dualism creates even more conflict. We see this on every hand in our world. We have the dualism of race, creed, countries, and beliefs. The perceived polarity of the male and female which is so prevalent in our society is also a program of duality. Yet, that is the very nature of the formed world and there is a great need to balance and harmonize all aspects of life and return to the realization that there is only ONE, and WE are IT. When we learn to accept things as they are and then work to bring change through harmony, we will accomplish unity without conflict.

Another factor is ***Separation from Love***–separation from the pure consciousness of I AM. The Scriptures state, "He who does not love does not know God; for God is love. ...God is love, and he who abides in love abides in God, and God abides in him" (1 John 4:8, 16 RSV). When you dwell in the consciousness of Love (I AM) and let Love guide your way, you will never go wrong and will have attained the I AM Consciousness.

The fourth factor is ***Light Realm Discordant Energy***. This was a natural result of the first three movements within the consciousness of the I AM, when discord was established.

The fifth factor is ***Dysfunction of Space-Time Energy***. High Self showed this to me as a ripple that was formed in the woof and weave of the fabric of the universe.

The sixth factor in the process of differentiation was a ***Dysfunction of Creative Energy***. This was a form of short circuit in the perfectly balanced energy of the super super universe (see Chapter 4–Infinite Service) that allowed for the infinite variety of vibrations that precede manifestation. This is like a tear in the fabric of the universe.

The seventh factor, ***Dysfunction of the I AM Level Consciousness***, represents the extending of the dream or illusion on all levels of expression.

The final factor, ***Programs Coming Up***, symbolizes all of the possible scenarios that can be set up so each soul may experience its own unique experiential path. Another way of stating the eighth item is that it is the ever-rising current of universal energy that brings forth the proliferation of dualistic ideas.

I know this is a very sketchy description of the terms on Chart 15, but the I AM does not want to give any more information at this time–it is material for a future book.

Chart 16—Fall of Consciousness

At the time of this writing, ONE is the final, ultimate, and absolute top level of consciousness listed on Chart 3–Levels of Soul Consciousness. High Self assures me that there is nothing higher than ONE, although there are 2,000 levels within ONE and each level is infinite. The GODHEAD or SPIRIT is at the top level of ONE. This is the point at which all things that we perceive in the physical world had their beginning. Behind SPIRIT, but not higher than, is LUMINOUS, WELLSPRING, and GRAND-I/WHOLE.

At the ONE level of consciousness, the energy of the ultimate universe is cubed and vibrating at an extremely high level. It is here, at the infinite consciousness of ONE, that SPIRIT began the process of forming, in consciousness, the divine blueprint of all that would become. Remember that this was only the inner picture, or blueprint, and had no physical substance. This is what is meant by the statement in Genesis 1:1-2 RSV:

> *In THE BEGINNING God CREATED the heavens and the earth. The earth was without form and void, and darkness was upon the face of the deep; and the Spirit of God was moving over the face of the waters.*

Water represents the unformed potential of all things that will become. Thus the items on Chart 16 had their inception as part of the divine blueprint held in the consciousness of SPIRIT when everything was formed 'in the beginning.'

ONE is made up of an infinite number of beings at infinite levels of consciousness, working as ONE consciousness. There is complete agreement, harmony, unity, and order at this level of being. Since the divine blueprint was created in perfection, the appearance of separation was set up, for as long as 'all that was formed' remained in the consciousness of SPIRIT, there would be only perfection—nothing less than SPIRIT, containing all perfect ideas, could exist. From these perfect ideas come the spiritual realms at the I AM or Yahweh level.

Rebellion to ONE

High Self states that, although there was not an actual rebellion, the process of separation appeared to be rebellion, and set up within the consciousness of individuals a belief that there was indeed open rebellion. The most important thing to remember when we talk about life is that all we perceive is illusion. High Self agrees with this and states that *in Truth* there has never been a separation and we are all one with the highest level of ONE at the GODHEAD.

Cast Out of Heaven

As long as we believe that we are cast out of heaven or the consciousness of SPIRIT, we must strive to change that belief, or we will continue to feel separated from SPIRIT and lost in a world of illusion. I have actually worked with people who have had a strong belief that they caused the war in heaven and were cast out of heaven into outer darkness.

Separation from ONE

The illusion of being cast out of heaven causes the belief that we have been separated from SPIRIT and are eternally lost and forever damned.

Fall from Grace

We believe that we have fallen from the grace or love of SPIRIT and are simply miserable human beings lost in a world of sin. Unfortunately, this false belief is promoted by many religions.

Shift into Unreality

Although we are still in the consciousness of SPIRIT, we have strong beliefs that God is unreal and that the only reality is what we experience through the five senses.

Fall into Darkness

This is a darkness of mind that keeps us bound to the illusion of separation from SPIRIT.

Loss of Spiritual Sight

Falling into darkness has affected our spiritual sight and to a large degree we see only the outer world. Until complete spiritual sight is restored, we will continue to wander in the darkness of the incarnational world, paying obeisance to the illusion of its false reality.

Loss of Spiritual Hearing

Jesus said, "Having eyes do you not see, and having ears do you not hear? And do you not remember?" (Mark 8:18 RSV). He was talking about looking beyond the outer appearances to the inner work of SPIRIT and knowing that SPIRIT is not only the SOURCE, but the substance of all things.

Blocks to Emotional Expression

Bob Toben and Fred Alan Wolf, in their book on quantum physics, *Space-Time And Beyond*, state that thoughts are particles and emotions are the wave forms that move the thoughts into expression. High Self agrees with this and further states that blocks to the emotions were set up as a damper on improper use of the creative energy of emotion. This concept also shows up on Chart 10–Miscellaneous Blocks in another form called 'inhibitors.' Should the emotions remain uninhibited, the negative ones could become so strong that they could destroy a physical world.

Blocks to Mental Expression

This final item is a natural result of the whole process of rebellion, separation, and fall, a belief that there might be something that seems to be different and apart from SPIRIT and has its own form of expression. It is part of the whole illusion or dream that SPIRIT is dreaming and we are major characters in the dream.

Chart 17—Fine Tuning

Once we have cleared programs listed on Charts 11 through 16, SPIRIT says *fine tuning* is in order. This is a harmonizing process and is of vital importance to the soul. Fine tuning could be likened to a mechanical tune-up of your automobile that makes it run and perform more efficiently.

Regardless of the makeup of the items on this chart, or when they were established, High Self can clear all of them in a matter of moments. It should now be obvious to you that the process of creation, formation, extension into incarnation and the lessons learned are interwoven and the soul is not completely free until all is experienced and learned and all the programs are cleared at depth back to SPIRIT.

Blocks to the Creative Force

I explained in Chapter 2–The Soul's Design that man has 18 bodies. These were created so that we could work with the ideas of consciousness (the mental) and bring those ideas into being through the creative energy (the emotions). All of the bodies have to be cleared of discord in order for the soul to return to the Light. Some of the blocks to be cleared include are beliefs in separation, discord, inharmony, duality, and limitation in all of their myriad forms.

Unwillingness

The next four programs–Unwillingness to Accept Change; Unwillingness to Let Go of Old Beliefs; Unwillingness to Cooperate with High Self; Unwillingness to Learn–are obvious in their meaning. So many people are unwilling to understand that every experience of life is part of the constantly expanding, changing, growing process of learning to work with High Self, and only by consistent, conscious effort to move into greater truth can we attain the ultimate goal of becoming one with SPIRIT. It is of utmost importance to understand that truth rises ever upward from a lesser truth to a greater truth, and eventually to the Truth of SPIRIT. A church, or for that matter, any spiritual movement or soul must have a constantly growing edge into higher spiritual consciousness or it is dead and founded on an old, outmoded belief system–a solidified monument to a partial truth.

Susceptibility to Lower Forces

Susceptibility to lower forces has to do with Chart 5–Blocks and Interferences listed on the chart as well as susceptibility to sense-consciousness or previous animal paths and animal programs.

Abdication of Spiritual Responsibility

This is a belief that someone else can 'do it for you,' such as a priest, savior, or God. Often this type of abdication is caused by adhering to parent's beliefs or old-time religion. There are two paths to higher consciousness. One is religion, or man's beliefs about God; the other is a spiritual walk with the High Self which is an inner attunement rather than a mental head trip. Unfortunately, religion and the spiritual path are often diametrically opposed. Most religions teach that a savior figure assumes your spiritual responsibility and your sins. A person on the spiritual path who is walking with the High Self knows that a savior is one who shows the way to spiritual freedom and not one who does it all for them. The effort of overcoming and walking in the wisdom of SPIRIT, under the direction of the High Self, and following the teachings of a savior who is in tune with his High Self is up to each individual.

Abdication of Mental Responsibility

When we abdicate our mental responsibility, we lack the understanding that we each create our own life and experiences through our mental patterns of thought and belief. Not realizing the importance of our thoughts, we allow them to run uncontrolled, thus creating chaos in our lives. Some people do not understand that their lives do not change after the clearing work is done simply because they are not taking on the mental responsibility for bringing about new and better patterns of thought and action.

Abdication of Emotional Responsibility

Abdication of emotional responsibility may cause a person to blame others for his or her uncontrolled emotional responses to life. The emotions are the catalyst, or creative energy, that moves thoughts into being. Therefore, it is important to look at the emotions, take charge of them, and change them as necessary in order to produce a more harmonious expression.

Abdication of Physical Responsibility

Abdication of physical responsibility indicates that the person believes he or she can use his or her physical body any way they wish without repercussion. Or they may believe that they can physically harm others without fear of personal or spiritual repercussion. The physical body is the temple of the soul and how it is treated is vital to the sojourn of the soul in the flesh. Also, how we use the physical body to bless or mistreat others is important. Anytime we blame someone else or something else for our condition of life, we abdicate spiritual, mental, emotional, and physical responsibility.

Reasons Behind Conscious Programs

These are set up at the level of Lord (see Chart 3). This is where we begin to work with the first level of our self-expression. At that level, we determine what we will experience in the future and how we will manifest that experience. It is there that the basic outline is formed for what we will experience and become. Once we have learned the lessons, we can release the reasons behind conscious programs and move into higher realms of being.

Belief in the Necessity of Meditation

In the beginning of our human path, the belief in the necessity of meditation is of vital importance, for that is the way to become still and listen to the "still small voice within"–the High Self. However, once you are working with the High Self and other spiritual committees, the moment that you pick up the pendulum, verify that you are clear, and start the questioning process, you are in tune with the still small voice of the Father within. From then on, meditation may be used simply to rest in the silence and renew your energy. My High Self says that I am at all levels of awareness (alpha, beta, delta, theta, and SPIRIT) the moment I tune in to my High Self to work for myself or someone else.

Desire to Reestablish Programs

This is the belief that we might lose what has been gained along the experiential path if our programs are cleared. We never lose the knowledge, wisdom, or understanding gained from any experience. What we lose is the discordant energy that causes pain, fear, anxiety, and so on.

Pick up Discordant Energy

A person can have a program to pick up discordant energy from the atmosphere or from others around them as a means of experiencing conflict, or as a way to create challenges that must be overcome in order to experience growth in consciousness.

Savior Complex

A person with a savior complex has a desire to keep others from experiencing the challenges, pain, and problems that are a part of the experiential path. They take upon themselves the other person's problems, never realizing that the other person still keeps them. The savior complex person has only increased their own painful load. A true savior is one who helps the other person understand that the planet is a school room for the soul and experiences are lessons that have been chosen in order to learn and grow. Then they encourage the person to learn, release, and move along the spiritual path.

Messiah Complex

A person with a messiah complex desires to make themselves responsible for another's pain. A true messiah is a spiritual teacher of Truth; there is no pain, only difficult lessons to be learned. Pain comes when a person chooses a particular lesson and then resists or refuses to learn and move through that lesson.

Desire to Suffer

This is the negative belief that lessons are better learned through suffering and that suffering makes one pure and holy.

Issues

These are simply the things we choose to experience along the path of spiritual unfolding. An issue can be the decision to encounter a difficult relationship with a particular soul along the path or a particular disease or diseases. Issues are individually-chosen, unique lessons of living.

Sensitivity to Others' Energy

This is a negative belief that we are callous and harsh if we do not suffer along with everyone else. It is also a belief that we are somehow responsible for another's suffering.

Hidden Vows

When explaining Chart 10—Miscellaneous Blocks in Chapter 14—Miscellaneous Blocks, we discussed heart vows which are made during religion-oriented lives. We also discussed how we set up vows that are part of the 'major beliefs' when we came out of anti-time into physical incarnation. You can also have hidden vows that are set up at the Majestic Consciousness level (see Chart 3) as your soul begins the development of its ruling consciousness, preparatory to incarnating. I have no clues as to what the vows actually are.

Chart 18—Higher Level Blocks

Chapter 4—Infinite Service, presents an outline of the groups of beings that preside over different levels of the universe, from the level of human consciousness to the ultimate universe. The final group is called ONE. There is a complicated process that takes place as all things are planned, modeled, and created. Everything starts at ONE and is filtered down and governed by the many beings who make up the divine hierarchy. The divine hierarchy introduces factors during our formative process that can have a lasting effect on our individual lives. We must nullify these factors as we return back up the spiritual ladder from soul learning to SPIRIT knowing, from the son of man to the Son of God, from darkness back to SPIRIT. The order of the items listed on Chart 18 may not seem like a logical sequence; however, High Self says it is correct. The blocks are explained in the order in which they appear on the chart, starting with blocks that appear on the left side.

Beings of God Consciousness Level Blocking

These are high level beings involved with the programs set up for the formation and creation of a universe and all that is contained within it.

This is where what the Eastern writers have called "the illusion" begins. It is necessary to clear the soul of all beliefs that the illusion, pain, and suffering are real or necessary.

Programs in the Conscious Mind of ONE

The programs experienced on all levels of being were initially blueprinted in the conscious mind of ONE or SPIRIT, so that is the next thing to be cleared.

Programs in the Subconscious Mind of I AM

The I AM presides over the super super universe. At this level, the spiritual prototype for all that will become the formed worlds is created. You do not need to know anything about these programs in order to have High Self clear them.

Ninth Level of Supreme Council Blocks

The ninth level of the Supreme Council is where the plans and directives for all of the super super universes are delineated and the formative process begins.

Programs in the Subconscious Mind of I AM THAT I AM, God of Planet

When a soul incarnates in a solar system, they are subject to the laws of the planet as set up by the God of the planet. We sometimes experience blocks at this level because this is the point at which we enter the physical realms after having partaken of 'the tree of the knowledge of good and evil.' We begin to work with the belief in good and evil and must turn to the God of the planet for guidance and a way out of the dilemma shaped by the duality of our human consciousness. For a more complete explanation of I AM THAT I AM. (For more information on I AM THAT I AM, see the explanation about the GOD level in Chapter 4—Infinite Service.)

Blocks from God Over Sun

When we incarnate in a solar system, the God over the sun in that solar system sets up blocks to wisdom and light so that we walk in darkness and ignorance as part of the learning process.

Programs in the Subconscious Mind of ONE

All that is formed (blueprinted) in the conscious mind of ONE is registered and stored in the subconscious mind of ONE. Since we are an extension of ONE, we have those programs.

Blocks from the Council within the 2,000 Levels

Clearing Infinite Council blocks attunes the soul to SPIRIT, so that we never again feel separated.

> *He who conquers, I will make him a pillar in the temple of my God; never shall he go out of it, and I will write on him the name of my God, and the name of the city of my God, the new Jerusalem which comes down from my God out of heaven, and my own new name. (Revelation 3:12 RSV)*

There we are totally at rest and work as ONE to draw blueprints for all that will become future universes.

Chart 19—How to Change Your Life

(See Chapter 20—Changing Your Life)

Chart 20—Refining Consciousness

Chart 20 contains a lot of odds and ends that need to be cleared up for the highest welfare of the soul and for complete attunement to the GODHEAD. The items on Chart 20 may be in levels, so make certain you ask High Self to clear all levels. Then check to ascertain that they are all cleared. Even after programs on this chart are cleared, you may run into hidden programs that are blocking a change in outer expression. I sometimes find higher level beings that are keeping a person from healing or experiencing a greater expression of life.

Programs Not on Charts at All Levels

These programs start at SPIRIT, in the beginning, and are encountered at every level of being, from SPIRIT into the lowest manifest level and back to SPIRIT.

Conscious/Subconscious: All DNA, Chromosomes, Paths, Compartments, and Levels at All Levels of Consciousness

These programs start at SPIRIT and interpenetrate all levels of both spiritual and manifest substance. These are subtle influences that may affect even rocks and plants, for all have life. Since there are 2,600 pathways, including the rocks and plants, by which we may eventually come to inhabit a physical body, all subtle influences that may be a carry-over from these paths must be cleared.

Hidden Programs at GOD Levels

GOD levels are the first seven groups of God at the level of GOD (see Chart 3–Levels of Soul Consciousness). They are responsible for solar systems and the programs that control and influence any soul that incarnates in the system. Many people have incarnated in more than one solar system and so may be carrying several sets of these hidden programs.

Inharmony at the ONE Level

Inharmony was set up during the blueprinting of all that would become the created heavens and earth.

Fine Tuning at the ONE Level

Fine tuning is done only after the soul has completed its learning process and has returned to SPIRIT from which it came. This brings the soul into complete harmony with its SOURCE.

Lessons to Accomplish Before Moving On, Working with ONE

Once the soul has returned to SOURCE, there it must learn before it is ready to join fully in the process of forming the divine blueprint for the next super super universe. Although time is not experienced as it is while we are in human form, it may take millenniums to prepare the I AM being (the soul who has returned to the GODHEAD) to take a full and complete part in the divine creative process.

Higher Level Issues by ONE

These are higher level issues that must be experienced and learned so that each soul who has returned to the GODHEAD and become an illumined being may be prepared for the work to be accomplished at the level ONE.

Imbalance of the Etheric Body at the ONE Level

The etheric body which was created for each individual at the ONE level was whole, perfect, and in complete harmony and balance. During the process of becoming, incarnating, and learning, the etheric body got out of balance and it is necessary to restore that balance at the ONE level.

Additional Programs Types I and II at the ONE Level

Type I and II programs have to do with the establishment of positive creative programming within both the conscious and subconscious minds of the soul. These are the higher teaching and refining processes that take place in order to completely harmonize all levels of soul to ONE.

CHAPTER 16

Charts 21 through 31

Chart 21—Final Items this ONE Universe

This chart, as with the other charts, developed gradually over a period of time as I worked with clients and taught classes. Some of these programs can be in levels. Ask High Self to clear the whole chart, all levels and all layers.

Programs Not on Charts

Sometimes there are items that fit no specific category, so High Self simply calls them programs not on charts.

Check List

There were a number of individual items that I was asking High Self about one by one. Tiring of this process, I asked High Self if we could refer to them collectively as "Check List" and put that on the chart. They indicated this would be fine.

Hidden Programs, Issues, 9,999

Sometimes there are hidden programs at various levels of soul consciousness and/or individual issues that require no research. Additionally, there is what High Self calls the 9,999 items at the level of One.

Raise the Soul and Committees to the Highest Level on Chart 3

When High Self indicates that there are no more programs to research or clear, it is necessary that the soul and the person's committees (Guardian Angels and High Self) be raised to the highest level shown on Chart 3.

The ALL Category

I was working with another set of individual items that High Self would not put on the "Check List," so I asked if we could call it "The ALL Category" and have all the items cleared without having to ask individually. They agreed.

18 Bodies and 90 Minds

After adding "The All Category" to the chart, High Self indicated that there are items in the 18 bodies and 90 minds that need clearing, so we added it to the chart as well.

Odds and Ends

High Self indicated there were still more odds and ends in this universe that need to be cleared and they were added to this chart.

Seven Seals and Bottomless Pit

High Self said that the symbolism referred to as the 'seven seals' and 'bottomless pit' in the book of The Revelation (4:1 and 9:1-2) also needs to be cleared. According to High Self, the book of The Revelation is 97% the process of SRT.

Alpha to Omega Search, Clear, and Harmonize

At this point, the old akashic record has been cleared and the new record written. However, there is still work to be done for the soul as this is not the final edition of the record. Thus, the current edition of the soul record must also be kept clear.

Something Else

When High Self indicated there was another program that was not already on the charts, I asked if it could be put on the "Check List" or "The All Category." They said no, but gave permission for it to be included on the chart as 'something else.'

Open to Receive Greater Good

This was the next item that High Self said to add to this chart. They gave no other information regarding it.

Desire to Suffer

High Self revealed that the soul sometimes has a desire to suffer because of a false belief that suffering pleases God. Suffering does not please God; it only causes pain to the individual. This program is different from the program on Chart 17–Fine Tuning.

Past Lives the Soul Does Not Want to Examine

Sometimes the soul has programs it does not want to look at because the pain that was involved is intense and there is a fear that looking at the lives will cause more pain. Rest assured that the programs have to be cleared so that they will not come up and cause pain. It is much simpler to clear the programs and get rid of them than it is to have them come up later, cause pain, and not know the source of the problem.

Chart 22—New ONE Universe

The new ONE universe began on April 24, 1993. High Self gave me Chart 22 exactly one Earth year to the day after the new ONE universe was begun. High Self says that it is already over 900 billion years old. Wow! Talk about there being no time or space in SPIRIT!

During a workshop in Michigan on April 24, 1994, High Self said there would be another chart with eleven items on it. They were referring to Chart 22. Once a soul has been cleared all the way to the GODHEAD, it has achieved the eighteenth or ALL mind. From then on, it is part of everything that is created and formed, including the new ONE universe. Once your soul is part of the new ONE universe, you can and usually do pick up blocks, interference, and energies from being so completely involved in the unfolding of that new ONE universe. These things need to be cleared and the soul blocked from ever becoming involved in the new ONE universe. This is what is accomplished when you ask High Self to clear Chart 22. You will notice that Chart 22 covers everything for the new ONE universe that was cleared for the soul as part of the process of becoming in this new ONE universe.

Past Lives at the I AM Level

These are the experiences of all souls and their various paths (past lives) of learning, growing, and experiencing in the spiritual realms before the first incarnation. The spiritual realms are created at the 2,000th level of the I AM level (see Chart 3–Levels of Soul Consciousness). These realms, called the garden of Eden in the *Bible*, extend all of the way down to the level of Light Status. From 96% to 99% of all the knowledge that the soul gains is through the spiritual beingness while living in the garden of Eden, not through the incarnational, physical body and its process. Thus 'past lives at the I AM level' or garden of Eden, needs to be cleared.

Past Lives in the New ONE Universe

You are the incarnational experience of every living soul who has been or will be incarnated in the new ONE universe. The past lives from the first incarnation to the last incarnation of every soul need to be cleared, renewed, and set in order.

Reservations to Expanding Consciousness Once Universal God Consciousness Is Attained

Many people and some souls believe that there is nothing higher than the level of Universal God Consciousness shown on Chart 3. This is made evident by the fact that most channeled material, if it is legitimate, is from the area of the arrows shown on Chart 3. Even I was excited when High Self revealed that category since I also believed that was the highest level of consciousness there was.

Breaking the Bonds of the 2,600 Pathways

There are 2,600 pathways that were established at the point of the divine plan at the GODHEAD. Our soul travels these incarnational pathways back up to the Queen of Life where we are spiritual bodies and living souls. During our incarnations, programs accumulate and they must be cleared.

Resolving Discord at All Levels of Chart 3

This relates to clearing Charts 10 through 31 in an ascending order as souls return up the path to the GODHEAD.

Remembering that the Soul's Purpose Is Spiritual Enlightenment

Most people believe that we were formed as physical beings when the living soul was created of the "dust of the ground" (Genesis 2:7 KJV). This is not true. We were created of the substance of SPIRIT, and did not become physical beings until we ate of 'the tree of the knowledge of good and evil' and the 'coat of skins' (physical body) was formed. When the soul enters the physical body to accomplish another step in its spiritual enlightenment, it loses sight of its spiritual nature. People are not aware that we are here to learn how to work with creative energy or that it is a trial and error method that eventually leads to knowledge, wisdom, and enlightenment. Only then are we ready to help design, create, and govern the new ONE universe. Thus, the statement, 'remembering that the soul's purpose is spiritual enlightenment' needs to be cleared in order to make way for the higher knowledge of SPIRIT.

Our Horizons Are Unlimited

After our soul has been cleared all the way to the GODHEAD, we become one with the GODHEAD working with and from that consciousness in an endless process of learning, growing, and experiencing all that the new ONE universe is. Thus, our horizons stretch infinitely before us and our belief that they are limited must be cleared.

Awareness of the Nine GODHEAD Councils

Before we can enter the GODHEAD and proceed through its 99 elevations, we have to be approved by the nine GODHEAD Councils. These GODHEAD Councils that take the idea for a new ONE universe, direct the formation of the plan, set the plan in motion, and oversee the creation of the spiritual realms and the formation of the physical worlds. They are at the GODHEAD and work directly under the GODHEAD to do all things the GODHEAD desires. So 'awareness of the nine GODHEAD Councils' must be cleared so that we can do the work the GODHEAD would have us do.

Awareness of the Entire Spiritual Process from SPIRIT to the Physical and Back to SPIRIT

The title of this program pretty much speaks for itself. It is everything we have learned about how to work with the new ONE universe as a result of working with this ONE universe.

Awareness That Love Is the Only Energy

The final two items are fantastic and vital to our total freedom as a living soul. Love is the only law of karma and all else is an illusion. What most people perceive as karma is the law of mind action that affects our lives when we partake of 'the tree of the knowledge of good and evil' and incarnate to experience, learn, and grow. It is the result of the individual's thoughts and emotions.

The GODHEAD is ALL; ALL is the GODHEAD

We come out of and are a part of the GODHEAD; we are the entire new ONE universe.

Chart 23—Spiritual Realms Programs

Root Causes

Sometimes when you clear past life programs, they do not clear completely. It is as though a weed broke off when you tried to extract it and left a root buried in the ground which can then grow and cause problems. This gets rid of those buried roots.

Clear the Soul

The soul may have discordant beliefs that it has accumulated while living and experiencing in the spiritual realms.

GODHEAD Elevations; Eleven GODHEAD Programs; Daily Accumulation of Discordant Energy; Odds and Ends into Infinity

There are 99 elevations of the GODHEAD and each of them is infinite in level. As the soul travels through the elevations discordant energies can be accumulated necessitating clearing the elevations from time to time. It is also important to clear any daily accumulation of discordant energy and odds and ends into infinity.

Alternate Life Paths and Root Causes

The soul, when it decides to incarnate, reviews a listing that contains 900,000,000 possible life paths. The soul can select from a combination of up to twenty as their final choice. This becomes the major life path. However the soul may also choose alternate life paths. All of these paths and their root causes have to be cleared.

Genetic DNA and Core Beliefs

Genetic DNA and core beliefs have to do with the spiritual body and living soul. Just as there is a genetic DNA that is part of the physical body, so there is a genetic DNA involved with the soul.

The soul also has its own core beliefs that were established as part of the learning process in the spiritual realms.

Spiritual Blocks 1 through 6

On Chart 13–Programs Before Creation we talked about Levels 1 through 6 that were established at the GODHEAD level. Clearing spiritual blocks 1 through 6 removes the energy established at that time.

Personal Soul Package

Each soul has its own 'personal soul package.' It is much like the persona of the human being which often needs harmonizing.

Emotional Body

I also find that the emotional body, which is created when the spiritual realms are created, also needs clearing of discordant emotional beliefs. One of the beliefs a soul may have is that it was separated from the GODHEAD when the mental and emotional bodies were formed.

Apply Chart 7

Once the former things are cleared, additional healing may be needed. High Self may indicate the application of Chart 7–Direct Healing Processes and Colors.

All Issues; Programs Coming Up

Although these programs have not yet been activated, they can be cleared and gotten out of the way before they do come up.

Soul Is Lying (Clear)

There seems to be several levels at which the soul can be found to be lying or covering up things that it does not want to look at as they may be considered by the soul to be too painful, and thus, better left alone. This is also one of the cross-checks I make when all of the programs and charts have been cleared.

Embryo of the ONE Universe

Everything that is experienced by the souls in a ONE universe becomes the egg or embryo which, with additional items inserted by SPIRIT, becomes the foundation upon which the next ONE universe is built. Any discordant energies and beliefs that have carried over from the previous ONE universe need to be cleared.

Lines of Love

High Self showed me little lines coming down from the nine GODHEAD Councils. These are called the lines of love and High Self indicated that each soul has one of these lines connected at the base of the neck between the shoulders. So we are all connected to the nine GODHEAD Councils and SPIRIT by one of these lines of love. Sometimes the lines of love can be sullied by the soul's beliefs while it is still in the spiritual realms. Therefore occasionally clearing the lines of love is important.

Cutting Edge of the Soul; Programs Not on Charts

The soul is always learning new things, so clearing the 'cutting edge of the soul' programs and 'programs not on charts' is vital to the well-being of the soul.

Chart 24—Rebirth Conscious Mind

The vows that we make, either consciously or without knowing we are making them, can and often do have a profound effect on our lives. There is a process listed on the inside of the chart whereby we make conscious vows that can have a very powerful effect on our lives for either good or bad.

First, we make the ***vow***. Perhaps it starts out as a New Year's resolution to do some particular thing. The vow becomes a ***goal*** which we ***reinforce with our thoughts***, until it becomes an ***obsession***. More ***reinforcing thoughts*** cause the obsession to become an ***active memory*** that may trouble us day and night because we have not fulfilled the vow. Next, our ***thoughts become obsessive*** and a further strong ***commitment*** is made and ***emotionally reinforced***. This ***manifests results***, although they may not always be of a positive nature. We may chastise ourselves for giving up and not fulfilling our vows. These vows then become ***buried beliefs*** and ***solidified patterns***.

It is better not to make vows, but simply be who and what you are and who and what you are not. Then work to bring about changes in your life that will benefit you and those around you.

High Self has presented a list of major vows that often are destructive and limiting. They say these vows are more common for women but, certainly not uncommon for men. One person vowed to be just like her mother whom she had taken as a role model. When this chart was revealed, she realized that her mother was ***subservient*** to her husband, chose him as her ***savior to follow***, and had ***abdicated her personal power***. She had ***religious vows of all kinds*** and had ***abdicated personal love*** and ***self-achievement*** in order to follow her husband's lead in all things. There were also ***vows to follow outmoded traditions*** in which the husband was the only authority. Her mother had all of the major vows on Chart 24 including ***vows to break a tradition***, ***vows of purity***, ***vows to annihilate evil***, ***commitments becoming vows***, ***vows to question status quo***, and many ***minor vows***, which the client had copied. When she had revoked all of these vows, she said she felt joy for the first time in many years.

Vows are sometimes made without our being aware that we have established them or even that we are in the process of establishing them, so it is beneficial to revoke vows every few days. Simply ask High Self to clear Chart 24 or repeat the statement: "I revoke any and all vows. I choose to stay open to daily guidance and decisions that are for my highest good here and now! I am okay as I am. I praise Universal Source."

Chart 25—Final Assurance

The name for this chart is actually a misnomer. There is no final assurance because we are never finished as spiritual beings. This chart is simply an attempt not to miss anything in the clearing process. High Self has indicated that there are many things on Chart 25 that are not listed on the chart. High Self says not to bother trying to write about these items. All you have to do is ask that everything on the chart be cleared.

Chart 26—Freedom Is Free

No Reality in the Fall

Everything is illusion except SPIRIT. There has never been a fall or separation from SPIRIT.

Mankind Is Blameless

Everything is simply the dream that SPIRIT is dreaming and we are the characters in the play.

Mankind Is Pure Spirit (Light)

We are created in the image and likeness of God and God is pure SPIRIT or Light.

There Is No Judgment

There is only the illusion of experience that is undertaken in order for the soul to learn and grow.

There Is No Separation

There is only a belief that we are separated from SPIRIT. The dreamer cannot be separated from the dream.

The Veil Is Broken

The veil was broken when Jesus went through the crucifixion and cannot be replaced although religion tries to recreate the illusion of a veil.

The Rim of Creation Is an Illusion; All Parameters Are an Illusion; Illness Is Only an Illusion

All things are part of the dream or illusion that the GODHEAD is experiencing.

The remaining items on this chart are statements of truth to which you may have blocks. The items are: ***All Is Perspective or Focus Point of View; All (every soul) Are Part of the Whole; All Are Vital to the Whole; We are Vital to SPIRIT's Understanding; We Share in the Love of ONE; We Are All in This Together; We Are the Healers of All.***

Just ask High Self to clear Chart 26 in depth at all levels and all layers.

Chart 27—Learning Is Fun

The Intention Is Growth

The process of the soul at all levels is to be a learning experience of SPIRIT. The soul experiences first in the garden of Eden (spiritual realms) where it receives up to 99% of its knowledge. Then the incarnational process begins and the ability to work at the physical level with creative energy is developed. Only then is the soul ready to return to the spiritual realms and take part in the creation and formation of new universes.

Experience Is the Process

This includes learning and gaining knowledge, wisdom, and understanding at all levels.

We Have Only Forgotten SOURCE

When we enter the physical body, a veil is drawn and the first thing that happens is we forget that our SOURCE is SPIRIT. We have suffered the first death as spoken of in Genesis when Adam and Eve ate of the forbidden tree and were given physical bodies.

We Are Involved in Planetary Energies

We enter the physical body to learn to deal with planetary energies called good and evil.

We Are Caught Up in Misbeliefs

During our time in the physical body, we forget our SOURCE and are involved in multiple forms of wrong thinking, believing, and discordant energies.

Learning Is a Continuous Process

Whether we are in the physical body, out of the body between incarnations, or finished with the physical body and no longer subject to incarnation and will remain forever in the spiritual realms, there is still learning at all levels for we are infinite beings.

Soul Beliefs

When the soul is created, there are certain beliefs that are part of the original programming by SPIRIT. They involve suffering, limitation, and other discordant processes of the soul's experience at all levels both in the garden of Eden and at the incarnational level.

Two Levels of Learning: Spiritual and Physical

This is explained in Chapter 2–The Soul's Design.

Ascension Is the Purpose

Educated souls return to SPIRIT with full knowledge, wisdom, understanding, and creative abilities so that they may take part in all that will be projected in the future.

Oneness with GOD/SPIRIT Is the Goal

We came out of SPIRIT and will return to SPIRIT.

Chart 28—Final Forgiveness

Memories, The Master Key

Memories begin with the embryo which is the foundation for the ONE universe, run throughout the entire creative process, include the experiential paths of each soul and never have an ending.

Personal Items

Each soul has its own personal items that it has experienced as it proceeds along its path from the beginning of creation to ascension and atonement.

Clear GODHEAD Plans

The GODHEAD plans contain all possibilities and since we were part of the whole and affected by all that was planned, the plans need to be cleared for each individual soul.

Clear for Integrity of Consciousness

Duality began when there was the idea for a new ONE universe and the plan was drawn for that universe. Duality causes a lack of integrity in spiritual consciousness and that integrity needs to be cleared and reestablished.

Integrate Multiple Programs in the Consciousness of ONE

ONE is where all of the plans for the ONE universe and for all souls were initiated and those plans and programs need to be integrated once the soul has returned to the GODHEAD.

Clear Memory Impingements

Memory impingements are caused by the creation of the illusion that seems to separate the soul from SPIRIT.

Multiple Pathways

Besides the possibilities of the 2,600 pathways previously mentioned in the discussion of Chart 13–Programs Before Creation, and the Levels 1 through 6, there are myriads of other possibilities which must be cleared.

Emotional Impingements

Fear is the greatest and most frequently encountered emotional energy that can restrict the free flow of creative energy on the soul's path of learning. Most other discordant energies are simply aspects of fear.

Release Anger at All Levels

Anger can even carry over from the previous ONE universe as part of the total consciousness of the souls who experienced in that ONE universe. This anger can be part of the embryo, the divine plan, the first draft, and the extension of both the spiritual and physical realms.

Cross Check List

This is simply another list of things that needs to be cleared as a part of the assurance that everything is completed; the soul is clean and in harmony with SPIRIT.

Clear the Void

"In THE BEGINNING God CREATED the heavens and the earth. The earth was without form and void" (Genesis 1:1-2 RSV). The soul had its first form of existence as part of the void and as a result it feels that it has never left the void and therefore does not exist in any meaningful way.

Chart 29—Final Blessing

Embryo

High Self has indicated that everything that was experienced by the souls in a ONE universe became the embryo of consciousness upon which the next ONE universe was based. Additional factors called Mother roots are introduced into the embryo by SPIRIT to cause the new ONE universe to be different and of a higher order of consciousness and experience than the preceding ONE universe.

A ONE universe may consist of eight quadrillion universes each of which may contain 900,000,000 super super universes. Each super super universe may contain 9,000 super universes with 700,000 universes in each one. A universe may have up to 126,000,000 galaxies of various sizes. Galaxies have numberless solar systems with planets in orbit around a sun or suns and every planet has life forms in one or more dimensions. High Self says our planet has sixty-nine dimensions and thirty-three of them have life forms. Besides all of this, each universe may have countless parallel universes.

Divine Plan

Once the embryo has been finalized, the divine plan is drawn which contains the potential for the extension of all that the embryo contains. According to the statement in Genesis 1:1-2, the heavens and the earth were without form and void for as yet nothing had been created or formed–only the plans had been drawn. The divine plan is much like the blueprint for a house that has not yet been built, but which contains all the details in the embryonic idea.

First Draft

The first draft containing all the elements of the divine plan is then written much as the specifications are written for a human home or place of business that is to be constructed. These are the specifications that will be followed by Creator beings at the GODHEAD level as the spiritual realms are created. All of the elements of the embryo will then begin to be enacted, first in the spiritual realms and ultimately in the physical realms in a trickle down process–as above so below.

Etheric Body; First Astral Body; Emotional Body; Mental Body; Idea (King of Kings); Spiritual Body and Queen of Life Factors; Living Soul Keys

These seven items are explained in Chapter 2–The Soul's Design so I will not repeat the discussions here. Just ask that they be cleared.

Majestic Consciousness Programs

The soul has its first level of self-expression at the level of Lord (see Chart 3–Levels of Soul Consciousness). This is the first point in the creative process where the soul has free will, whereas, prior to this there was mostly (for 99% of the souls) preprogramming of the various paths of creation. Once the soul has reached the Majestic Consciousness level, it lives in the garden of Eden where it develops its ruling consciousness by partaking of all of the trees in the garden except for 'the tree of the knowledge of good and evil.'

Two thirds of the created souls decided that incarnation was not for them and remained in the spiritual realms. The one third who decided to incarnate partook of 'the tree of the knowledge of good and evil,' took upon themselves a physical body, and began the process of learning to work at the physical level with creative energy.

Holy Spirit Body

The Holy Spirit body witnesses everything that has gone before, so it needs to be cleared also. This body is a recording device and is both a conscious and subconscious mind.

Spirit Body

The Spirit body is much like the physical body in that it is the vehicle for the previous bodies. Just as our physical body registers and records all that the human consciousness experiences, so the Spirit body registers and records all that the nine previously created bodies experience.

Holy Spirit Consciousness

The Holy Spirit consciousness is the breath or living witness to all that has gone before or that follows the incarnational, learning process. Holy Spirit means breath of God, so the breath needs to be cleansed of all discord that it has witnessed.

Portals to Parallel Universes

A universe may have any number of parallel universes connected to it. My picture of this situation is that of a cover on a book which is the universe and the pages within the book are parallel universes. There may be portals or openings between universes that need to be cleared and closed to keep discordant energies that are being experienced in those universes from bleeding over and causing problems.

Infinity Programs

These are the myriads of little nit-picky experiences that do not seem to have any specific connection to a major issue that has been researched and cleared. Therefore, they need to be eliminated for greater balance and harmony of the soul. It is like a thorough dusting and cleaning of the physical house.

Consciousness Expressing (SPIRIT)

Each soul is one of the infinite multiplicities of SPIRIT seeking to expand its awareness of itself. Thus we are consciousness expressing. Everything that is less than the consciousness of SPIRIT must be cleansed, harmonized, and perfected.

Encoding Physical DNA

Once the soul has decided to incarnate, there are certain codes that are planned to go into the DNA of the physical body. The purpose is to establish those codes in the body that will cause certain physical results. For example, if the soul needs to face the challenge of a Down Syndrome-affected body or some other form of deformed or limited body, they would encode those factors that would cause the parents (according to the human and the medical industry's perception) to produce such a body for the soul's needed and chosen experience. Once the soul has completed the experience it has chosen, the codes need to be removed or they can affect later experiences of the soul.

Miracles

There is no order of difficulty in miracles. However, many believe that some miracles—expressions of SPIRIT—are more difficult than others. This is simply a matter of limited beliefs and these must be cleared and removed.

Chart 30—Final Light

Soul Fingerprints

These are set up by the 17th group at the GOD level on Chart 3–Levels of Soul Consciousness. This is the group in Genesis 1:26 RSV that said, "Let us make man in our image, after our likeness." Just as the physical body of each human being has its own identifying fingerprints, so the soul has its own identifying characteristics.

High Self says they cannot explain what these are–just ask that they be cleared.

Personal Soul Package

This is, as implied, unique to each soul and has its start when the soul partakes of 'the tree of the knowledge of good and evil,' preparatory to incarnating. Remember that there is a catalog containing 900,000,000 possible life paths and the soul may choose a combination of from one to twenty as their major path. Minor paths are also chosen, but not always lived. Should any minor paths be lived, they would register as a 'personal soul package.' These packages would be lived when the soul wants a change from the major path that was chosen. The biggest number I have found so far is seventy-eight but High Self says there is no limit.

Head to Toe Search and Clear

Once the programs are cleared, I want High Self to give me the assurance that all illnesses or any possibility of illness that the soul may be planning is completely eliminated so I ask them to do a head to toe search and clear. Almost always they find either illness or programs for illness and clear them. There may also be programs set up to experience accidents and injury which can be cleared.

Life Stream

The life stream is from SPIRIT which flows through the embryo, divine plan, spiritual realms, and into physical expression. All of the elements, and factors, and experiences of this stream need to be cleared and harmonized for complete resonance of the soul with SPIRIT. This stream was shown to me as sparkles indicating the countless particles that are involved in the makeup of this stream, most of which involves the education of the soul in the garden of Eden before it became physical.

Light Stream

This light stream is the knowledge gained through the physical experience and between incarnations, when the soul returns to the spiritual realms to assimilate and harmonize what was experienced in the physical. This stream of light rises from the lowest level on Chart 3 to the GODHEAD and into the GODHEAD elevations and contains all the experiences of the soul as it returns to SPIRIT from which it sprang.

Infinity Stream

This stream is at the GODHEAD when the soul has completed its learning path and extends backward and forward without end. What is done at any point in what we call time affects that which went before to a lesser degree and that which comes after to a greater degree. Since the now affects all things, the infinity stream must be kept clean at all times.

Nine Councils in this ONE Universe

These are the most important councils in the entire process of creation, formation, and experiencing of the soul. They are the hub or center around which the whole creative process revolves–the network center which sends out the signals, receives the return signals, and assimilates them into the working whole. It is important that they stay balanced and neutral in all of their work.

Finished, Wrap-up

This was not the end. They later gave me Chart 31–Memory Clearing. I don't believe there is an end as the soul is infinite in possibility.

Chart 31—Memory Clearing

The inside of this chart covers elements to be cleared up to and including the GODHEAD and SPIRIT levels. The outside of the chart clears elements at the level of SPIRIT, LUMINOUS and WELLSPRING. The items in the inside of the fan are explained first.

Factors

Factors are the creative codes that go into the makeup of each word that is thought or spoken regardless of language. It is the idea behind the language. These creative codes are strings of numbers and letters.

Embryo

The embryo for each ONE universe is based on the accumulated knowledge and experiences of the souls from the preceding ONE universe. SPIRIT then places additional factors (an infinite number) in the embryo to make it different and a little bit higher in consciousness than the preceding ONE universe. Both carry-over energy from the previous ONE universe and the additional factors need to be cleared and harmonized.

Divine Plan

The next step is to draw the divine plans for the new ONE universe. This plan contains all of the elements of the embryo. This plan contains all possibilities including the basic primal fears carried over from the previous ONE universe

First Draft

This is a complete list of the specifications for the ONE universe and involves the preparation for the advent of new souls, created in the image and likeness of God, and their process of becoming. Just as there is a set of specifications for the creation of a house, automobile, or factory, so there is a set of specifications for the ONE universe. The first draft for a ONE universe is beyond imagination. In the book of The Revelation (9:1-2) the first draft is referred to as 'the bottomless pit.' Both SPIRIT and High Self state that the process of SRT and the book of The Revelation are synonymous and signify the cleanup of the soul and the reestablishment of its connection to the GODHEAD and SPIRIT. The clearing of the first draft may take considerable time, so ask for infinite guarantees that all is completed.

83 Waves of Expression

The GODHEAD is central to the ONE universe and is the Prime Mover of all that is contained in the embryo, divine plan, and first draft. These waves are set up by the GODHEAD and sent out in concentric circles to create the spiritual realms and eventually form the physical universes, galaxies, and planets. These waves contain all of the elements that have gone before.

2,600 Pathways

There are 136 major categories involved in the 2,600 pathways. One of the major categories is the animal paths and there are 540 of those paths. All paths are prior to and preceding the creation of mankind as a spiritual body and living soul. The paths (in total) contain everything that is in the embryo, divine plan, first draft, and 83 waves of expression. SPIRIT expands Itself as the GODHEAD, Life, Love, and all-that-is through many steps in the creative process.

Council of 13

High Self calls the Council of 13, "The Ring Council." This council is central to all of the spiritual beings who make up the GODHEAD. They are responsible for the creation of all-that-is and will-become and they are reluctant to make changes unless asked to. When you ask for the clearing of Chart 31, it brings about many of the changes necessary for the complete freedom of the soul being cleared.

Rim of Creation

The rim of creation was shown to me during 1992 and looked like a wagon wheel with twelve lines through it. Eleven of the lines are support systems for the advent of mankind which is the twelfth line.

Principles of Creation

This is a separate record that contains everything so far covered on this chart.

Eighteenth Group of Gods

This is an Elohim Council and is an Infinite Council of Gods responsible for the formation and government of a physical universe and the creation of all spiritual bodies and living souls. They assist with the basic programming of the soul and the process of their experiences and education first within the spiritual realms (garden of Eden) and then at the physical incarnational level.

King of Kings

This involves the final clearing of the 45,000 possible elements that go into the Queen of Life to form the spiritual body.

CREATOR Consciousness

This involves clearing the 56,000,000 elements that can go into the makeup of the physical body when the soul chooses to incarnate.

99 Elevations

There are 99 elevations of the GODHEAD which must be cleared. Also, check to make certain that your soul and your spiritual committees are in the 99th elevation once High Self indicates that the clearing work is completed.

Archeprints

Archeprints can come up again and again, even after Chart 8–Inner Archetypes is cleared. High Self says these are statements about archetypes and these negative statements need eliminating.

Archetypes

Blocks to the inner child are found in the first astral body, the living soul, and the Spirit body. These blocks are another aspect of the archeprints just discussed. The inner child at these three levels of creation contains the elements of all the archetypes on Chart 8.

Additional Items Chart 31 (Outer Ring)

These items do not usually come up until the basic soul programs are researched and eliminated. They are involved with the divine plan and have their beginning at the level of SPIRIT. SPIRIT is that which lies above and behind all that is. SPIRIT is all life, substance, and intelligence that extends Itself as all of creation and formation. SPIRIT is like the ocean and each soul is like a wave or movement of the ocean. Each wave is because the ocean is. Since we are part of and an extension of SPIRIT, these items on the outer ring of Chart 31 must be cleared in depth or they will come up again and again. I ask for an infinite number of guarantees that they are cleared (an infinity is 90,000 digits). Then I ask that the infinite number be raised to the infinite power an infinite number of times. Once that is done I ask that the whole figure be again raised to the infinite power an infinite number of times. Do this until High Self indicates that you have gone far enough. This is like clearing every drop of water in the largest ocean imaginable.

Hidden Vows

Hidden vows are involved with the divine plan, the first draft (specifications for the divine plan), and the spiritual creation which takes place at the 2,000th level of the I AM level. Hidden vows can be registered in any of the first four bodies: etheric, first astral, mental, and emotional. They can be both positive and negative but only the negative ones need to be cleared. High Self says that when a person has hidden vows, it is extremely difficult for them to change and establish a balanced life until the vows are cleared.

High Self gave two examples. A female had hidden vows of hate of God, fatigue, and depression in the etheric body. A male had hidden vows of hate, alcoholism, and failure. High Self said their lives were controlled and affected 100% by those vows which are now cleared.

Root Causes

One root cause is in the embryo that was the basis for this ONE universe. Another is in the divine plan for this universe that was formed at the GODHEAD. Another is in the 2,600 pathways by which we come into being. Another is at the 2,000th level of the I AM level where the spiritual realms are formed. Another is at Queen of Life and another at Lord of Lords. However, High Self says there are an infinite number of root causes, all of which can be cleared.

Elevations

There are 99 elevations of the GODHEAD, and each elevation has infinite levels within it where the soul resides within the GODHEAD. These need to be cleared from time to time as the soul never stops learning and growing. There are other elevations on Chart 3–Levels of Soul Consciousness that extend from the top of the Universal God Consciousness level up to and including the GODHEAD level. As the soul is cleared to higher and higher levels on Chart 3, these elevation programs must be eliminated for the full, unlimited expression of the soul.

Issues and Challenges

Issues and challenges are a carry-over from the previous ONE universe and are a part of the makeup of the embryo that formed this universe. High Self says about 49% of all souls have issues and challenges of this nature. There can be any number of these and they can be in layers. Unfortunately they can come up one at a time over many years, causing a person to experience a lot of ongoing turmoil in their life. Make certain your High Self is educated and aware of these programs and that they know they can clear them in depth at all levels. Issues and challenges include all of Chart 2–Themes and Challenges and countless other possibilities.

The 'issues' listed on Chart 17–Fine Tuning and the 'all issues' listed on Chart 23–Spiritual Realms Programs are different programs and are cleared when you clear the respective charts. Information on them is included in the explanations of Charts 17 and 23.

Items Not on Charts

These have their origin at the 2,000th level of the I AM level when the spiritual realms are created. They can come up a few at a time over your entire lifetime. By asking High Self to research and clear all of them they can be eliminated once and for all.

Factors

These are different from the factors on the inside of Chart 31. Every word that is created to be used in the ONE universe has its own creative factors. When a word is held in mind, even before it is spoken, these creative factors go into play and begin to produce a result which may be positive, negative, or of mixed value depending on the person's thoughts. A person may pray for healing while also holding in mind a fear of illness. When this occurs, the mix of creative factors may tend to maintain the illness, or even increase it, rather than bring about a cure.

Factors on the inside of Chart 31 involve combinations of positive and negative words (like those in a sentence) while factors on the outside of Chart 31 involve a single negative word or a collection of negative words. For example a female held everything on Chart 6A–Discordant Energy and more, a total of 139 negative words and their factors which were accumulated over 126,389 past lives. High Self just gave me the symbolism of a whole string of garbage trucks filled to overflowing.

More

There are a lot of things that come up that are not specific in nature. It is simply a hodgepodge of stuff. High Self simply calls it More.

Archetypes

Chart 8–Inner Archetypes lists twenty archetypes and these are involved with the incarnational experience. Archetypes are also involved with the divine plan. High Self says there are 386 of them, which are characteristics much like and including the twenty listed on Chart 8. These are in layers so make certain they are all removed or they will come up repeatedly.

Archeprints

Archeprints are statements about the characteristics of archetypes that the soul can encounter in its process of development and expression.

There are three major areas in which both archetypes and archeprints are found: the first draft, the 83 waves of expression, and the 2,600 pathways. These will come up again and again if they are not cleared in depth.

Jacob's Ladder

One day while working on a client's programs, I had an inner vision of a ladder standing and reaching to heaven. There was a landing at both the top and bottom. I called it Jacob's ladder after the story in Genesis 28:12. The platform at the bottom is earth life. The platform at the top symbolizes the spiritual realms. The ladder is the channel of communication–SPIRIT descending to mankind and mankind ascending to SPIRIT. This channel must be kept open at all times for clarity of communication with SPIRIT.

Mind of SPIRIT

SPIRIT is CONSCIOUSNESS that formulates ideas in Its mind. Each soul is an extension of an idea held in the mind of SPIRIT. The metaphor I use is SPIRIT as the ocean and each soul as a wave or expression of the ocean moving in the mind of SPIRIT. The ocean affects the wave and the wave affects the ocean, so both must be cleared for complete harmony and freedom of soul expression.

Integrate 18 Bodies

It is of vital importance to ask for the complete integration of the 18 bodies with LUMINOUS and WELLSPRING. This is the final atonement and ascension spoken of by Jesus. We do have a physical body as one of the final 18 bodies after completion of the incarnational learning process. However, it is not the corruptible physical body that is subject to illness, dissolution, and death that we experience through while incarnated. It is, rather, a spiritualized body energized by spiritual life.

Blocks to LUMINOUS

LUMINOUS IS SOURCE OF ALL. It is LIGHT beyond, above, and behind all Light. LUMINOUS gives rise to consciousness which is SPIRIT and SPIRIT works through mind to ideate and extend all that is, first the spiritual realms and eventually the physical universes, galaxies, and planets.

Programs to Keep the Soul Clear

The soul never stops experiencing, learning, expanding, and growing. Ask that positive programs be set up at all levels of Chart 3–Levels of Soul Consciousness and above and below to keep the soul clear

Duplicate Programs

High Self says that the records of everything experienced while in the physical body is duplicated in both the second and third astral bodies. Everything that is experienced by the soul while out of the physical body in the spiritual realms is duplicated in the I AM body, the Christ body, and the Holy Spirit body. These must be cleared or they will come up and cause problems. High Self also indicated that the embryo, divine plan, and first draft also need a final clearing.

Programs Coming Up

Before you came into this incarnation, while in the bardo, you designed a basic plan for your life. There were plans to encounter certain trials or challenges at specific times during your journey on the planet. You may have chosen to meet someone who had killed you, or whom you had killed in a past life, in order to face and work through the accumulated energy. Once your past life programs are cleared, these future, preprogrammed incidents may be cleared because there is no longer any energy from the past to face, work through, and release.

Guarantees

After clearing everything through Chart 31, I ask for seven levels of guarantees that the records are completely cleared. These are the questions I ask:

1. Does the soul agree that it is clear?
2. Does High Self agree that all is clear?

3. Does SPIRIT agree?
4. Does LUMINOUS agree?
5. Does WELLSPRING agree?
6. Does GRAND-I and WHOLE agree?

Once I have agreement of these seven levels, I am confident that all is cleared up to this point. That does not mean that nothing else will ever come up to be cleared.

Miscellaneous Information

High Self says the specifications for the entire ONE universe is called the first draft. Jesus says that the 'bottomless pit' in Revelations is referring to the first draft. Several years ago High Self showed me little squiggly lines. When I asked what they were, they said they were waves of expression and that there were 83 of them. That is all I know about the waves. Then the picture showed little short legs extending down from the bottoms of the waves. I was told that they were paths and that there were a total of 2,600 pathways that precede the creation of the living soul (mankind). There are 136 major categories and one of the major categories is the path of animals which consists of 546 paths out of the total 2,600 pathways. Once an animal soul has completed its learning it can evolve toward human. Depending on its level of consciousness it can be transformed to pre-Neanderthal, Neanderthal, or human. There are further steps that take the pre-Neanderthal to Neanderthal and then to human.

Even after all charts and all items on all charts are completed, I encounter problems that are not on charts. These are usually cleared very quickly and High Self says they are placed on one of the existing charts so that if someone else comes up with the items they will be cleared automatically when the chart is cleared. Remember that the soul is infinite in nature and that it is never finished with the process of learning and expansion. Even SPIRIT, which is our SOURCE, is never finished.

During October of 1996 I was given a picture of what looked like a large sheet of glass. It was not a sheet of glass, which became apparent as an object was dropped into the left side of the picture. The object sent out concentric rings that continued beyond the edge of the picture just as it would if dropped into a body of water. Questioning revealed some important information.

Water in the *Holy Bible* symbolizes infinite potential as it can fill any shape. It can also take the form of solid (ice), liquid (water), and gas (vapor). The object dropped into the water was the soul, so the water symbolizes the infinite possibilities for soul expansion. The concentric rings moving beyond the edge of the picture indicates that there is no stopping point for the expansion of the soul.

Working with SRT and developing new possibilities has been a real challenge for me as I am a person who likes to complete any task I undertake. There is not a point of completion for the soul or for SRT as the soul is constantly expanding to gain new knowledge, wisdom, and understanding in the development of its infinite potential.

The Maze

The first time I ran into the 'maze,' I thought Spirit was playing games with me or that I had blocks or interference. As I researched, the pendulum was moved from one chart to another between Charts 11 through 20. There did not seem to be any order or logic in the process. High Self says a maze is the convoluted path that a soul travels from the point of the divine blueprint to the point where the spiritual body and living soul is created. The maze contains a record of all the experiences encountered along the paths regardless of which of the 2,600 pathways have been taken. Thus it would include the record of being an atom of an earthly element, a plant, a bird, a fish, and so on. Since Charts 11 through 20 concern the paths of creation that all individual souls follow, from the drawing of the divine blueprint to the present moment, and all beliefs, perceptions, and judgments accumulated along the way, the blocking or limiting beliefs must be cleared for complete freedom of the soul that has returned to SPIRIT.

At the GODHEAD level, or top level of ONE, the energy of the universe is cubed and vibrating at an extremely high level. It is far beyond the visible realms but lies behind all that is formed. At the GODHEAD, the divine plan for all that would become the spiritual realms and the manifest realms was formed. That constituted the blueprint which was drawn upon the etheric fabric of the ultimate universe. The blueprint or pattern contained all substance, life, and intelligence. We were present in the beginning and it was there that we experienced the past lives in other dimensions (listed on Chart 4—When) that need to be cleared. These lives were in the beginning of all things and long before the spiritual universe or the formed worlds came into existence.

At the I AM level, the energy, as we know it here in the physical realms, was squared. There we were created as spiritual beings, and lived, experienced, learned, and grew in knowledge and wisdom. Finally, the physical universe, galaxies, planets, and all they contain were formed, and we left the spiritual realms and incarnated. The vibration of energy at the physical level is low enough for us to see with our human eyes which are designed to work with this vibratory level.

There are many other bits and pieces that have been revealed to me by my High Self regarding the formative process, the structure of the universes, and the government that directs the whole process of creation and formation, and the paths of unfolding life. However, they are not needed to clear programs and are subjects for a future book. There is sufficient information in this book to clear all programs that have directed and affected the path of the soul from alpha to omega.

Final Draft

This is a final harmonized rewriting, redesigning of the entire ONE universe based on new insights gained by SPIRIT because of the clearing work that has been accomplished through SRT. SPIRIT and the GODHEAD wish to extend their grateful thanks to all who have assisted and persisted in the process of clearing and harmonizing the many souls in this ONE universe, it has made a profound difference at all levels of expression.

CHAPTER 17

Creating Health

Disease, according to several dictionaries, is a disorderly or incorrectly functioning organ, part, structure, or system of the body resulting from the effect of genetic or developmental errors, infection, poisons, nutritional deficiency or imbalance, toxicity, or unfavorable environmental factors. Disease is any illness, sickness, or ailment.

Health is physical and mental well-being. The healthy person is one who is free from disease, pain, or defect. There is complete normality of all physical and mental functions. Health is a condition of body and mind.

While this is correct to a point, these definitions are incomplete. Working with SRT reveals that a person may be diseased (out of ease) physically, mentally, emotionally, and in the soul. The two greatest causes of disease are the programs chosen by the soul as part of the learning experience, and emotions that are out of control, balance, or harmony. The medical profession does a magnificent job of treating the symptoms of disease. However, too little is known about the causes of disease and how to cure them. There is an increasing awareness on the part of the medical profession that most disease has its basis in psychosomatic disorders and not genetics. Although they are getting closer to the truth, there is much more involved than that. Here are some questions and answers from Spirit regarding illness, disease, or lack of health.

Q. Do we inherit disease? (-)

Q. Do we inherit genetic tendencies toward disease? (+)

Q. Are these tendencies registered in the genes? (+)

Q. Do people (souls) enter the physical body with the intent to experience illness and disease? (+)

Q. Would the soul that has chosen to experience ill health as a part of their learning process pick parents who had experienced disease and had registered in their genes the illness patterns that the soul wishes to face and work with? (+)

Q. Does the intent to experience illness always have to be fulfilled? (-)

Q. Then the soul, even after it enters the physical body, can change or alter the path he or she has chosen? (+)

Q. May the soul also choose a path free from disease? (+)

Q. Is that the reason why one child may manifest the tendency for disease they have picked up from their parent's genes record and another may not? (+)

The process of picking up the gene record from your parents is similar to holography.

In holography, every part contains the whole. In a similar way, every cell of the body contains all of the patterns, tendencies, and programs of the person. When your body is formed as a result of the union of your mother's egg and father's sperm, the cells contain all of their programs, good and bad. Whether you run those programs or not is up to you and the decisions you make on the conscious, subconscious, and soul levels. Clearing your soul programs and cellular memory of all discordant energies can dramatically alter your mental, emotional, and physical expression and can prevent disease.

You clear the negative energy of disease, just as you do other programs: by researching and clearing past lives.

Case Studies

Although the following client has given me permission to use his real name, I will not do so. I shall call him Jerry. The doctors discovered that Jerry had cancer in his esophagus and told him they would have to remove the cancerous growth or it would completely close off the esophagus and he would not be able to swallow. Near the end of January, 1989 they performed the necessary operation to remove the cancer. When they opened Jerry up, they discovered that his abdomen was filled with cancer and it had attacked the liver. They sewed him up and sent him home with the expectation that he would die within one to two weeks.

A mutual friend called me and asked if I would work with Jerry. I checked with High Self to see if I was allowed to work with him and received a positive response. The friend gave me Jerry's phone number and I called him and made an appointment for February 6. When I arrived, he was lying in a recliner in the living room. He was very weak, his color was poor, and he was very listless. Rather than trying to set Jerry up to use a pendulum, I asked permission from my High Self to do the research work myself, and permission was given.

Jerry had a self-hate program and there were eight past lives we had to research and clear. (Later questioning revealed that there were a total of 648 past lives in the program.) I had Jerry repeat clearing statements that I gave him. By the time we were finished with the clearing statements, Jerry was sitting up in the recliner, his color was good, and his energy had increased dramatically. He practically jumped out of the recliner and moved briskly to the bathroom. His action concerned his wife and she said, "For heaven's sake, Jerry! Take it easy. You just had an operation." Jerry's response was, "I feel great! I feel terrific!" Jerry *was* feeling great and he was on his way to complete healing of the cancerous condition in his body. It took six weeks for the cancer cells to be completely replaced with healthy cells.

Several months later Jerry came to me for additional clearing work. He told me the doctors had informed him that the reason they sewed him up and sent him home was that when they opened him up and looked at what was going on inside of him, they could actually see the cancer growing on the liver, filming it over as they watched.

The doctors gave him up for dead. However, the root cause for the cancer, a self-hate program, was found and removed and the body healed itself. Jerry's expected life in the body was found (by questioning High Self) to be another seventeen years. At this point, Jerry is still alive and according to his doctors, in excellent health.

Cancer does not always dissolve after the client's programs are cleared, nor does the soul always stay in the body. Sometimes the soul has already decided to leave the physical world and has chosen cancer or some other disease as the means of making that exit. When the soul decides to leave, it is going to leave regardless of any clearing work, prayers, or medical treatment.

Many times, when the soul has already made the choice to exit, High Self can clear all of the programs without research, because there is nothing for the person to know or learn on the conscious level. The learning takes place on the inner or soul level, so the programs are simply cleared by High Self. I tell people when their loved one has made a decision to leave, "At least they will go over clean and will not have to incarnate again to face and clear unresolved discordant energy."

The effectiveness of the clearing work in this next case was also later verified. Sharon is a gentle, loving, kind, considerate, wise, intelligent, and wonderful woman. I could go on listing her positive qualities and still not do her justice. You would have to know her personally to understand what she is really like. Still, Sharon was diagnosed as having breast cancer by her doctor and he wanted to perform a double mastectomy. Sharon said, "No! I know that I can be healed and will be healed without surgery." When I heard that Sharon had cancer, I called her and asked if she would work with me to determine the cause of the cancer and remove it. She agreed and we set up an appointment.

When Sharon came in, I told her I wanted to clear all of the discordant energy she held on everyone in her life. She informed me that she did not hold any negative energy on anyone, because she had spent forty years forgiving and praying for people. I suggested that we do some checking to verify that she was clear and she agreed. Working with High Self, we found that she was clear on her mother and father and held only positive energy toward them. However, when we asked for the discordant energy on her stepfather, we got a figure of 100%, with zero positive. The energy was established in a past life in which Sharon was a female and her stepfather was a male.

At this point I saw the past life and knew what had happened. Sharon was a black slave in the deep south. Her stepfather was her owner. He abused her mentally, emotionally, physically, and sexually tortured her to death. Although I was not completely aware at the time, I had an inkling what form the torture took and later asked some questions to clarify my inner perception.

Q. *Did Sharon's master attack her with a knife? (+)*

Q. *Did he slice her breasts? (+)*

Q. *Were other parts of her body cut also? (+)*

Q. *Was she stabbed to death after the torture? (+)*

Q. *Was the intense hate she held for the man who tortured and killed her the cause of the cancer in this life? (+)*

Q. *When there is cancer in the human body, is hate always involved? (+)*

I was curious why the cancer created by the hate started in the breasts and not in the female organs.

Q. *Was there some reason why the cancer was located in the breasts? (+)*

Q. *Because that is where the slaver started the torture? (+)*

Q. *The breasts were the focal point for the pain and hate? (+)*

Sharon started to cry when we researched the past life and found what had happened. She could not understand why, for as she informed me, she had "finished with crying and had not cried for forty years." I told her the reason was because she had not known about the past life and the energies had come up to be faced and released, and tears are a catharsis and a wonderful way to wash away the pain.

Once the clearing work was done, it took five weeks to dissolve the cancer cells and replace them with healthy cells. The body will usually heal itself when the cause for dysfunction is removed. Sometimes the healing process can be speeded up by asking for help from Higher Beings (use Chart 1—Contact or Help), or by using a color, which we will discuss later.

Based on my past experiences of seeing the wonderful results of working with SRT, I was confident that clearing the past life was the reason the cancer dissolved. About sixteen months later my belief was verified. Sharon went to a meeting where two psychics, a husband and wife team from Denmark, were speaking. When she walked in the door, the man approached her, and said, "There is a tall gentleman in your life who has given you a wonderful gift, there is not even any scar tissue." When next I saw Sharon, she gave me a hug and told me what the man had said.

Janice had cancer cells in her body, although they were not yet attacking any particular area or organ. The cancer program (belief in cancer) was inherited through the genes. Her maternal grandfather had cancer and his cellular memory was passed on to his daughter who passed it to Janice. Now Janice was dealing with a conscious fear that she might get cancer, because it had been experienced by at least one member of the family. Her fear had the potential of triggering the program registered in the genes, thus causing the cancer cells to attack the body. The energies that caused the cancer in the grandfather were hate, hate of God, hate of self, and self-punishment, and Janice picked up the energy. Since the programs are cleared High Self assures me that Janice needs to no longer fear that she might have cancer.

Lottie had four programs which triggered her cancer. They were self-punishment, bitterness (intense hate), inheritance, and anger, all involving past lives. The bitterness program was the first one to research and clear. In the first life she was a female who was harmed by her father. He sexually molested her from seventeen months old until she was thirteen. Lottie was extremely bitter, violently angry, hated her father with a passion, and was depressed. In the second life, she was an older male (grandfather) who was being cared for by an aunt. The aunt was filled with hate and anger, was stingy and hated caring for Lottie, so she killed her. Lottie was violently angry, bitter, and had extreme hatred of the aunt for ending that life. In the third life Lottie was a Cherub. God, the Council of Nine, and a lot of discordant thoughts created by Lottie were involved. She was starting the process of incarnating for the first time. She believed that God did not want her to incarnate, nor did she want to. However, the Council wanted her to incarnate so she believed she was in conflict with them, committed spiritual suicide, and cut herself off from God (wholeness) when she incarnated.

Anger was the next program researched for Lottie, and in the first life she was a male. There was an aunt, daughter, mother, and male doctor involved. Lottie had terminal cancer and the family and doctor conspired to put her to sleep. Lottie saw it as murder, and after she was killed she set up the energies of anger, bitterness, cruelty, and depression. In the second life, she was androgynous playing the part of the female, and two males were involved. There was a love relationship between Lottie and one male. The other male was jealous and killed them. Lottie registered hate of God (twice), hate, and bitterness.

In the first life we researched to clear Lottie's self-punishment program, she was female with a husband (who is also her current husband), a male (who is a friend in the current life), and a group. Lottie's husband attacked the male and the male killed him. Lottie, in anger and hate, stirred up a mob who lynched the man. The reason she set up the self-punishment program was that she knew it was a miscarriage of justice because her husband was at fault. In the next life, Lottie was male and her father was involved. She was born deformed and her father killed her at birth. Lottie hated her father for killing her, felt guilty because of her hate, and set up the self-punishment. In the third life, she was a mother with a son and grandfather. Both Lottie and her son were depressed, hated life, and committed suicide.

Lottie also had an inherited belief in cancer from her mother's father through the gene memory. He had cancer in 350 lives and had retained a lot of hate energy.

Maude wanted to know why she was blocked in health and freedom of physical movement. There were 772 past lives involved and we had to research three. In the first one, she was a Light being and God was involved. Her twin flame, to whom she was addicted, had incarnated and she wanted to follow them. Her soul record indicated she believed that God would not let her incarnate. She believed God had held her captive, bound her, restricted her, and limited her.

In the second past life, Maude was male with a mother and son. She caused an accident in which her mother and son were killed. Since she limited their lives by accidentally killing them, she believed she had to punish herself and was doing so by limiting her own expression in this life. In the third life, Maude was an invalid female who was being cared for by her father and aunt. She was very angry because she believed they caused her pain and conflict. This third past life was the root cause of the program causing ill health in the present life. She was punishing herself for any reactive energy in this current life by limiting her freedom of expression as she was limited in the third past life.

Polly had stomach problems and wanted to clear up any subconscious programs she might have that could cause them. There were two very interesting past lives involved. In the first, she was High Self for a female who is a flame mate. The female was possessed by discarnates and she had two Guardian Angels. One of the angels was of Spirit Status and the other Light Status. They were in conflict with each other, which was causing the female problems. The discarnates also caused conflict in the female which resulted in stomach problems. Polly, as the High Self, was having difficulty 'stomaching' the whole situation and she picked up the female's stomach problems, which were manifesting in this life.

In the second past life, Polly was an androgynous soul in the Como Berneces galaxy. Polly's soul petal did not split, (see Chapter 3—The Soul Family), so she is both the male and the female halves of the soul. The other cast member was a Spirit Status guide. The guide was her flame mate and wanted her to leave the galaxy and incarnate on the earth. Even though the idea of incarnating on earth turned her stomach (symbolically), she decided to do so anyway. Now, she cannot stomach earth and has been trying to get out of the physical body and off the earth by having stomach problems. Polly had lost her sense of purpose here and wanted to die and go home to her family in Como Berneces.

The following past life scenario comes up quite frequently when researching back problems. The client was a priest accused of heresy. He was strung up by his wrists and heavy weights were tied to his feet. He was literally pulled apart and his back was broken. His back was broken in 121 past lives.

Another client was having problems with his knee. He had a past-life memory of an injury that occurred when he was a knight in battle in the British Isles. The knee caused him pain and problems the rest of his life. He experienced depression, hate of self, and fear of starving, and he killed himself. In the second life, he was a mother riding in a wagon with her son. The wagon tipped over and broke both of the son's legs. The mother felt guilty, wanted to punish herself, and tried to do so by committing suicide. The suicide only locked the energy into the client's subconscious causing it to come around again in this incarnation.

Cheryl had a host of physical problems, none of which were life-threatening, but were making her life miserable. First was a problem with her hands which began when she was four. Her arms and hands were held by a man so she could not move while her father molested her. Second, she had a problem hearing words correctly. This resulted from a past life in which she was a female child born deaf because her father had syphilis. Cheryl believed that the syphilis and the deafness were her fault so she set up a self-punishment program for herself. Then she was having rectal and posterior pains because of past lives where she was homosexual, practiced sodomy, was diseased with syphilis, and caused others pain.

Cheryl had ichthyosis. The energy attached was the result of being burned as a witch. Her nose staying clogged most of the time related to her nose being crushed in battle when she was hit in the face with a shield. Circulation problems in her legs were traced to a past life experience as a member of the Byrd expedition to the North Pole where she got her legs wet and froze to death. She decided it was a stupid thing to do and has been punishing herself ever since. The pain in her breasts was connected to her nurturing, feeding, and nursing her daughter who was draining her and causing her pain. When we cleared this program, we also cleared a problem she was having with her ribs.

Cheryl had a lot of mucus drainage. This was organ language and originated at birth. She was placed on a cold metal surface and the nurse stuck a straw up her nose to clear the mucus. Cheryl was very angry at everyone and set up self-punishment energy.

The pain in her knees started in past lives in which she was a cowboy. She was bulldogging a steer and her horse fell on her, crushing her left knee. In another life, her right knee was crushed. She decided to punish herself in a future incarnation because it was a stupid, careless thing to do.

Cheryl also set up spleen and liver problems because of 237 past lives as an alcoholic in which she had cirrhosis of the liver. The problem with her jaw was a past life injury. Researching why Cheryl's eyes were too dry brought up a death experience in which she was burned at the stake and the resulting anger caused self-punishment. Her migraine headaches were connected with a life in which she hanged herself and died very slowly. Cheryl's problem with balance resulted from an imprint in which she told herself that she was confused and lacked balance in her life.

Cheryl had a lot of pain in her toes. We had to research six lives to clear it. In the first past life, she was a young male. She and an uncle were carrying supplies to some family members during a severe winter. She suffered frostbite and lost three toes on her right foot and four on her left. In the second life she was a sailor on a whaler. Cheryl's foot became tangled in the rope and she was pulled overboard and drowned when the whale sounded. In the next life, she was a male who lived in the Gobi desert. Through her own negligence, she sustained an injury to her feet that cost her life. In the fourth life, she was born with a club foot and everyone teased her about it. Cheryl was filled with anger, hated the people, and killed herself. Finally, she was a male traveling with a wagon train. Cheryl accidentally started a prairie fire in which she and several other people from the wagon train were killed. Every one of these past lives had self-punishment involved, and Cheryl has been doing very well at fulfilling that program. Now she can let go of self-punishment and be free.

Asthma is often tied to past lives in which the person dies in a fire or causes someone else's death by fire and then sets up a program of self-punishment. Drowning, smothering, and hanging are other energy causes for asthma. Of course there are other reasons that I will not list because the possibilities are unlimited. Neck problems are often connected with lives in which there has been an injury in battle, an accident, hanging, beheading, and so on.

There are many causes of aches and pains, ill health, and other physical challenges. Some of the aches and pains can be attributed to physical stress, strain, overwork, or injury, while other aches and pains are expressions of subconscious programming and can be researched and cleared as we have shown through the examples presented. Once you have learned to work with SRT, you can keep yourself clear by checking yourself daily, for it only takes a few minutes. For example, I was experiencing sharp needlelike pains in my stomach and could not consciously think of any reason for them. A quick check revealed that I was running the energies of hate of self, hate, self-punishment, and anger. I asked High Self to clear the energies and when the clearing was accomplished, the pain stopped immediately.

Some physical symptoms, like my stomach pains, are healed almost instantly; other symptoms may take several hours, days, or weeks. It usually takes about six weeks for the body to be cleared of cancer cells. Other symptoms may require an even longer period of time, may require assistance from a medical practitioner, or may require a change in your mental, emotional, and physical diet, exercise, vitamins, or minerals.

Using Colors—Chart 7

There are times when High Self suggests the use of a color to change the vibrations of the body and speed up the healing.

A friend called me one day to inform me that his High Self had asked him to design a color chart, which he did. They gave him the colors and he placed them on Chart 7–Colors. He brought copies of the chart to me and we discussed the possible uses of color. We were not certain of how to use the chart to the best advantage, but we knew that High Self would reveal the information as needed.

Within an hour of the time the friend left my office, High Self presented the first opportunity to use color. A member of our congregation, Pearl, came to the church and wanted to see me. I invited her into my office and asked her what the problem was. She informed me that she was having trouble thinking clearly, her mind seemed to be confused and fuzzy, and she was fearful that she was losing control of her mind. I asked my High Self if there was something on the charts that would help her, and received a positive response. The charts I had been using were stacked in front of me on my desk. The color charts the friend had just brought were to the left. I reached for the pile of charts directly in front of me, and a strange and fascinating thing happened. I could not pick up the regular charts, instead, my hand was moved to the left and I picked up the color chart. I began to ask my High Self some questions.

Q. *Would the use of color help Pearl clarify her thinking? (+)*

Q. *What color should she use? (Orange)*

Q. *How long should she use it, in minutes? (3)*

Q. *How many times a day? (6)*

Q. *How many days should she use color? (Continuously) (This is shown by a circular motion of the pendulum.)*

Pearl was to sit quietly and comfortably and imagine the color orange. She was to imagine the color flowing into her with every breath, filling her whole head to harmonize and clarify her thinking.

Pearl said, "Oh! That's easy. I will use an orange and imagine the color from that flowing into my head."

She went home and began the process as directed. The next time I saw Pearl, she was ecstatic. She informed me that using the color orange really worked, her thinking was clear, she was more at peace, and the fear had evaporated.

Later, the same day, another person came in for her counseling appointment. She asked me to check and see if there was still something wrong with her thyroid (we had previously cleared many issues causing problems with her thyroid). There were no programs causing problems, just something additional we needed to do. Investigation revealed that she needed to use the color white to purify and harmonize the thyroid. The program was set up; she used it and immediately felt the change.

Paul had suffered from narcolepsy for many years. (Narcolepsy is a condition that is characterized by the sudden onslaught of deep sleep.) The first thing we did was research and clear all subconscious programs that were causing the problem. We verified that there was no longer any reason for Paul to experience narcolepsy and asked how long it would take for a complete healing of all symptoms. The High Self moved the pendulum in a circular motion, which indicated that the time was ongoing or uncertain. We asked if there was something on one of the charts that Paul could do to speed up the healing process and received a positive response. We used Chart 1–Chart to Use, to determine what chart to use and were led to the color chart (Chart 7–Colors).

Q. *What color should Paul use? (Indigo)*

Q. *How many times a day should he use indigo? (5)*

Q. *How many minutes each time? (7)*

Q. *How many days should he use it? (25)*

Q. *Should the use of color be continued longer? (+)*

Q. *How many more days? (22)*

Q. *How many times a day? (4)*

Q. *How many minutes each time? (5)*

Q. *Will Paul be healed at the end of the 47 days? (+)*

Paul was healed at the end of the forty-seven days. The last time I spoke to him, which was about a year later, he was still free from narcolepsy and was delighted.

Another client wanted to know what her spiritual color was. It was indigo, which has a very high spiritual vibration. There was nothing she needed to do other than to 'know' it was her color. Your spiritual color should be the predominant color of your aura when you are centered and balanced in High Self. Several years ago, I was told that my aura was silver. When I learned to use the color chart, I asked what my spiritual color was and my High Self indicated that it was silver.

Using the color chart is easy. Just follow the examples given. The first question to ask is, "Can a color be used to speed up or enhance the healing process, or improve the situation I am working on?" When a "yes" response is received, ask how many minutes the color is to be used, how many times a day, and how many days. Then ask if that will complete the process. If it will not, ask if color needs to be used additional days. Simply ask questions until you have a complete process.

Using the Health Charts

Several years ago, I had a very vivid dream. There was a friend in the dream who told me she had just received a medical diagnosis that she was dying. I told her that her statement was interesting because I had received the same information from my doctor. When morning came, I checked it out.

Q. *Am I really dying? (+)*

Q. *Is there something I need to do to change that? (+)*

Q. *How many things are there? (5)*

My wife, Mary Ann, and I sat down and brainstormed what the five things were. High Self revealed: prayer and meditation, exercise, diet, fresh air, and recreation. Then we sat down and working with High Self created charts to help in determining what a person needs for maximum health and well-being.

There are two health charts in Appendix B: Chart 9A–Vitamins and Minerals and Chart 9B–Food or Diet; Health and Well-Being. These may be used to find out what is needed for you to establish and maintain your body in the highest condition of health, strength, and vigor. Here is how to find out if there is anything you need to do to improve your mental, emotional, or physical health. I will use the charts to see where I am now as I write this.

Q. *Is there something listed on one of the health charts that I need to do to improve my health? (+)*

Q. *Which chart is it on? (Chart 9B)*

Q. *How many things are there? (3)*

Q. *What are they? (Spiritual support and meditation, recreation, and fresh air)*

Q. *Is the spiritual support a church or religion? (-)*

Q. *Is it more prayer and spiritual reading? (+)*

There was snow on the ground and the roads were icy and extremely hazardous, so I had not gone out for my usual morning walk and I needed fresh air and exercise. For the past several years I have been so deeply involved with SRT that I seldom indulge in anything of a recreational nature. So I was not surprised when recreation came up as something I needed for my mental, emotional, and physical balance.

Chart 9A—Vitamins

There is much controversy over the value of specific vitamins: which ones are best, and what quantity each individual needs to take for best results. No hard and fast standard can be established because every individual is different and their requirements vary. You cannot even set up a program for yourself and continue it without variation over a long period of time. Your body's requirements change from time to time and your vitamin intake needs to be varied to meet its changing needs. One person may need 200 units of vitamin E and another person may need 400 units. High Self wants me to take 600 units which is an unusually high dosage. Even then, I occasionally check the amount to make certain my requirements have not changed. Use the charts to determine what you need to take for maximum well-being.

The subconscious is in charge of all the autonomic functions of the body and does a marvelous job directing the digestion and assimilation of food and elimination of waste material. However, it does not have an understanding of vitamins and minerals. Neither does your High Self automatically have this knowledge. When I first started working with my High Self to determine what was required for maximum well-being, I asked them if they understood my physical requirements and they said, no. I asked them to research, and if necessary call in a staff of spiritual nutritionists to assist in determining what I needed for maximum health, strength, and vitality. Once my High Self had knowledge of my body's needs, I asked them to inform my subconscious mind what those needs were. Ask your High Self to research what your body needs for maximum well-being. Once you have confirmed that the research is completed, you are ready to use the health charts.

Q. *Is there anything on Chart 9A I need to change? (+)*

Q. *What is it? (C (ascorbic acid))*

Q. *Do I need to take vitamin C? (+)*

There are many forms of vitamin C and you want the one that is the best for you. Go to a store where a variety of vitamins are sold and have your High Self research all of the vitamin C on the shelves. I use my pendulum and ask a series of questions.

Q. *Is there a vitamin C on one of these shelves that is best for me? (+)*

Q. *Is it on the first shelf? (-)*

Q. *Is it on the second shelf? (+)*

Q. *Please point it out? (The pendulum is moved to point in the direction of the vitamin; pick up the bottle.)*

Q. *Is this the best vitamin C for me? (+)*

Q. *What is the quantity I need to take in milligrams? (Use any chart with numbers.)*

Before you go to a store to purchase supplies, research every vitamin you need and determine the units or milligrams. Most health food stores carry a wide variety of vitamins and are used to people coming in and using a pendulum to make selections. They will be happy to make suggestions and provide information on standard units of size. Learn to work with and trust your High Self; it knows more about you and your needs than you do. Do not assume that everyone in your family will use the same forms of vitamins you do. Mary Ann, my wife, has a different digestive system than mine, and does not easily digest the same vitamin formulas my system does. Once she had X-rays taken as part of a medical checkup and her intestines were full of calcium tablets that had not dissolved. Now she makes certain that the vitamins she uses can be absorbed and utilized by her body.

Chart 9A—Minerals

A healthy diet will usually provide all of the trace minerals you need. However, do not assume you are getting enough–ask your High Self. Here is what I just asked of my High Self.

Q. *Am I getting enough minerals with my diet? (-)*

Q. *Would food provide the minerals I need? (-)*

Q. *Would blackstrap molasses provide all of the necessary minerals? (+)*

Q. *Would one tablespoon daily be enough? (+)*

Additional charts could be developed to fit specific purposes. The possibilities are endless. Just check to ascertain your needs, and then follow through. Good intentions are great, action is better. I just went to the kitchen and took a tablespoon of molasses.

Q. *Am I now taking the correct amount and types of vitamins and minerals I need? (+)*

Spiritual Response Therapy is a wonderful tool to assist you in researching and clearing any blocks to health and well-being and determining what you need for your body. Use it!

Chart 9B—Health and Well-Being

There are eleven things listed on Chart 9B–Health and Well-Being that, if properly used, can enhance your health and sense of well-being. First, determine how many things you need to do. (Note: the following examples are not necessarily actual case histories but are included to illustrate the questioning process.)

Q. *How many things are there on this chart that I need to change? (3)*

Q. *What is the first one? (Diet)*

Q. *Is my diet basically bad and in need of drastic change? (+)*

Q. *What is the second thing I need to change? (Positive emotions)*

Q. *What is the third thing? (Constructive thoughts)*

These three things–diet, positive emotions, and constructive thoughts–constitute our physical, emotional, and mental diet. All three are extremely important for every person's health and well-being.

Water is another factor that is of vital importance to everyone. It is the major ingredient in the human body, the solvent that carries nutrients to the cells of the body through the blood, and a carrier of waste material to the elimination organs. Unfortunately, much of the water on the planet is being contaminated and drinking it may be detrimental to health. Knowing that drinking our water may be risky, I listed several sources and types of water and asked my High Self which was the best for me and my family. You may want to check your own water. Here is how. Take a sample of water and using a chart with numbers; ask your High Self what the value of the water is for you. For example, I will use my tap water and the water we purchase in bottles.

Q. *What is the positive value of this tap water for me? (100%)*

Q. *What is the discordant value? (10%)*

Q. *What is the positive value of distilled water? (93%)*

Q. *What is the discordant value? (11%)*

Q. *Is the only reason for the discordant value the lack of minerals? (+)*

Q. *Am I getting enough minerals from other sources? (+)*

Chart 9B—Food or Diet

Quality gasoline and oil are vital for the efficient operation and long life of your automobile. Quality food and water are essential to the body if you expect to have good health, vitality, and a long life. Most people, especially in the United States, eat a lot of low-quality junk foods, and many of them are destructive to the human body. Here is my own example.

Q. *Is there anything on Chart 9B I need to change? (+)*

Q. *How many things are there? (4)*

Q. *What is the first one? (Sweets)*

Q. *Have I been eating too many sweets? (+)*

Q. *What percent should I eliminate? (100%)*

Q. *What is the value of sugar, in any form, for me? (0)*

Q. *What is the destructive value? (700%)*

When I first started working with SRT, and had the dream in which I was dying, I asked many questions about the value of different food and drink for me. The destructive value of sugar led me to ask other questions.

Q. *Is the reason I should not eat sweets because I am diabetic? (-)*

Q. *Is it because I am borderline diabetic? (+)*

Q. *If I eat sweets, will I become diabetic? (+)*

Q. *What is the second item I need to change? (Vegetables)*

Q. *Should I increase or decrease them? (Increase)*

Q. *Increase by what percent? (60%)*

Q. *Cooked or raw? (Raw)*

Q. *What is the next thing I need to change? (Grains)*

Q. *Should they be increased or decreased? (Increased)*

Q. *What percent? (30%)*

Q. *What is the fourth thing I need to change? (Bulk)*

Q. *Will increasing my consumption of raw vegetables a full 60% give me the required bulk? (+)*

Food combining is one of the most important things you can check out using SRT. Most dietitians recommend that you have foods containing starch and protein for every meal, plus fruit. My High Self says that diet is completely wrong for me. But you are not me and your food requirements may be different. Starch requires an alkaline system for proper digestion and protein requires an acid system. Fortunately, the human body can provide either. Unfortunately, when you put both starch and protein in your stomach at one time your body produces both acid and alkali, mixing them together, and they neutralize each other so you do not get proper digestion. Eat all of the meat and vegetables you desire for they digest well together. Or, eat all of the starch and vegetables you desire. Just don't mix starch and proteins. Check with your High Self to see what kinds of meat, if any, are good for you. My High Self gives me a very high rating for fish, zero for beef, and a high negative factor for pork. Do not assume that you will get the same figures I do. Everyone is different and only you or a trained response therapist can determine through spiritual means what is right for your body. After several years of restricted diet, I can now eat anything I desire as long as it is in moderation and with good judgment.

Fruit requires about thirty minutes in the stomach for the first stage of digestion, and then it moves into the intestinal tract for further processing. Do not eat fruit with a meal for it does not digest if put with other foods; it ferments. Eat fruit thirty minutes or more before a meal or two and one half hours after. That way it will not interfere with the normal digestive process for other foods your body requires and you will receive the maximum benefit from your food. This is also advocated in the book *Fit For Life* by Harvey and Marilyn Diamond.

You can use a number chart to determine the value of any food or combination of foods for your body. When Mary Ann and I were married in 1977, I did not drink coffee or tea. However, I liked to have a hot drink when I came in from working in the yard on a cold day. She would fix me a drink made from whey and molasses dissolved in hot water. After starting to work with SRT, I did some questioning regarding the value of these two ingredients for my body. Whey had a 40% value and molasses 145%. Asking what the value of the hot drink was, I got a zero reading! The two taken together were not compatible.

Sometimes one food can enhance the value of another food. I love corn chips and hot salsa. I get different values on different brands of corn chips. The brand I was using had a value of 81% and the salsa a value of 110%. The combination of corn chips and salsa had a value of 100%.

Direct Healing Processes—Chart 7

Every part and organ of our bodies has its own vibrations and when those vibrations are in harmony and balanced, there is health and vitality in the whole system. When they are out of balance and inharmonious, there is disease. Discordant thoughts, emotions, and programs set up harmful vibrations in the body which can cause headaches, ulcers, and other diseases. We have found while working with SRT, that, after the basic programs are cleared, the vibrations of the body can be changed by applying direct healing processes. Chart 7–Direct Healing Processes, shows a list of things that can be processed by High Self directly into the body as vibrational medicine. There are 42 items shown on the chart. There is another 83 items on the chart that are not typed in. You simply ask High Self if any of these things would be of benefit, and if so, to please apply all of them as needed. I will discuss some of them here.

I asked if any of the crystal books currently on the market would be of value in healing and balancing the energies of the body and received a "yes" response. I then asked that four crystal books, with corrections, be set up for listing on the chart, and this was done. I did not ask what the four books were; they were simply set up by High Self.

Wheels of Light, by Rosalyn L. Bruyere, is another book that has been of great value in balancing the chakras, and this book is listed on the chart. We have also listed several other books that High Self said would be valuable in the healing process.

Many people have heard of and may even have had occasion to use the Bach Flower Remedies. They are powerful and may be programmed in directly as vibrational medicine.

The Brain Tuner is a small black box that puts out an electrical impulse. It is applied behind the ears at the base of the mastoid bones, and is used to attune the brain. One young girl, who had never been to school because of a learning disability, needed 400 applications of the brain tuner. We (her father, who was taking my workshop at the time, and I) asked High Self if the tuner could be applied directly and they said "yes." The next day, when the father returned to class, he was very excited because his wife said the daughter had picked up a child's book the previous afternoon and started to read by herself.

Many people have had one or more parts of their body severed in past lives. Or, they have had major wounds which pierced vital organs of the body. These dismemberments or wounds can cause the etheric body, which is the pattern body for each incarnation, to have a permanent break or tear. These breaks in the etheric body can and often do cause problems in the physical body in subsequent incarnations. For instance, one of the major reasons for carpal tunnel syndrome is having a hand cut off in a past life (a common punishment for thieves). The person may have carried a lot of discordant energy on the event which manifested in a subsequent life as carpal tunnel syndrome. Even major surgery can wound the etheric body. High Self, upon request, can heal the etheric body by performing psychic surgery.

Some people have blocks to receiving their greater good, so we have placed that on the chart under *Remove Blocks to Direct Healing.*

Many people pick up discarnates again and again because their auric or physical vibrations are too low, so we ask High Self to raise them sufficiently to keep discarnates out. Your vibrations should be at least 2,000 cycles per second or higher to protect you from discarnates. Ask your High Self to keep your vibration up.

Wait until all of the client's programs and issues are cleared before asking High Self to apply the direct healing processes found on Chart 7. Ask that Holy Spirit beings be assigned to apply the direct healing processes to the client as needed for maximum well-being. Later, the client has to ask the Holy Spirit beings to apply the direct healing processes when they feel the need.

CHAPTER 18

Dreams: A Sure Guide

Many people long to have God speak to them and assure them they are loved and okay. Others wish that God would communicate with them and tell them how to conduct their lives moment by moment. Then there are those who desire assurance that God does not punish, and that they will go to heaven when they die, regardless of how many mistakes they have made in this life or how misguided they have been. What assurance do you have that there even is a God? How do you know that there is any meaning to life at all?

Does life really have a purpose beyond everyday living and the experiencing of challenges that must be faced and overcome? Are you forced into life by some unseen power? Perhaps you arrive here because of some whim or mistake of your parents for not taking proper precautions to avoid pregnancy and that is all there is to it. How do you know that birth is not the beginning of life and death the end? Has some great God or perhaps some lesser god created all of this, placed all forms of life here and then abandoned it? Are you really a miserable sinner slated for hell or are you a beloved child of God? Working with your High Self using SRT is one way to receive answers. Another way to receive answers is to pay attention to your nightly dreams and learn to interpret them. Dreams are another way that your High Self communicates important information.

Using SRT to Interpret Dreams

There are many dream books on the market and each one gives guidelines to the correct interpretation of dreams. Excellent clues can be obtained from them. Some of the books are better than others. Most of them require long study of the symbols found in dreams and many attempts at interpretation before some degree of accuracy is acquired. Even then, there is no guarantee that you have chosen the correct interpretation, as each person has his or her own unique meaning for even universal symbols.

SRT is the fastest and most accurate method yet devised to interpret dreams. It is completely accurate once you have learned to get the conscious mind into neutral so that the answers are not influenced by your conscious desires for particular meanings or your fear of what the dreams are trying to tell you. You can also find out where dreams come from. Here are some questions I asked my High Self regarding dreams.

Q. Do dreams come from the High Self? (+)

Q. Do they come from some other level of consciousness such as the conscious or subconscious mind? (-)

Q. Can they be interpreted by questioning the subconscious mind? (+)

Q. *When the High Self communicates with you in dreams, is it always through the subconscious mind? (+)*

Q. *So a person can gain an interpretation from the subconscious mind because it is always aware of what the High Self is doing? (+)*

Q. *Does the subconscious ever interfere with the dreaming process or block the interpretation of a dream? (-)*

Q. *Are there ever blocks in the subconscious mind that can interfere with the receiving and remembering of dreams? (+)*

If you do not remember your dreams, and want to do so, make certain there are no subconscious blocks causing you to blank them from conscious awareness. When these blocks exist, you can research and clear them using SRT. This will then allow you to remember your dreams.

When you retire in the evening, tell your subconscious mind that you desire to remember your dreams, and to cooperate with you, so you can use your dreams for guidance in living your life better and to develop spiritual awareness. Keep a pencil or pen and a pad of paper by your bed so you can record the dreams after they are received. Have a light handy so you can see to write. When you awake from a dream, do not jump up and start writing. First, go over the dream in your mind so that it is firmly fixed, then start writing. You may want to review your dream while you are sitting up so there is no chance for you to drift off to sleep before you get it written down. Or, you may wish to use a tape recorder and recount the dream onto tape.

Once the dream is recorded, you can take your time interpreting it, for the information is permanently recorded in the subconscious and always accessible. Start by interpreting the dream by asking the subconscious what specific people or things mean. The following dreams are some that have been received by me and interpreted using the questioning process developed through SRT.

Case Studies

Dream Received May 19, 1986

In this dream, I was at a home where a man was either crippled or injured. He moved with great difficulty into the house and sat down. I followed and stood beside him laying my hands on him. There was a strong sense of inner movement going on within me. I felt like I was going within the center of my being more deeply than ever before. It was a very profound feeling. The man was healed. I asked the following questions about this dream.

Q. *Is there any significance to the dream? (+)*

Q. *Does the feeling of going deeper within mean I am becoming more in tune with High Self? (+)*

Q. *Is this a result of the training I am taking in Response Therapy and the work I am doing with it? (+)*

Q. *Is the man who is crippled or injured me? (+)*

Q. *Does this dream signify that my own physical and spiritual healing is taking place? (+)*

Q. *As I go deeper within, getting closer to my spiritual center, will the healing be accomplished? (+)*

Q. *Is there anything else I need to know about this dream? (-)*

Dream Received May 20, 1986

In this dream, I was working at a new Sears store that was being set up for business. (Prior to becoming a minister, I worked for Sears.) Employees from other Sears stores were coming in to help set up displays. I worked with one crew to set up a gazebo-type clothing display they were having trouble with and was called to task for helping them. However, the display did very well with an exceptional return. Later, I was in the restroom changing from work to dress clothes. A urinal was overflowing, and I was trying to stay in a dry area to change. There was a man who was mopping the floor.

This dream was given to me as a form of encouragement. I had begun to get deeply involved in using SRT as my major form of therapy. There was some negative feedback from a few of the people in the congregation who heard what I was doing. Because of the negative feedback, two members of the Board of Directors were concerned, fearful that SRT was not spiritual, and objected to my using the method.

Q. *Does working for a new store in an old firm relate to states of consciousness? (+)*

Q. *I am taking an old work place, Sears (consciousness), and helping others set up a new consciousness through using SRT? (+)*

Q. *So, using SRT is helping people establish new ways of displaying or living their lives? (+)*

Q. *The resultant returns of the changed consciousness are high? (+)*

Q. *Am I being called to task because I changed my method of counseling? (+)*

Q. *Does the exceptional return also have to do with the substantially increased income to the church from this form of counseling? (+)*

Q. *Changing from work to dress clothes means my conscious is being upgraded in the process of helping others using SRT? (+)*

Q. *Trying to stay out of the mess from the urinal means I am trying to stay out of the discordant energies that are being expressed by some people at church? (+)*

Q. *Does the man cleaning up signify that I am being given some assistance in handling the situation? (+)*

Q. *Is this assistance being given by a spiritual guide or guides? (+)*

Q. *Are these guides also working with the other people who are upset over what I am doing? (+)*

Q. *Is there anything else of significance I need to know about this dream? (-)*

This dream was very encouraging. It helped me to weather the storm until the tremendous value of SRT, for both the church and the people, became clearly evident.

Dream Received May 21, 1986

Many dreams do not have any spiritual significance. They are simply a method the High Self uses to help you release tensions that have built up during the day. Here is an example of such a dream.

I was driving a car, much older and larger than the one I had, along a narrow road with my brother, Don, as a passenger. I sensed that the car was not in the best shape, so we parked it and went into a building. We got on a vehicle like an elongated auto-repair scooter with me sitting in front. We went down a long hall into a large room. I was going to make a sharp turn and cause the vehicle to do a crack-the-whip. It did not work. Someone came along and said he saw the car belch some smoke as I turned the sharp corner.

Q. *Does the car represent my physical body? (-)*

Q. *Does it represent an old state of consciousness? (-)*

Q. *Did the car belong to me in the dream? (-)*

Q. *Does this dream contain anything of significance for my life right now? (+)*

Q. *Is it simply a release of tension from yesterday? (+)*

Q. *Anything further I need to know about it? (-)*

Dream Received May 24, 1986

Physical health and well-being are not always easy to maintain when from youth you have been used to going full blast and refuse to believe that age has anything to do with stamina.

This next dream was telling me I had overtaxed myself and to take it easy. I dreamed that my automobile was overheated. The radiator was boiling and overflowing. I pulled into a service station and ran water from a garden hose into and over the radiator to cool it.

Q. *Does the car represent my physical body? (+)*

Q. *Did I overwork and overheat my physical body? (+)*

Q. *Did my strong desire (ego) to work with SRT cause me to overwork my physical body? (+)*

Q. *Am I okay now? (-)*

Q. *Will a nap restore my energy? (Weak "yes" response.)*

Q. *Will it be best for me to take it easy today? (+)*

Q. *Will my energy be restored by tomorrow? (+)*

Q. *Is there anything else I need to know about this dream? (-)*

Dream Received May 25, 1986

High Self may use some very interesting dreams to inform you of what is taking place in your consciousness.

In another dream I had, a school was to be constructed on a lot near our old home in Michigan. Just before the engineers arrived, I walked through the edge of the lot and sank almost to my knees in the soft ground. The engineers arrived and, seeing the condition of the ground, wanted to move the structure to the lot immediately adjacent to the house. I told them they would have to obtain my mother's consent. I sent someone to get her and when they did not return at once, I went to get her myself. Even then she delayed and wanted her hat and gloves, which I found on a shelf. By the time we returned to the construction site, the pile driver crew had already installed the piles on the back part of the lot that was adjacent to the house. Mom gave her consent and the work proceeded.

Q. *Does building the school represent building consciousness? (-)*

Q. *Does it represent building spiritual consciousness? (+)*

Q. *Building the school on the second lot represents trying to move too fast without proper preparation and the help of spiritual guides (pile driver crew) in building a firm spiritual foundation? (+)*

Q. *Does constructing on piles mean building on a stronger spiritual base? (+) (I was to build on solid ground.)*

Q. *Does my mother represent High Self leading me into spiritual knowledge and growth? (+)*

Q. *So getting her consent means getting the permission and cooperation of the High Self? (+)*

The heady excitement I was experiencing as a result of working with SRT caused me to be overly-enthusiastic and in some instances was causing me difficulties, conflict, and even emotional pain. This dream was telling me to stay centered in High Self and to build the foundation slowly and firmly. Also, many years ago I was told that my guides wanted to work with me and would do so whenever I would allow them to. In this dream the indication was that at last I was allowing them to work with me.

Dream Received September 1, 1986

High Self lets us know when we are making progress on the spiritual path. This next dream was very wonderful and came at a time when I needed encouragement.

I was fishing, accompanied by two men. I made a very long cast and the lure hardly hit the water before I hooked a fish. I started reeling it in but made little progress, so I started hauling it in by hand, assisted by the two men. As we worked together, the fish rose out of the water and became a model airplane that flew very high. When the plane landed, we found it had no motor and I was amazed that it could fly. The line was all tangled up and I could not find the end, so I left it. (Note: For me, fish represent divine or spiritual ideas.)

Q. *Does going fishing represent seeking divine ideas? (+)*

Q. *Have I come a long way in spiritual growth (represented by the long cast)? (+)*

Q. *I caught a divine idea (fish) in consciousness? (+)*

Q. *Does hauling it in by hand mean I have a better grasp of things? (+)*

Q. *Does the fish changing to a model airplane and rising high into the air symbolize a higher, more enlightened spiritual idea or consciousness? (+)*

Q. *Does the missing motor symbolize that the idea is moved by High Self and flies solely by High Self? (+)*

Q. *Does the line being so tangled that we could not find the end mean that we are not to try? (+)*

Q. *Will High Self take care of it? (+)*

Q. *Am I just to follow my inner guidance and act? (+)*

Q. *Do the two men helping me bring in the fish (idea) have a special significance? (+)*

Q. *Does one of them symbolize my High Self? (+)*

Q. *Is one of them Ra Kesh, my Guardian Angel? (+)*

Q. *Am I releasing my self-will and allowing them to assist and guide me more? (+)*

Q. *Anything else I need to know about this dream? (–)*

Dream Received September 7, 1986

How very easy it is for most of us to give up when life becomes difficult or confusing. We get caught up in our emotions and feel trapped and overcome and give in to frustration and despair. When this happens, we can look to High Self for encouragement and balancing of the emotions. Never give up something you believe is right and beneficial to you or your brothers and sisters on this planet. The following is a dream of confirmation and encouragement.

Two girls were cutting up lettuce to make a salad. The lettuce was in bad shape and one of the girls was upset. I started singing cheerful songs but could not remember all of the words. A young man was upset because I would not lead the people in singing, as I did not know all of the words. There was a lot of string on the ground which I was going to wrap on a stick. He did not want me to and tried to pull the stick away from me. I took the stick and began to hit him over the head with it. Another young man stepped in to help take the stick from me. I kept hitting first one and then the other until they gave up. The second fellow said, "You never give up, do you?" I said, "No!" He replied, "Don't." People said I would be arrested, but I refused to give up.

Q. *Does this dream have anything of spiritual significance for me? (+)*

Q. *Do the girls represent my emotions? (+)*

Q. *Have I been upset over the struggle of working with SRT and trying to get it accepted by the church as a viable and productive counseling method? (+)*

Q. *Does singing symbolize keeping up my courage and strong spiritual desire to see SRT accepted? (+)*

Q. *Does the young man represent others who want me to follow their desires? (+)*

Q. *Does the string on the ground symbolize the tangled affairs and confusion of the worldly intellect I was trying to wind up? (+)*

Q. *Does hitting in the head mean overcoming the intellect? (+)*

Q. *When the people said I would be arrested, does it signify that people said I would get into trouble using SRT, but I refused to give up regardless of threats? (+)*

Q. *Am I to keep on using SRT regardless of threats? (+)*

Many times I have been tempted to discard SRT, not because of the negative reaction of others, but because of the difficulty and confusion I experienced in developing it. In the beginning, there were no charts and very little information about how to proceed. Every time (and there have been many) I was tempted to trash the whole thing, an inner voice would say, "Wait a minute. Has it helped anyone?" Of course, my reply was an emphatic "Yes!" Then the inner voice would respond, "Then keep it."

Dream Received February 11, 1987

What we think and feel are of vital importance if we want to walk the spiritual path. The following is a dream reflecting the need to keep a pure consciousness.

In the dream, my house was being pumped full of sewage.

Q. *Is the house my physical body? (–)*

Q. *Is the house my consciousness? (+)*

Q. *Does sewage represent contaminated thoughts? (+)*

Q. *Am I allowing contaminated thoughts into my consciousness? (+)*

Dream Received December 2, 1988

Procrastination is often detrimental and destructive. This dream was given to me after I had started working on this book. I had a general idea for the book but no concise plan. I knew that, like the first book, as soon as I started writing, High Self would reveal the material I was to present. This is of vital importance, since I have little or no skill as a writer. Neither do I have full knowledge of the material that Spirit wants brought to the attention of people with minds open enough to receive it. That is exactly what happened. The moment I started writing, it seemed like the work I did with every client brought new insights and information that was to be included in the book.

Then I stopped working on the book. About two months later, I received the following dream. When I awoke the next morning, I was very reluctant to find out what the dream meant, so refused to search out the meanings. Finally, twenty-four hours later at breakfast the dream came so strongly to mind I decided I better check it out. (High Self was really nudging me on this one.)

In this dream, my fish tank was low on water and some of the fish had died. They were floating on top of the water and seemed made of transparent, crystalline glass. The water was low and dirt had settled in the bottom.

Q. *Is there anything of spiritual significance about this dream? (+)*

Q. *Do the glass-like fish represent spiritual ideas? (+)*

Q. *Are the spiritual ideas given to me dying of neglect? (+)*

Q. *Is there something I need to do about this? (+)*

Q. *Does it have to do with the new book? (+)*

Q. *Am I neglecting the writing? (+)*

Q. *Are some of the concepts dying (being lost) because I have not written them in the book? (+)*

Q. *Is there anything else I need to know about this dream? (–)*

Dreams Recounted By Others

A client, Robert, wanted to find out about two dreams that kept recurring when he was a child and young man. In the first dream he felt like he was being possessed and overcome by a discarnate. We used Chart 4—When; Cast of Characters to help determine the reason.

Q. *Is this dream a memory of a past life? (+)*

Q. *What were you in this life? (Guide)*

Q. *Who else was involved? (Female)*

Q. *Someone else in the cast? (+)*

Q. *What were they? (Dark energy)*

Q. *Was the dark energy bothering the female? (-)*

Q. *Was the energy trying to overcome you so it could possess the female? (+)*

Q. *Were you fearful that you would be overcome? (+)*

The second dream also occurred when Robert was a child. He saw the colors black and yellow and heard a sound that kept getting louder. This also was past life recall.

Q. *What were you in this life? (Androgynous)*

Q. *Someone else involved? (-)*

Considerable questioning was needed to bring out all of the factors in the dream. Robert had designed and constructed a color machine used to control people. This was not negative control, but was devised to promote healing through the use of color. Robert was testing the equipment and it malfunctioned. Part of the equipment was a band around the chest.

When the machine malfunctioned, the band tightened and started to crush Robert. The agony was intense and the sound getting louder was a result of the pain he was experiencing—Robert was trying to call for help. Fortunately, the machine burned out and Robert was released.

Here are three dreams related to me by Suzanne. "In the first dream I was in a jewelry store and was told that there was a secret room which contained treasures. Somehow I knew that lights reflecting off coins were the key to the room. So I took two coins and tried to reflect light off them to open the door. However, it did not open. When I added a third coin and placed them in the right position so the light would reflect off them, the door opened. The room did not contain objects with monetary or earthly values such as gold or jewels, but contained characteristics like happiness, love, understanding, and greater spiritual awareness. There was a man in the room like a wizard. He said all of the treasures were available to me and I could have anything and everything in the room if I chose to have it." Suzanne was using her pendulum and the charts as I asked the questions.

Q. *Is there anything of spiritual value for you in the dream? (+)*

Q. *Are you the jewelry store? (+)*

Q. *Is the secret room your spiritual being? (+)*

Q. *Does the hidden treasure represent values that lie dormant within you? (+)*

Q. *Do the coins represent levels of consciousness? (+)*

Q. *Are the first two levels the conscious and subconscious mind? (+)*

Q. *Is the third coin the superconscious mind? (+)*

Q. *Is the wizard your High Self, who will help you get the treasure? (+)*

Q. *Is there anything else you need to know about the dream? (-)*

"In the second dream, there were three fire-breathing dragons. One of the dragons was on top of a tall building trying to get free. The dragon was not trying to hurt anyone, it just felt tied down and wanted loose. The other two dragons were trying to keep the one on the roof from going anywhere. There was fire caused by the dragons and the building was shaking loose but there was not a deliberate attempt on the dragon's part to destroy anything or cause any harm."

Q. Do you need to understand this dream? (+)

Q. Does it have spiritual significance to you? (+)

Q. Are the three dragons' aspects of self? (+)

Q. Are the three aspects the conscious, subconscious, and High Self? (+)

Q. Is the dragon on the roof your High Self? (+)

Q. Are your conscious thoughts and subconscious programs keeping your High Self from fully expressing? (+)

Q. Is your High Self shaking you up, trying to make you more aware of your potential? (+)

"In the third dream, I was presented with a drawing of a male lion by a woman who seemed to be either a psychic or very wise. However, I did not actually see the woman; I just felt her presence. The drawing was like a paint-by-number painting. The woman told me that each numbered section had a meaning behind it, and the ones on the head of the lion were the most significant. One area on the head kept drawing my attention, the area around the mouth. I was told that was the most important section."

Q. Does the dream have any spiritual significance? (+)

Q. Does the lion represent spiritual power? (+)

Q. Was the woman your High Self? (+)

Q. Does the significance of the area around the mouth mean you are to express your power through speaking positive words? (+)

Q. Are you to use your head to develop your spiritual power and to live your life with power? (+)

Q. Are you to become more aware of and work with your High Self? (+)

Q. Does the dream signify that you have the power to color and control your own life? (+)

Q. Anything else we need to know about the dream? (-)

Darlene asked me to interpret the following dream. She was on a bus. There was a black man on the bus and several small children. The black man drove the bus up on the embankment where it exploded into flames. In the next scene, Darlene was in her apartment and there was a mulatto friend in another room. The bus driver was in the same building but not visible to her. She locked the doors to protect herself and her friend. Darlene changed into a black woman. Fire started in the room where the friend was, and he came bursting through the wall. It was almost as though Darlene disappeared at this point and the friend was very angry.

Q. Does the black man represent dark energies? (+, Fear and panic)

Q. Are the children new ideas, more God-like, that can lead you to a more spiritual expression? (+)

Q. Are the black energies of fear and panic trying to kill the God-like ideas? (+)

Q. Does the bus represent the physical body? (+)

Q. Fire means that both the physical body and spiritual ideas are being burned up? (+)

Q. Does the mulatto friend represent dark energy, but not as dark as the black man? (+)

Q. Does this have anything to do with a past life? (+)

Q. Is this a precognition of meeting Joe (a new friend) and his dark energies? (+)

Q. Does locking doors mean trying to lock out fear and panic? (+)

Q. Does changing into a black woman mean your fear and panic is overcoming you? (+)

Q. Does disappearing mean you have been overcome by the dark energy? (+)

Q. Was your friend angry because you are not doing more to clear yourself of fear and panic? (+)

Q. Is there anything else Darlene needs to know about the meaning of this dream? (-)

These examples will give you enough understanding of the questioning process to get you started on interpreting what *your* dreams are saying to *you*. Know that your own inner mind is the best source of knowledge about you—not some book. Use SRT to expand your knowledge of dream meanings. You can become aware of and follow your dream guidance to a greater expression of life.

CHAPTER 19

Examples of Complete Cases

We have discussed many different programs in the earlier chapters of this book. As you may have guessed, the clearing process for each person can take any of an infinite number of paths. The case studies presented in this chapter are designed to provide you with an overview of the research process required to clear your programs or your client's programs from beginning to end.

When a client comes to me and wants research and clearing done, the first thing I ascertain is that I am clear up to and including the level of GRAND-I/WHOLE (see Chart 3–Levels of Soul Consciousness) and that I am working with my High Self. I verify that they are in the 99th elevation of the GODHEAD (see Chart 3) and at GRAND-I/WHOLE. When you begin working with this system, your High Self committee and your other committees and councils may not be at the level of the GODHEAD. You can still work with your High Self even though it may not be at the GODHEAD level.

Next, I make certain that all my committees and councils are clear all the way to the level of WHOLE and that they are at the minimum size for maximum effort. Remember a soul never stops learning and growing and even at the higher levels may pick up some programming that needs to be cleared. Ask for this clearing as a gift to those on your committees and councils and to ensure that you will receive accurate answers. Since no research is needed to clear those out of the physical body, this happens very quickly. The pendulum moves in a clearing circle, returning to a yes movement when the clearing is finished. If there are some souls on your committees and councils that are not at the level of the GODHEAD, the clearing you ask for on their behalf will enable them to move up through the levels of soul consciousness with greater speed and ease.

Using Chart 1–Contact or Help, I ask them to indicate with whom I am working. The pendulum is moved in a clearing circle and when completed, points to High Self. Should High Self not be indicated I ask that additional clearing be done until I can work with my High Self and until the High Self is indicated.

Case Study 1: Alberta

Here are one client's programs. I shall call her Alberta. Alberta was having mental stress, emotional difficulties, and physical problems. Her relationships were always a disaster and she had several health problems. Alberta had many of the problems commonly involved with clients, and her case presents a good cross section of programs that often have to be researched and cleared.

As always, I ask permission to work on the client's programs.

Q. Can I do the research work for Alberta? (+)

Then, using Chart 1—Chart to Use, I ask what the first program is that we need to research and clear for her.

Q. *On what chart will we find the first program that needs to be cleared? (The pendulum indicates Chart 5— Blocks and Interference; Negative Motivations)*

Because there are two sets of programs on Chart 5, I hold the pendulum below and halfway between the Blocks and Interference and the Negative Motivations on Chart 5 and ask which set it is. The pendulum indicates Negative Motivations.

Q. *What is the negative motivation? (Coercion)*

When negative motivation is indicated, always research past lives (for a review of this process, see Chapters 5—The Basic Steps of SRT and 13—Negative Motivations). The first person you identify in the past life case is the client. Using Chart 4—Cast of Characters, I ask the following questions.

Q. *Who was Alberta in the first past life? (Mother)*

Q. *Mother as in what? (Using the options sheet in Appendix B, mother superior was indicated).*

When High Self moves the pendulum to indicate a character listed to the left of the center line on Chart 4, this nearly always indicates the cast is made up of religious figures. High Self says I am given many religious lives to research and clear because, as a minister, religious lives are important to me, and religious lives, because of the high expectations and demands to be the perfect example, carry a higher negative charge if those expectations and demands are not fulfilled.

Q. *Was someone else involved? (+)*

Q. *Who were they? (Group, 48 brothers or priests)*

When I ask "Who were they?" and the pendulum moves in a circle, High Self is indicating that there is more than one person involved—a group. I then use a chart with numbers to get the total involved. In this case, the pendulum moved between 40 and 50, which indicates more than forty and less than fifty. The second digit was 8, so the complete number was 48. When I asked what they were, High Self indicated brother, which means priest.

Q. *Was someone else involved? (-)*

The next thing I do is determine if there was any form of harm, and if so, who was harmed, what form the harm took, and the seriousness of that harm.

Q. *Was there harm? (+)*

Q. *Who was harmed? (Alberta. I held the pendulum below where mother superior and group of priests were written in my notes and the pendulum pointed to mother superior.)*

Q. *Was it physical harm? (+)*

Q. *Was it serious? (+) And was it death? (+)*

Q. *Was she accused of heresy and burned? (+)*

I knew to ask this last question because this is a common cause of death in this type of past life situation, and because my intuition suggested it. Then I make sure there is nothing more to research in this past life.

Q. *Is there anything else we need to know to clear this past life? (-)*

Q. *Do we need to research another past life to clear this negative motivation completely? (-)*

Q. *What was the total number of lives involved in this negative motivation? (963 ½)*

Please clear and replace with good. Thank you.

The ½ indicates that some of the same energy was running in Alberta's current life. Alberta believed that she was coerced in that past life, and even more interesting, she believed that she deserved to be coerced in this present life. I proceeded to research by asking if there was another negative motivation on Chart 5 to clear. There was, and it was self-punishment.

Q. *Who was Alberta in the first past life involving self-punishment? (Chart 4, Female)*

Q. *Was someone else involved? (+, Sister, a relative)*

Q. *Was someone else involved? (-)*

Q. *Was there harm? (+)*

Q. *Who was harmed? (The pendulum moves halfway between female and sister, indicating that both were harmed.)*

Q. *Who did the harming? (Alberta)*

Q. *Was it physical harm? (+) Serious? (+) Death? (+)*

Using my intuition, I guessed at the circumstance surrounding the death.

Q. *Was it murder and suicide? (+)*

Q. *Does Alberta believe she must punish herself for what she did? (+)*

Q. *Can this life be cleared now? (+)*

Q. *Can the negative motivation be cleared? (+)*

Please clear and replace with good. Thank you.

Q. *What was the total number of lives involved? (837)*

Q. *Is there another negative motivation to research or clear? (-)*

I then return to Chart 1 to begin researching the next program.

Q. *What chart is the next program on that needs clearing? (Chart 6A– Master Programs, Discordant Energy)*

Since the program can be either master programs or discordant energy you have to ask which it is.

Q. *Which category is the program? (Discordant energy)*

Q. *What is the discordant energy? (Self-punishment)*

Q. *When was the program established? (Chart 4 - The pendulum moves in a circle, which means it is in the present life and ongoing.)*

Q. *Can you clear without further research? (+)*

Please clear, replace with good and give me a "yes" response when you are finished.

The pendulum moves in a circle indicating that High Self is clearing, and finally moves into a "yes" position indicating the clearing is finished. Once again, I use Chart 1 to determine whether or not there is another program to be cleared.

Q. *Is there another program to be cleared? (+)*

Q. *What chart is the next program on? (Chart 7–Direct Healing Processes)*

Q. *Do you want to apply direct healing? (+)*

Please apply now.

Again, the pendulum moves in a circle, indicating that the work is being done, and finally swings in a "yes" position, indicating they are finished. It is unusual for High Self to indicate this early in the clearing work that direct healing processes are to be employed. However, they understand the proper procedures, so I just ask them to do what is indicated.

Then I use Chart 1 to see if there is another program to be cleared.

Q. *Is there another program to be cleared? (+)*

Q. *What chart is it on? (Chart 6A–Master Programs)*

As you may recall from Chapter 8–Master Programs, you may need to find which elements of master programs the client has.

Q. How many of the eight elements does Alberta have? (8)

Q. What level of consciousness did Alberta attain? (900)

Q. How many master programs does Alberta have? (The pendulum moves along bottom of the number chart indicating there is an infinite number)

When there are an infinite number of master programs, the number of hidden agenda and backup programs is also infinite.

Q. Can you burn all of them, root, branch, and seed? (+)

Please burn and replace with good. Thank you.

Q. How many master programs remain after burning? (373)

Q. What is the first master program that we need to clear? (Chart 6A, Murder)

Q. Who was Alberta in the first life? (Chart 4, Father, head priest)

Q. Is someone else involved? (-)

When the cast consists of the client only, I go directly to Chart 6A–Negative Energy, to find the negative energy they accumulated in the past life.

Q. What is the energy? (Negativity, spiritual suicide, murder, unforgiveness, intolerance)

Questioning revealed that some of the nuns were having sex, getting pregnant, and killing the babies at birth. The murder energy was actually witness to murder. Alberta felt she was in rebellion to the Church and to God because she did not agree with what was happening. She could not tolerate the death of the babies, was unforgiving of the Church and the people involved in the pregnancies, and in the killing of the babies.

Q. Is there another life to research? (-)

Please clear and replace with good. Thank you.

Q. Is there another master program? (+, Chart 6A, Negativity)

Q. Who was Alberta in the first past life? (Chart 4, High Self)

Q. For whom was she High Self? (Mother superior)

Q. Someone else involved? (+, Priest)

Q. Anyone else? (+, Son, a child)

Q. Was the son born to the mother superior? (+)

Q. Was the child killed at birth? (+)

Q. Was Alberta, as High Self, angry, upset, and negative, and did she see the killing of the child as murder? (+)

Q. Can you clear this master program now? (+)

Q. What is the total number of lives involved? (2,414)

You do not have to find the number of lives involved in each program researched. The major value of finding the number of lives, to me, is to see if energy has carried over and if the client recognizes that the energy has been affecting their life in a discordant way.

Q. Is there another master program to research? (-)

Please clear all remaining master programs and replace with good. Thank you.

Once again, I return to Chart 1 to ask if there is another program to research and clear.

Q. Is there something else to research? (+, Chart 4–Programs)

Q. What is the program on Chart 4? (Self-punishment)

Q. When was the self-punishment established? (Past lives in other dimensions)

Q. Who was Alberta in the first life? (Male)

Q. Is someone else involved? (-)

Q. What was her energy? (Chart 6A, Intolerance, negativity, fear, spiritual suicide, injustice, black magic)

Q. Can you clear the program? (+)

Please clear and replace with good. Thank you.

Return to Chart 1.

Q. Is there another program? (+, Chart 2—Themes and Challenges; Soul Qualities)

Q. Which program is it, themes and challenges or soul qualities? (Soul Qualities)

Q. Which quality do we need to research? (Understanding, love)

Q. Who was Alberta in the first life? (Chart 4, Brother, priest)

Q. Is someone else involved? (-)

Q. What are the energies? (Chart 6A, Injustice, frustration, fear, lying, spiritual suicide, alcoholism, self-punishment, negativity, unforgiveness, addiction to lying, hate of self, hate of God, hate of self, hate of life, suicide)

Q. Do we have enough information to clear this? (+)

Please clear and replace with good. Thank you.

Return to Chart 2.

Q. Is there another soul quality to clear? (+, Unity, compassion)

Q. Who was Alberta in the first life? (Chart 4, Mother superior)

Q. Is someone else involved? (-)

Q. What was her energy? (Chart 6A, Anger, hate of women, hate of God, hate of men, hate of men, self-limitation, and suicide)

Q. Can you clear the program? (+)

Please clear and replace with good. Thank you.

(***Note:*** If you wish, you can wait until all programs are researched and then clear everything at one time. However, I find that if I clear each program as it is researched, there is less energy that might block the questioning process, and answers seem to come more quickly. Also, you may or may not wish to get the total number of lives involved in each program. Just make certain you have an agreement with your High Self that they will clear all lives in the situation.)

Once again, I return to Chart 2 to make sure we have cleared all soul qualities.

Q. Is there another soul quality to clear? (-)

Return to Chart 1.

Q. Is there another program to clear? (+, Chart 1)

Q. What is the program? (Conscious mind)

Please clear and replace with good. Thank you.

When High Self points to Chart 1 as the location of the problem, it is one of the items found on the inside of the fan. In this case, High Self wanted to dissolve the discordant energy accumulated in the conscious mind. There are compartments in the conscious mind (High Self says eighty-nine) that can hold individual programs. It may be necessary to clear one or more of those separate compartments in order to bring about a specific change in a person's life. For instance, one person had difficulty losing weight and although we had cleared all of his programs regarding excess weight, he was not reducing. When we asked why he was not losing weight, we found a belief in the conscious mind that had to be cleared.

Once High Self has cleared the program, return to Chart 1.

Q. Where is the next item to clear? (Chart 10—Miscellaneous Blocks)

When High Self indicates Chart 10, I simply ask High Self to clear the entire chart. Here is my questioning process. For a review of clearing programs listed on this chart, see Chapter 14—Miscellaneous Blocks.

Q. *How many levels of genetic beliefs does Alberta have? (4)*

Q. *How many forms of toxic streams? (2)*

Q. *How many decaying universe programs? (3)*

Q. *Does she have loss of subconscious integrity? (+)*

Q. *Does she have multiple souls? (+, 38,752)*

Q. *Is Alberta a transfer student? (-)*

Q. *Do you need to clear cellular memory? (+)*

Q. *How many major beliefs does she have? (12)*

Q. *Does she have anti-time conflict? (+)*

Q. *Does she have soul programs? (+)*

Q. *Does she have everything else on the chart? (+)*

High Self, please clear everything on this chart and replace with good. Thank you.

Return to Chart 1.

Q. *Is there something else we need to do? (+, Chart 11–Soul Energy Programming)*

Q. *Does Alberta have everything on Chart 11? (+)*

Please clear in depth and replace with good. Thank you.

Return to Chart 1.

Q. *Is there something else we need to do? (+, Chart 12–Spirit Energy Programming)*

Q. *Does Alberta have everything on Chart 12? (+)*

Please clear in depth and replace with good. Thank you.

Return to Chart 1.

Q. *Is there something else to clear? (+, Chart 13–Programs Before Creation)*

Q. *Does she have everything on Chart 13? (-)*

Q. *Which ones does she have? (Chart 13, Idea, thought, infinite levels before thought, levels 1 through 6, fire planet energy)*

Q. *Do we need to determine the depth? (-)*

Please clear and replace with good. Thank you.

Return to Chart 1.

Q. *Something else we need to clear? (+)*

Q. *What is it? (The pendulum moves in a circle indicating that the rest of the remaining charts, programs, energies, and items can now be cleared.)*

Return to Chart 1.

Q. *Is there something else to clear? (-)*

Q. *Is there something else we need to do? (+, Chart 9B–Health and Well-Being)*

Q. *What is it that Alberta needs to change? (Recreation)*

Recreation, in this case, means self-nurturing—doing things that will provide excitement, a sense of self-value, self-esteem, and fulfillment. There is nothing to clear here; this is a recommendation to Alberta that she consciously change her routine.

Q. *Is there something else to be done? (+, Chart 7–Direct Healing Processes and Colors)*

Q. *Do you wish to apply the direct healing processes? (+)*

Please apply. Thank you.

Q. *Is there something else to be done? (-)*

Q. *What percent of her onion is peeled? (100%)*

High Self gives me the picture of an onion as the symbol for the person's programs. It is a good symbol, as the programs do seem to peel off in layers. Sometimes, after a lot of clearing work, there is only a small amount of the onion that appears to be peeled. The onion may be eight feet tall. I see the outer skin, a gap of about eight inches where the onion is peeled (programs cleared), and the rest of the onion that still needs to be cleared. This means there is more work to be done, as I am not finished with the client until there is not even a nucleus remaining.

Case Study 2: Chester

Chester had a lot of problems in relationships. He could not seem to develop any sense of closeness or harmony with women. Although he had a strong desire for a loving relationship, nothing seemed to click for him.

Q. Can I do the research work for Chester? (+)

I begin with Chart 1.

Q. What is the first program to be cleared? (Chart 2—Themes and Challenges; Soul Qualities)

Q. Which of the two sets of programs is it? (Themes and Challenges) (Sex, sexual relationships)

Q. Who was Chester in the first past life? (Chart 4, Mother superior)

Q. Was someone else involved? (+, Male)

Q. Anyone else? (-)

Q. Was there harm? (-)

Q. Was there a sexual relationship with the male? (+)

Q. Was Chester blocking his sexual expression in this life because of this past life? (+)

Q. Can you clear this program? (-)

Q. Do we need to research another past life? (+)

Q. Who was Chester? (Head priest)

Q. Someone else involved? (+, Group of 37 nuns)

Q. Was there harm? (-)

Q. Was there a sexual relationship with each of the nuns? (+)

Q. Can you clear the program now? (+)

Please clear and replace with good. Thank you.

Return to Chart 1.

Q. Is there another program? (+, Chart 4—Programs)

Q. What is the program? (Past lives)

Q. Who was Chester in this life? (Female)

Q. Is someone else involved? (-)

Q. What were his energies? (Chart 6A, Panic, spiritual suicide, abandonment, self-destruction, unforgiveness, suicide)

Q. Can you clear this program? (-)

Q. Who was he in the next life? (Priest)

Q. Someone else involved? (+, Group of 2,862)

Q. Someone else involved? (-)

Q. Was there harm? (+, to Chester)

Q. Was it physical, serious, and death? (+)

Here, again, intuition helped. I knew psychically that he was accused of heresy, tortured, and burned at the stake by the group.

Q. Can you clear all of the past lives now? (+)

Q. What is the total number of lives involved? (2,911)

Please clear and replace with good. Thank you.

Q. Is there another program? (+, Chart 11—Soul Energy Programming)

Q. Can you clear everything in depth on Chart 11 without further research? (+)

Please clear Chart 11, in depth, and replace with good. Thank you.

Q. Is there another program to clear? (+, Chart 4–Programs)

Q. What is the program? (Imprint)

Q. When was the imprint set up? (The pendulum swings in a circle indicating it is ongoing.)

Q. Can you clear without further information? (+)

Please clear and replace with good. Thank you.

Q. Is there something else to clear? (+, Chart 11– Soul Energy Programming)

Q. Are the programs in layers (levels)? (+, 38,000,000)

Please clear and replace with good. Thank you.

High Self then had me return to Chart 11, indicating that all items could not be cleared when I first asked for them to be cleared in depth. So I asked Spirit to clear the remaining levels.

Q. Is there something else to clear? (+, Chart 12–Spirit Energy Programming)

Q. Can you clear all programs and all levels without any further research? (+)

Please clear and replace with good. Thank you.

Q. Is there something else to clear? (+, Chart 13–Programs Before Creation)

Q. What are the programs on Chart 13? (Idea, thought, infinite levels before thought, levels 1 through 6, levels 7 and 8, imprint of brain damage, Creator programming)

Q. Can you completely clear all of these now? (+)

Please clear and replace with good. Thank you.

Q. Is there something else to be cleared? (+) (The pendulum moved in a circle indicating that any remaining items could be cleared without research.)

Q. Can you clear the rest of the charts through Chart 31, all programs, all discordant energies, and miscellaneous items? (+)

Please clear and replace with good. Thank you.

The application of Chart 7–Direct Healing Processes, is usually done at this point as it is one of the last things that High Self wants to do when clearing a person's programs.

A check revealed that Chester was now infinitely cleared and there was nothing further to do. This does not mean that other bits and pieces of programs might not come up in the future.

Case Study 3: Anthony

When I first started working with SRT, I would have to research a person's programs in detail. Later, as I gained more knowledge of the system, I was able to clear in greater depth with less and less detail. Now, sometimes High Self will clear all of a person's programs without any research at all.

Many people have asked me if I can research and clear a person without them knowing. My answer is: "Sometimes without their conscious knowing, but never without their soul knowing and approving." When I work with my High Self and ask for permission to research someone's programs, they work with the person's High Self, who works with the person's soul and obtains the soul's permission. Sometimes the soul will not give permission because they have major self-punishment programs and are not ready to give them up. The self-punishment can be broken by asking that the soul be given a spiritual kick. I have worked for many people I have never met. This next case involves such a person.

I wanted a special case as an example to put in the book; a case that would show much of the variety of programs that you can run into while doing research work. High Self said they would give me a good example. Here is what was given. High Self revealed that the subject is a sixteen-year-old male living within five miles of my home whom I shall call Anthony. Much of the information received I will put in narrative form. After asking permission to work, I always start with Chart 1—Contact or Help.

Q. *What is the first item to be cleared? (Guardian Angels)*

When High Self indicates that a person's guides, Guardian Angels, High Self, or another council needs to be cleared, I often ask what soul level the client and the offending guide have attained using Chart 3—Levels of Soul Consciousness. Anthony's level of soul when he came into this life was at the Incarnational - earth level. When I started researching his programs, he had risen to the level of Holy Spirit Consciousness. This indicated that since incarnating, Anthony had experienced considerable soul growth through his own daily efforts. When he incarnated, his Guardian Angels were at the top level of Ascended Masters, and a check revealed that his High Self was at the same level. Anthony had actually grown enough in soul level to make him higher than his two committees. The committees thus needed to be cleared. I asked that the work be done. A subsequent check using Chart 3 revealed that the new committees were at the level of Supreme Consciousness. They were now high enough in soul consciousness to be of further assistance to Anthony.

Then I returned to Chart 1.

Q. *What is the next program to clear? (Chart 6A—Master Programs)*

Anthony had all eight of the elements involved with master programs. He had attained the 144,000 or top level of the Ascended Master level on Chart 3 as a result of his first round of incarnations. He returned to the physical incarnational process to gain his advanced degree of soul consciousness and had an infinite number of master programs. I asked High Self to burn all elements root, branch, and seed and they did. After burning, there were 1,276 master programs remaining, although it was necessary to research only three. I used Chart 6A—Master Programs, to determine the first master program we needed to research; it was injustice. Then I went to Chart 4—Cast of Characters, to determine the cast of characters in the first past life we needed to research.

Q. *Who was Anthony in the first life? (Mother superior)*

Anthony was mentally and emotionally unjust to himself, drove himself insane, and committed suicide in this past life. In the next life he was a monk and a group of 837 people were involved. Anthony was channeling information from his High Self and was healing people. He was accused of witchcraft, blasphemy, and heresy. They threw him into a dungeon where he was tortured. When he would not recant, they burned him at the stake. The number of lives involved was given as 2,650 ½. The ½ indicated he was running some energy in the present life. He had a belief that life would treat him unjustly, and he was helpless to do anything about it, and unforgiving of everything about life. These programs were set up after he was burned in the past life, so they were soul programs and very strong.

After asking Spirit to clear these programs, I returned to Chart 6A to determine the next master program that needed to be researched.

Q. *What is the next master program we need to research? (Unworthiness)*

Q. *Who was Anthony in the first past life? (Chart 4, Sister)*

I used Chart 6A—Discordant Energy to determine the negative energies Anthony had retained from this life. The first energy was guilt, set up as a result of sexual coveting. This resulted in a sense of helplessness because he could not overcome his strong desire for sex. Anthony was unforgiving and unjust to himself because of his uncontrolled desire, so he built up a lot of self-hate. He felt unworthy of God's love and was filled with terror that he would be eternally damned. These energies and a strong sense of shame led him to commit suicide. The number of lives was given as 89 ½. The current-life energies he held were envy of men who are sexually active, guilt, self-limitation, helplessness, mental illness, hate of men, hate of life, and suicide.

Q. What is the next master program we need to research? (Chart 6A, Illness)

I used Chart 4 to determine the role he played in the first past life we needed to research. Questioning revealed he was a monk and there was a female involved. The female is a sixteen-year-old female in this life and Anthony's twin flame, on whom he holds addictive energy. The female failed to nurture or give herself credit as a viable human being. In the current life, she is stingy toward others, self-centered, demanding of attention, and self-nurturing at the expense of others. Anthony felt helpless to change or help her and was unforgiving of her stinginess to herself. He developed ulcers because of the tension, and felt she was being sadistic to herself. He had a strong sexual desire for the female which he found difficult to handle and committed suicide. He went into that life with his twin flame with the desire to break the addictive energy. After he left the physical body, he felt like he had failed and was helpless to break the addiction; and he felt ill. He ran the feeling of being ill because he was addicted for 6,898 lives.

After Spirit cleared all of Anthony's master programs, I returned to Chart 1 to determine the next program to research.

Q. What is the next program? (Chart 2–Themes and Challenges, Health, fitness)

In the first life, Anthony was a monk who had tuberculosis, was filled with shame because of the illness, and killed himself.

Anthony's second theme and challenge was money and income. Again he was a monk. His energies were health abuse, unforgiveness for having cut himself off from God, a belief that he was unworthy of God's love because he was ill, unhappiness because he was unable to heal himself, and a belief that he was unworthy of ever experiencing good–money, income, life, friends, God's love, and so on–in that life or any future life.

Q. What is the next program? (Chart 2–Soul Qualities, Understanding, love)

In the first past life researched, Anthony was a mother and there was a family group of sixteen. His energy was hate of life and suicide, which caused his family mental and emotional pain.

The second soul quality was faith and joy. In the past life researched, Anthony was a mother. He felt helpless against the problems of life, unworthy to experience any good, had a hate of women, was emotionally ill and felt it was unjust, and became involved with alcoholism. This framework of mind led to unhappiness, health abuse, and suicide.

The next thing we cleared was discordant energy on his younger brother. In the past life Anthony was male and a head monk. His brother was another head monk. Anthony's brother accused him of heresy and he was crucified. In the second life, Anthony was a wife to his brother, who stabbed Anthony to death.

The next program was an imprint that Anthony gave himself when he was born into this life. He told himself that he would suffer physical illness, would be helpless to live life in a productive manner, would be unforgiving of life and all of its difficulties, and would commit suicide.

The next program was a future life in which Anthony was a monk. He had hate of life and God, unworthiness, health abuse, intolerance of life and God, injustice to himself, self-destruction, sexual promiscuity, intolerance, and injustice to himself regarding his sexual urges, unhappiness, unworthiness, and colon cancer. When the future lives were cleared, I asked if he would be healed of the cancer and received a positive response.

Q. Is there something else to clear? (+, Chart 4–When, Parallel universe)

Anthony had only one life in the parallel universe as a head priest. He ran the energy of hate, saw God as sadistic, had a blood disease, and committed suicide.

Q. What do we work on next? (Chart 10–Miscellaneous Blocks)

Anthony had everything listed on the inside of the chart. He had all twelve heart vows, three forms of curses, six forms of contracts, six generations of genetic beliefs, twenty-three blocked chakras, and three forms of toxic energies. He had everything listed on the outside of the chart, except major beliefs and transfer student. This chart can usually be cleared without finding the specific items. Just ask!

The next program we cleared appeared on Chart 19–How to Change your Life was 'other.' I have no idea what the 'other' was, I simply asked High Self to clear it. High Self then pointed to Chart 11 and indicated everything on the chart. Then they wanted to clear programs listed on Charts 12 through 18, and Chart 20. It was necessary to clear each of these items, even though the details did not have to be researched.

High Self then pointed to conscious mind on Chart 1. They wanted to clear eighty-three of the eighty-nine compartments of the conscious mind, and baptize with the Holy Spirit. Next, High Self pointed to the subconscious mind, listed on Chart 1, and wanted it cleared and baptized. I asked High Self if there were compartments in the subconscious mind and they said yes–900,000,000. Anthony had programs in 86% of them.

I was surprised when High Self pointed to Chart 9A–Minerals and Vitamins, and indicated that Anthony needed vitamin A. When asked if they could assign beings to apply vitamin A direct as a vibration, they said yes, and told me to ask for Angels of Light, which I did.

High Self pointed to Guardian Angels and High Self, indicating that they needed to be cleared to higher levels.

Q. Is there anything else we need to do? (+, Chart 4–Programs, Past lives)

Anthony was a father in the only life researched. He had health abuse, unhappiness, felt life was intolerable and unjust, was unforgiving of himself and others, felt women were unjust, had terror of God whom he saw as sadistic, had tuberculosis, and committed suicide.

High Self indicated that Anthony had a program on Chart 20–Refining Consciousness, 'programs not on charts at all levels'; and that the 'fine tuning at the ONE level' needed to be completed for Anthony. They also indicated 'hidden vows,' listed on Chart 17–Fine Tuning.

The next item indicated was that I was to ask that Anthony be raised to the 99th GODHEAD elevation along with his committees, and to see that they were in order and harmony. That was done. Then I asked them to edit his entire soul record from alpha to omega making certain that all of the rest of the charts through Chart 31 were cleared together with all programs, energies, and miscellaneous items. Then I asked for the application of Chart 7–Direct Healing Processes. I asked if there were any hidden programs or issues to be cleared, and was assured that there were not. When I asked what percent of Anthony's programs were cleared, the pendulum was moved to indicate "infinite."

Anthony was at last clear. When I questioned if the work would have a profound positive effect on his current life, I was assured it would. The addictive energy on his twin flame was cleared, he would not commit suicide, and his belief that life would treat him unjustly was gone. He was literally born again.

Case Study 4: Clearing an Animal

I have cleared all kinds of animals with programs: cats, dogs, horses, birds, and others. High Self says the next-door neighbor's cats have some programs. I used Chart 1–Chart of Use, to find where the first program is located. (Note: Many times I can simply ask that all programs be cleared for the animal without any research necessary).

Q. *What chart is the program on? (Chart 4–Programs)*

Q. *What is the first program? (Self-punishment)*

Q. *When was it established? (Past lives in other dimensions)*

I saw an inner picture of a saber-toothed tiger.

Q. *Was it a saber-toothed tiger on another planet? (+)*

Q. *Was it a planet in this galaxy? (+)*

Q. *Was someone else involved? (+)*

Q. *What were they? (Chart 4–Cast of Characters, Female)*

Q. *Was there harm? (+)*

Q. *Did the saber-toothed tiger kill the female? (+)*

Q. *Is that the reason the house cat wants to punish itself in this life? (+)*

Q. *Any other reason or program? (-)*

Please clear the program and replace with good. Thank you.

Q. *What chart is the program on for the second cat? (Chart 4–Programs)*

Q. *What is the program? (Identification)*

Q. *When was it established? (Past lives in other dimensions)*

I had an inner picture of a very ugly hippopotamus type animal.

Q. *Does the cat identify itself as being very ugly? (+)*

Q. *Anything else to clear? (-)*

Please clear the program and replace with good. Thank you.

The programs for animals are not nearly as complex and expansive as they are for humans. Usually they only have one or two things to clear, although I know of one dog that had ten programs. Any living creature can have programs, so you may wish to check all of the dogs, cats, birds, horses, cows, and so on that you have around.

Whether the program is for a human or an animal, you simply follow the charts and the examples as shown, and you will be able to do the work for yourself, for others, and for other creatures. You can even ask High Self to clear programs for people who have left the physical body and have not reincarnated yet. Usually, when a person out of the physical body has their programs cleared, they do not have to incarnate again, because there is nothing further for them to work on.

CHAPTER 20

Changing Your Life

By following the procedures outlined in this book, you can clear all of your discordant energies and blocks so that you are free to live a more successful, harmonious, prosperous, and happy life. Sometimes the results of clearing the discordant programs are dramatic and seemingly miraculous. Other times nothing seems to change in the client's life. When nothing seems to change, and I ask High Self why, they often show me a picture of the Grand Canyon in the middle of the person's forehead. This means that his or her conscious mind is deeply grooved by the habitual negative thoughts, beliefs, and actions; the conscious mind is set in stone to the degree that much work with the conscious mind will be required to bring about the desired changes in the client's life.

Some people expect SRT to be the magic wand they can wave so that all their past, present, and future challenges will be dissolved instantly. In many instances, these people believe that others are responsible for the total condition and direction of their life and what happens to them. Others believe they are how they are because of the problems and training of early childhood. And since they cannot go back and change how they were raised, they believe they are stuck. Since they believe they are stuck, and they cannot personally do anything about improving their lives, they are unwilling to make the effort to bring about the necessary changes.

Each person can and must learn to take responsibility for him or herself, unless, of course, that person is mentally retarded or has some disease that limits and inhibits them. However, even then these souls chose on the soul level, before coming into this life, to encounter what they are experiencing. Since each soul determines its own path and plans the situations it will encounter, they can either walk their chosen path with understanding and balance, or they can change the path by using the power of their conscious mind. I have seen illness, allergies, aches and pains, relationship tensions, and many other mental, emotional, and physical conditions healed or dramatically altered by using SRT to research and clear discordant programs. After the clearing work is accomplished, the client can use his or her conscious mind to bring forth continuing good in life.

Use Chart 19– How to Change Your Life, provided for you in Appendix B, to locate areas in your life you need to consciously change.

Clear Blocks to Growth

Chapter 9–Octaves of Learning and Soul Qualities, outlines eight basic steps called octaves of learning. The steps are also listed on Chart 19–How to Change Your Life. The steps are awareness, desire, faith, willingness to change, setting goals, working on goals, and completion (of the goals) and rest. Every aspect of our moment by moment walk through life is associated with these steps. Let's say you have awareness that you are hungry. The desire to eat is the next automatic step. You have to have a willingness to prepare food and to eat that food or nothing will happen; your appetite will not be fulfilled. Your faith is that you can find food that is already prepared, or that you can prepare at home, or you may determine that you will go to a restaurant to obtain what you desire to eat. You plan out what you desire and how you will fulfill that desire to accomplish the satisfying of your appetite. You prepare the food and eat at home, or go out and eat at a restaurant; your hunger is satisfied. Then you are at the next point of awareness: "Boy, I ate so much my stomach is upset." These eight steps are in some phase of being at every moment of our lives. It is important that you become aware that these steps exist and can be used to focus and change your life for greater good.

You may need to clear blocks to taking these steps in your own life. Here is an example.

Q. *Do I have blocks to my awareness of life? (+)*

Q. *What chart is the block on? (Chart 5–Blocks and Interference, Discarnates)*

Q. *Any other blocks to awareness? (+, Chart 5–Negative Motivations, Fear of change [This was intuitive.])*

Q. *Any other blocks to awareness? (-)*

Q. *Is there some reason why I fear change? (+)*

Q. *What chart is it on? (Chart 5–Negative Motivations)*

Q. *What is the negative motivation? (Conscious control)*

Q. *Must I always be in control? (+)*

Q. *If I were experiencing change, would that indicate that I was out of control? (+)*

Q. *Can you clear this energy and help me stay open to change without fear of losing control? (+)*

Please clear and replace with good. Thank you.

Q. *Are any of the other steps blocked? (-)*

Another step to growth is to use clearing statements because the spoken word is very powerful and some people need to hear themselves speak words of release. For instance, in the above example, the client could use the following releasing statements.

> "I release all belief, perception, and judgment that experiencing change would indicate that I was out of control, or that I was allowing someone else to control my consciousness. I release all fear that I am, or might be, out of control. I release all need and desire to believe that experiencing change would mean I was out of control."

Once the clearing statements have been used, it is important that replacement statements be made, as a vacuum has been created that needs to be filled. Here are typical statements that you can put into the subconscious mind in order to set a new pattern for life. "I now completely believe and accept, and instruct my conscious and subconscious minds to believe and accept, on every level of my being, that I am open to change and free from fear. I live in complete awareness that I am always in control of my life. I am open and receptive to the guidance and direction of SPIRIT, confident that whatever is revealed will bring about positive changes in my life. I am at peace."

Taking a Break

Self-nurturing is of vital importance if we want to avoid overload and burnout in life. Some people become very enamored of and caught up in SRT. Their desire to help themselves and others becomes an obsession and they encounter all kinds of blocks to working with the system. They are simply overloaded and need to take a break. Many times, while working with and for others, I have worked twelve- to fourteen-hour days, seven days a week. When I am that involved without a break, I start getting a lot of crazy answers. Questioning my High Self as to what is happening, I find that they are deliberately giving me wrong answers in order to get my attention; they want me to take a break and renew my energy. It does not make any difference whether it is SRT or some other work we are undertaking to help others or simply to earn a living. We can become too involved for our own mental, emotional, physical, or spiritual good. Then it is time to take a break before life breaks us.

Draw in Energy

Life can be tiring and exhausting and can drain our vital energy. While working with SRT, I have depleted my physical energy to as low as 5%. Taking a break, lying down for a rest, or getting a full night's sleep can recharge my energy. Another way I recharge is by sitting quietly and drawing in energy from the universe. When I do this, I rub my hands briskly together, extend my arms above my head with my palms up, and visualize drawing energy in from a central sun. After doing this for a few minutes, I can feel the change in energy. Using a number chart, you can check the increase in the level of energy. Another way to increase energy is simply to ask High Self to increase the energy. Your mental or emotional energy can also be depleted. When either of these is low, ask High Self to raise the energy level.

Practice Orderly Thinking

Few people realize that the thoughts they hold in mind and the energy they attach to those thoughts produce results–good or bad–in their lives. Some people expect the worst thing possible to happen to them and they are seldom disappointed–it usually happens. They are simply experiencing having their emotionally charged thoughts fulfilled. Replacing habitually disorderly and destructive thinking and emotions with orderly thinking and positive emotions can dramatically change a person's life. Try it. It works.

Replace Worry

Worrying is a habit that is learned and developed. Fortunately, anything that a person has learned and habitualized can be changed. Effort is required, for things that are worthwhile take practice to make them a part of life. Sometimes it is easier to fall into bad habits than it is to learn good habits, for bad habits do not require as much training and discipline to acquire. If a person is smart enough and patient enough to learn to tie their shoes, dress themselves, drive a car, and so on, they are, or can be, smart enough and disciplined enough to get rid of bad habits and replace them with good ones. Change worry into the expectation of good and you will not be disappointed. Be persistent in well-doing.

Meditate

According to the dictionary, to meditate is to engage in continuous and contemplative thought, to muse, or to cogitate. The purpose of meditation is to expand the consciousness inward; to center oneself in Spirit awareness. From time to time it is important to remove the attention from the outer world and contemplate the presence of the High Self. This brings about a heightened state of consciousness in which you become aware of the still small voice of High Self. In this state of consciousness, you can see inner pictures, hear inner words of counsel and instruction, and know the truth beyond human wisdom. When you are able to enter into this altered state of consciousness, you will find answers too many things. I have found that it makes the process of research through SRT faster and easier, for I see, hear, and know things that I never knew before, especially when the problems involve past lives.

Pray

Prayer, quite simply, is communion between God and man. True prayer is never supplication; it is the affirmative action of mind and heart based on an understanding of the Truth of our being–an affirmation that we are spiritual beings. We are created in the image and likeness of God.

Inhabiting the physical body is simply the means we have chosen to experience, learn and grow, and to become aware that we are one with SPIRIT.

Never supplicate or beg God, for that reinforces a belief that God is not interested in helping change the human condition. Instead, become still and meditate on the truth that God is the source and substance of all good that is everywhere present. This substance of SPIRIT is inexhaustible and will move into being according to the individual's belief in the right to receive in both quality and quantity. The Scriptures point out, in many ways, that we receive according to our belief. Ask yourself what you really believe and you will gain a greater understand of why your life expression is limited or unlimited.

The good we are seeking always exists as the 'perfect idea' of expression before it appears in the manifest form. There is a great reservoir of unlimited good that fills all space. There is a conduit that connects to that reservoir and carries to us an infinite supply of all good. That conduit, or supply hose, is our beliefs. Many people do not receive from that unlimited source, because they do not believe they are worthy of God's good or they have very limited views of themselves, seeing themselves only as erring human beings—not as children of God. The good we seek already exists in God Consciousness as divine ideas, and we bring ideas into manifestation through the positive prayer of faith, affirmation, praise, and acknowledgment that it but awaits our expressed desire. I often see people asking for good and then standing on the supply hose with their discordant thoughts and beliefs.

Manifest Good

There are fourteen steps listed on Chart 19–How to Change Your Life, that a person can follow to manifest greater good. However, the first thing is to determine if the individual has any blocks to using these steps to produce greater good. Here is an example.

Q. *Do I have any blocks to using these principles? (+)*

Q. *What chart is the first block on? (Chart 11–Soul Energy Programming)*

Q. *What is the block? (Preprogramming)*

Q. *Can you clear it? (-)*

Q. *What chart do we use to discover the blocking energy? (Chart 4–Programs, Imprint)*

Q. *Was the imprint set up when I was created as a living soul? (+)*

Q. *Do I need to know what the imprint is for you to clear it? (-)*

Q. *Is there any other block to using the fourteen steps? (-)*

Please clear in depth and replace with good. Thank you.

Believing—Examine Your Beliefs

Have you ever sat down and analyzed what your basic beliefs are about life? If you have not, do so. Take a large piece of paper and draw a line down the center. List on the left side of the line all the negative beliefs you have about life, people, government (city, county, state, federal), the world, God, the devil (if you believe in the devil), and so on, and do not forget what you believe about yourself. Take several days to work on the list. Keep the paper handy and as something pops into your mind, write it down.

On the right side of the paper, list all of the positive things you believe. Be completely honest in compiling your list—no one is keeping score. You may be very surprised by the awareness of some of the things you believe, and if you are like most people, you will be shocked at how many negative beliefs you have. Yet your beliefs determine the course of your life, especially when they are emotionally charged. The *Bible* puts it this way, "For as he thinketh in his heart, so is he" (Proverbs 23:7 KJV). Thoughts mirror beliefs, and emotions are the catalysts that move into being the thoughts that are held in mind.

The people that believe they are the way they are because of the influence of others are sadly mistaken and may seriously be limiting themselves in their life expression. It is true that your early childhood experiences and training (or lack of it) have had, and may still be having, an influence on your life. However, when we believe that we are victims of circumstances and that there is no possibility to change those circumstances, we are indeed stuck. The circumstances are not the problem; it is the belief system (thoughts held in mind) as well as the emotional energy we attach to the belief that creates more of the same. A person who is born on the wrong side of the track has to stay there only if their beliefs and emotions say they have to, and they refuse to change those beliefs and emotions. A person first has to break the prison bars made up of their own limiting beliefs and emotions before they can walk tall and free.

1 Corinthians 13:11 RSV states, "When I was a child, I spoke like a child, I thought like a child, I reasoned like a child; when I became a man, I gave up childish ways." We are children of God, unlimited, capable of great things, free to be and to become one with God and all good.

Establish a new, positive belief and hold it firmly in consciousness. Nurture and sustain that belief with positive emotions. Never let the belief or the energy fade, and your life will be transformed–it is your choice. Set some goals that stretch your mind and your faith. Believe that the goals are possible and can be accomplished by YOU. Stretch and grow. Work toward your goals. Keep them firmly in mind. Get excited about them and hold that excitement regardless of outer appearances. Break the habit of negative belief by being aware of what you are thinking (*and* believing), and then change your thinking. Do it again and again until you have built a new way of looking at life and at your own potential.

Imaging—Imagining Your Life

Imaging is dreaming, fantasizing, sensing, knowing, and seeing with the inner mind the desired goal as having already been accomplished. In the Scriptures, Joseph, the son of Jacob, was known for his coat of many colors, the clarity of his dreams, and for his ability to interpret the dreams of others. Joseph represents the power of imagination. The coat of many colors symbolizes the power the imagination has in coloring, shaping, and determining the direction of life–good or bad. Few people are aware that the pictures they hold in mind form much of the basic elements of life. All great artists, engineers, musicians, athletes, inventors, mathematicians, business men and women, architects, and other highly successful people have vivid imaginations and use the power of the imagination to mold and shape their lives.

All spirit beings, which includes all living souls, have been given the spiritual gift of imagination as part of their basic coding (see Chapter 15–Programming Before Formation and the "Twelve Aspects of Spirit as Genetic Coding" that are listed under Chart 12–Spirit Energy Programming). This gift of imagination can be deliberately used by you to enhance your life. Sit quietly, relax, and begin to image in your mind the greater good you would like to experience in your life. When others are involved, do not encroach on their right to live and express their life as they are guided and directed. You can image them as peaceful, wise, orderly, harmonious, healthy, loving, supportive, understanding, and so on, but do not try to mold them to fit your own beliefs as to what they should be, how they should act, or what they should do. Just hold the highest image of good for them. Change yourself, image your own greater good, and you will draw to yourself all the power of heaven to create good in your life.

Accepting— Abundance and Prosperity

Many times when a person's blocks to prosperity have been cleared, they do not receive because they are not open to receive. They may have a subconscious program blocking their ability to receive, or they may have developed a habit of rejecting good. Some people are martyrs. They are able to give, and give they do, but they block their own receiving by refusing to accept what others offer for the services they render. To accept would be contrary to their martyr complex. Never turn down payment that is sincerely offered for some service performed unless the payment is from someone you feel could not afford to give. You can always take the offering and then find some way to return it in the form of something they can use, or as a gift. Acceptance is one aspect of the law of prosperity, and acceptance begins in the mind. Of course, if you do not believe you have the right to accept you need to look at your belief system and change it.

Knowing—Know that You Know

I used to know a lady who, when questioned why she believed something that others did not, would simply say, "I know that I know that I know." Do you know absolutely that the world is round or do you just believe it is? Do you know that there is an infinite Source that is willing to supply all of your needs? Do you know that you have the right to receive from that Source? And, do you believe that you *will* receive from that Source? Knowing is having enlightened faith in an unlimited universe.

Letting Go of the Old

Have you ever tried to break a habit such as smoking, biting your fingernails, or being angry? Sometimes it isn't easy letting go of the old habits because the patterns are deeply ingrained and automatic; they are done without thinking. At the beginning of the chapter, we mentioned that awareness is the first key to making changes. Once we are aware that something needs to be changed, that there needs to be a letting go of the old, we can begin the growth process. Let go of the belief that you have to smoke, bite your nails, be angry, and so on, and you are on the way to success and freedom.

Forgiveness means giving up the old for a new and better way of seeing, believing, and doing. Many people never receive anything new because their lives are completely cluttered with the old and they are afraid to let go. Letting go of the old, cleaning out, makes space for the new. One simple way to start cleaning out is to pick one catchall drawer or closet and clean it out. Give away, throw away, or have a garage sale to free yourself of anything that you have not used in the past couple of years. Do not save those things for a rainy day, let them go, because that makes room for the new.

Affirming

To affirm means: to make firm, first in mind, then in word, and finally in action. There needs to be a firm idea in mind of what you want before it can be brought into the physical. Before the heavens and earth were formed, they consisted of a divine blueprint in the consciousness of Spirit, "without form and void" (Genesis 1:2 RSV). Then God began to speak forth the power of the word and creation began.

> *And God said, "Let there be a firmament in the midst of the waters..." (Genesis 1:6 RSV)*

'Firmament' means faith in the creative process. Affirming, even before the desired effect is made manifest, sets in motion the formative energy that will produce the desired results. When there is firm belief coupled with the spoken word, things begin to happen, because what the mind can conceive and believe, it can achieve as the necessary inner and outer steps are taken.

Always make your affirmations in a positive, firm manner. Let go of all doubt and the fear of all appearances to the contrary. See the desired end result as already accomplished, and it will be. You can speak the affirmative word and write it. Sometimes the written word has the effect of making things clearer, almost like a written contract between you and the Creative Principle.

Loving

Love is the greatest creative energy there is, for "God is Love" (1 John 4:16 KJV). The Scriptures tell us to love God. Therefore, when we substitute the word Love for God, we are really being told to love, Love. Love God, love your fellow beings, love life, and Love and you will never go wrong. Too many people hate and thus create more things to hate. Hate and fear are the two strongest discordant energies and they create more discord and negativity. Love is capable of dissolving all things unlike itself. Try it!

Taking Action

We can have all the best intentions in the world and still not accomplish anything of value. Remember the saying, "The road to hell is paved with good intentions." Hell is consciousness or states of mind that keep a person from experiencing their greater good. When we have good intentions, but never follow through because of fear or doubt, we are living in a state of mind called "hell." Any journey begins with the first step. Then each succeeding step, whatever it may be, must be taken until the goal is achieved.

Acting As If

Live with the attitude that the positive good you seek is already on its way. However, make certain that the good you seek will not harm, restrict, or cause anyone else pain, and that it is not at another person's expense. When prosperity is your goal, always see your bank account unlimited and your purse full. Remember that imaging is a prime ingredient in success. The story is told of one woman who wanted to travel in foreign countries, "to see the world." She had no means to travel so she went to a travel bureau and got brochures of the foreign countries she would like to see. She studied the materials until she was completely familiar with the countries. Then a dear lady friend who was very wealthy asked her to be her companion as she traveled in the very countries the woman had studied. Act as if and it shall be accomplished.

Visual Programming

You can change your outer world, allowing it to become a reflection of greater good, as you begin to visualize that good. Getting your outer world in order as much as possible and then organizing your inner world creates miracles. Create your own good by visualizing that good. Everyone is familiar with stories of people who have accomplished great things because they had an inner vision that they held on to despite all outer appearances. You can deliberately picture that which you desire. However, whatever you picture must be visualized without doubt or hesitation. Hold steadfast to the truth that this is a very prolific universe in which we live, that we are all children of God, and that it is the Father's good pleasure to bless us.

What the mind can perceive and believe, it can achieve. Pictures of the good desired can be cut out of magazines and pasted on a poster. Then hang the poster on a wall where you see it often. Every time you see it, give thanks that what you desire is already accomplished in Spirit and will quickly be manifested in the outer, material world to bless your life.

Giving

The tree draws nutrients from the air and soil so that it can grow and expand. In return, the tree returns oxygen to the air, moisture from its leaves, and nutrients through the fallen leaves that decay and enrich the soil. We draw substance from the planet, life from SPIRIT, and the means to support ourselves through our mental, emotional, and physical efforts. However, all of our efforts would be of little or no effect if it were not for the fact that, whether we know it or not, we live and move and have our very being in SPIRIT. SPIRIT gives to each one of us life, substance, and intelligence, and the guidance (if we will allow and seek it) to direct our lives in positive ways. We need to return part of what we receive to the source of our good; where we receive our spiritual nurturing. Many arguments have been presented regarding the need to give.

The simplest argument is that all things are based on cycles of giving and receiving. Without giving and receiving, all things would come to a standstill. One important aspect of giving is that the return, call it a tithe or whatever, must be to the place or instrument through which your spiritual good is received.

Praising

Fasting from negative thoughts, beliefs, and emotions is vital to the law of praising. Praising the good even before it manifests in the physical is an important factor in experiencing ever expanding good. See your bank account, purse, or pocketbook overflowing, praise them for providing a constant flow of abundance into your life.

Enjoying

Never make abundance a burden. Do not hoard it but share it with others freely and abundantly without strings attached "freely ye have received, freely give" (Matthew 10:8 KJV). Participate in the joy and happiness of being in the flow of all good.

Effort is required to accomplish all things in life that have any value. Do all of these things, read, study, work, laugh, love, and enjoy, for that is what life is all about.

Re-Create the Soul

I have talked to many people who have experienced a rebirthing process that has carried them back to the womb and the trauma they may have experienced. Other people have undergone hypnotherapy to discover buried problems and release the negative energies. Still others have had psychic readings to reveal problem areas, or had spontaneous realizations that have helped them understand and work with life in greater harmony, peace, and productivity. However, all of these methods and others that have been devised do not equal what can be accomplished by using the principles and process outlined in this book. The process called SRT goes to the very depths of our being. SRT rebirths the entire soul, not just the mental, emotional, and physical expressions. It clears all programs and prevents further discordant energy from accumulating, and if it does accumulate, it can easily be cleared.

Study the book and work with the process until it becomes second nature to you. When you research to clear your own programs and ask your High Self for permission to work for others, they may be blessed. Ultimately we are all one and what affects one affects the whole. When you work to clear even one person—to whatever degree of your awareness and expertise—you have to some degree raised the consciousness of the entire universe and everyone in it. I find that the people I work with have undergone such a complete soul re-creation that they do not need to incarnate again; they have gained the required knowledge and understanding. The soul is complete and has returned to the GODHEAD. I check daily to keep myself and my entire family clear of all programs of accumulated discordant energy, and ask High Self to apply any healing vibrations that may be needed. You can do the same as you re-create your life and soul and develop your cosmic potential!

APPENDIX A

Glossary

Akashic record: The record of everything the soul (spiritual body and living soul) has experienced from the instant of the divine blueprint formed at the level of the GODHEAD until the present moment and beyond. Another name is soul record.

Androgynous: Of neutral gender, used to describe the physical body type of a person when researching past lives in other dimensions. Depending on the planet where the past life was experienced, 'androgynous' may mean the body form is both male and female. At other times High Self indicates that it is neither male nor female. This form could be part human and part animal or sea creature or other form of creature which SPIRIT does not consider as having gender. The third form is when the male and female aspects of the soul do not split and they are incarnated in one body. There are times when High Self says the body form is both male and female, and when I ask if they are androgynous, they give me a negative response.

Angel: From the Greek, meaning *"messenger; messengers of God"* (MBD). Angels are spiritual beings that can be from many levels of consciousness and have many functions.

Angels of Light: An angel that has attained the level of Light Status or higher. Angels of Light serve in many ways and are usually assigned to an incarnated being for a specific purpose, such as healing, guidance, or protection.

Anti-time conflict: As a divine idea, we go through a gestation period in the womb of creativity. There we are created as a spiritual body, and given a working consciousness called the living soul. When the soul is ready to leave the womb of creativity (anti-time) and incarnate, he or she may experience a conflict regarding the purpose of incarnation, and may be traumatized by leaving a pure state of soul and entering into the consciousness of good and evil.

Ascended Master: Is a level of soul consciousness. There are eighteen offices in each level of Ascended Master, and there are 144,000 levels. High Self also indicates that there are many levels where you find Ascended Master groupings, especially in the area of the Universal God Consciousness level. (Also, see *Masters.*)

Astrological beliefs: The planets do have an influence on our lives. Unfortunately, many people establish beliefs that the primary influence is negative. These beliefs, accumulated over many lifetimes, need to be eliminated from consciousness so they have no further destructive effect.

Bardo: A Tibetan term meaning "between lives." After the soul has left one life, and when it is ready to incarnate for its next lessons, it stands in the bardo and communicates with its High Self. The soul reviews its akashic (soul) record and determines what needs to be worked on during the next incarnation.

Belief of beliefs: Belief in voodoo, curses, black cats crossing your path, broken mirrors, four leaf clovers, and so on, all fit this category. They only have power because we believe they do. The positive beliefs are great! Get rid of the negative ones. You could have accumulated thousands of these beliefs from past lives.

Cellular memory: Every cell is a minicomputer which contains a complete record of all that has transpired as the soul learns and grows. Once the programs have been cleared of discordant energy, the cells need to be cleansed of harmful memories.

Chakras: There are seven major chakras, or energy centers that run up the spine of the physical body. They can be blocked by discordant programs. There are eighteen additional chakras that extend upward into the spiritual realms. These can also be blocked.

Cherub or Cherubim: According to the *Metaphysical Bible Dictionary*, "The "cherubim" of 1 Kings 8:6-8 were symbolic figures representing the attributes and majesty of God." They stand for unlimited, unfettered truths of being. They are also souls who hold an angel office or level of consciousness. They may serve as guide, Guardian Angel, or High Self. When Cherub is indicated, I always ask if they are serving in an office. If a "yes" response is given, I ask what the office is: guide, Guardian Angel, or High Self. Cherub is also one of the first forms of consciousness we take prior to our first incarnation.

Christ Consciousness: The level of soul consciousness attained once the soul has come to a complete awareness that it is the Son of God, the perfect Christ idea. Jesus grew "in wisdom and in stature" (Luke 2:52 RSV), until He was the fullness of the divine potential. At that point, He became the expression of the perfected divine spiritual idea man and was called Jesus Christ.

Christ Status: A level of soul consciousness where the soul is first beginning to realize that it is spiritual in nature, with an infinite potential to learn and grow into the full image and likeness of God. The soul realizes that it is a divine idea on the path of gaining knowledge, understanding, and wisdom.

Conscious memories: The often discordant experiences recorded in the two levels of conscious mind (spirit body and physical body) that can be erased (only the discordant memories) for the greater peace and harmony of life.

Conscious mind: There are two forms: first, the conscious mind of the spiritual body is the living soul (Genesis 2:7 KJV); second, there is a conscious mind, of the physical body, that functions as part of the human expression. Through the five senses, it is the observer, decision-maker, and the programmer of the subconscious mind. The conscious mind does have storage capabilities and sometimes holds discordant beliefs even after programs are cleared from the subconscious. When you are searching for a reason why something has not changed, there may be a special area of the conscious mind that needs cleaning out, much like a closet under the stairs that is seldom used or entered. The conscious mind can have compartments (up to eighty-nine) which can hold specific messages that can restrict a person's greater expression of life.

Contracts: A soul that incarnates for a second round of incarnations and convinces others to incarnate with them may have contracts to pick up the other souls' programs. Another form of contract has to do with decaying universes, where a soul has a contract to pick up the discordant energy of the young souls living in the decaying universe, so the souls in that universe can be taken out and placed in an expanding universe (see Chapter 14—Decaying Universe).

Council of Seven: A group of seven souls at the level of Light Status or higher who serve as counselors. There are also seven Ascended Masters who serve as a council for this planet. They work directly under the God of planet Earth. There are other Councils of Seven who serve other functions. They are found throughout the governing structure of the planets, galaxies, universes, and super universes.

Creator Consciousness: Beings at this level of soul consciousness take part in creation of a planetary system and its solar system. They work under the direction of souls at the Universal God Consciousness level.

Curses: One form of curse is when you curse someone else–you always keep the original energy you send out. Another form is when someone has cursed you, and you accept and believe it. You may also feel cursed by God or life. Curses have no power except that given them by the individual.

Dark energy: The soul is created of the substance of SPIRIT, or Light, and dwells in SPIRIT or Light. When the soul decides to incarnate, it may have the sense that it left the realms of Light and became dark energy–that it took upon itself the belief in good (light) and evil (darkness). Spirit through High Self may also indicate that a person has dark energy when the person is caught up in any of the energies listed on Chart 6A. These energies 'blank out' the person's spiritual Light.

Dark energies can also be discarnates with discordant energy that they carried with them when they left the physical body. The energies can be comprised of (but not limited to) any or all of the items on Chart 6A. All dark energies can be cleared by High Self.

Dark forces: Beings, either in or out of the physical body, who carry a lot of dark energy such as hate, anger, and so on (anything listed on Chart 6A). When out of the physical body, they band together and may cause problems for people in the physical realm.

Death: A belief that, when we leave the physical body, we die. In truth, death (annihilation) does not exist–there is only change.

Decaying universe: High Self says that each universe is first created by a method called coagulation from pure energy. That energy is formed and shaped into the galaxies, suns, planets, and so on. The planets eventually support diversified forms of life. The universe goes full circle, eventually decays, collapses into a black hole, and is recycled with a big bang out of a white hole, and a new universe is formed.

Demonic: Any soul that has left the physical body, has become earthbound, and carries with it a lot of bad energy. Demonics can often have been murderers, rapists, drug traffickers, and so on. Demonic energy is worse than that of satanics.

Demonic forces: A group of souls that have left the physical body, and are earth bound. They have not left the physical vibrations for one reason or another. They carry bad energy and have banded together, usually with the purpose of causing incarnated souls problems. They are vindictive and destructive. However, demonic forces cannot harm anyone unless that person allows it. For example, when a person has a program of self-punishment, he may open himself to discarnates of various temperaments in order to fulfill that program. The energy of demonic forces is worse than that of satanic forces.

Desire to escape: A desire to learn without experience, effort, difficulty, struggle, or pain. Other forms include the desire to escape life and its hardships and responsibility, and a desire to escape divine judgment or eternal damnation. The desire to escape should be cleared because it interferes with our motivation to move forward on our spiritual path.

Devil: The aggregate of discordant thoughts and beliefs that have been built up in race consciousness through many generations of earthly experiences. The devil is simply an archetypal representation of the carnal mind which opposes and rejects God or Truth.

Discarnate: A soul that has left the physical body, but has not left the vibrations of the physical realm within 90 hours of exiting the body. Discarnates become earthbound and cannot leave without help. Just ask High Self to remove them and take them into their right and perfect place.

Discarnates in the aura: Discarnates may enter a person's auric field because the field may have holes in it caused by drugs, alcohol, anger, or other discordant energy; or the auric field may be weak because it is vibrating at a low frequency. If the field vibrates at a rate under 800 cycles per second, the person may be open to discarnates. Ask the High Self to raise and keep the vibration at several thousand cycles per second, and heal any holes in the aura.

Discarnates in possession: Discarnates who have entered the vibrations of the physical, emotional, mental, etheric, or first astral body. For a description of the energy bodies, see Chapter 2.

Discarnates from past lives: When a person is hypnotically regressed to a past life, they encounter all of the energy of the past life and relive the whole experience. While working with SRT, you actually open the past life to the present time, although you do not usually re-experience the pain and trauma of the past life. However, if there were discarnates attached to the past life, they can come into the present time and be felt. Just ask High Self to remove them and take them to their right and perfect place.

Dissipation of vital energy: The soul is provided with the vital energy of SPIRIT. This energy can be dissipated by becoming involved in discordant programs. Involvement with any of the energies on Chart 6A can cause loss of vital energy. High Self says there are over 470 ways a soul can dissipate vital energy.

Elevations: There are 99 elevations, each one infinite in levels, where the soul resides within the GODHEAD, and these need to be cleared from time to time.

Elohim: El means the strong and ever-sustaining one—God. Elohim means Gods many, or Gods plural. Elohim is another name for Yahweh or I AM.

Energy imbalance: Everything has a positive and a negative pole, every leaf, blade of grass, house, animal, person, and so on. Those energies may need to be balanced and brought into harmony.

Essence: The fundamental nature or quality of a thing. A substance that is distilled or subtracted from another substance and having the special qualities of the original substance. For instance, a person may have the soul essence or nature of several musical artists who have previously lived, and thus may have an inherent musical genius that unfolds naturally and easily.

Extra Souls: Second round, advanced souls may have extra souls in their physical body. There are past life connections that need to be resolved, so the host allows the extra souls to enter at birth. Then, when the host soul is cleared, the extra souls are discovered. When they are cleared and removed, they do not have to incarnate again as they are clean and have returned to the GODHEAD.

Forces of Light: A group of Light beings at the Universal God Consciousness level or higher, who may be called on by the person's High Self for specific purposes such as healing, instruction, and protection.

Free: A being at the level of soul consciousness one level below the Vector level. There are 756 offices in each level and infinite levels of Free. One function of Frees is to be in charge of a planetary system under the supervision of the God of that solar system.

Future lives: Future lives are simply an alternate reality, or dream state, in which you face and work through situations that you either need or want to work on for soul growth, but do not want to experience in the current life. Future lives (if indicated) are being lived now, and they will be completed before you leave the physical body.

Genetic beliefs: These are made up of the beliefs a person's parents and grandparents have established, and which the person inherits through the genes. The programs can be passed on for as many as eight generations. For example, if your own illness programs reinforce the genetic programs, you can run the diseases that your parents or grandparents had.

God: As a designation for soul consciousness, God represents any soul that has reached the soul consciousness level of GOD that is high enough to serve as the God of a planet. The God of each planet is called "I AM THAT I AM" (Exodus 3:14 KJV). Moses was provided this name by God while on the mountain of Horeb (Exodus 3:13-15 KJV). This is the only instance in the Scriptures where the God of the planet actually names itself.

GOD: A level of soul consciousness which has infinite beings at infinite levels. GOD is Creative Intelligence, Spiritual Life, Spiritual Substance, and Prime Mover of All That Is. Beings at this level are called God (see God). For an explanation of the levels of service in this hierarchy of soul consciousness, see Chapter 4.

GODHEAD: The Trinity of the Father (Infinite Consciousness), the Son (Divine Idea of Self Expression), and the Holy Spirit (the Breath or movement of the Idea of Self Expression). Your return to the GODHEAD is attained once the soul has overcome your challenges and risen to the level of ONE. ONE is the highest level of soul consciousness for the GODHEAD. The GODHEAD is not a 'being'. It is many beings working as ONE.

GRAND-I / WHOLE: This is the culmination of all that is; the grand finish of the whole creative process.

Guardian Angel: A being that is assigned to guard and protect an incarnated soul. Guardian Angels cannot act against the will of the individual they are to protect, and have greater ability to help when the individual asks. They can be found at levels from Spirit Status on up. An incarnated being may have from one to an infinite number of Guardian Angels. Too large a number of Guardian Angels can be a detriment. I always ask that the committee be not more than 90.

Guide: When a soul is out of the incarnated body and in spirit form, it can serve as someone's guide. Under certain circumstances, a soul can also serve as a guide while still in the incarnated body if his or her soul consciousness is high enough. A soul can serve as a guide when his or her soul level is Spirit Status and higher. The higher the guide's level of soul consciousness, the purer the soul and the better they are able to guide and help.

Heart vows: These are normally taken during religious lives. They are called heart vows because they register in the emotional center located in the heart. Because of their emotional charge, there is a strong potential for manifestation. For instance, vows of poverty can stop a soul from prospering lifetime after lifetime.

Hidden vows: These are set up as possibilities in the GODHEAD elevations, before the divine plan is even formed, but have no effect on the souls that are later created until they incarnate. They are actually a carry-over of error beliefs from the previous ONE universe. A soul may have one hidden vow or many.

High Council: A special group of very advanced souls, of no definite number, who work on special assignment. They work under the office of Christ Consciousness. High Council may be assigned to a particular incarnated being for special protection and to help that person learn and grow.

High Self: Jesus referred to His High Self as 'the Father.' High Self is the master teacher within, and is made up of from one to an infinite number of beings. A soul has to be at the level of Light Status or higher in order to serve as another's High Self. Too many members in your High Self committee can be a detriment. I ask that there not be more than 900.

Holy Spirit, The: One of the aspects of the GODHEAD. The Holy Spirit means the movement, or the breath of God. The Holy Spirit causes to move into being the divine ideas that the GODHEAD forms in consciousness.

Holy Spirit Consciousness: A soul that has grown to the level of soul consciousness called Holy Spirit Consciousness. Souls at Holy Spirit Consciousness are one with the active and creative forces of the universe.

Holy Spirit Status: A level of soul consciousness. The inner teacher, an aspect of self that begins to lead the incarnated individual toward the path their own divinity or Light that is within each person.

I AM: A level of soul consciousness. This is a beingness which becomes Itself through extension; Yahweh, the self-existent One.

I AM THAT I AM: All beings at the level of GOD. See Chapter 4 for a more complete explanation.

Ideas: The flow or movement of intelligence. In the beginning, the GODHEAD ideated all that was, is, and shall be within Its consciousness.

Imprint: A belief that is imprinted upon the subconscious mind during an emotionally charged time. The imprint can be given to you by yourself or by someone else. For example, perhaps you were born during the depression of the late 20's and early 30's, and your grandmother said to your parents, "You shouldn't have a child. You can't afford it. How will you ever provide for it in these trying times?" As a result of this conversation, you may have given yourself an imprint that you should not have been born because you were a financial burden on your parents.

Imprint of brain damage: An imprint, often registered at birth, to the effect that the person sustained brain damage. The doctor may have used forceps in the delivery process and thought, "I hope I do not damage this child's brain." The soul may have understood this as actual brain damage, and later expressed life as though there was actual brain damage. Seldom is there actual brain damage.

Imprint other: This is usually an imprint of brain damage as a result of disease (Alzheimer's, Downs syndrome, and so on), statements by others, head injury, or messages of insanity in past lives. Some people were accused of insanity in past lives and were incarcerated in an institution. High Self says that most of the time, they were not insane.

Incarnational Status: A level of soul consciousness where the soul's entire energy is focused on the physical, incarnational world. He or she knows little or nothing of the higher aspects of man or man's spiritual potential. They are caught up in and follow the 'ways of the world.'

Infinite Council: A group of souls who are infinite in number, spiritual level, and ability. They have attained a level immediately below the 2,000th I AM level. Incarnated beings who are high enough in soul consciousness may have the Infinite Council working with them.

Inhibitors: A defense mechanism which prevents the incarnational body from reacting under certain circumstances. Inhibitors are like gate keepers in the sense that, when stimulus is presented, they cause the body to react in a specific way. Inhibitors are set up by the soul to prevent destructive reactions from occurring when the stimulus is experienced. Inhibitors need to be cleared because the person under the control of an inhibitor can never really know their true, spontaneous response and the inhibited response may no longer be beneficial to the soul.

Jehovah: This is one of the names for the Christ, the Son of God. Jehovah symbolizes the perfect expression of the GODHEAD expressing Itself as all life, substance, and intelligence. When mankind has developed his creative nature through the process called incarnation, and has returned to the consciousness of SPIRIT with full awareness he is the Jehovah, the Christed One, the Son of God.

Karmic beliefs: Karma is a belief system like in the *Old Testament* teachings of an "An eye for an eye and a tooth for a tooth" (Matthew 5:35 RSV). In Hinduism and Buddhism, karma is the belief that what you have done in previous lives, good and bad, will bring a reward or punishment in the current life. Karma is based on the belief that we must suffer for our misdeeds, rather than realizing that all experiences are simply steps in our growth. High Self informs me that the only karma is love. Negative karma is simply the beliefs that we set up when we partook of 'the tree of the knowledge of good and evil' and incarnated.

King of Kings: King represents a ruling level of soul consciousness, the executive faculty in every person whose life is guided, governed, and directed by SPIRIT. King of Kings represents the perfect idea of spiritual man or woman, the Christ, ruling in consciousness. It is at this point that the divine idea is formed and we are differentiated. This idea is then placed in the womb of creativity or the Queen of Life where it undergoes its gestation period, and becomes a spiritual body. (Also, see *Queen of Life.*)

Ladder: Jacob's ladder with platforms at top and bottom is the process of communication from heaven to earth and earth to heaven.

Light: The essence of God as the highest form of creative substance. This is the very ground of our being as symbolized in Genesis 2:7.

Light energy: God is Light and we are created of this Light as spiritual bodies and living souls. Thus, when Jesus said, "You are the light of the world. ... Let your light so shine" (Matthew 5:14, 16 RSV), He was speaking of the truth of our very being. Our goal is to regain the knowledge that we are indeed Light of the ONE LIGHT, and magnify it in all that we do.

Light Status: The level of soul consciousness of a soul who has entered the realms of Light, and is working at one of the levels called Ascended Master or higher. The Light realm is an ever-ascending spiral of expanding consciousness. Another path that the soul may travel once it reaches the Light realm is the Savior Path.

Lord: A level of soul consciousness where Light beings work with newly incarnating souls. They help them design their basic soul path, which then becomes the pattern or law (Lord) of their expression. The Lord level is made up of an infinite number of beings at infinite levels of consciousness.

Lord of Lords: Lord means law or ruling level of soul consciousness. Lord of Lords means that the divine idea man (the living soul) is programmed with the ultimate laws of its expression. These are the ruling elements that will govern and affect the soul's existence and determine its experiential path through many incarnations. (Also, see *King of Kings* and *Queen of Life.*)

Loss of subconscious integrity: This occurs any time a person takes into the subconscious a negative belief or emotion, which all of us have done at one time or another.

LUMINOUS: LUMINOUS is LIGHT beyond, above, and behind all Light. LUMINOUS gives rise to consciousness which is SPIRIT and SPIRIT works through mind to ideate and extend all that is, first the spiritual realms and eventually the physical universes, galaxies, and planets. Through using SRT everything that the soul experiences are cleared back through LUMINOUS to GRAND-I/WHOLE.

Majestic Consciousness: The major function of souls at this level of soul consciousness is to work with other souls who are planning their second round of incarnations, and to help them set up and accomplish their master programs. There are infinite levels within this level.

Major beliefs: Major beliefs are set up when we are coming out of the womb of creativity into physical expression. They are often called separation beliefs, because they are set up as we incarnate, separate from the Light (spiritual awareness) and come into darkness (the physical).

Masters: Sometimes called Ascended Masters. These beings are of Light Status or higher. Masters serve souls both in and out of the physical body as teachers, counselors, and guides. They work under the office of the Holy Spirit at the level of ONE and are assigned to the individual by Holy Spirit beings.

Mentor Consciousness: A soul symbolizes the combination of the divine idea man (Christ) and the perfected knowledge (Holy Spirit) that the soul is, and is able to communicate that knowledge to other souls who have not yet reached their level of understanding. A soul at the soul consciousness level of Mentor Consciousness is in charge of a universe from the aspect of teaching others what they have learned along their own spiritual path.

Multiple souls: Often referred to as 'piggy-back souls,' because they attach themselves to the incarnated body of another soul at the time of birth. There is always an agreement with the host soul. Their purpose is to have their programs cleared so they will not have to incarnate again to work on their own stuff. Sometimes their energy is so intense that they interfere with the host and is a possible cause of schizophrenia. Only second-round souls might have multiple souls.

Negative motivations: Discordant programs that have their roots in past lives. When High Self indicates a person has a negative motivation, they mean the soul has a desire to misuse their spiritual talents and abilities, or, those talents and abilities were sacrificed and there was failure to use them in a constructive manner. For example, an individual may have used their spiritual power to control, manipulate, and harm others in past lives. On the other hand, they could have given up their own power (as in the case of a slave) and become apathetic and lacking in self-determination or self-will.

Negative thought forms: Every thought we think is an energy form. The duration of the form and its strength depends on the amount of energy involved.

Octaves: The eight-step process that we encounter every day of our life as part of the experiential path of soul evolvement. They include an *awareness* that something needs to be changed, *desire* to make the change, *willingness* to change, *faith* to accomplish the change, *setting goals* and *starting work*, *completing* the goals, and *rest* after a job well done. Then with an awareness of the next task that is to be accomplished, we start the process again.

ONE: That which is above all things. ONE is the Supreme Consciousness, Creator, Prime Mover, Source, Creative Energy, Spiritual Substance, All.

One: The next level of soul consciousness above the Ascended Master level. There are seventy offices in each level, and there are 70,000 levels within the One level. One of the functions of One is to act as a council member for a planetary system. The council consists of seven members and works under the direction of the God of the planet. They assist in directing and balancing the physical functions of the planet. There are Councils of One for all planets in all solar systems.

Parallel lives: An incarnation that is being lived at the same time you are living the present one. A parallel life can be lived on this planet or another planet; in this galaxy or in another galaxy. The number of parallel lives a person can be living may be from a single life to many thousands. A person can be living parallel lives in several different galaxies at the same time.

Parallel universe: A universe parallel to this one, but invisible to us because it is vibrating at a different frequency. Each life lived in a parallel universe can have a record of past lives that were lived within that universe, as well as past lives in other dimensions.

Past lives: Any life in a physical body lived anywhere in the universe. It is still considered a past life if the soul is out of the incarnated body and serving as a guide, Guardian Angel, High Self, or in some other capacity. When you have picked up the essence of another soul, their past lives register as part of your total number of past lives (see *Essence*).

Past lives in other dimensions: These past lives have not been experienced as an incarnation on the planet Earth. They may be at other vibratory levels or dimensions. They could also be in the spiritual dimensions where you are serving as a guide, Guardian Angel, High Self, or in some other capacity.

Polarity beliefs: Any belief that tends to polarize concepts into opposites: good and bad, right and wrong, one race as better than another, one religion as better, and so on.

Prime Mover: The Supreme Consciousness that is above, over, and through all things seen and unseen. (See *ONE.*)

Queen of Life: The level of soul consciousness that is the womb of creativity where the ruling idea called man is placed during its gestation or formative period. The divine idea of mankind, the Christ, goes into the womb of creativity (Queen of Life) for its gestation and formation into the 'spiritual body' which was created in the image and likeness of God (Genesis 1:26-27).

Race beliefs: These beliefs, carried over from lifetime to lifetime, are about the value and qualities of others. Race beliefs encourage discrimination, and can be very destructive. Non-judgment and forgiveness is a vital ingredient to a balanced life. I know I have, and I am sure you have, in other incarnations been about every race, nationality, color, and creed known to us here on this planet and many that are unknown.

Root causes: One of the root causes is in the embryo that was the basis for this ONE universe. The second is in the divine plan for this universe that was formed at the GODHEAD. The third is in the 2,600 pathways by which we come into being. The fourth one is at the 2,000th I AM level where the spiritual realms are formed. The fifth one is at the Queen of Life level and the sixth one is at the Lord of Lords level. There are many root causes although you do not need to know how many or where they are established. Just ask that they be cleared in depth.

Satan: Any soul whose power is derived through the unlawful use and expression of their spiritual potential and abilities.

Satanic forces: A group of discarnates with bad energies that have banded together.

Satanics: Discarnates with bad energies. Just as there are people who have different degrees of good and bad energy, so there are discarnates who have different degrees of good and bad energy that they carry with them when they leave the physical body. (Also, see *Demonics* and *Discarnates.*)

Savior: A spiritual path that I call 'the greased pole,' because it is the most difficult path to follow. The requirements are stringent and demanding and often difficult to accomplish. The Savior path is made up of two levels of savior, first and second. There is one second-level savior for each planet in the universe, but there may be many first-level saviors. A first-level savior is any spiritual teacher who comes to bring greater knowledge and wisdom. First-level saviors may be teachers, writers, healers, and so on. There are many on Earth, and they are under the direction of Jesus, who is the second-level Savior of this beautiful planet. A person can serve as first-level savior on one planet and still be a second-level savior on another planet, since the soul and its expressions are without limit.

Scarring: The soul itself has been wounded in some fashion. The wound has been healed, but scarring remains. High Self can remove the scarring so there is no trace left.

Separates: These are beings from the level of One who do not want to work within one of the seventy offices in the level of One. They enter the earth vibrations and independently try to help people. Unfortunately, they do not help and actually may cause problems because their high vibrations interfere with the incarnated person's vibrations. They, like souls that leave the physical body at death, must not stay in the earth vibrations for more than twenty-seven days or they become stuck. Once this happens, they need help to leave. Other separates deliberately enter the earth realms and attach themselves to people who are using SRT, as they want to have their programs cleared.

Seraph or Seraphim: Heavenly beings that Isaiah saw in his vision, described in the sixth chapter of Isaiah. They represent wholeness or completeness, ideas of purity or the cleansing power of spiritual ideas. Seraph is often indicated as the form of the soul before first incarnation. Seraphim may serve as guides, Guardian Angels, High Self, and other offices at countless levels throughout the spiritual realms. The lowest level for a Seraph is first-level savior or Christ Consciousness level.

Serpent: An archetypal representation of a soul who desires to incarnate for a second round to increase his or her knowledge and convinces other souls to incarnate as well. The serpent also represents any soul that incarnates into sense consciousness.

Siamese souls: When the soul is created, it may have a string of souls attached to it like a string of paper dolls of which there may be a maximum of nine. They need to be separated and cleared of all programs that the soul has experienced or the programs will bleed over from each soul that is attached.

Soul programs: These are strong discordant programs that are set up after the physical body has been vacated but while the soul is still within the planetary vibrations. They are usually established after a person has been seriously harmed such as by torture or sexual abuse, and then killed.

SPIRIT: That infinite SPIRIT which lies behind all things. It is all life, substance, and intelligence which work through an infinite mind. It is the SOURCE of SOURCES, the Alpha and Omega of all that is. Another name for SPIRIT is Yahweh.

Spirit Status: As a level of soul consciousness, it is the spiritual state of a soul that is just beginning to search for higher truth, rather than follow the ways of the world.

Subconscious clutter: The odds and ends that remain in the subconscious after programs are cleared. They are like the wrappings that the programs came in. High Self revealed this by showing a Christmas tree with the presents unwrapped and stacked under the tree and the floor covered with the wrappings.

Subconscious mind: There are several forms (see Chapter 2 regarding the 18 bodies and 90 minds). The first form is the subconscious mind of the etheric body. The next subconscious mind is of the spiritual body. This is where all the wisdom and knowledge that is gained on the soul path is stored; it is the repository for the akashic record. Another form is that of the human expression. This is where all of the incarnational experiences are recorded and stored. Those records, along with the akashic record, which is programmed into the cellular memory of the physical body immediately after birth, determine the process and quality of the soul's life. The information picked up as a result of the incarnational process is stored there until the soul leaves the incarnational body. Only then are the records transferred to the akashic record repository.

Supreme Consciousness: The level of soul consciousness that is above the infinite levels of the Ultimate Consciousness level. The Supreme Consciousness level has infinite levels within it. One of the functions of beings at this level is to work with souls at lower consciousness who are newly incarnated to help them establish and work with the inner archetypes listed on Chart 8.

Thought: This is the first form of manifestation and starts at the GODHEAD long before physical expression. A soul may be identified as 'thought' when it is planning to incarnate for the second round to work on its master programs. Thought, in this case, is what the soul is holding in consciousness as the curriculum for its second round of incarnations. Thought can also be indicated when the incarnated person's consciousness is filled with bitter or dysfunctional thoughts, such as anger, bitterness, fear, hate, or unforgiveness.

Toxic streams: Energy streams running under the surface of the earth that carry discordant energy. Where two streams cross, they set up a vortex of energy that can be very harmful to a person's mental, emotional, and physical bodies. High Self can fill them with light so they are positive and constructive. Other names are *geopathic lines* or *lay lines*.

Transfer student: Some sources call these 'walk-ins.' The original inhabitant of the physical body becomes disillusioned with life and decides he or she wants out. Another soul, usually an advanced being, decides they want to enter the physical body, so an agreed-upon exchange takes place. Usually, the new soul has something of great value to bring to the inhabitants of the planet. Sometimes the transfer student is made up of a group of souls who work together as one soul.

Transition: A major change in consciousness. High Self has given three examples: transition brought about by moving from one environment to another, leaving the physical body in death, or one soul leaving the incarnated body and another entering.

Tree: An archetypal representation of any structure of consciousness that has life and is added to in the process of experiencing, learning, and growing. A tree may be formed of good only or it may be a mixture of good and evil. It is always the soul's choice what tree (knowledge) it will partake of. The trees in the garden of Eden represent structures of consciousness, or living beliefs within the consciousness of God. We partake of different trees (beliefs) of consciousness lifetime after lifetime as our soul learns and grows. It is best to look at the experiences of life as lessons to be encountered and knowledge to be gained. We separate the wheat (positive energy) from the chaff (discordant energy) and eat of only the highest order of trees (beliefs).

Twin Flames: Every person has a soul family just like we have human families and relatives.

Ultimate Consciousness: A level of soul consciousness a soul reaches after going through the Universal God Consciousness level along whatever path the soul has chosen. There are infinite levels within this level. Souls at this level, having overcome their own challenges, work with other souls on the spiritual path to help them with their themes and challenges (listed on Chart 2).

Universal God Consciousness: Souls at this level of soul consciousness take part in the creation and manifestation of a physical universe. There are many levels and groups of beings throughout the Universal God Consciousness level. There are also many paths of learning and soul expression that open up to the soul when they reach this category.

Vector: Souls at this level of soul consciousness are creative forces and work with the formation of physical expression, especially fire planets that are in the formative or molten state. They also serve as council members for a complete solar system. Vectors are mentioned twice in the Scriptures, as "sons of God" (Genesis 6:2; Job 38:7 RSV).

WELLSPRING: WELLSPRING lies behind LUMINOUS and is that from which all life, substance, and intelligence springs. That is the only information that High Self will or can give at the present time.

World Energies: These are comprised of any discordant energy picked up while living in the physical body (energies listed on Chart 6A).

Yahweh (Hebrew): The self-existent One that reveals Itself to Its creation, through Its creation, as Its creation; Elohim, God over the super super universe. Yahweh at the GODHEAD is all life, substance, and intelligence seeking to express Itself. Yahweh at the top level of I AM is the extension of all life, substance, and intelligence as the spiritual realms.

APPENDIX B

Charts

The charts in this appendix are provided to help you identify and clear the negative blocks and programs described in the earlier chapters of this book. For an explanation of how to use these charts, see Chapter 5The Basic Steps of SRT. To locate an explanation of the programs listed on each chart, see the following table.

Figure B-1. Where to Find Information About the Charts

For information about	See
Chart 1	Chapters 4, 6, and 7
Chart 2, Soul Qualities	Chapter 9
Chart 2, Themes and Challenges	Chapter 12
Chart 3	Chapters 4 and 6
Chart 4	Chapter 7
Chart 5, Blocks and Interference	Chapter 6
Chart 5, Negative Motivations	Chapter 13
Chart 6A	Chapter 8
Chart 6B	Chapter 10
Chart 7	Chapter 17
Chart 8	Chapter 11
Charts 9A and 9B	Chapter 17
Chart 10	Chapter 14
Charts 11 through 18	Chapter 15
Chart 19	Chapter 20
Chart 20	Chapter 16
Chart 21-31	Chapter 16

Chart 1	Chart to Use; Contact or Help
Chart 2	Themes and Challenges, Soul Qualities
Chart 3	Levels of Soul Consciousness
Chart 4	Programs, When, and Cast of Characters
Chart 5	Negative Motivations, Blocks and Interference
Chart 6A	Master Programs, Discordant Energy
Chart 6B	Blocks to Positive Expression
Chart 7	Direct Healing Processes and Colors
Chart 8	Inner Archetypes
Chart 9A	Minerals and Vitamins
Chart 9B	Food or Diet, Health and Well-Being
Chart 10	Miscellaneous Blocks
Chart 11	Soul Energy Programming
Chart 12	Spirit Energy Programming
Chart 13	Programs Before Creation
Chart 14	Pre-Fall of Consciousness, Creating the Illusion
Chart 15	I AM Level Consciousness Programs
Chart 16	Fall of Consciousness
Chart 17	Fine Tuning
Chart 18	Higher Level Blocks
Chart 19	How to Change Your Life
Chart 20	Refining Consciousness
Chart 21	Final Items this ONE Universe
Chart 22	New ONE Universe
Chart 23	Spiritual Realms Programs
Chart 24	Rebirth Conscious Mind
Chart 25	Final Assurance
Chart 26	Freedom Is Free
Chart 27	Learning Is Fun
Chart 28	Final Forgiveness
Chart 29	Final Blessing
Chart 30	Final Light
Chart 31	Memory Clearing

Chart to Use *(Outside)*
Contact or Help *(Inside)*

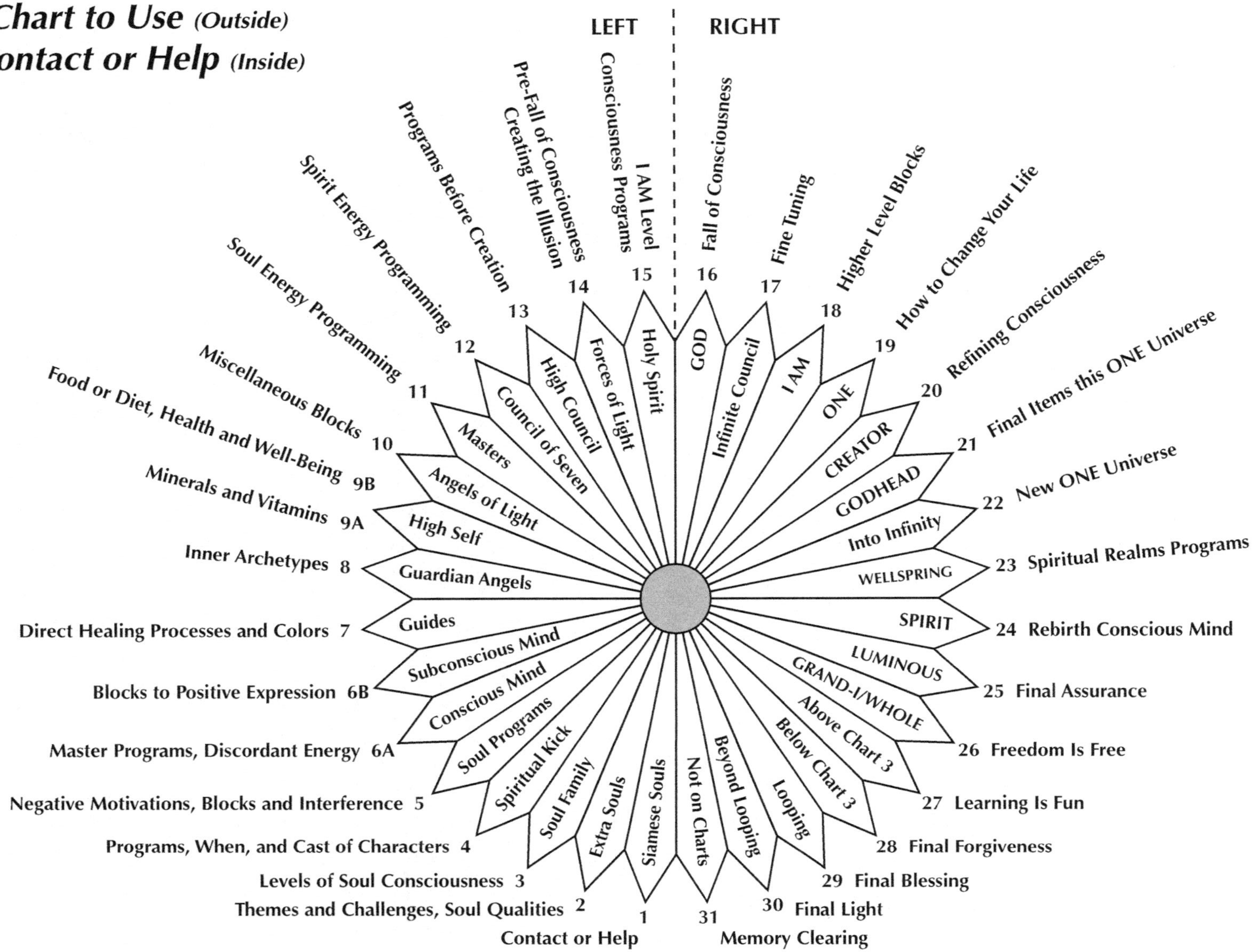

Chart 1

Themes and Challenges, Soul Qualities

Chart 2

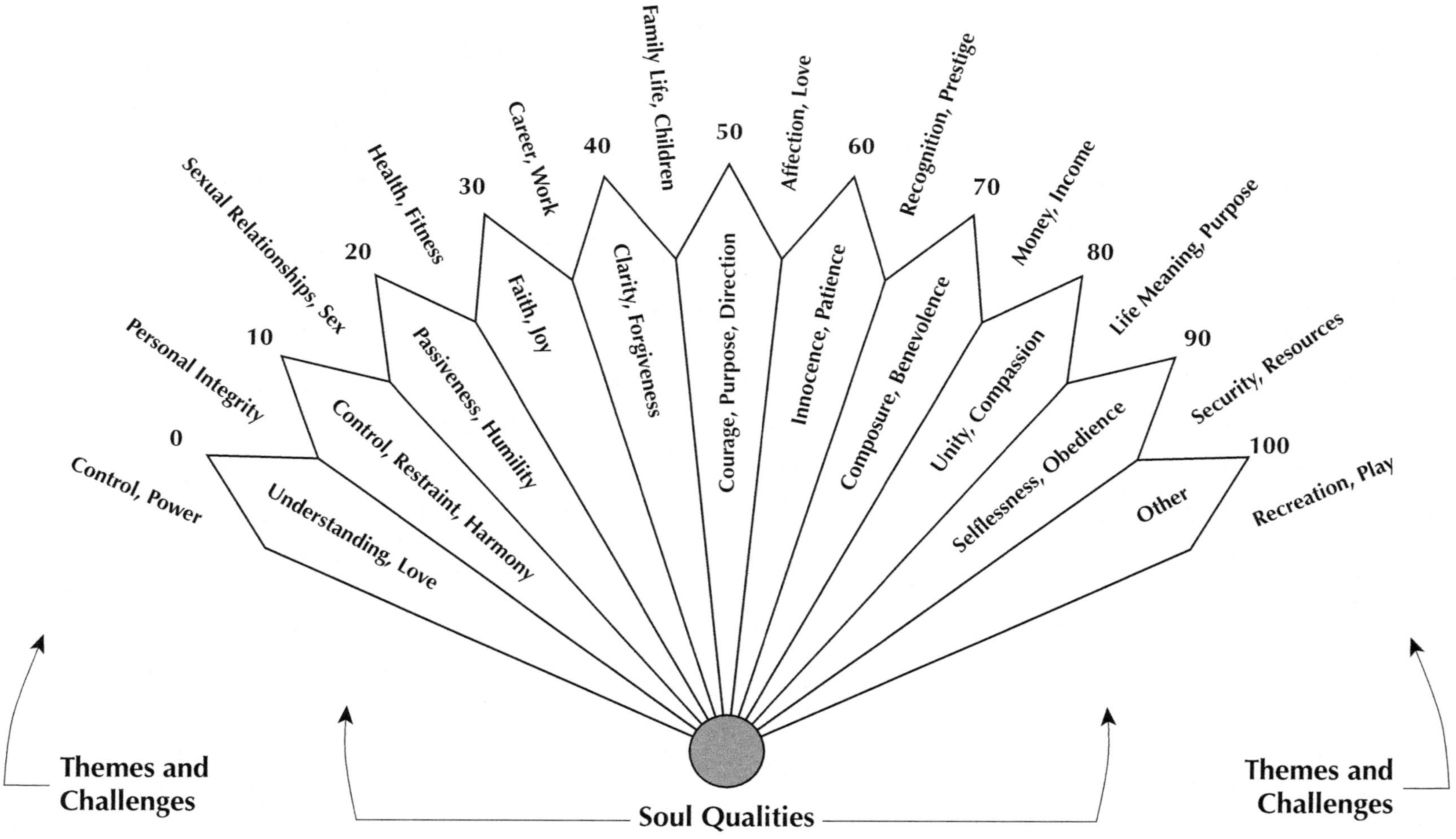

Levels of Soul Consciousness

GRAND-I/WHOLE

LUMINOUS SPIRIT (c) WELLSPRING

GODHEAD	Ten Levels	1 - ONE	1 … 2,000	Etheric Body (sc), 1st Astral Body (c) (Father Province)
		9 - Supreme Council		
I AM	Two Thousand Levels	2,000th I AM Level		Mental Body (c) and Emotional Body (c) I AM (Father of Knowledge)
		1,999 Infinite Council Levels		

GOD - Infinite Beings at Infinite Levels (18 Groups)

Level	King of Kings	[45,000]	Idea (egg and sperm)
	Queen of Life	[150]	Spiritual Body (sc)
	Lord of Lords	[5,000]	Living Soul (c)

Lord/1st Eden	1st level of self-expression, 900,000,000 choices of life patterns.
Majestic Consciousness Levels	Choose one life pattern to develop a ruling consciousness.
Supreme Consciousness Levels	I AM Body (c)
Ultimate Consciousness Levels	Christ Body (sc)

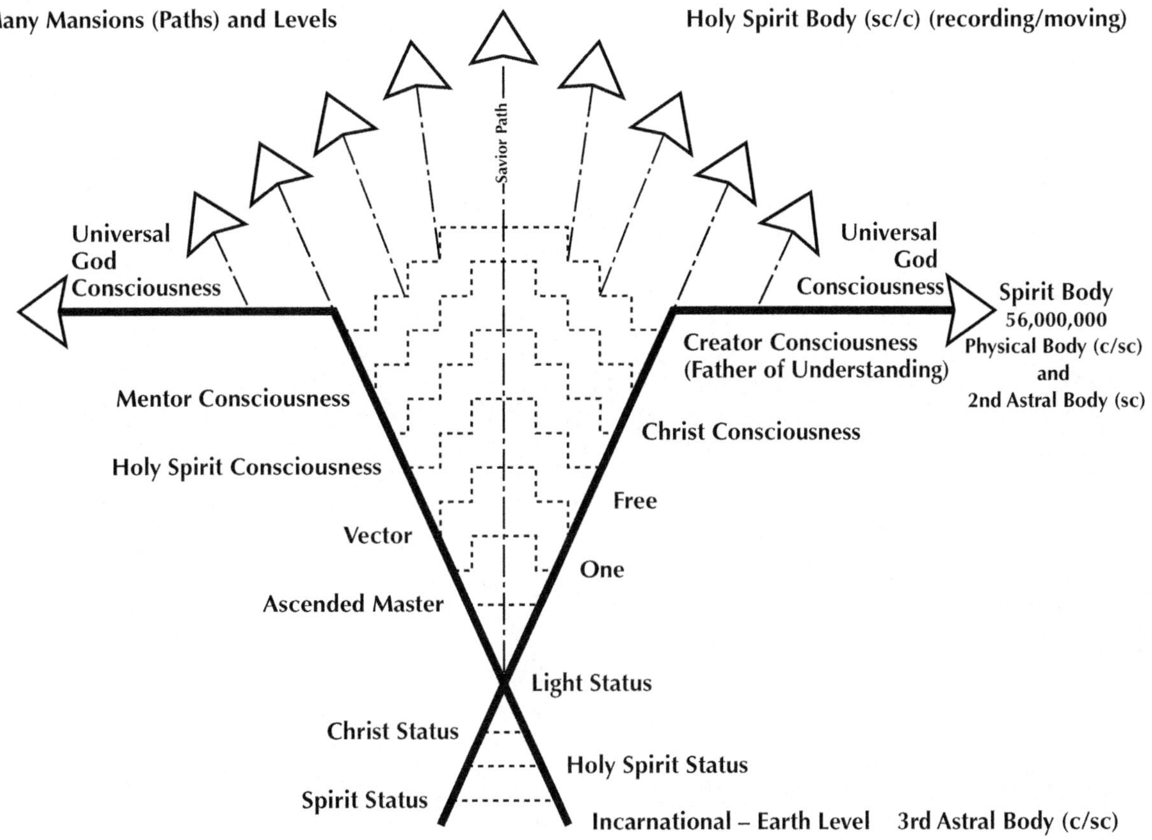

Below Incarnation there are 2,600 pathways (consisting of 136 major categories)

Key:
c = conscious
sc = subconscious

Programs, When, and Cast of Characters

Chart 4

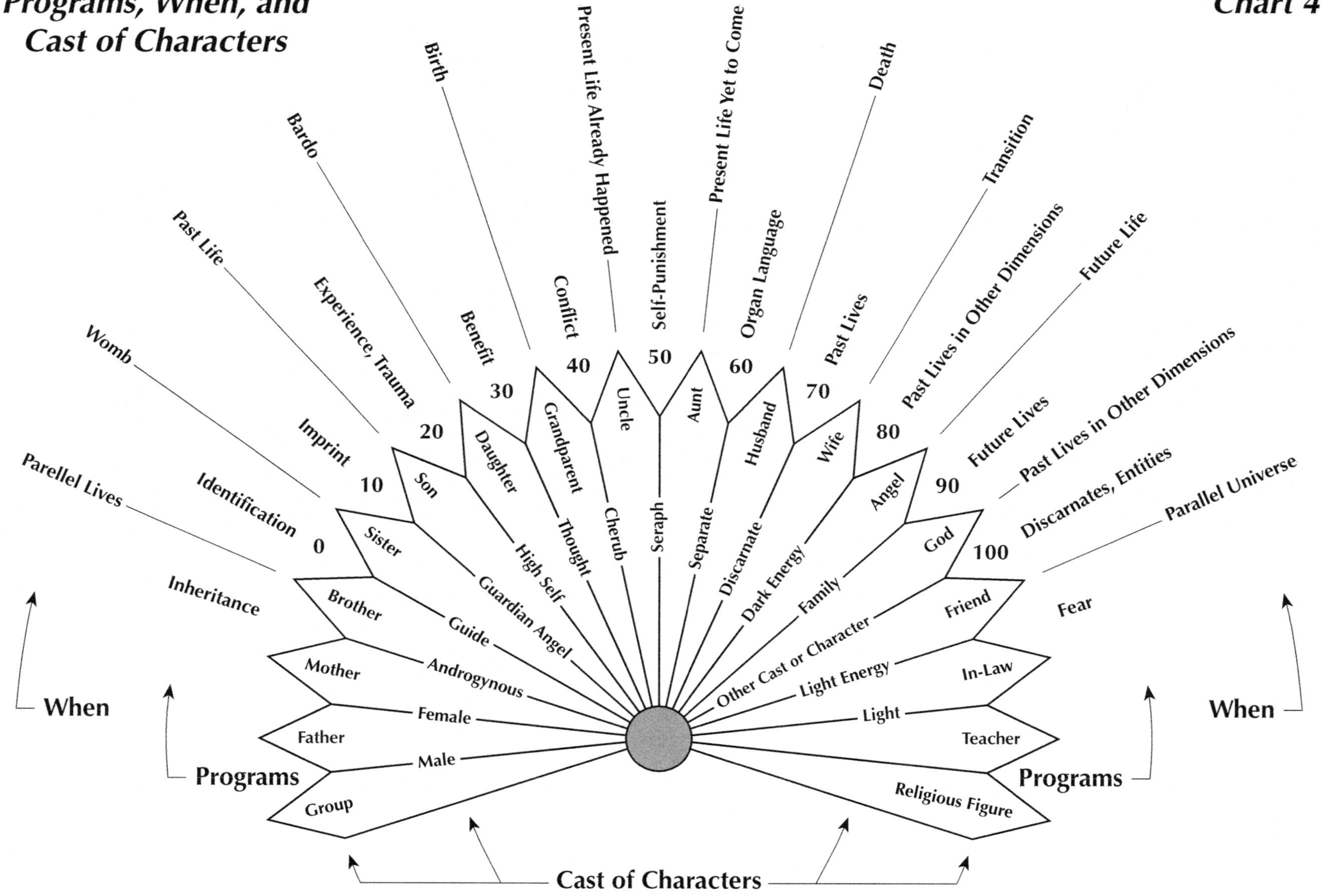

Negative Motivations, Blocks and Interference

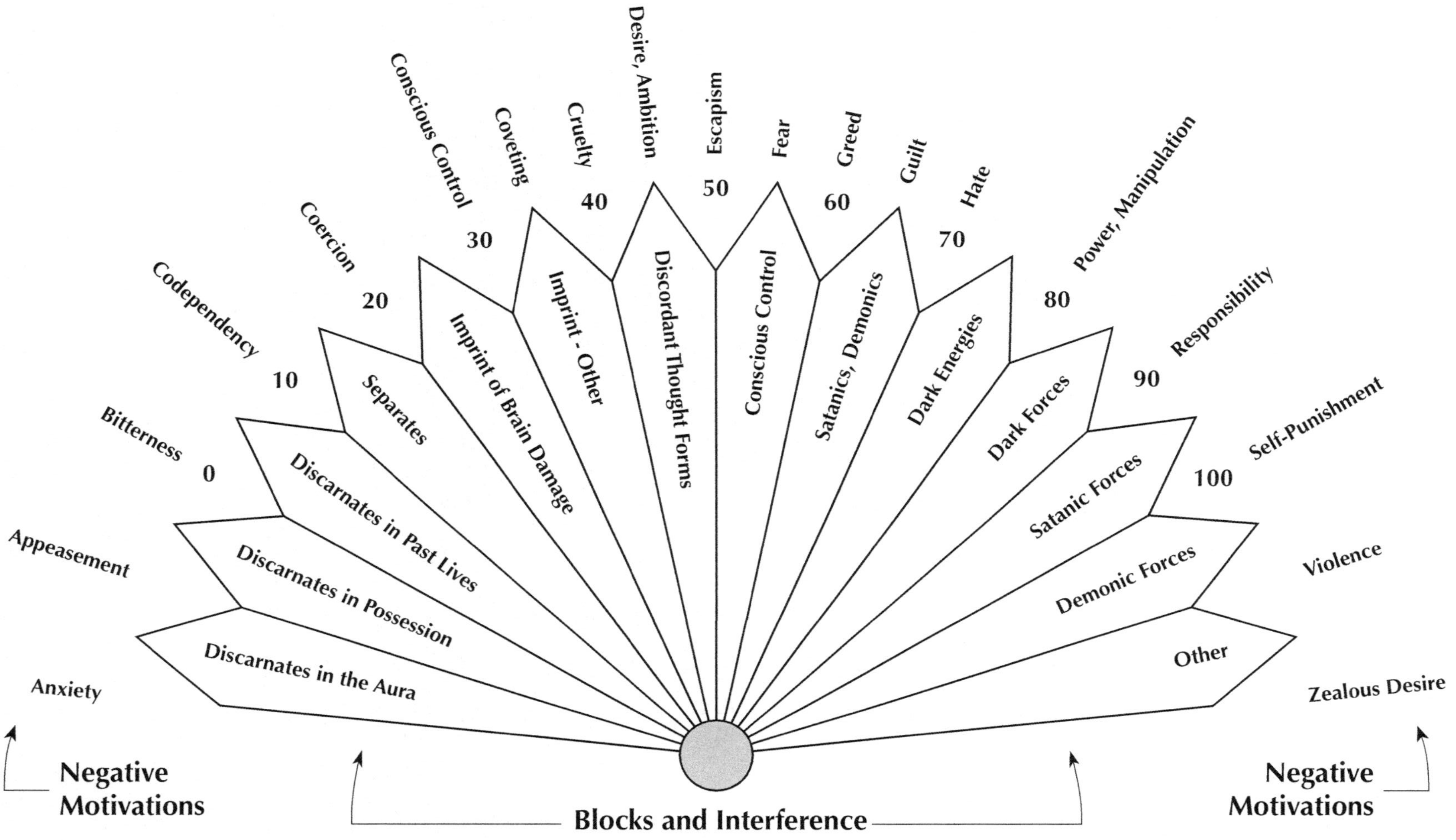

Chart 5

Master Programs, Discordant Energy

Chart 6A

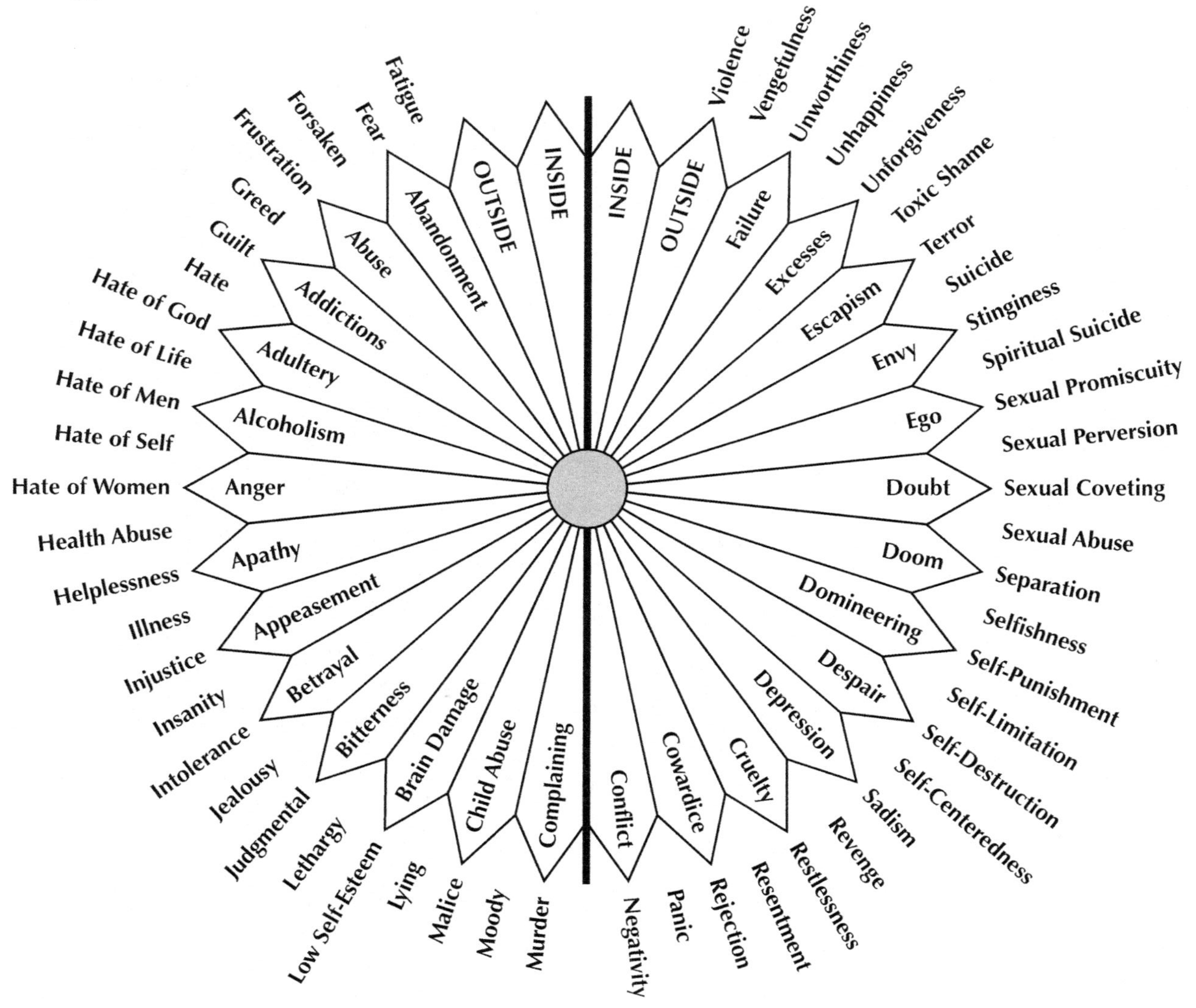

Blocks to Positive Expression

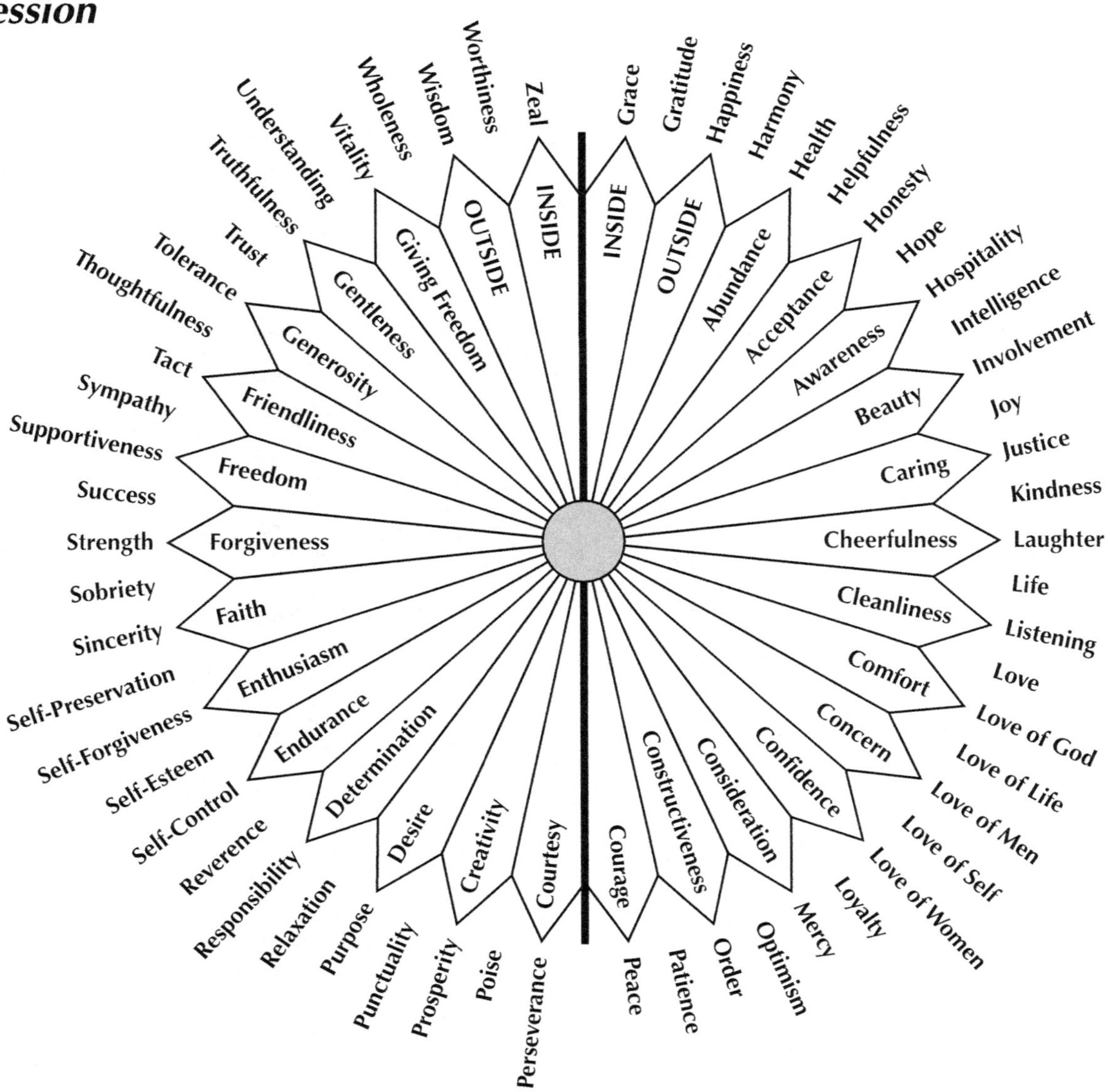

Chart 6B

Direct Healing Processes and Colors

Chart 7

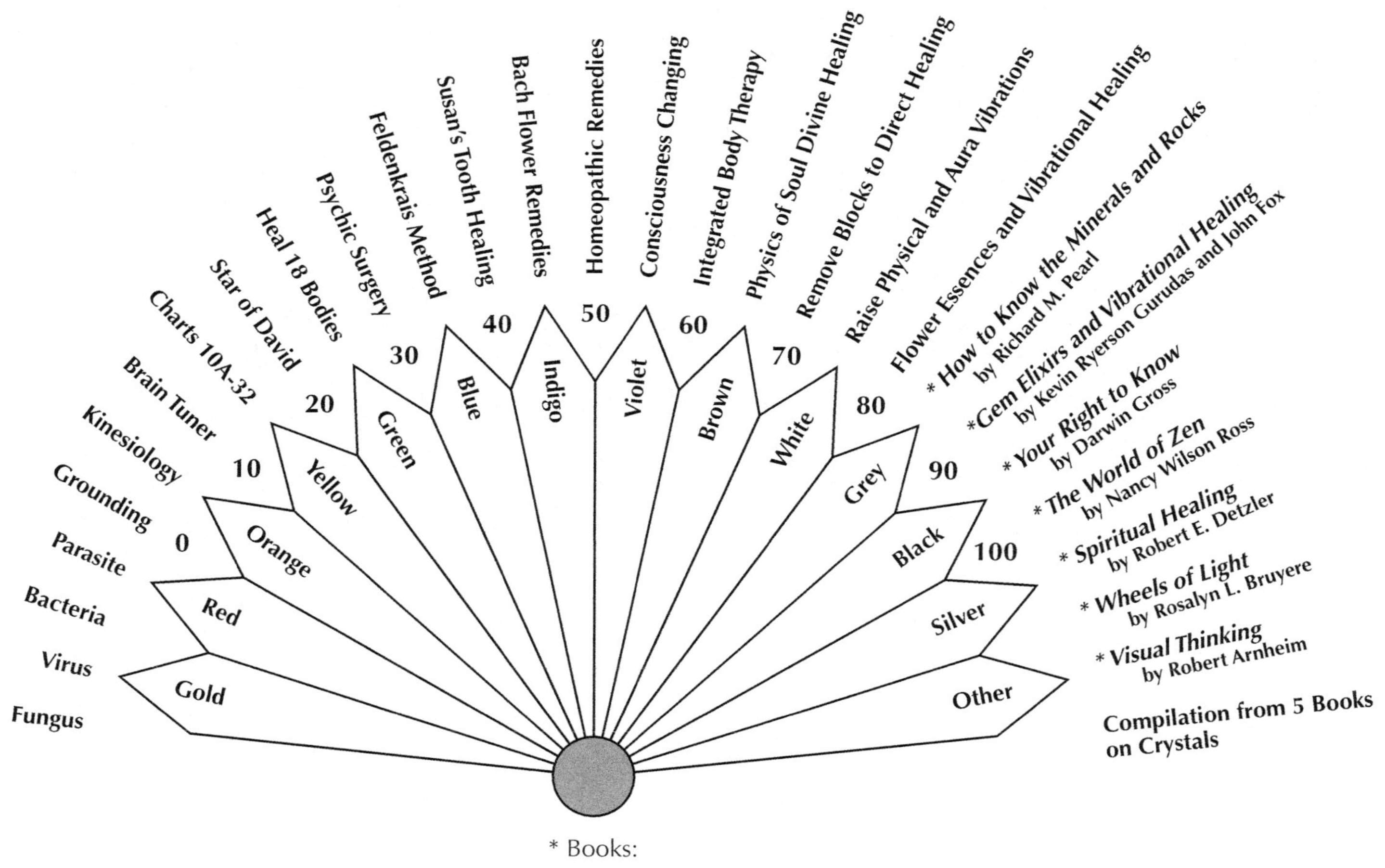

Inner Archetypes

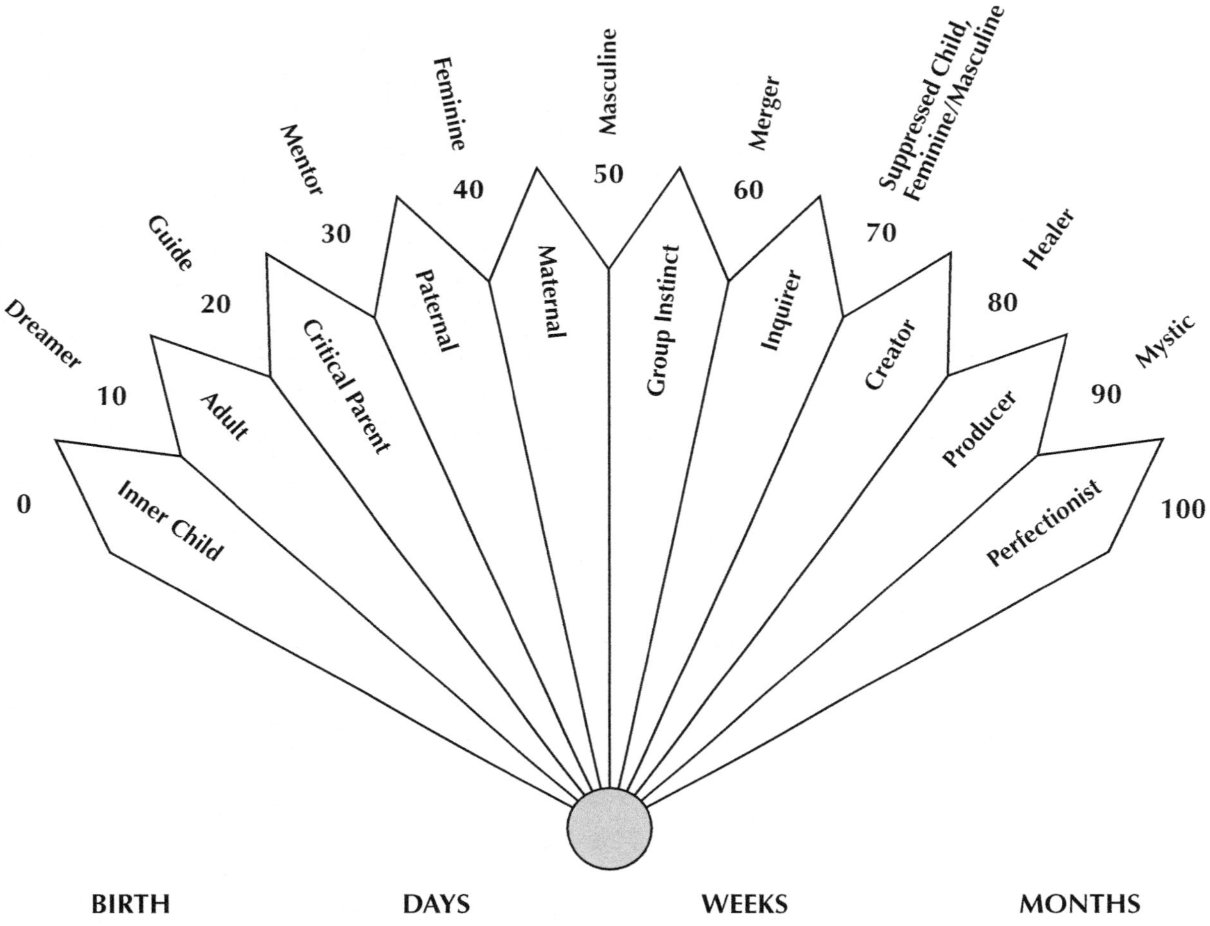

Chart 8

Chart 9A

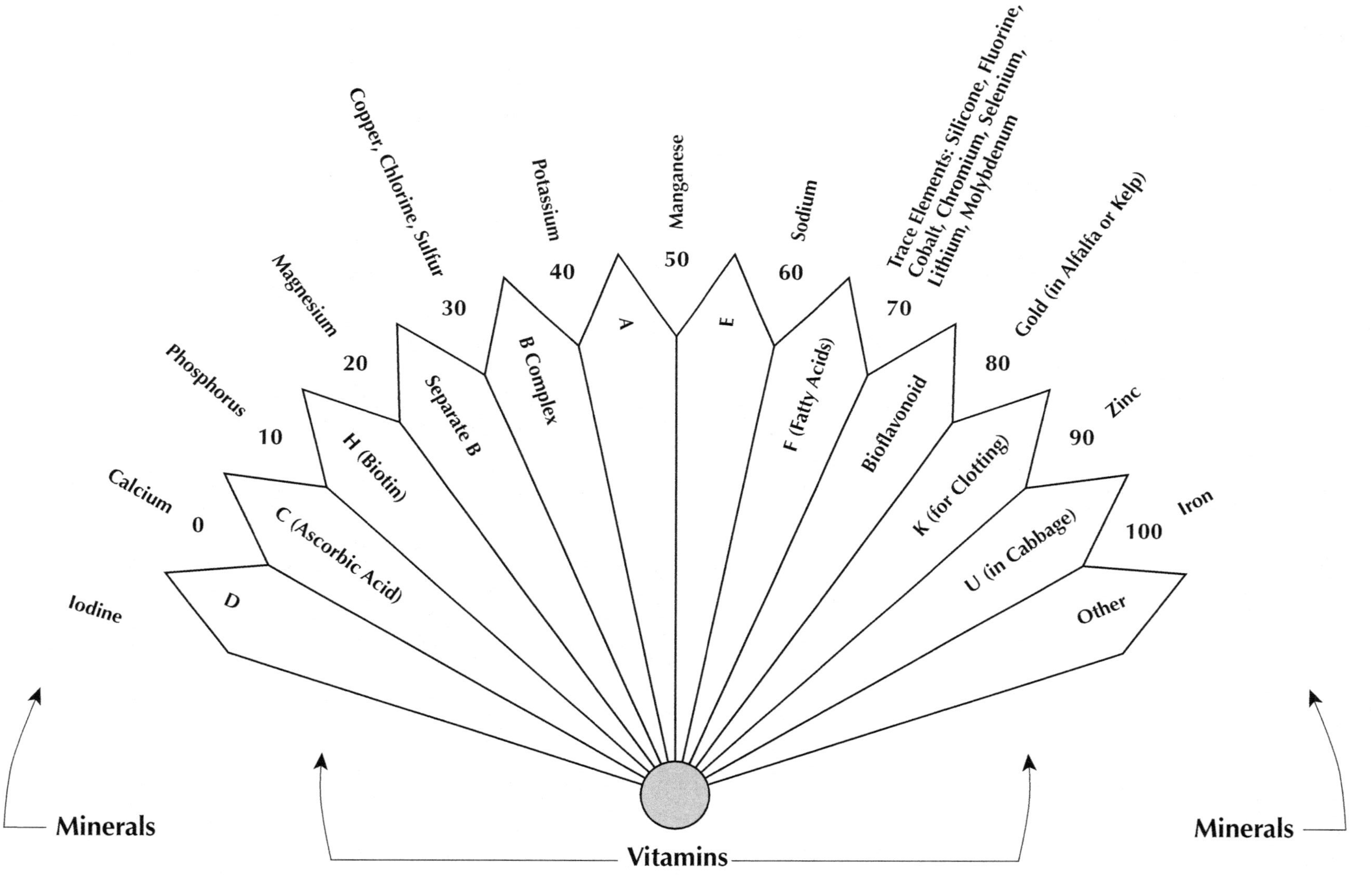
Iodine
Calcium
0
Phosphorus
10
Magnesium
20
Copper, Chlorine, Sulfur
30
Potassium
40
Manganese
50
Sodium
60
Trace Elements: Silicone, Fluorine, Cobalt, Chromium, Selenium, Lithium, Molybdenum
70
Gold (in Alfalfa or Kelp)
80
Zinc
90
Iron
100
D
C (Ascorbic Acid)
H (Biotin)
Separate B
B Complex
A
E
F (Fatty Acids)
Bioflavonoid
K (for Clotting)
U (in Cabbage)
Other
Minerals
Vitamins
Minerals

Food or Diet, Health and Well-Being

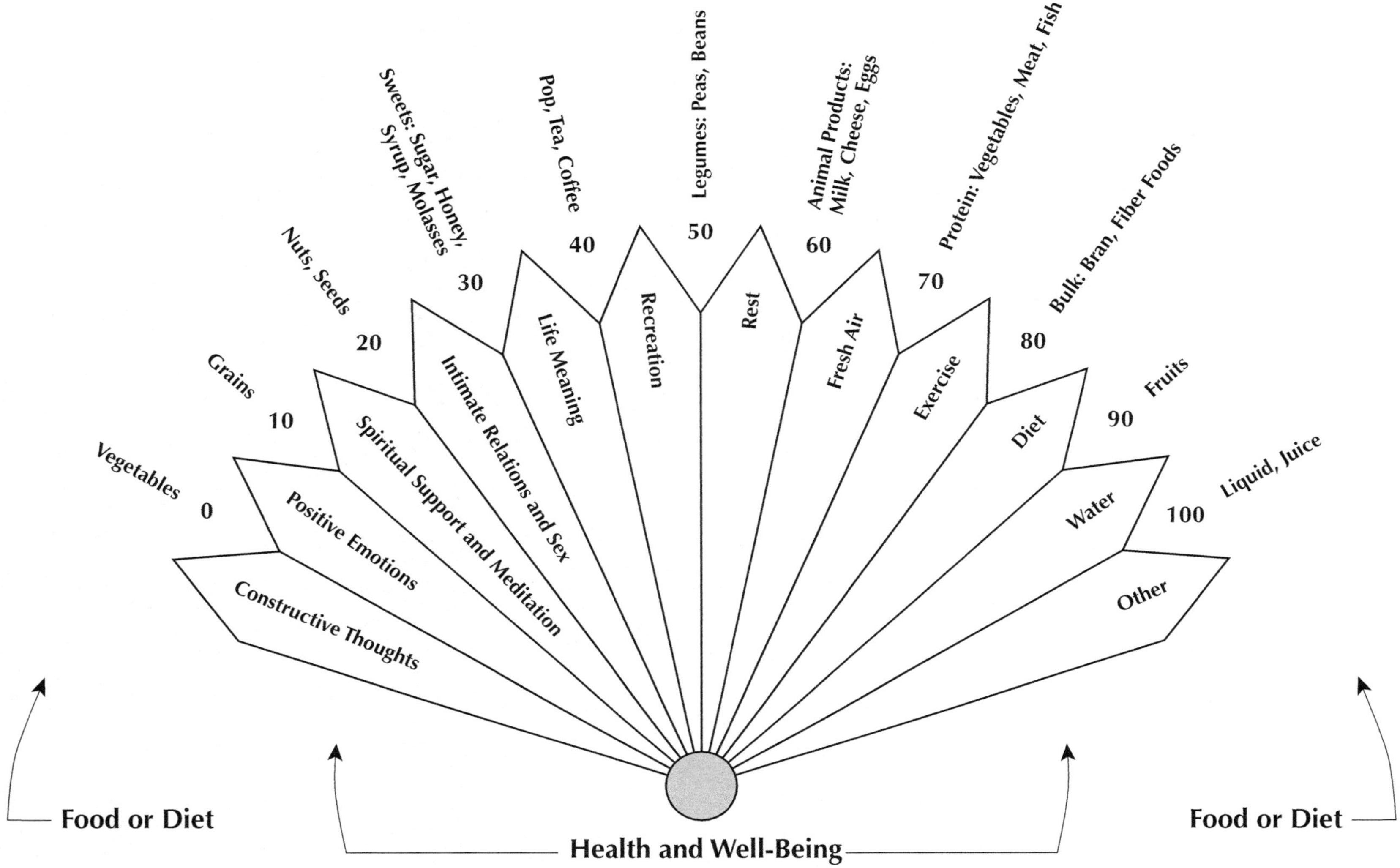

Chart 9B

Miscellaneous Blocks

Chart 10

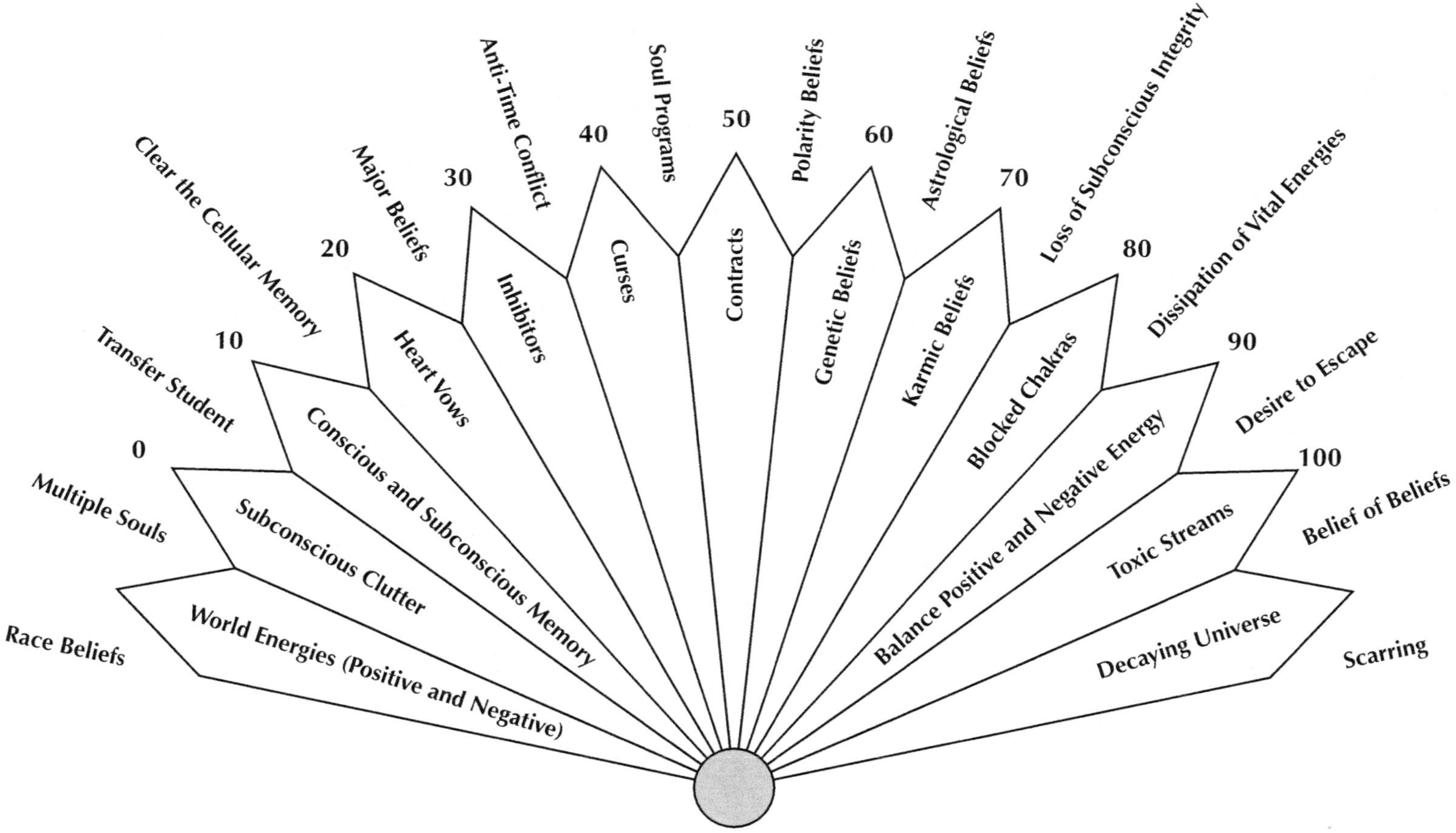

Soul Energy Programming

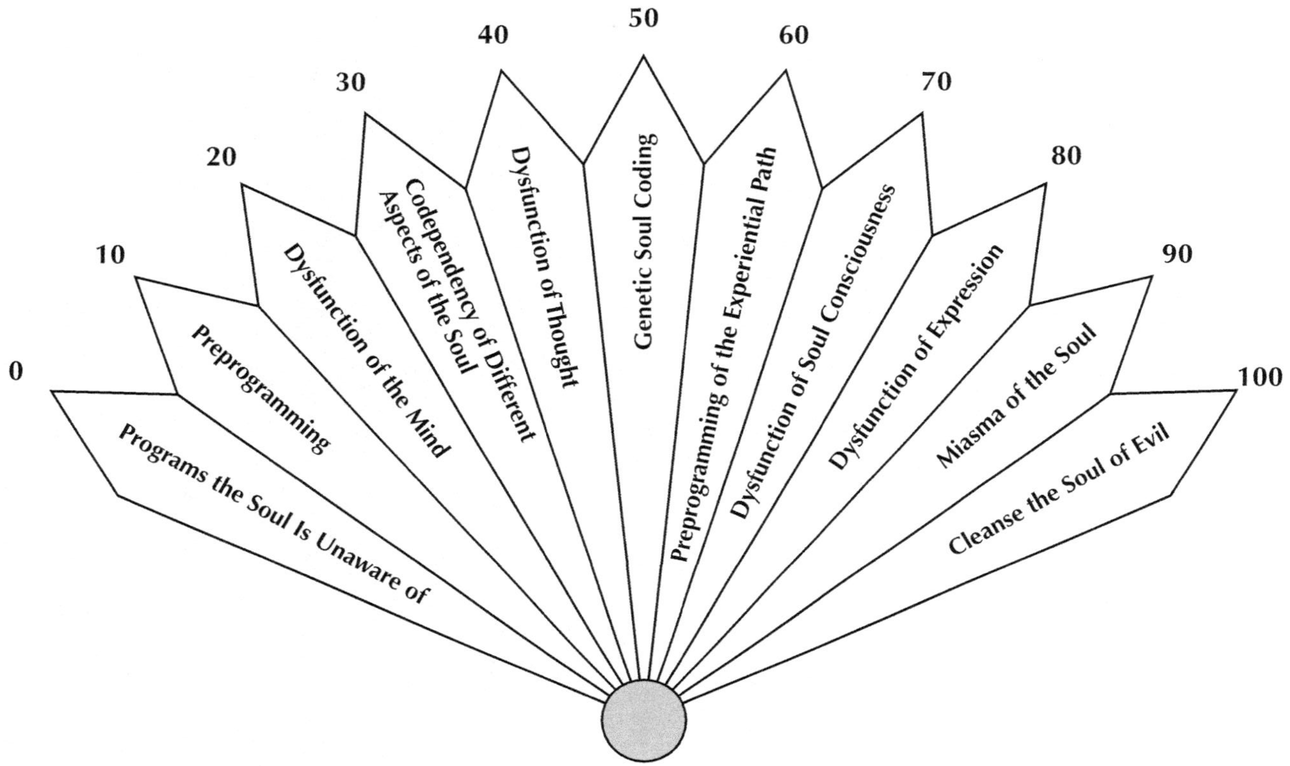

Chart 11

Chart 12

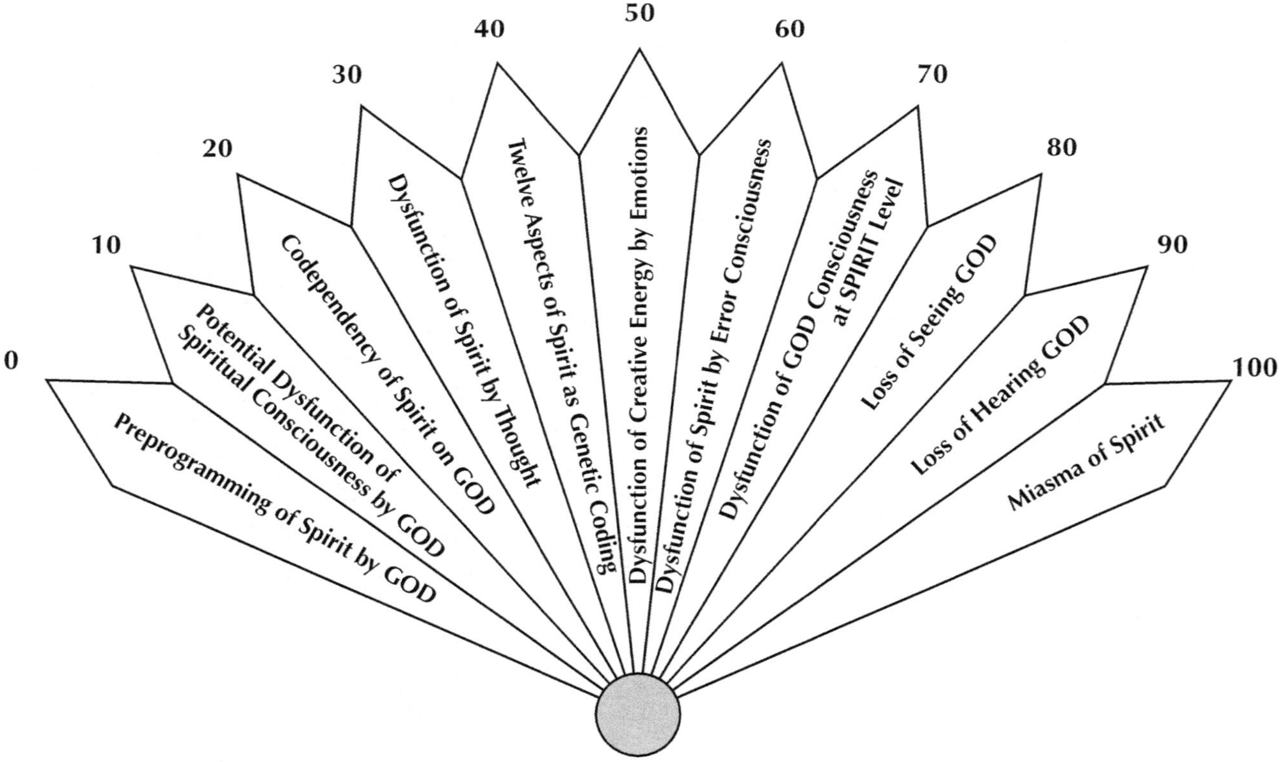
0
10
20
30
40
50
60
70
80
90
100
Preprogramming of Spirit by GOD
Potential Dysfunction of Spiritual Consciousness by GOD
Codependency of Spirit on GOD
Dysfunction of Spirit by Thought
Twelve Aspects of Spirit as Genetic Coding
Dysfunction of Creative Energy by Emotions
Dysfunction of Spirit by Error Consciousness
Dysfunction of GOD Consciousness at SPIRIT Level
Loss of Seeing GOD
Loss of Hearing GOD
Miasma of Spirit

Programs Before Creation

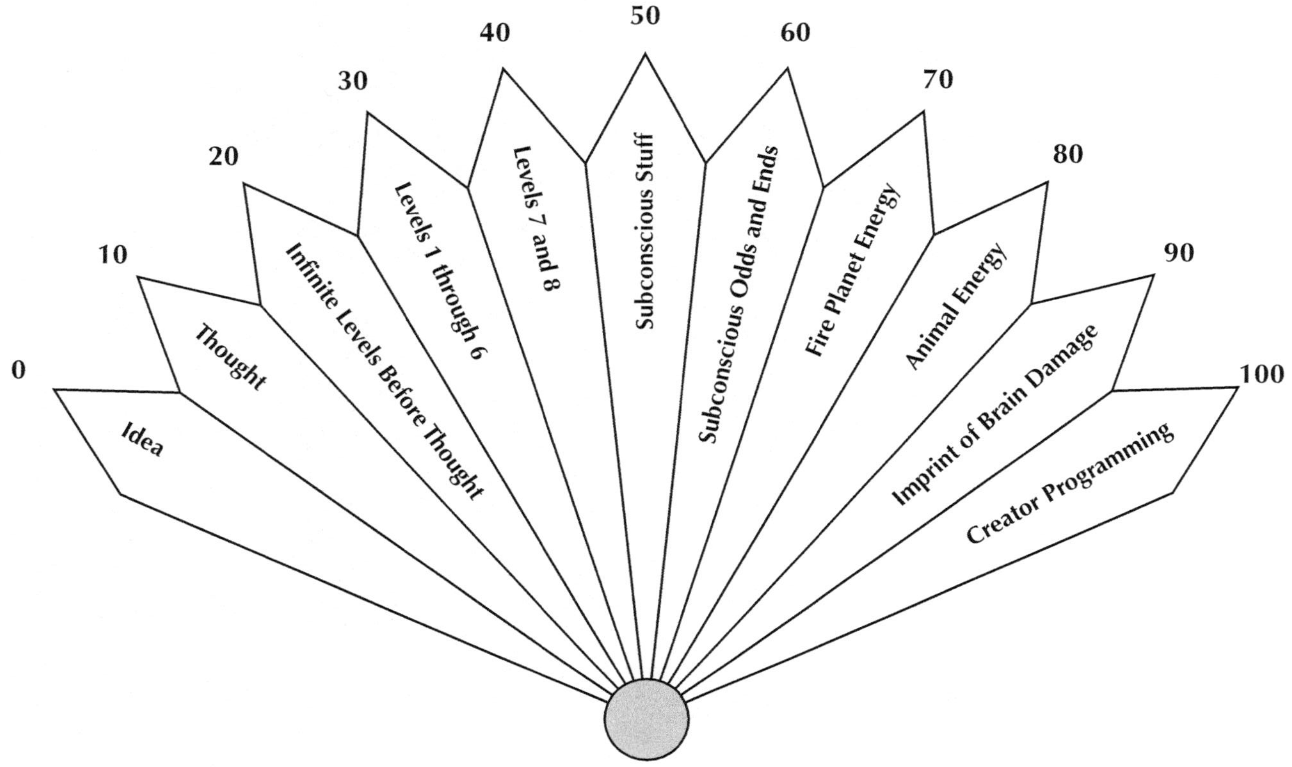

Chart 13

Pre-Fall of Consciousness, Creating the Illusion

Chart 14

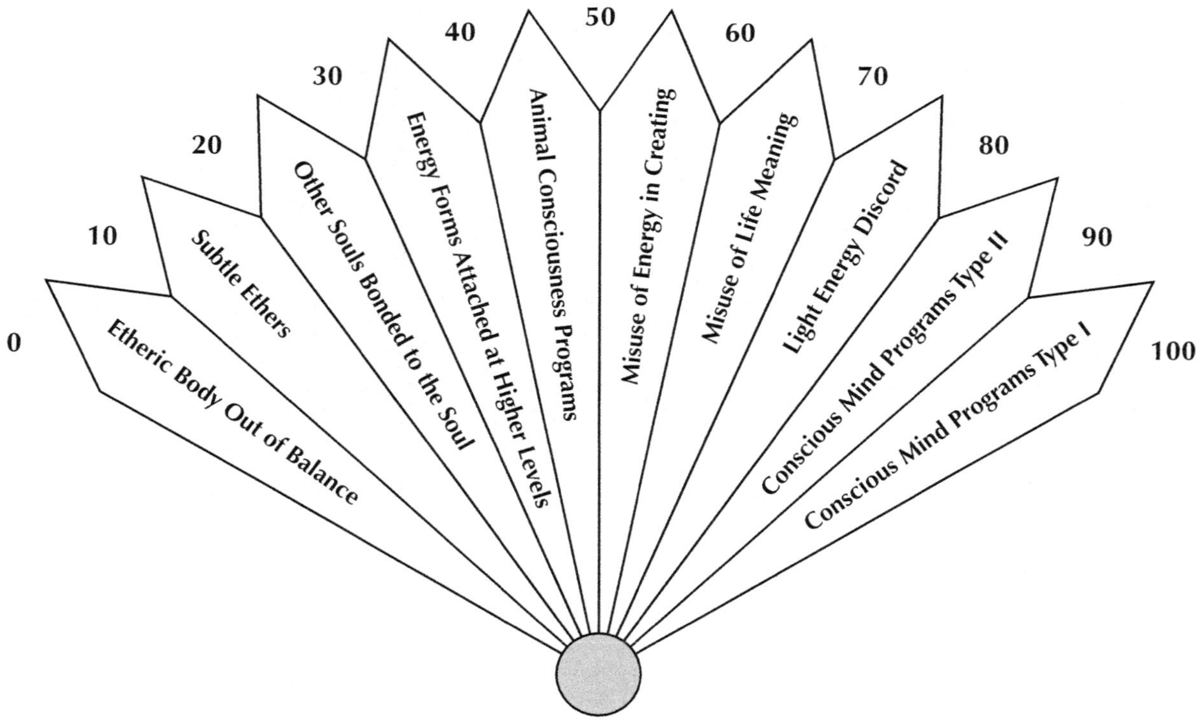

I AM Level Consciousness Programs

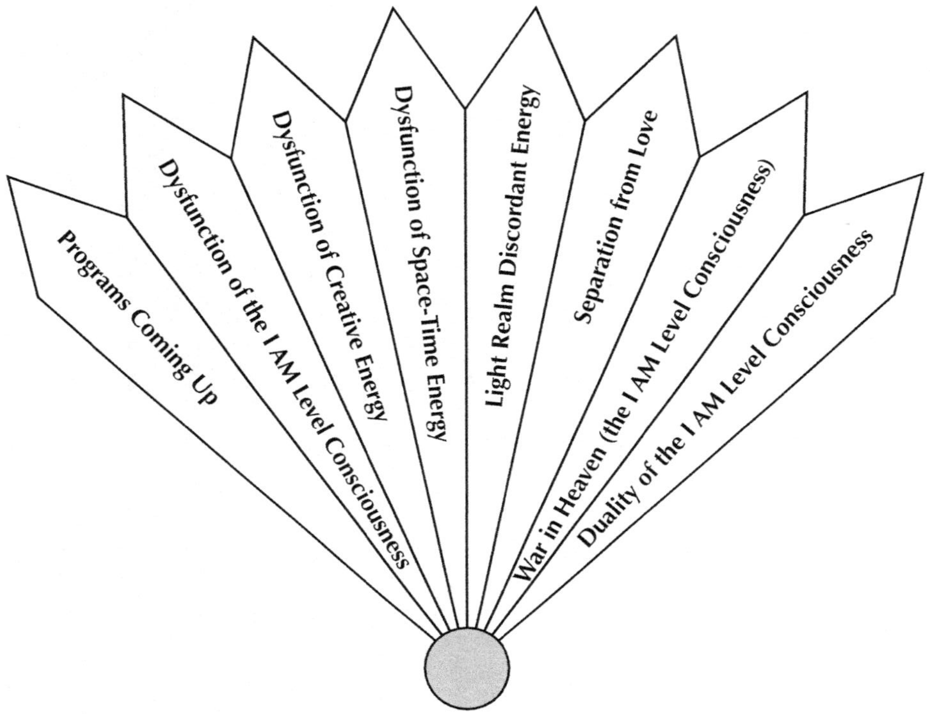

Chart 15

Fall of Consciousness

Chart 16

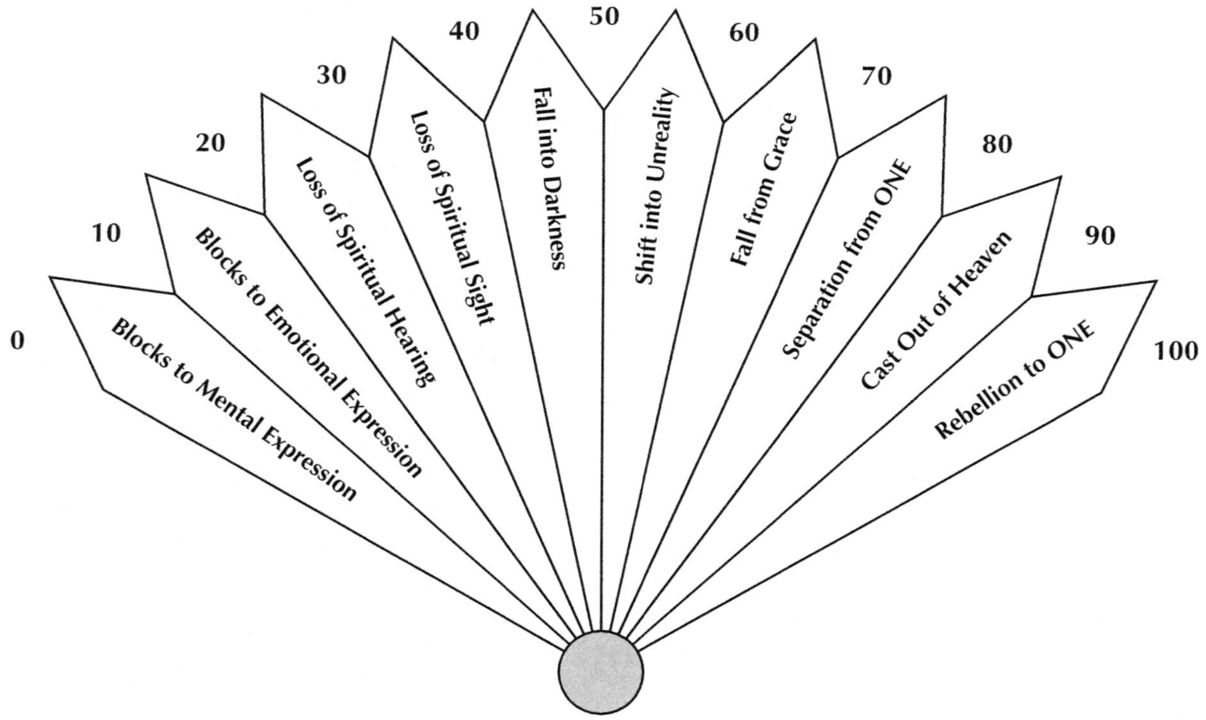

Fine Tuning

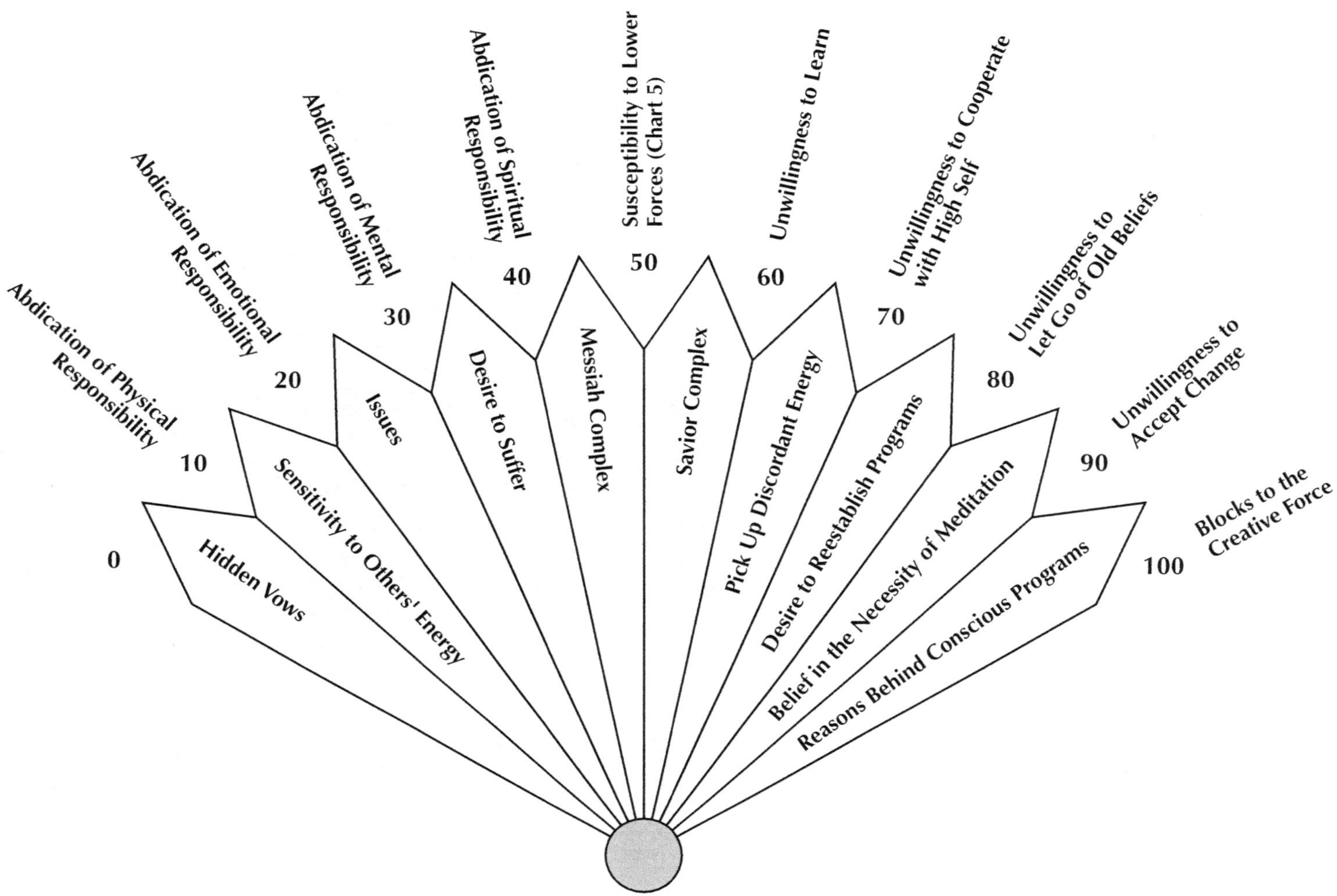

Chart 17

Higher Level Blocks

Chart 18

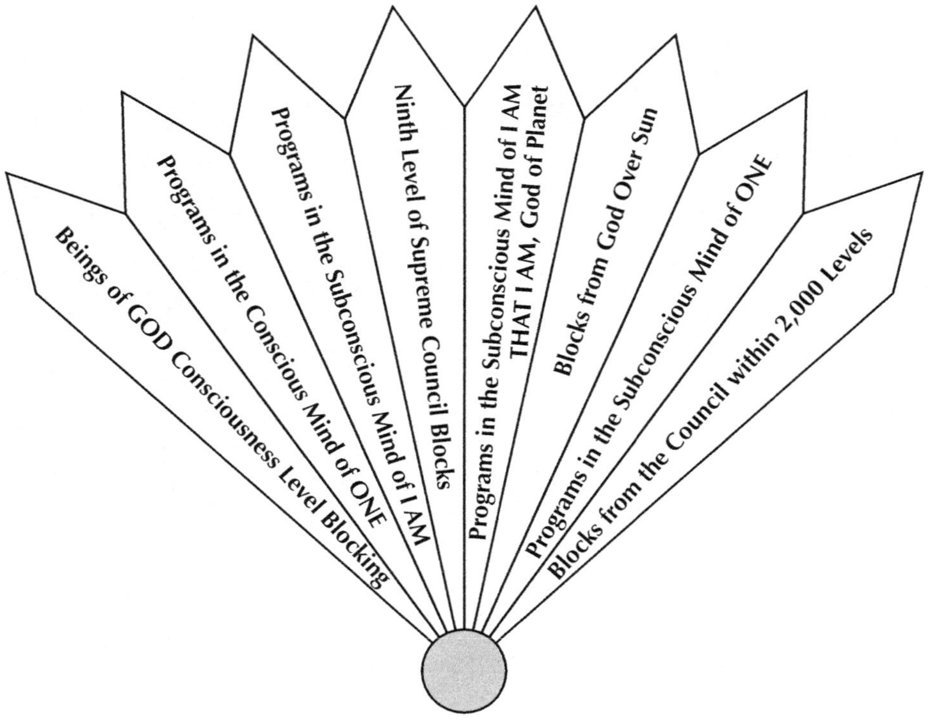

How to Change Your Life

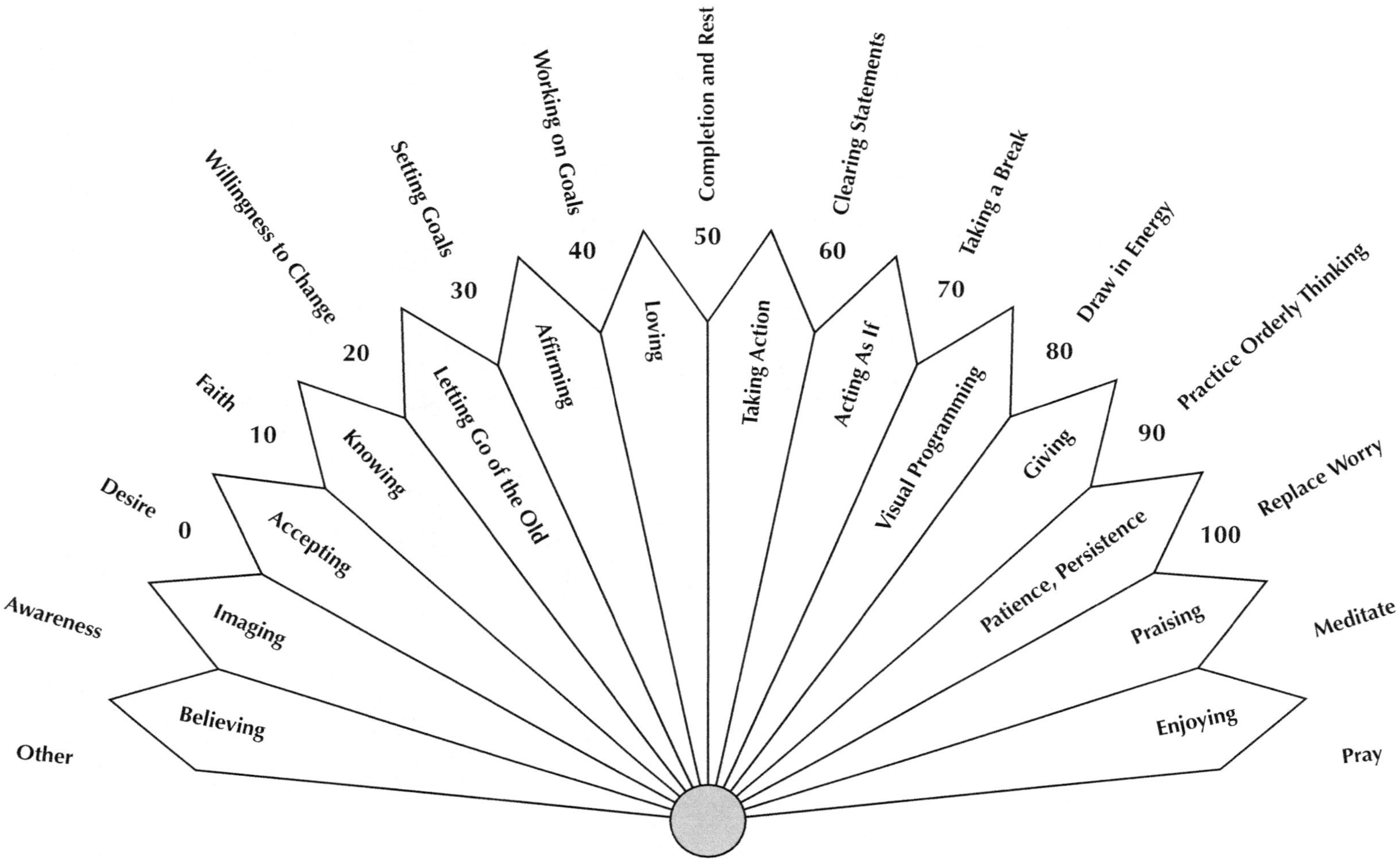

Chart 19

Chart 20

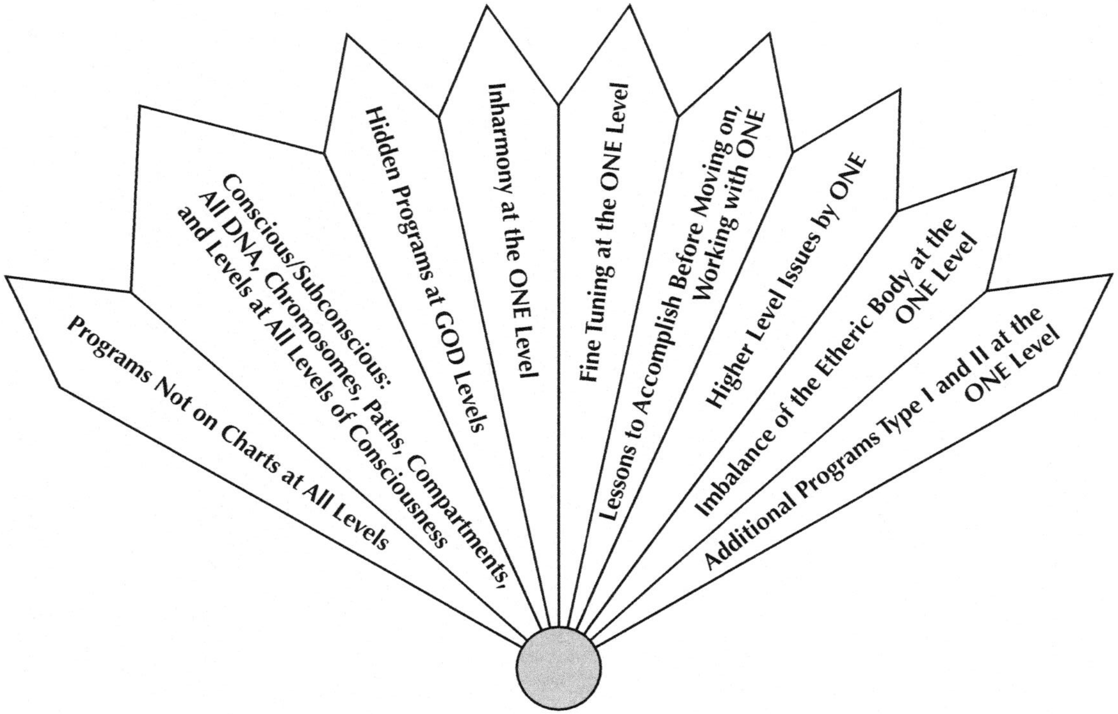
Programs Not on Charts at All Levels
Conscious/Subconscious:
All DNA, Chromosomes, Paths, Compartments,
and Levels at All Levels of Consciousness
Hidden Programs at GOD Levels
Inharmony at the ONE Level
Fine Tuning at the ONE Level
Lessons to Accomplish Before Moving on,
Working with ONE
Higher Level Issues by ONE
Imbalance of the Etheric Body at the
ONE Level
Additional Programs Type I and II at the
ONE Level

Final Items this ONE Universe

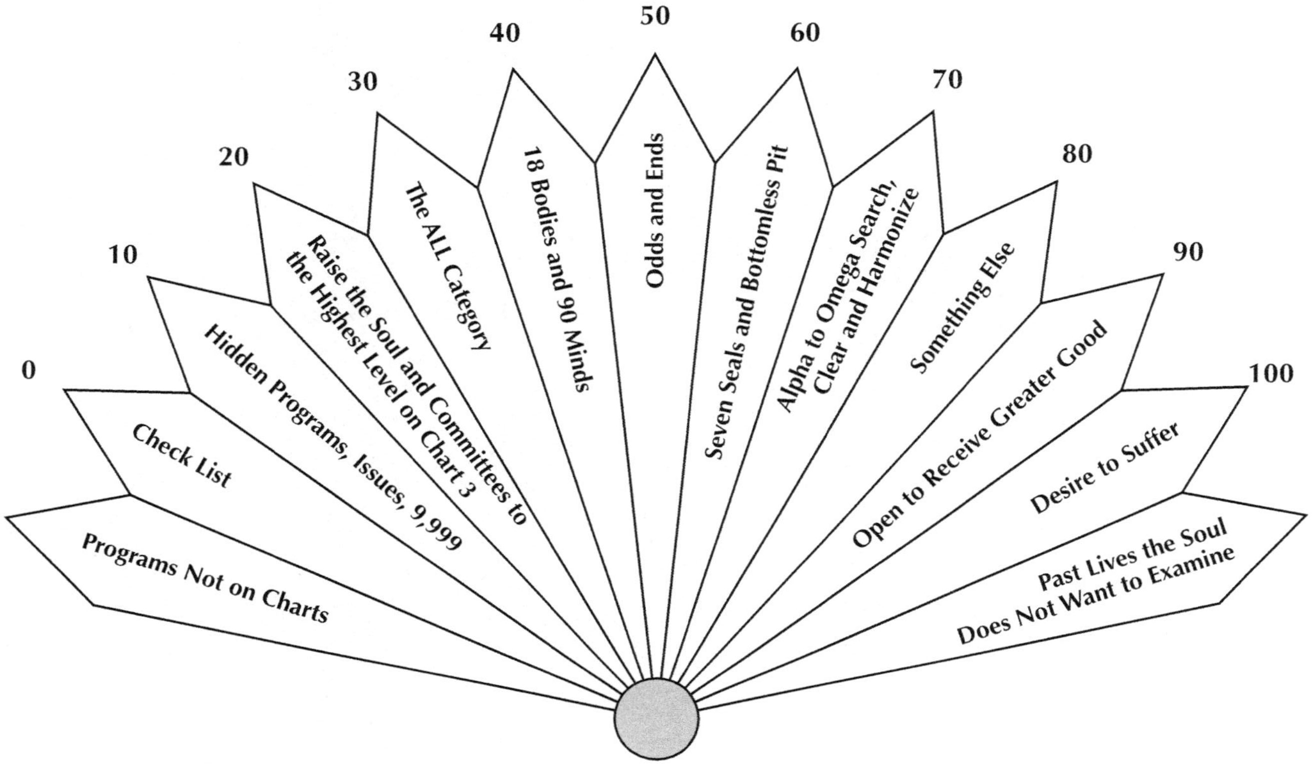

Chart 21

Chart 22

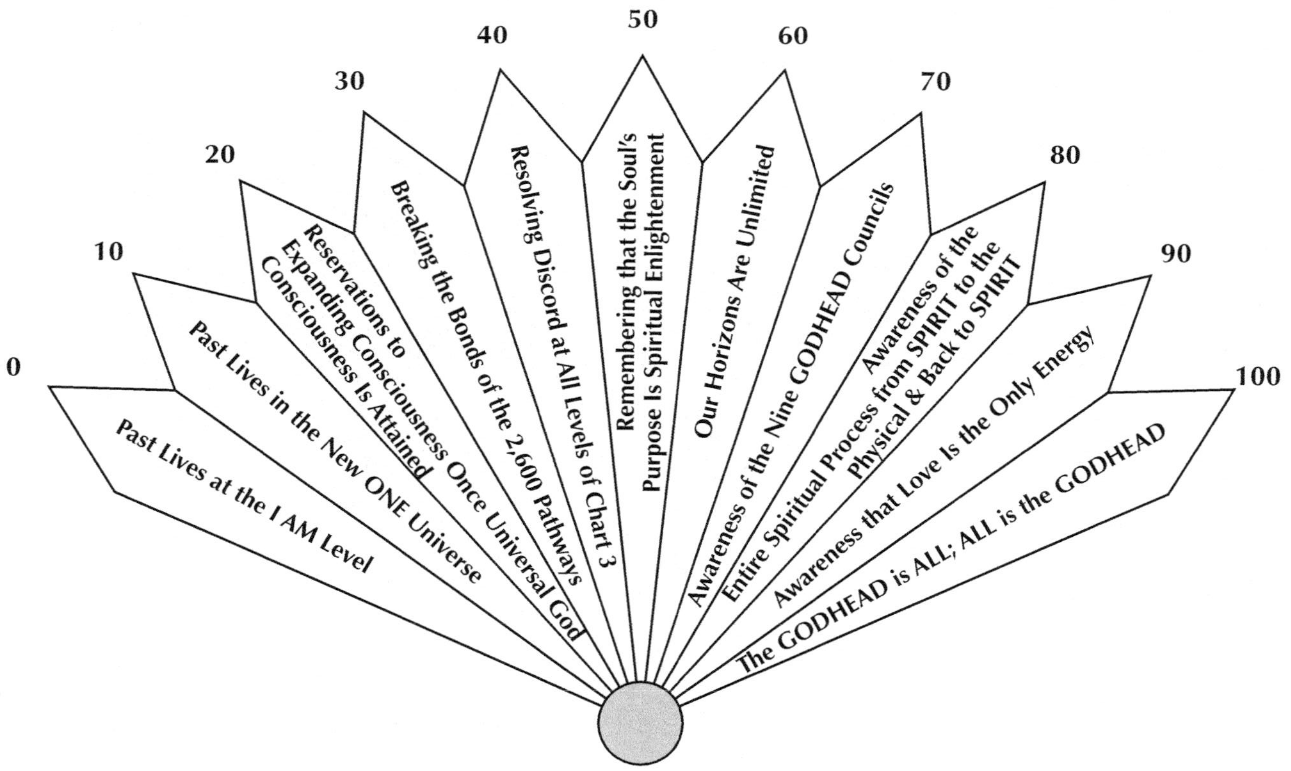
0
10
20
30
40
50
60
70
80
90
100
Past Lives at the I AM Level
Past Lives in the New ONE Universe
Reservations to Expanding Consciousness Once Universal God Consciousness Is Attained
Breaking the Bonds of the 2,600 Pathways
Resolving Discord at All Levels of Chart 3
Remembering that the Soul's Purpose Is Spiritual Enlightenment
Our Horizons Are Unlimited
Awareness of the Nine GODHEAD Councils
Awareness of the Entire Spiritual Process from SPIRIT to the Physical & Back to SPIRIT
Awareness that Love Is the Only Energy
The GODHEAD is ALL; ALL is the GODHEAD

Spiritual Realms Programs

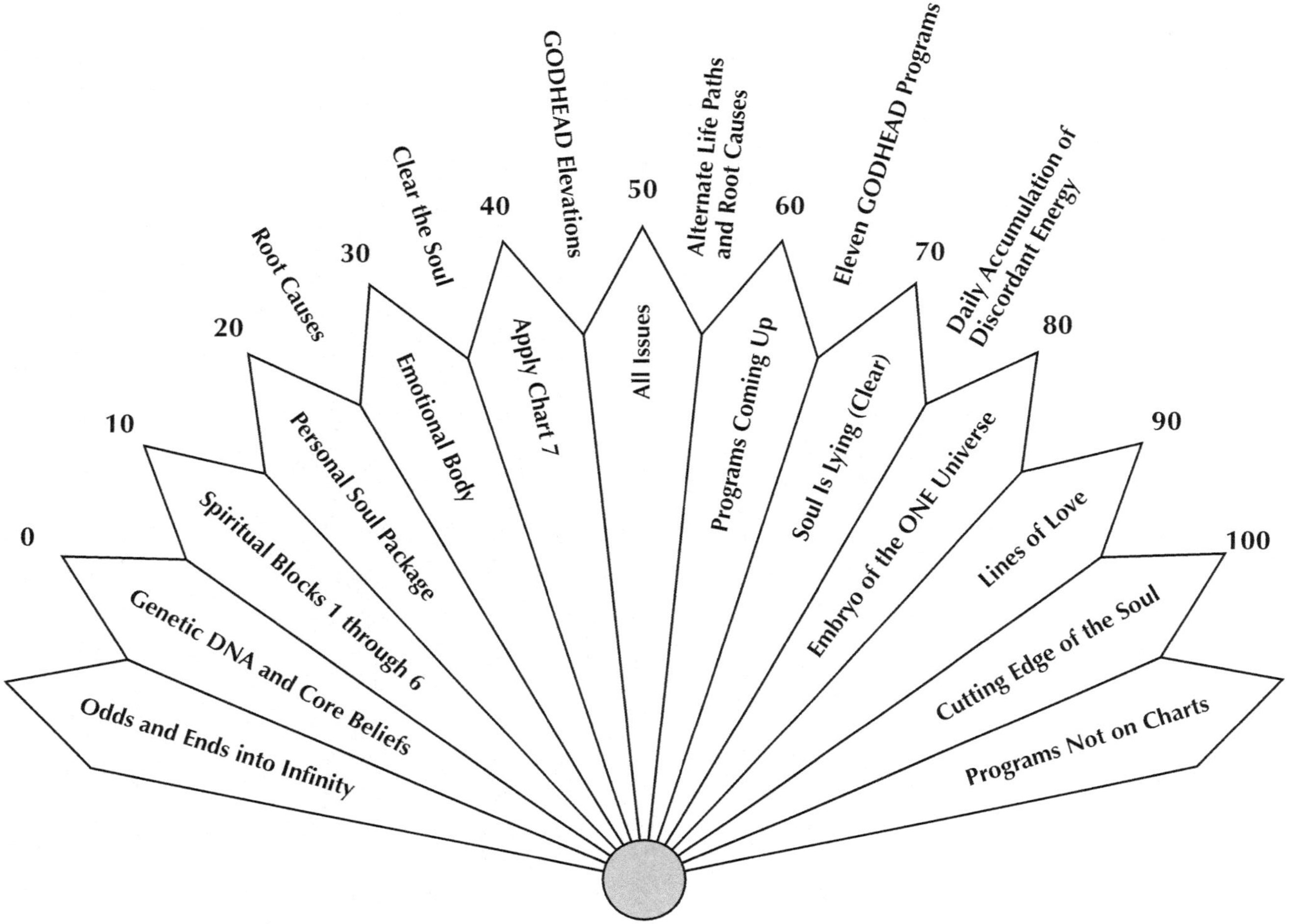

Chart 23

Chart 24

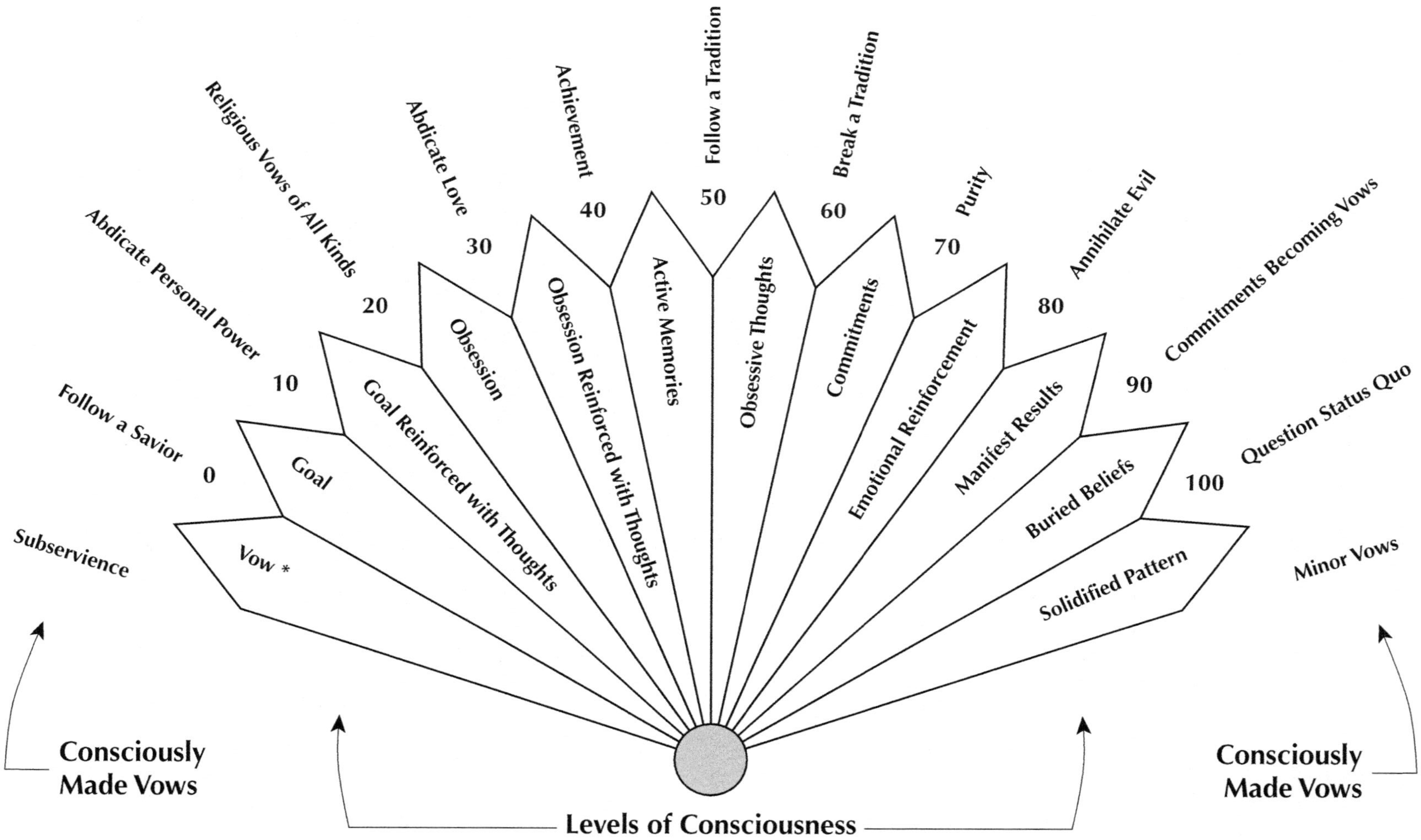

* Recognize or identify the vow, discharge the locked energy by revoking the vow.
"I revoke any and all vows to __________ and I choose to stay open to daily guidance and decisions that are for my highest good here and now! I am okay as I am, I praise Universal Source."

Final Assurance

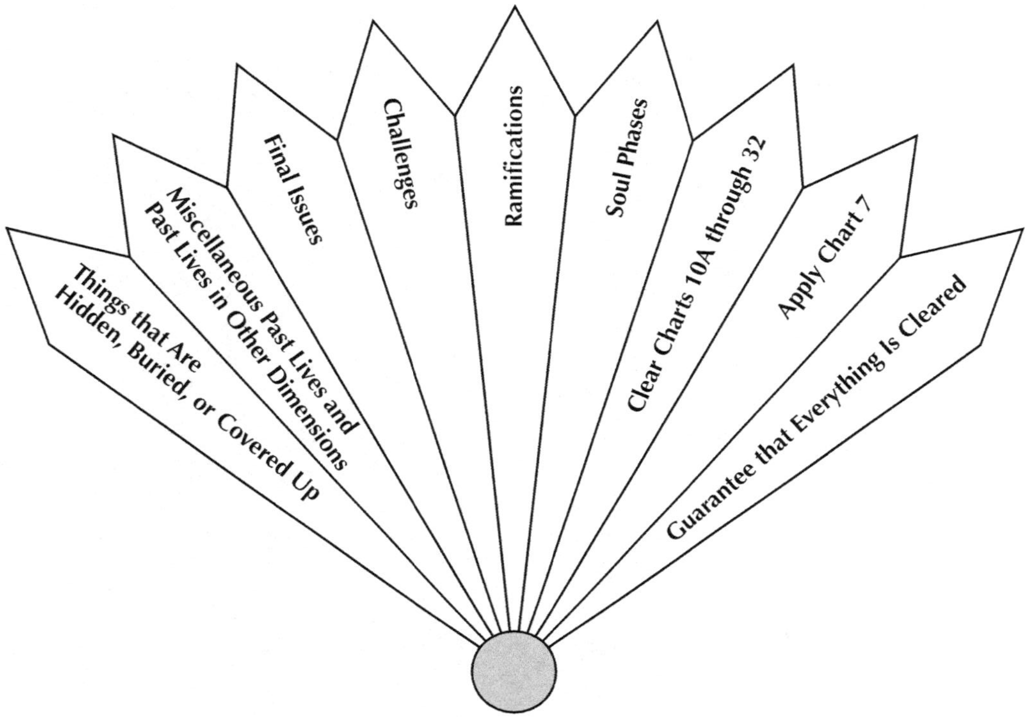

Chart 25

Chart 26

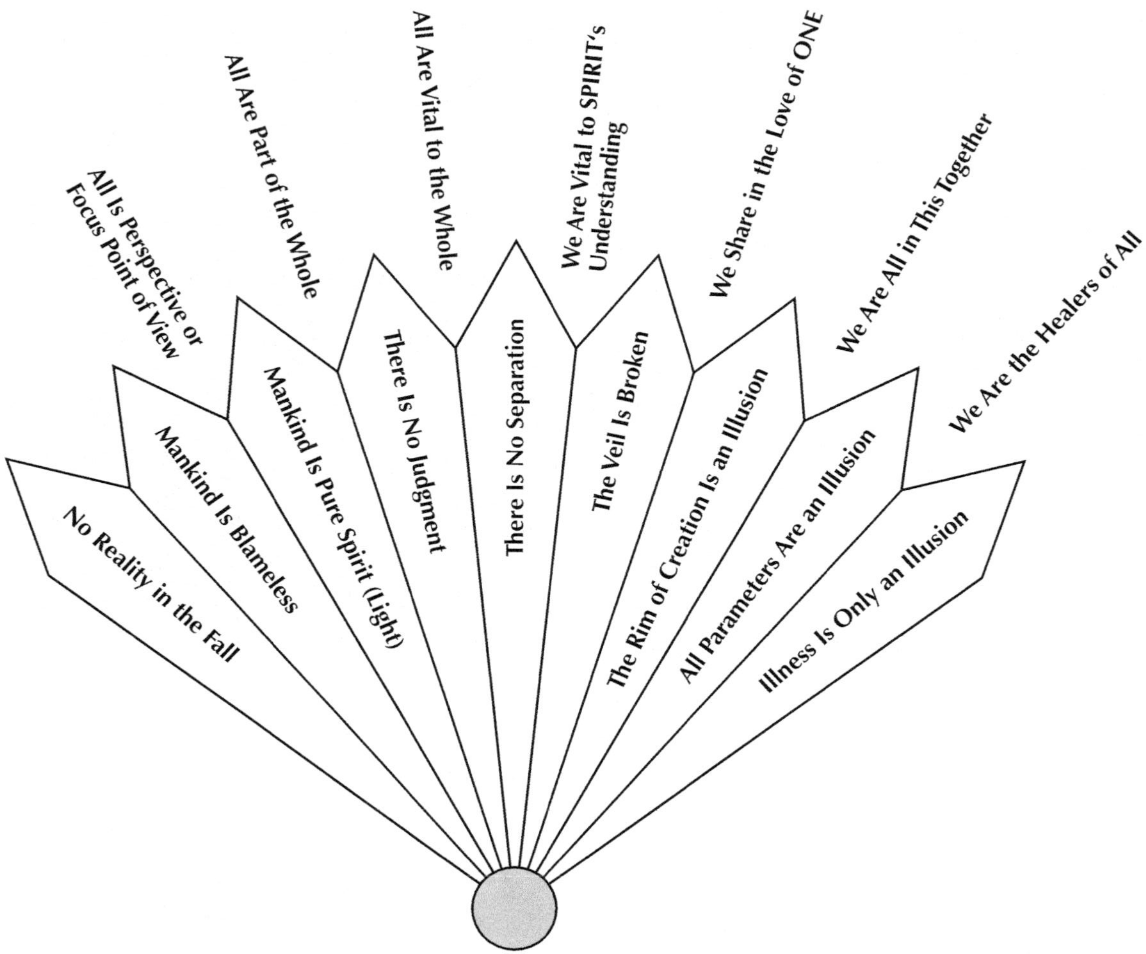

All Is Perspective or Focus Point of View
All Are Part of the Whole
All Are Vital to the Whole
We Are Vital to SPIRIT's Understanding
We Share in the Love of ONE
We Are All in This Together
We Are the Healers of All
No Reality in the Fall
Mankind Is Blameless
Mankind Is Pure Spirit (Light)
There Is No Judgment
There Is No Separation
The Veil Is Broken
The Rim of Creation Is an Illusion
All Parameters Are an Illusion
Illness Is Only an Illusion

Learning Is Fun

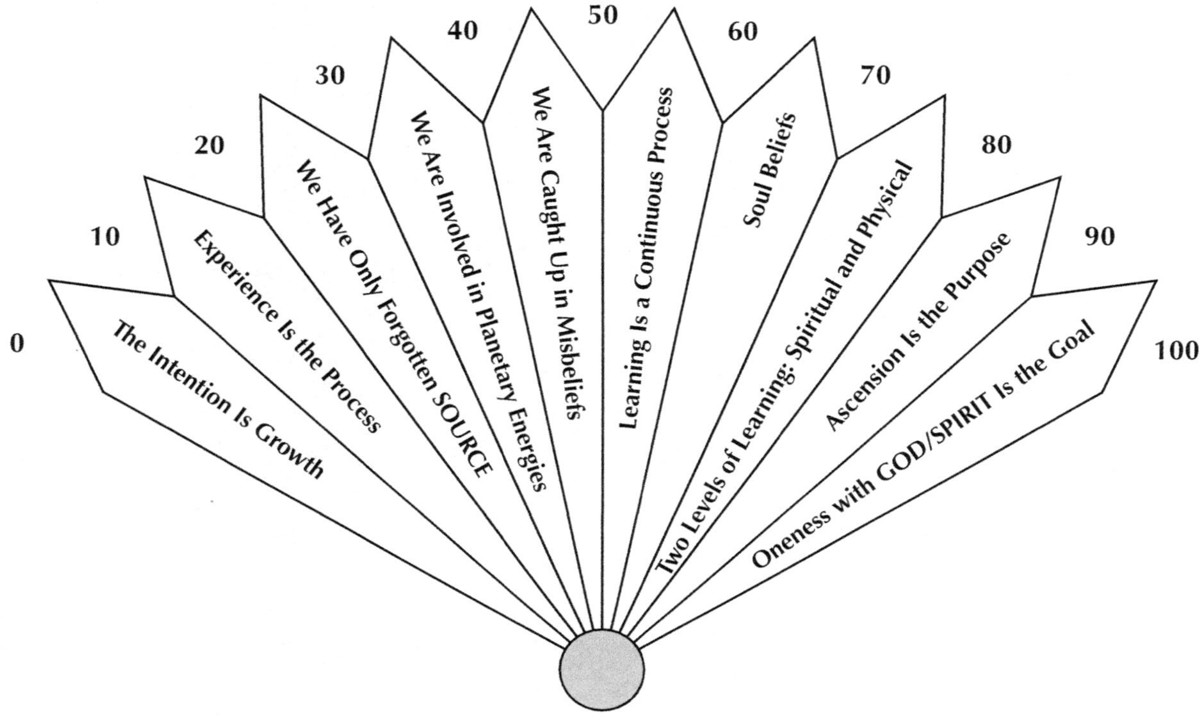

Chart 27

Final Forgiveness

Chart 28

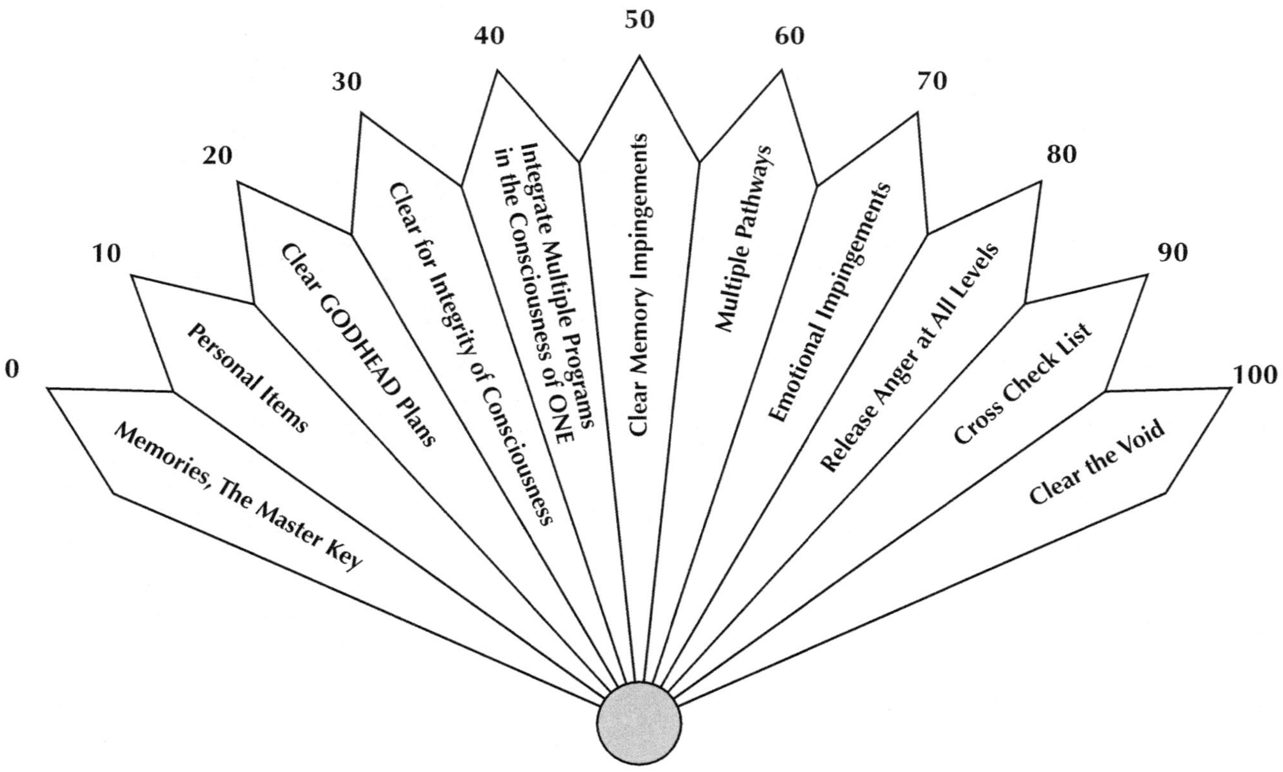

Final Blessing

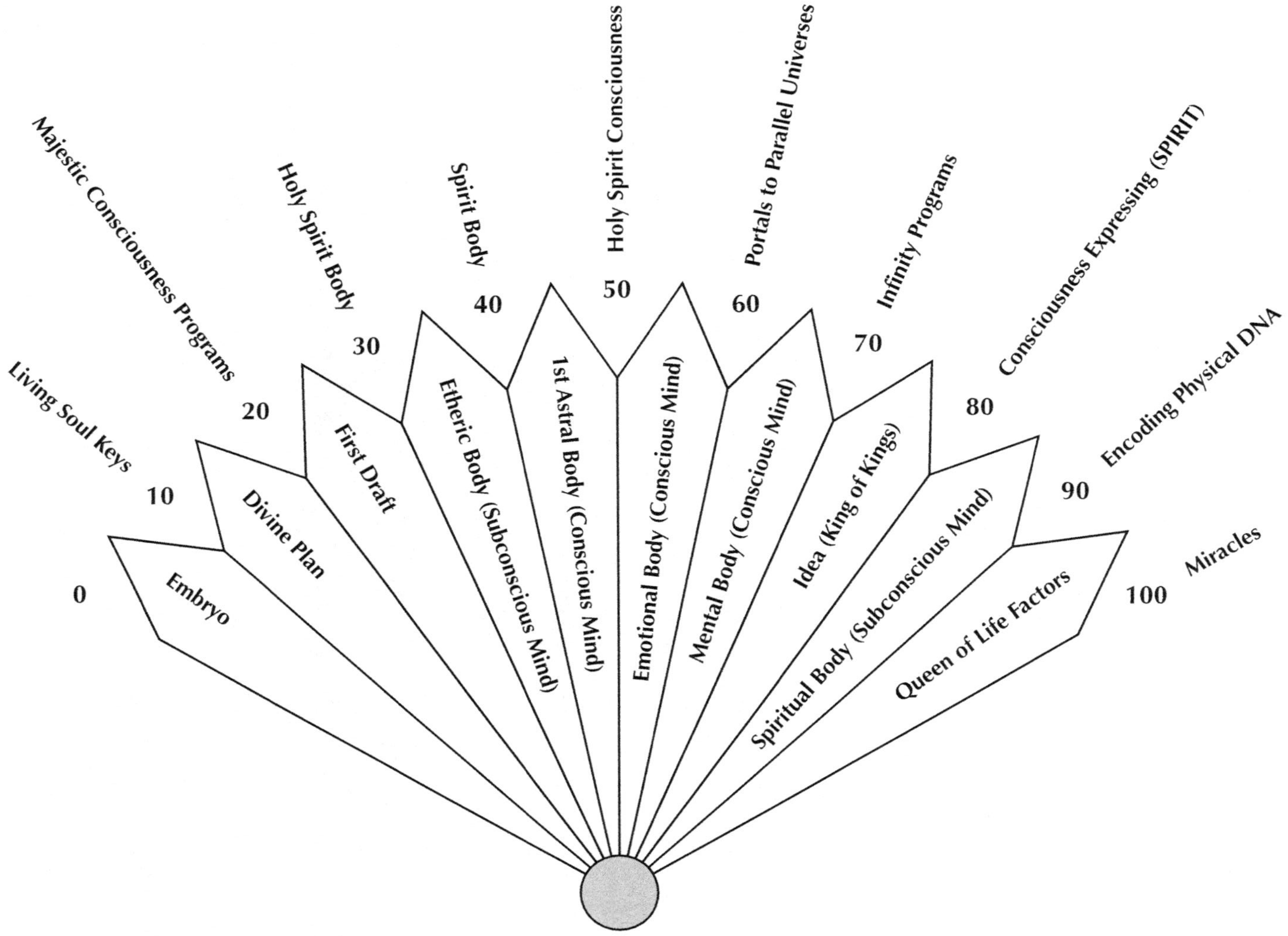

Chart 29

Chart 30

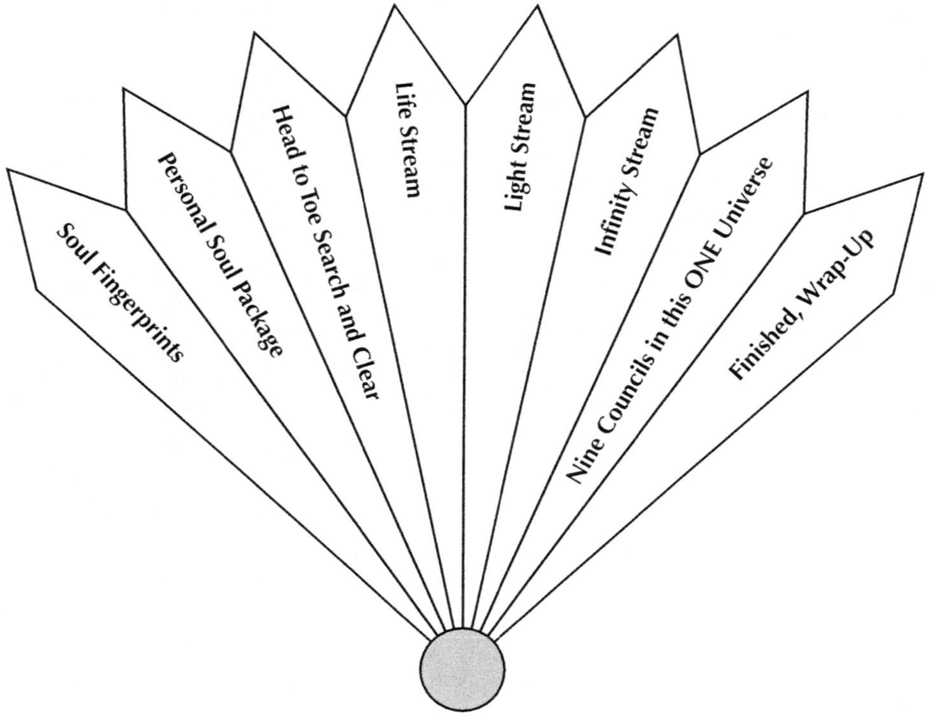
Soul Fingerprints
Personal Soul Package
Head to Toe Search and Clear
Life Stream
Light Stream
Infinity Stream
Nine Councils in this ONE Universe
Finished, Wrap-Up

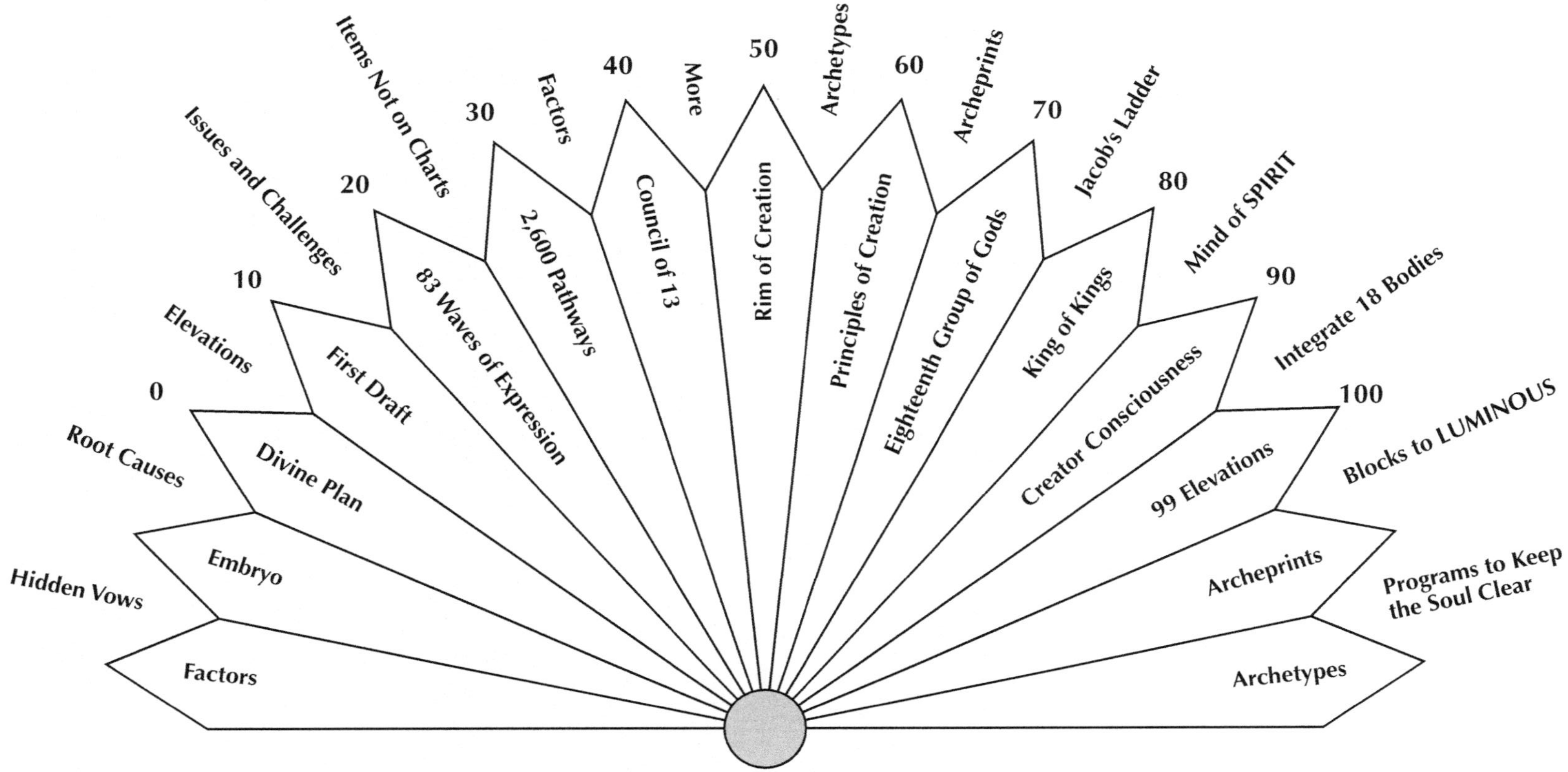

Outside: Through SPIRIT, LUMINOUS, and WELLSPRING
Inside: Through GODHEAD and SPIRIT

Chart 31

Bibliography

Arnheim, Robert. *Visual Thinking.* Berkeley: University of California Press, 1969.

Bentov, Itzhak. *Stalking the Wild Pendulum.* New York: E.P. Dutton, 1977.

Bruyere, Rosalyn L. *Wheels of Light.* Sierra Madre, Calif.: Bon Productions, 1989.

Detzler, Robert E. *The Freedom Path.* Redmond, WA: SRC Publishers, 1988.

Detzler, Robert E. *Spiritual Healing.* Redmond, WA: SRC Publishers, 1998.

Diamond, Harvey and Marilyn. *Fit For Life.* New York: Warner Books, Inc., 1985.

Evans-Wentz, W.Y. *The Tibetan Book of the Dead.* New York: Oxford University Press, 1960.

Fillmore, Charles. *Metaphysical Bible Dictionary (MBD).* Unity Village, Mo.: Unity School of Christianity, 1931.

Gross, Darwin. *Your Right To Know.* Menlo Park, CA, Illumined Way Press, 1979.

Gurudas, Kevin Ryerson, and John Fox. *Gem Elixirs and Vibrational Healing,* 2 vols. Boulder, CO: Cassandra Press, 1985.

The Hebrew-Greek Key Study Bible (KJV). Edited by Spiros Zodhiates. Chattanooga: AMG Publishers, 1986.

The Holy Bible, King James Version (KJV). Nashville: Thomas Nelson, Inc., 1976.

Maynard, James. *Transpersonal Hypnotherapy.* p. 38, Seattle: Transpersonal Press, 1989.

Montgomery, Ruth. *Strangers Among Us.* New York: Fawcett Crest, 1982.

Pearl, Richard M. *How to Know the Minerals and Rocks.* New York: McGraw Hill Co., Inc., 1955.

The Oxford Annotated Bible with the Apocrypha, Revised Standard Version (RSV). New York: Oxford University Press, 1965.

The Random House Dictionary. Edited by Stuart Berg Flexner. 2nd ed. New York: Random House, 1987.

Roberts, Jane. *Seth Speaks.* Englewood Cliffs: Prentice-Hall, 1972.

Ross, Nancy Wilson. *The World of Zen.* New York: Random House, 1960.

Toben, Bob and Fred Alan Wolf. Space–Time and Beyond. New York, Bantam Books, 1982.

Whitton, Joel and Joe Fisher. *Life Between Life.* New York: Doubleday, 1986.

Suggested Reading

Bachler, Kathe. *Earth Radiations.* Manchester: Wordmasters Ltd., 1989.

Bradshaw, John. *Homecoming.* New York: Bantam Books, 1990.

Fiore, Edith. *You Have Been Here Before.* New York: Ballantine Books, 1979.

Fiore, Edith. *The Unquiet Dead.* New York: Doubleday, 1987.

Ospensky, P.D. *In Search of the Miraculous.* New York: Harper and Row, 1974.

Pennington, M. Basil. *Centering Prayer.* New York: Doubleday and Co., Inc., 1982.

Speeth, Kathleen. *The Gurdjieff Work.* New York: Pocket Books, 1976.

Wambach, Helen. *Life Before Life.* New York: Bantam Books, Inc., 1981.

Products and Services provided by the Spiritual Response Association (SRA)

Other Books Published by SRC Publishing

The Freedom Path: Your Mind Net to Clear Your Soul Records (formerly titled: *Your Mind Net: Reprogramming the Subconscious*) by Robert E. Detzler, 1988, second edition 1996. This book provides basic how-to information for researching and clearing negative subconscious and conscious mind programs, including past life records, using Spiritual Response Therapy (SRT). This textbook is required reading for the Basic Spiritual Response Training Class.

Spiritual Healing - Expanded Edition, by Robert E. Detzler, 2008. *Spiritual Healing* presents specific steps on how to apply 201 vibrational patterns for spiritual healing. Fourteen other diagrams and charts for help in transforming your physical-emotional health. This is an adjunct technique to SRT, no class is needed to use.

Training Classes

Basic Training in Spiritual Response Therapy (SRT) is a twenty-four-hour class, demonstration, and practice workshop given over a three to four-day period. In the introductory time you will receive instruction in the pendulum dowsing used for SRT. Specially prepared curriculum materials and the basic edition of primary SRT Charts will be included. The required textbook is *The Freedom Path.*

Classes can be scheduled anywhere a group of interested students are located. Contact any of the certified teachers listed on the Spiritual Response Association website. Note that some of these classes may be in that country's language.

Advance Training in Spiritual Response Therapy is a twenty-four-hour class that reviews the research and clearing process of the Basic Training class and provides Advanced Training in clearing soul programs, dream interpretation, and clearing for unusual and exceptional situations. This instruction and supervised practice is open to students who have completed the Basic Training. Specific curriculum and all the up-to-date advance charts will be included. The required textbook is *Soul Re-Creation*.

Private Sessions and Counseling

Private sessions of this Spiritual Response Therapy (SRT) method are available with Spiritual Response Association certified consultants and teachers. Long distance clearing can be arranged by telephone by contacting the Spiritual Response Association or checking their website for certified consultants in your area.

Ascension Newsletter

The network of Spiritual Response students, teachers, and clients is maintained through a monthly newsletter consisting of articles on SRT methodology and practical suggestions for improving your life and enhancing spiritual growth and healing. For information about the *Ascension* contact Spiritual Response Association.

Spiritual Response Association, USA

Email: srtmail@spiritualresponse.com

Telephone: (360) 413-7881 Pacific Time

Fax: (360) 413-7882

Website: www.spiritualresponse.com

Please call or email for additional information on ordering books and individual SRT clearing or to register for classes.

A general brochure on the Spiritual Response Association, a non-profit religious educational organization, further explains other available products and services. Training Class brochures and information on how to set up a class in your area are also available upon request.

Printed in Dunstable, United Kingdom

63388924R00152